PRECARIOUS FORTUNES

Best Wishes

Ian Gonsul

PRECARIOUS FORTUNES

IAN TOWNSEND

2016

First edition published in 2016 by Mandy Townsend Publishing
12 Granby Road, Harrogate, North Yorkshire, HG1 4ST

© Ian Townsend 2016

Ian Townsend asserts the moral right to be identified
as the author of this fictional work.
www.precariousfortunes.com

A catalogue record of this book is available from the British Library.

ISBN 978 0 9935893 0 0

Edited by Tamara Hartley
www.tamara-hartley-editing-services.co.uk

Designed and typeset by Croft Publications
The Croft, 8 St James Meadow, Boroughbridge YO51 9NW
www.croftpublications.co.uk

Printed and bound by York Publishing Services
64 Hallfield Road, Layerthorpe, YO31 7ZQ
www.yps-publishing.co.uk

List of Illustrations

For my grandfather and great-great grandfather.
Together, they provided the inspiration (and name)
for my adventurous protagonist,
Captain George Townsend.

Acknowledgements

As with just about everything else I have ever achieved in life, this work would not have been possible without the love and support of my family. In particular, I cannot thank my wife Mandy enough for all the hours of research she donated to this cause. Thanks also go to my daughter Georgina, in reading the story and being so thorough in her assessment of its content. This book is also dedicated to my sons James and Peter, who are a constant source of material. And not forgetting my sister Susan, who is probably my only living relative who can appreciate the degree of surprise that this work would have brought to my parents and in particular our brother Gordon. They are never far from our thoughts.

And finally, without the technical expertise of Tamara, together with her boundless enthusiasm for this project, the finished article would have been one of immense frustration to my former English teachers.

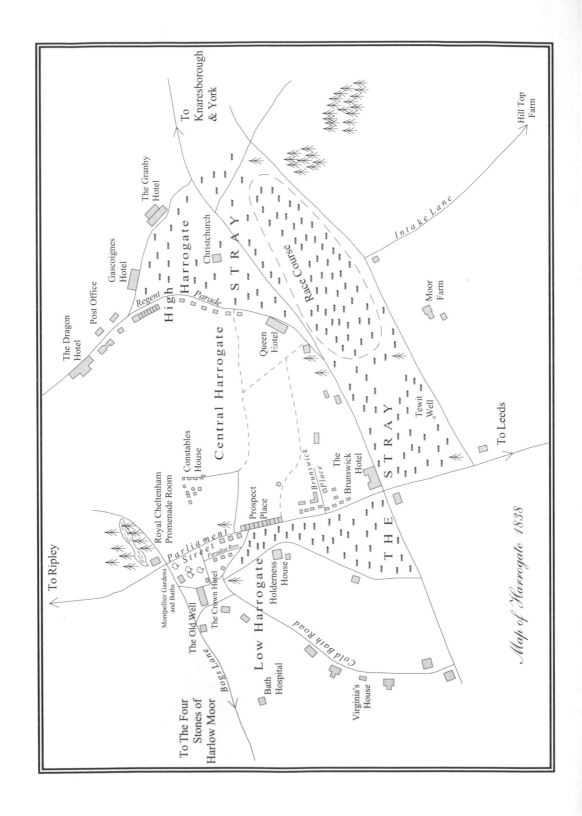

To Knaresborough & York

Hill Top Farm

The Granby Hotel

Intake Lane

Gascoignes Hotel

Christchurch

High Harrogate

S T R A Y

Race Course

Post Office

The Dragon Hotel

Regent Parade

Moor Farm

Central Harrogate

Queen Hotel

Constables House

Tewit Well

To Leeds

Royal Cheltenham Promenade Room

Brunswick Place

The Brunswick Hotel

T H E   S T R A Y

Prospect Place

To Ripley

Montpellier Gardens and Baths

The Old Well

Parliament Street

Paradise Row

The Crown Hotel

Low Harrogate

Holderness House

Cold Bath Road

Bogs Lane

To The Four Stones of Harlow Moor

Bath Hospital

Virginia's House

Map of Harrogate 1838

Prologue

Sir William Hamilton eased back into his leather armchair in a quiet corner of his London club. He cupped a glass of brandy in his left hand and a large Cuban cigar in his right. He drew on the cigar and then spoke to the man in the adjacent chair.

"Do we have an agreement then?" he said ambivalently.

"You can guarantee that you are able to deliver what we have asked for?" came the reply.

"Of course," said Sir William taking a draw on his cigar, allowing the smoke to rise hypnotically from his mouth as he exhaled.

"Then we have a deal," replied the man.

"Just one more thing," added Sir William whilst carefully placing his cigar in an ash tray.

"There is someone who is a great irritation to me and headed your way."

"Then say the word, Sir William, and we will do our damnedest to ensure that they have a visit to remember," replied the man.

"Excellent. You shall be hearing from me. Then let me know when you have everything in place and I will take care of the rest. And now sir, I will bid you goodnight."

Sir William put down his brandy and the man made his way out of the near deserted club.

A deal had been struck.

Chapter 1

I was trying to remember if I had packed everything in my trunk as I rode my horse steadily along the northern turnpike road to Harrogate. If I had forgotten something then it was my misfortune as everything had probably already arrived at my aunt's house, having made its way there independently, courtesy of the much faster Royal Mail coach.

At the insistence of a rather cynical government minister, I was riding this day in August 1838 to what is reputed to be the best spa town in Europe. Despite having been born in the north of England, I had not been to Yorkshire for many years, and were it not for my unfortunate encounter at Gordon's Club on St James's Street in London, it may have remained many more years before I returned. Even though we were living in changing times following the Reform Act and a new young Queen, the country was still run by the affluent members of the aristocracy. And I suspected one or two of them may have had a hand in my swift relocation north.

Nonetheless, here I was and although summer was upon us, the temperature was far from warm and the skies far from clear. Having ridden through a number of showers on the long ride north, I was confident there were enough breaks in the clouds to suggest that the day would remain dry.

I stopped briefly at a small stream which ran gently by the side of the road, allowing my horse a well-earned drink. I patted Tribune's neck as he lapped up the cool, clear water as it rippled over smooth cobbles. We had travelled many miles together and I trusted him as much as any man or woman I had ever met. He was a strong horse with a strong name and had never failed me. After four days on the road we were now only a few miles from our destination and I was starting to feel a few pangs of hunger as several hours had passed since breakfast.

I twisted around in the saddle and gazed at the countryside which was awash with different shades of green. Kites soared majestically overhead. We were in a basin-like valley and I could see cattle and sheep grazing peacefully on the gentle slopes. Mature oaks and sycamores graced the landscape as if designed by that 'Brown' fellow, the one everyone fusses about. The road ahead meandered aimlessly through pasture land dotted with freshly gathered haystacks. Behind me and to my left were the hills surrounding Leeds and Bradford and ahead of me were the hills leading to Harrogate.

Having refreshed himself, Tribune raised his head and I urged him on. With any luck I should be at my aunt's house in thirty minutes or so. Not for the first time on my long ride north from London I found myself wondering just what trouble and dangers might be lying in wait for me. Then a grumbling noise from my stomach had me reflecting equally on what my aunt's cook might have prepared for lunch. Suitably motivated at the imminent prospect of the latter, I dug my heels in and Tribune kicked on.

As we galloped around the next bend, I pulled up sharply on the reins as I could see a carriage blocking the road a mere one hundred yards ahead. My heart rate quickened. Surely this couldn't have anything to do with what had happened at Gordon's? No one knew I was headed for Harrogate other than the powers that be at the Foreign Office. I pushed my right hand into my saddle bag looking for the reassurance of my pistol. It was there but not loaded. Should I place it in my belt or was I overreacting? After all, I was on my way to Harrogate for pity's sake, not Calcutta. I steadied myself. This was not Bengal or Afghanistan and I was no longer riding on patrol with the 11th Light Dragoons but in the most genial of England's countryside without a bandit in sight. I had been through the areas where the Chartists were stirring up trouble but surely there was nothing to fear in this most affluent part of northern England?

Standing on the roadside by the carriage were four people. There were three ladies who had moved a short distance away from the carriage and a man who was bellowing orders to two coachmen as they fussed around one of its rear wheels. I inched Tribune forward taking care to keep all my wits about me. As I drew closer it became apparent that the coach had a damaged wheel and was incapable of progressing in its present condition. All seemed to pose no threat to yours truly unless this was an over-elaborate plot to waylay me, which looked doubtful. There wasn't a weapon in sight.

Having moved to within fifty yards of this gathering I could see a crest on the carriage door which rested half open. I didn't recognise the emblem but the carriage was one of the finest I had ever seen. The coat of arms displayed a bright red stag's head. The carriage was fully laden with baggage and, given the short distance we were from Harrogate, I took it that they were heading there for the season.

I continued to edge closer and the sound of Tribune's hooves on the hard road announced our arrival on the scene. Servants and gentry alike turned their heads towards me. Although I was not in my finery I was still respectably attired and I bargained that Tribune was as good as any horse that would be seen in Harrogate this season.

Moments earlier it had been I who had been wary at the sight of someone else on the road but irrespective of my innocent appearance, it was evident that they were the ones now feeling uneasy.

"Good day, sir," I said to the gentleman who was clearly in charge, endeavouring to speak to him in as reassuring manner as possible. He looked up at me, hatless, his furrowed brow betraying years of anxiety, and proceeded to reply in a vexed and suspicious tone.

"Good day to you too, sir."

From his attire he displayed all the characteristics of the aristocracy but his accent revealed a good deal of time spent in the north. Given our location this did not strike me as unusual considering the north of England was full of successful factory owners who had, one way or another, acquired titles for themselves.

I acknowledged his greeting and then turned to his travelling companions raising my hat. They bowed their heads in response and all the while the expression on their faces barely moved. One of the ladies was much older than the other, who would have been little more than twenty years old and the third was a lady's maid and by far the prettiest. I took the elder to be the wife of the gentleman and the other to be, perhaps, their daughter. Having said that I could be mistaken, as there seemed little resemblance of the younger girl to either of her travelling companions. A niece perhaps or maybe a friend?

My mind was rapidly taking in every detail. This may be an entirely harmless incident, however my years in the Dragoons had taught me to evaluate situations quickly and my ability in this department of soldiering had saved my life on more than one occasion. They were all dressed extremely well which, together with the fine craftsmanship of the coach, led me to conclude that there was no reason for me to reconsider drawing the pistol resting in my right saddle bag.

It was clear that the coach's wheel would require the services of a blacksmith and given the apparent innocence of the situation I volunteered my assistance, though not as a blacksmith.

"Is there anything I can do to be of assistance?" I enquired, adding quickly, "I can ride ahead and return with help."

I was on my way to Harrogate in any event and with all the coaches and horses that would undoubtedly have made their way to the spa town, I was confident a blacksmith would not be hard to find.

"That would be most kind sir," replied the gentleman, resting the furrows on his over worked brow. I kept glancing at the coat of arms hoping that the name of its owner would spring to mind.

"I was going to send one of these two," he said, pointing to the two coachmen, adding in a mocking tone. "But it would be faster to walk myself."

He was clearly very frustrated at his situation and having to wait around for a solution was doing nothing to improve his temperament. The coachmen looked lost and were clearly well out of their depth. I doubted they had ever been marooned with a broken wheel before, leastways not five miles from the nearest town. I surmised that they were probably more used to carrying out their duties in London where the roads were more predictable and assistance more readily available.

As a consequence, my arrival on the scene now appeared to be universally welcomed by the inconvenienced travellers and their spirits seemed to rise as a resolution to their predicament was close at hand.

"If I ride now sir, I should be back within the hour," I said, readying myself to gallop away at high speed with the shameless intention of drawing the full attention of the young lady who had seemed completely disinterested in my presence. She intrigued me and although not a stunning creature she had a certain gravitas despite appearing shy and unassuming. She was tall, slim and instinctively I wanted to learn more about her.

"I would appreciate that very much sir, but please do not waste your time with blacksmiths and spare wheels. If you will, I would be grateful if you could ride to the Queen Hotel. Upon arrival there, you should seek Mr Jonathan Dearlove who is the owner of the establishment and advise him of the misfortune that has befallen the Lord Redmayne and his party. Having been acquainted with the facts, I am sure he will promptly dispatch his own carriage for our recovery and no doubt his blacksmith to attend to our wheel."

"Very good, sir," I nodded.

All the same, the introductions remained incomplete and Lord Redmayne promptly rectified this.

"And now, having advised you of my name, perhaps you would be kind enough to tell us yours?"

"Captain George Townsend of Her Majesty's 11th Light Dragoons," I replied in an instant, straightening my back in the process.

"Then we are very fortunate to have made your acquaintance this day, Captain," said Lord Redmayne, looking somewhat relieved to hear of my military pedigree. Then, turning to the two ladies he added, "Lady Redmayne and Miss Coutts, permit me to introduce Captain Townsend," at which point I bowed my head and they followed suit. I raised my eyebrows when Miss Coutts's name was mentioned.

"Now Captain, we all wish you a swift and safe return."

Lord Redmayne was finished with the formalities and his manner now portrayed that of a man who desired a prompt resumption of his journey. Having learned that he was escorting one of the richest women in Europe it was little wonder. Miss Coutts was the talk of London and a target for every bachelor in search of a fortune. Her grandfather had founded one of the most prestigious banks in Europe and, even though I had no idea how it came about, she had inherited a fortune reputed to be two million pounds within the last twelve months. I now felt that the coat of arms on the carriage was more likely to be that of the Coutts's family than the Redmayne's and would surely present a tempting target for some enterprising villain.

Before riding off I leant down from my horse and spoke to Lord Redmayne as quietly as I might for fear of alarming the ladies.

"Perhaps you would welcome the loan of a pistol in case some rogue or Chartist seeks to take advantage of your compromised position sir?"

"Perish the thought, Captain! And fear not, as we do have weapons with us. You have not seen them as I did not judge you to be a threat," replied Lord Redmayne, nodding reproachingly to his coachmen, suggesting that they had shared a different view as to my intentions. Perhaps they had suspected me of being some sort of highwayman akin to the famous Dick Turpin who repeatedly terrorised travellers on the roads in the north until he met his end at the gallows in York.

There was nothing more to be said. It was now time for me to take my leave and ride the last few miles to Harrogate hoping there would be no further distractions along the way.

I was now in something of a flap as I assimilated the reality of this chance encounter. I had just met one of the richest women in Europe and would certainly be seeing her again. This was an incredible stroke of good fortune and my excited mind wandered fancifully as to where this may lead. I was simply fascinated by her, but not in a mercenary way.

I spurred on my horse and within a few minutes I was leaving the turnpike road at Buttersyke Bar. As I approached the toll house I saw a miserable looking fellow standing at the door watching me closely. He had no reason to be interested in me because I was leaving the road and had already paid the toll in Leeds. Nevertheless, I needed him to remove the bar which stretched across the highway, which he proceeded to do – giving me a brief wave in the process. As I rode on, I turned in the saddle and glanced back. The surly gatekeeper's expression had not improved, his sour expression seemed to be burned into his face.

For a moment I wondered if this expression was solely for my benefit, but assuredly, this man had no reason to single me out for special treatment.

My destiny was moving in a most unlikely way and it occurred to me that perhaps I wouldn't be here at all if had I stayed away from Gordon's Club or had resisted the temptation to expose that drunken aristocratic whelp of cheating. But having reflected on this a number of times on my journey north there was no doubt in my mind that, given a chance to revisit the situation, I would do the same thing all over again. If for no other reason than to see the look on the whelp's best friend's face as I demonstrated how he had just been taken for a thousand guineas. But maybe I am wrong to connect the events at Gordon's with this assignment as I could have been sent here regardless. It has also spared me the possibility of an unpleasant reunion with the Light Dragoons' 'glorious leader' Earl Cardigan. He remained in London awaiting orders and apparently had not thus far forgiven my indiscretion of repeating to my fellow officers the commander in chief's comments that the Earl was constitutionally unfit for command. So perhaps being ordered to Harrogate may not be so bad after all.

With those rambling thoughts leaving my mind, I returned to the task in hand. In spite of the need for speed it would have been foolhardy to continue to gallop all the way to the Queen Hotel and so, as the incline of the land increased, we reduced our pace. It was at that point it dawned on me that I was not completely certain as to where the Queen Hotel was. I had been so swept along with the prospect of a 'Light Dragoon officer effecting daring rescue' that I had not asked the simplest of questions. I had, of course, heard of the Queen Hotel and knew it had a fine reputation but that was all I could remember. The last time I had been in Harrogate I was probably no more than twelve years old. Confound it all! I had been a presumptuous fool. I had promised to return within the hour without the slightest idea as to whether I was going to High Harrogate, Low Harrogate or somewhere outside Harrogate.

As we reached the top of the hill, I could see a scattering of buildings ahead together with the occasional farm worker going about their daily duties. Then, on my right, we passed the Travellers' Inn which had an old farmer sitting outside at a table with a jug of ale and pipe in hand. Behind him a girl was taking a basket of eggs into the inn. A young man was tending a horse and he looked up as I rode by. I urged Tribune on, trotting along nicely as we neared the town.

Ahead of me to my right and left lay the famous 'Stray' – two hundred acres of common grassland, free from any buildings as ruled by parliament in order to allow public access to the myriad of wells which lay within the area. It was the alleged therapeutic properties of these wells that drew people to Harrogate, although rumour has it that just as many came solely for the social gatherings. As serene a picture as you could imagine with sheep keeping the grass trim all the while peacefully bringing the countryside to the front door of the town.

I could now distinctly make out a large hotel which was a veritable hive of activity with several coaches lined up outside its front door. A bit busier than the poor old Travellers' Inn and, with luck, this will be the Queen Hotel but the closer we came I could see a sign clearly spelling out the name of the Brunswick Hotel.

Carriages were arriving and passengers alighting, bags were being passed down to doormen and guests were led into the grand entrance of this fine looking three storey hotel.

There was a queue of various horse drawn coaches including one or two of those new hansom cabs, all waiting to take guests elsewhere in the town. I drew up alongside the last carriage in the line. The driver seemed a likely fellow, covered in whiskers and wrapped up against the northern winds which stole the warmth from a pleasant August day.

"Excuse me, my good man, could you be so kind as to direct me to the Queen Hotel?"

Pleasingly I received a cheerful response whereupon I was directed to ride east whilst continuing to keep the vast grassland of the Stray to my right.

I thanked the driver and headed east as he had directed. My spirits rose as, after one hundred yards or so, I saw a handsome building standing proudly on my left. Yet again my eagerness was left wanting, as handsome as it might be, the Queen Hotel it was not. A mild sense of concern flashed through my mind at my inability to find the hotel. I suddenly reflected on the image of Lord Redmayne and two ladies marooned and at risk on the turnpike road to Harrogate. They were depending on me and I was determined not to fail them.

To my right, in the vast green expanse, I could see traces of a racecourse and, if there had been more time, I would have had a gallop around but that would have to wait for another day. I was now peering ahead like a ship's captain looking for land. Time was of the essence and it seemed to be taking me an age to arrive at the Queen Hotel. A church came into view a further two hundred yards ahead together with a collection of buildings, but these resembled a small inn with stables.

As I started to think that I must have misunderstood the directions from the cab driver, there on my left, neatly set back and nestled amongst some trees was the Queen Hotel. It was indeed a beautiful stone built property which, like the Brunswick Hotel, was three storeys high. Two fine gate posts stood at either side of the sweeping drive allowing carriages to drive easily in and out of the hotel. Even though I had only seen a few properties it was hard not to appreciate that whatever else Harrogate had to offer, it at least had some very fine buildings.

The Queen Hotel, Harrogate.

Chapter 2

I was now outside the gates of a hotel expectant of the imminent arrival of Lord Redmayne together with the richest woman in England. I was carrying a vitally important message which I fully expected would precipitate a good deal of frantic action. I had delivered many important messages in my time in the 11th Light Dragoons, however this was probably the most important message I had ever been asked to deliver as a civilian. During my time in India with the British Army, I was surrounded by seasoned officers and, save for a few notable exceptions, panic was a rarity in times of trouble. Panic can be the undoing of any situation and I hoped that Mr Dearlove was not liable to such failings. With that thought firmly planted in my mind I rode through the entrance gates up to the front door and within a few seconds a young boy came to my aid and held Tribune whilst I dismounted. My desire to return to the damaged coach on the turnpike road must have given the impression that I was irritated by having to wait, albeit briefly, as the young boy appeared to express some disquiet under his breath.

In jumping down, I asked the boy where I might find Mr Jonathan Dearlove as I had an urgent message for him from Lord Redmayne, whose carriage had met with a most unfortunate accident. No sooner had I finished mentioning Lord Redmayne's name when a more senior doorman appeared.

"Please wait here, sir," he said, as he led me towards a seating area in the entrance lobby. Inside the hotel a log crackled on the fire as, despite this being summer, the air circulating the town was a trifle bracing. The fireplace was flanked by surprisingly modern pilasters decorated with classical urns and swags. A number of brass chandeliers hung from the ceiling. Unfortunately I was in no mood to sit patiently admiring the décor and proceeded to pace around oblivious to the most splendid surroundings in which I now found myself. I was concerned for the safety of Lord Redmayne and the ladies. Further, my body was reminding me that lunch was due which was most unfortunate, but happily there was no-one within earshot of the tune my inners were now playing.

No-one came and my impatience grew. I was just about to instil some urgency into the situation, when a gentleman in a light grey jacket and dark grey trousers appeared, walking purposely towards me. He was reasonably tall, middle-aged, had neat, dark brown whiskers and a rosy complexion.

He walked up to me and, dispensing with any formalities, said in a calm tone of voice, "Now sir, what is this about Lord Redmayne?" Whereupon I recounted the events of the last half an hour and, most particularly, the message I was asked to relay to Mr Dearlove. He listened most diligently and I could see that the more he became appraised of the situation, the more anxious he became to react promptly. As I was finishing my tale he was almost completing my sentences for me.

"Quite, quite," he said, urging the words from me. "Well sir, you have found me. I am Jonathan Dearlove." Then, turning to an assistant who had now appeared at his side, he took command of proceedings.

"Dawson! Follow this gentleman and take my carriage to meet up with Lord Redmayne and send someone around to Simpson's blacksmiths and have them proceed to the scene of the accident on the turnpike road from Leeds… and hurry man!"

Lord Redmayne and Miss Coutts had obviously been expected, however an expression of concern suddenly flashed across his face and, turning back to me, said, "And what did you say your name was?" Without hesitation I replied, "My name is Captain George Townsend of Her Majesty's 11ᵗʰ Light Dragoons."

Seemingly reassured as to my bona fides, Mr Dearlove moved his left arm forward motioning me to the door.

"Well, Lord Redmayne is indeed fortunate that it was yourself and not some unscrupulous villain that happened by when you did. I suggest we make haste, Captain, and remove them all back to the safety and comfort of this hotel without further delay."

I nodded in agreement, feeling relieved that we would be shortly retrieving Lord Redmayne and his ladies from their precarious plight. Why, their baggage alone would present a great temptation to many!

I was once again outside, where the sun had now broken through the clouds causing the boy who still held the reins of my horse to squint and hold his free hand to his forehead to shade his eyes. I moved to re-mount just as a carriage pulled by four stout horses came from around the back of the hotel and pulled up alongside us. It was a grand coach although it lacked the finesse of the one carrying Lord Redmayne and Miss Coutts.

Dawson was sitting with the driver and he looked down at me as we all readied ourselves for the rescue. He was slightly older than me, probably in his late twenties and possessed a muscular build not dissimilar to my own. And then it was as if time stood still for the briefest of moments, during which I could have sworn I saw a flicker of recognition in his eyes. This struck me as strange as I was certain we'd never met before.

"We will follow you, sir," said Dawson breaking the moment's pause and placing a rather insincere emphasis on the word 'sir'. "And having led us to the carriage your assistance will no longer be required, whereupon you can leave everything to me," he added dismissively.

Before he could add anything else to his lecture, I was in the saddle and turning Tribune back towards the turnpike road to Leeds. Damn cheek! I was happy to help anyone in such circumstances as I found Lord Redmayne nevertheless I was more than a little disappointed to be shown such scant respect by the hotel. I had to remind myself that I was helping people who were stranded and vulnerable and they were not to blame for this apparent lack of common courtesy. Maybe I was prejudging Dawson, but my first impressions of others were generally sound and there was something distinctly unpleasant about him. Perhaps the lack of food was making me irritable but either way I was running on a short fuse as we sped past the Brunswick Hotel and headed back towards Buttersyke Bar.

The chase was on as I galloped ahead turning in the saddle at regular intervals to see the coach bouncing along with Dawson clinging on for all he was worth. It may be unkind, but the sight of him being bounced around brought a smile to my face. His discomfort amused me. My mother would have been very disappointed in me as sadly, in spite of all my best efforts, I often lacked the powers of forbearance which she'd possessed.

We were now back at the turnpike and the miserable gatekeeper crept out of his 'lair' as we fast approached. I pulled up at the gate and moments later the coach did the same causing a great cloud of dust to fill the air. The horses were breathing heavily, their muscles twitched and their hooves clawed at the ground as we waited for the gatekeeper to raise the bar. Before I could speak the gatekeeper said, "That'll be two shillings if you please."

Well, that topped it all! I was endeavouring to be a good Samaritan, had been dealt with most dismissively by the hotel and was now being charged two shillings for my trouble. Even though I was by no means poor, I was equally by no means rich, nonetheless, before he died, my father had at least managed to teach me the value of money. I was in no mood to be parted from it needlessly.

"You cretinous imbecile! We are on our way to rescue Lord Redmayne and his party who have been much inconvenienced by their carriage encountering an accident, no doubt as a result of the poor condition of your road – the road you are supposed to keep maintained, and you are now seeking to charge two shillings? I should take a whip to you!"

Unfortunately I had not been able to contain my anger, whether it was due to fatigue or the absence of my lunch, or just the pure irritation of the situation, it mattered not.

Before he could respond, Dawson interjected, "Dick! Pay no heed to the Captain here. I have the toll." With that, he tossed down a coin which was duly caught and both Dawson and the gatekeeper looked towards me with a certain amount of disdain and satisfaction written across their faces.

I had only just met them and yet they both appeared to have taken an instant dislike to me. Perhaps this was because I was a cavalryman? Had brown hair and brown eyes? Who could say? In any event whatever the reason, it seemed fanciful to suppose that it could be connected to the true purpose of my visit to Harrogate.

With his toll duly collected, the gatekeeper raised the bar and the coach went through the gate with me following close behind. I then rode past Dawson's coach whereupon Lord Redmayne and his party soon came into view some four hundred yards ahead. The servants had set up a makeshift shelter for the ladies keeping their fair complexions out of the midday sun, weak and hazy though it had become. I galloped on and Lord Redmayne spotted me and moved a few steps away from the ladies. A broad smile appeared on his face when he also saw Jonathan Dearlove's personal carriage following close behind.

"We are in your debt, Captain," he said as the ladies, too, could see that the discomfort they had endured for the last couple of hours was soon to end.

Dawson arrived and after alighting from the carriage proceeded to show a side of himself which was clearly only reserved for fee paying guests. He was full of grace and consideration as he fussed around Lord Redmayne and the ladies as they made their transition to the hotel's coach and four.

Paying no heed to Dawson's request that I should leave everything to him, I dismounted and gave assistance where it was appropriate. Dawson looked particularly irritated as I was on hand to assist Miss Coutts and Lady Redmayne whilst he was left to attend to their baggage. It took no time at all for the ladies to be comfortably seated and as Lord Redmayne moved to join them he turned to me and held out his hand.

"Captain, we have a private dining facility at the Queen and we would all be delighted if you would allow us to repay your kindness by accepting our invitation to join us there for dinner this evening. It will present us all the opportunity to become better acquainted. Shall we say seven o'clock?" said Lord Redmayne, his warm smile portraying a sincerity I could not refuse.

Having accepted his invitation and after a couple of 'splendids' Lord Redmayne sat down in the coach and his coachman closed the door.

"We will see you at seven then," and with that the coach sped off leaving Lord Redmayne's two coachmen to wait for the blacksmith.

I was straight back in the saddle and contented myself in following the coach. I wasn't going to pass it until we had been through the toll gate. Remembering my last conversation with the gatekeeper I felt that discretion was in order. I had no wish to cause a scene in front of such august company.

We passed through the toll gate without incident as Dawson once again nodded to his friend and for the second time in less than an hour I found myself riding up the hill into Harrogate. I spurred Tribune on and we eased past the coach at a wide section of the turnpike road.

I never looked back but I could hear the coach clattering away behind me as I galloped past the imaginatively named Travellers' Inn. The same old farmer was still at the same table with a drink in one hand and a pipe in the other. He looked so comfortable and at peace that as he looked up at me, I nodded to him in admiration. What more could a man wish for than to be sitting peacefully with a drink and a smoke, in the warmth of an English summer's day? Well, it wasn't really all that warm and perhaps a pretty girl might have capped it all off, all the same the old farmer looked a picture of contentment.

A cart came towards me heading for Buttersyke Bar and glancing at the spare coach wheel, hammers and blocks stacked behind the driver, I presumed that this was the blacksmith on his way to repair the disabled coach.

At long last I was now heading for my aunt's house. All she had told me was that it had recently been built in Harrogate pink stone and overlooked the Stray in the low part of Harrogate. My aunt was a lady of some means and so I assumed that the house would be easy to find. Holderness House, as it was called, was named after the area in Yorkshire where my uncle previously had an estate.

I passed the Brunswick Hotel for the third time in an hour, noticing that it still possessed a long line of carriages and hansom cabs. I looked out for the man who had guided me to the Queen Hotel, but there was no sign of him. Unlike that occasion, I was now passing the hotel on its left-hand side as I looked at it, heading north along Prospect Place towards Low Harrogate. Low Harrogate was hardly lower, being for the most part virtually on the same level as High Harrogate. Having said that, the landscape did eventually fall away from the town houses on Prospect Place creating a little valley that ran down towards a number of wells around which several grand hotels had been built. There was the Crown Hotel, the White Hart, the Swan as well as many smaller boarding houses. The Crown Hotel was sited close to one of Harrogate's most famous sulphur wells which was legendary for its curative powers in treating a variety of ailments.

Prospect Place, Harrogate.

In particular the sulphur waters were extremely effective in checking gout and the tendency to it as well as rheumatism in its various chronic forms. It was also reported that patients afflicted with the frequent eruption of boils and other skin conditions benefited greatly from these waters.

My aunt had advised me in her letter that if I reached those hotels near to the well then I had passed her villa and gone too far. The further I rode, the more people I encountered; some walking towards Low Harrogate's wells and some returning. A positive hive of activity lay before me, a production line of the great and the good carrying out their daily rituals in search of better health.

As I rode by Prospect Place my thoughts turned towards my aunt. I hadn't seen her for almost five years. She came to see me in London just before I set sail for India and seeing all these people taking the waters made me pray that the good health she had always enjoyed was undiminished. Her last letter had made no mention of any problems but I hoped that there was no unfortunate purpose to her having a house built so close to all these wells. My uncle had died some years ago, leaving my aunt exceedingly well provided for. She was my mother's sister and they resembled each other so closely that they were often mistaken for twins.

I heard a dog barking and saw a black cocker spaniel running in front of me giving both Tribune and myself a start. Before I could reflect any more on the past, a large villa fitting the description of Holderness House came into view on my left. It had a most pleasing aspect, surrounded by a stone wall with elegant wrought iron gates through which I could easily see a short drive to the house and a longer drive to the left leading to the coach house and stables.

I felt very proud of my aunt as I rode up to the gates, all the while keeping a watchful eye on the black cocker spaniel which was now being patted and fussed over by a pretty young girl. Before I could dismount to open the gate a voice called out, "No trouble, Captain, I will get those for you."

It was Benson, my aunt's faithful servant who had been with her for years. As he appeared, pulling the gate inwards, I could see that the years were catching up with him. Although at least fifty years old, he was still blessed with a kindly face and his back remained as straight as a rod of iron.

"Your aunt was expecting you earlier, Captain; your luggage arrived a couple of days ago," he said as I dismounted.

"It's a long story Benson but I'm here now and it's so good to see you." He smiled at this and readied himself to lead Tribune away.

"How is my aunt, Benson? Well, I trust?" I enquired.

"Fit as ever, Captain. Don't know how she does it!"

"I think it could be that she's got you to look after her Benson," I said, raising a smile. "And where will I find her at this time of day?"

"I should try the library to start with, Captain, but I am sure as soon as she hears you in the house that she will find you."

I gave Tribune a last pat on his neck and asked Benson to make sure he was

15

Holderness House, Harrogate.

well looked after following which he was to bring my saddle bags up to the house. I then walked through the doorway of the impressive Holderness House.

A weight was being lifted from my shoulders as I closed the door behind me and walked inside. The house was light with a warm and welcoming feel which belied the fact that it had been built in stone. The corridors were wide and the ceilings high, the latter being beautifully decorated with garlands of leaves and flowers.

I walked past the first reception room where a maid was tending to a fire. I then opened the door to the next room which was indeed the library, only to find that, although splendid in its presentation of reading matter, it was lacking of one aunt.

Before I could call her name she burst into my presence, throwing both arms around me.

"My dear George, you sweet boy, it is so very good to see you." As our embrace relaxed I could see that even though she, too, was past fifty years old, she had fared better than Benson and her features showed little sign of ageing.

"The years have been kind, Aunt; you look just as you did when I last saw you in London. This Harrogate well water must agree with you."

She smiled and took both my hands in hers and looked me up and down, much as my mother used to do. "You have grown into a very handsome man, your parents would have been so very proud."

Her eyes glistened with the hint of a tear at the mention of her dear departed sister. This momentarily interrupted our joyous reunion but in an instant we were back embracing.

"Where have you been? I expected you hours ago."

We separated but she still held both my hands. "I was attempting to be a good Samaritan, Aunt, and in the process met the wealthiest woman in the country and, as my reward, I am to dine with her and her travelling companions tonight at their hotel, the Queen," I said.

My aunt looked fit to burst as she instinctively knew that unless I had met Queen Victoria that I must be referring to Miss Angela Coutts.

"Angela Coutts, granddaughter of Thomas Coutts?" she exclaimed.

"Yes, Aunt, I do believe it is the very same," I replied.

"How absolutely marvellous, you must tell me everything," she exclaimed, clapping her hands together and urging me to sit down. "I remember reading about her inheritance in the *Morning Herald*. They estimated that her fortune equated to some staggering amount of gold. Almost fourteen tons, they said. Someone apparently calculated that if her fortune was converted into gold sovereigns and then laid in a line, the line would stretch for twenty five miles or more!"

"That's unbelievable!" I said, marvelling at both the comparison and also my aunt's recollection of the amounts involved.

"How was it that she came to inherit the Coutts' fortune? Weren't there any male heirs?" I asked.

"There may have been a grandson," she said. "But unfortunately for Thomas Coutts he only had daughters. Anyhow, when his first wife died, he married a famous actress by the name of Harriot Mellon. Then, on his own death, left absolutely everything to her. If that wasn't enough, she then went on to marry the comparatively poverty stricken Duke of St. Albans, at which point the Coutts family must have thought they'd seen the last of Thomas Coutts' bank. Surprisingly, on Harriot's death everything reverted to Angela Coutts and the bank once again rested in the hands of the family."

"How extraordinary," I replied. "They must have been mighty relieved when they learnt that the Coutts' fortune was not left to the Duke and his heirs."

"Quite so, George. And it's so refreshing to see so much wealth entrusted to a lady. Men have had it all their own way for too long," said my aunt, with a smile.

"So why didn't the Duke of St. Albans inherit everything?" I asked.

"Well, I suspect Harriot had promised Thomas Coutts that she would ensure only his flesh and blood ultimately inherited his bank. In which case he must have thought a lot of her to trust her with so much wealth."

"And she must have thought a lot of him not to betray that trust," I added.

"Absolutely, and from what I have read, Angela Coutts is a wise and sensible choice, nevertheless I expect the fortune will be a heavy burden for one so young to bear. Did I ever tell you that I met Harriot, Duchess of St. Albans whilst she was staying at the Granby Hotel in Harrogate?"

"No, Aunt," I replied.

"Well I did, but that is a tale for another time. Now tell me, who did you say she was travelling with?"

"The Lord and Lady Redmayne," I replied.

"Really? Lord and Lady Redmayne? I am not completely certain but I believe that they own a number of mills across the Pennines. That might explain why they are staying at the Queen and not the Granby. The prosperous industrialists from Manchester tend to descend on the Queen Hotel in the season," she said, and then after a moment's pause added, "I wonder why Sir Francis didn't accompany his own daughter to Harrogate rather than Lord Redmayne?"

She was excited by this news and wasn't satisfied until I had given her a full account of the morning's events including my best recollection as to how the ladies were attired. I left nothing out save my momentary loss of patience with the surly gatekeeper and the somewhat curious reception I received from the arrogant Dawson.

"Now you must away to your room, have something to eat and when you feel refreshed we must talk more as you have so much to tell me." And after a moment's reflection added, "It is so good to see you George."

With that, my aunt rang the servant's bell and in an instant Benson's protégé, Cookson, arrived on the scene and escorted me up the stairs to my room.

With his duty done and the door closed, I let out a great sigh. I had arrived at last. It seemed a long time since I had left London. I ached from riding constantly and my back still cursed my choice of beds these last four nights.

I threw down my coat on the bed and moved over to the window. I surveyed the famous Harrogate Stray which stretched out in front of me. Little over one hundred yards away, directly opposite and facing me were the elegant townhouses of Prospect Place. As my senses absorbed my new surroundings, I relaxed for the first time since that night at Gordon's.

I then moved over to the small desk which was on the left hand side of the room. My aunt had left me a local publication to amuse myself. I picked it up and started to thumb through a few pages. Even though it was nothing to set my pulse racing it was nonetheless quite illuminating. The publication was the work of Pickersgill Palliser. At first glance it seemed incredibly useful, including every conceivable category of information a visitor to Harrogate could reasonably wish to know. How extraordinarily inventive of Mr Palliser, I said to myself, hoping that his publication would prove very useful in the furtherance of my assignment.

I read on. There were details of the weekly balls, the spas and the wells, in addition to the timings of the stage coaches in and out of Harrogate. There was a directory listing who resided permanently in Harrogate as well as details of all the shops, businesses and professionals in the area. I searched for the Harrogate equivalent to Gordon's only to have my hopes dashed. The most exciting club seemed to be the Clothing Society closely followed by the United Order of Ancient Druids and, the most foreboding, the Temperance Society and the Bible Association. All in all I appeared to be a long way from the gaiety and excitement of London. But surely there must be something livelier or was my assignment here a disguised punishment?

Still reflecting on this I unpacked my trunk which had been placed at the end of the bed and then changed clothes. I now needed to talk to my aunt at length, as, if I was to make a success of my mission in Harrogate, I would most surely need her help.

Chapter 3

Dawson quickly had Lord Redmayne and his party safely transported to the Queen Hotel. No sooner had the carriage pulled up at the main entrance, than Jonathan Dearlove came running down the steps to ensure he was the first person his famous guests would encounter.

A footman opened the door to the carriage and unfolded the steps allowing first, Lord Redmayne and then his ladies to disembark, one by one. As each alighted, they were met by the ebullient proprietor who sympathised greatly with the misfortune they had encountered on their travels that day.

"We are most grateful to you, Mr Dearlove, in coming so swiftly to our rescue," said Lord Redmayne. "We were indeed fortunate that Captain Townsend happened by and was able to bring our dilemma to your notice."

Jonathan Dearlove did not like the notion of sharing any credit with anyone, despite his only contribution in the proceedings being to bark orders to his staff. Consequently, he politely dismissed the Captain's contribution, causing Angela Coutts to raise an eyebrow.

"Welcome back, Your Ladyship, and also to yourself, Miss Coutts," he paused in a solemn moment and then continued. "We were so sad to hear of the passing of your grandmother, the Duchess. She was a great lady; her visits were always memorable." Angela smiled in a kindly fashion, though doubted that Mr Dearlove knew the Duchess that well, as she invariably stayed at the Granby – a hotel reserved entirely for the aristocracy and owned by her good friend Jonathan Benn. As he finished, he passed her a letter. "This arrived for you earlier today."

Angela thanked Mr Dearlove asking if she could now be excused, as she wished to retire to her room. At which point she was led away by a servant, with her lady's maid following on behind.

She entered her room and suddenly found that the familiarity of Harrogate brought back the memory of many happy, and yet also sad times. She sat at the dressing table and turned her head to look across the Stray towards the racecourse and thought about her benefactor, Harriot, Duchess of St. Albans. She recalled her describing how she had walked to Harrogate as a young girl with her own mother to see a performance at the theatre by Mrs Jordan, mistress to the Duke of Clarence, after which she determined she would become an actress.

Angela smiled as she further recalled newspaper articles describing Harriot's unbridled success on the stage, the stories she'd told of great parties and the theatre, as well as the times they spent playing together as they opened up her old theatrical boxes. Harriot had seen life from the very rich to the very poor and this gave her an appreciation of her position in life, which found such favour with her grandfather. A tear formed in each of her eyes blurring her view of the racecourse. She wished she knew more about how her step-grandmama had dealt with all the begging letters and unscrupulous marriage proposals that she herself had received after inheriting the bank from Thomas Coutts.

Angela sat at her dressing table whilst her lady's maid, Emily, fussed around attending to her luggage. Wistfully she turned her head away from the window and looked at the letter given to her by Mr Dearlove; she let out a short sigh, wiped her eyes and then carefully opened it. It was from her father and her sad expression changed to one of concern as she absorbed his message. He had received a warning from a well informed source that she might face even more unwanted attention in Harrogate. He could not specify from whom this attention might come, but the message which had been relayed by a government minister urged her to be on her guard.

"Is everything alright, miss?" said Emily, as she contemplated what her mistress would be wearing for dinner. Following which, she would take such items away and rectify any deterioration brought about by their long journey from London. With Emily in full flow, Angela gathered her thoughts together and then, after carefully folding the letter she replied. "Yes, Emily, although I fear we may not be staying in Harrogate quite as long as we planned."

"But you need to get your strength back, miss, and you know that the waters here do wonders for your complexion. I promised Miss Meredith before we left that I would make sure you took the waters each day. She said you needed complete rest away from all those beggars and fortune hunters."

Angela heaved another sigh and then placed her father's letter in her travelling bag. As she accustomed herself to her surroundings, she noticed on the table in front of her a local publication, which she picked up and read. It was written by Pickersgill Palliser and claimed to be a history and directory of Harrogate including a variety of useful information. Having been to Harrogate on a number of previous occasions, this was something new and being somewhat intrigued, she read on.

She noted that balls were still held weekly at the Crown Hotel on Mondays, the Dragon Hotel on Wednesdays and the Granby Hotel on Fridays (all commencing at nine o'clock). There were even occasional balls at the Cheltenham Pump Room which, given the magnificence of the building, she felt would surely make it an excellent venue. She was not averse to balls, but since the world became acquainted with the extent of her inheritance, she had shied away from unwanted attention. As Angela Burdett she could go anywhere un-noticed but having changed her name to Coutts, as decreed by the terms of her legacy, such anonymity was no longer possible. She continued to read in the hope she would come across information about the theatre, but sadly this wasn't mentioned even cursorily. She surmised that this was because the publication was intended as a guide for the whole season and theatrical performances depended very much on which travelling players passed through from time to time.

Her thoughts were interrupted by a knock on the door. She put down Palliser's companion for visitors and turned to see Emily admitting Lady Redmayne.

"Hello my dear," she said as she strode purposefully into the room. "I was wondering if you would like to accompany me on a short walk before dinner?" Angela smiled and was grateful for the offer but declined, wishing to rest more fully ahead of the dinner engagement with Captain Townsend.

"Are you sure my dear? I feel certain that a brisk walk will have you positively glowing."

"It is so kind of you to think of me, Lady Redmayne, but I fear I would be poor company as Harrogate holds many memories of the time I spent here with my step-grandmama. In fact I was considering returning directly to London."

"My dear Angela, if it is the memories that are bothering you then there is nothing better than a walk. The air here is quite bracing and I feel sure the breeze will blow all unhappy thoughts from your mind," said Lady Redmayne as she caringly took hold of Angela's hand.

"I do appreciate that, but just not now. Emily will prepare me for dinner and we will all put our best faces on, for if nothing else, our Captain Townsend is deserving of a pleasant evening and not one with a sad young girl who is feeling a little sorry for herself."

"As you wish my dear, but please remember that if we can help in any way we will be most pleased to do so. Your father, and in fact all your family, have been very good friends to us all." With that, Lady Redmayne left the room and

Angela turned her attentions to preparing for dinner and the arrival of Captain Townsend.

Emily now returned to help her mistress. The two of them had known each other for many years and were both twenty four years old. To a large extent they had grown up side by side but in very different circumstances. They got along famously, and regardless of their difference in circumstances, Angela trusted Emily almost as a friend rather than a servant. Her thoughts then returned to the letter from her father who urged her to take care.

"So, what do you make of our gallant Captain, Emily?"

The Captain intrigued her. She had only seen him briefly but she liked him.

"Well," said Emily pausing to collect her thoughts. Then smiling she replied, "He's a Light Dragoon and very handsome, Miss"

"Is that all you see? I see a caring man of strong character; noble and chivalrous. He offered to assist us, complete strangers, without giving a second thought as to how that may inconvenience himself. I think my grandfather would have liked him immensely."

"So, you like him then?" asked Emily looking at her mistress in the mirror as she stood behind, gently brushing her hair.

"He seems very nice. He reminds me of my brother and yes, he's handsome. I wonder if he's rich too?"

They both laughed. The thought that she would marry anyone for money was the one thing that would never happen. And with the laughter, Angela began to feel a weight being lifted from her shoulders. It was almost as if her step-grandmama's spirit had suddenly entered the room.

The Duchess of St. Albans had enjoyed every minute of her custodianship of the Coutts fortune whilst also managing to look after it competently. Angela hoped to do the same, but unlike the late Duchess, she had led a sheltered existence. Added to which, her present predicament was one encountered by so very few women over the centuries. No-one, other than maybe Queen Victoria herself, could appreciate her circumstances. The only difference between the two of them was that the Queen had expected her responsibilities whereas Angela had not. Being incredibly rich made Angela's search for an honourable spouse virtually impossible.

Chapter 4

Having refreshed myself, I went in search of my Aunt Violet who I found drinking tea in the orangery gazing over Montpellier Hill. She had created some magnificent gardens, which extended to a full acre. It seemed as if the loss of my uncle and the absence of any children had spawned a deep fondness for nurturing and tending to flowers. Beyond the neat stone walls which surrounded the house and between the trees, we could just make out people, bath chairs, horses and carriages gathering at the bottom of the hill. As the day was drawing to a close most had finished their twice daily rituals of taking the waters, and were either returning to one of the Low Harrogate hotels or were starting to make their way up the hill into town, or on towards High Harrogate where the Queen, the Dragon and the Granby were situated.

"I love my view. The flowers are magnificent this time of year, are they not?" she said as she beckoned me to join her. "Tea?"

"Thank you, Aunt," I replied.

"Now George, tell me why you are really here. It's wonderful to see you but I suspect there is more to it than visiting your old aunt."

"Perceptive as always, Aunt. A great deal has happened since I returned from India but because of the far reaching consequences that could result from my visit I am somewhat restricted in what I can disclose, even to you, Aunt."

"How very intriguing!" she replied, shuffling in her chair. "Perhaps, before you go into anything too alarming, you could begin by telling me what has happened between you and that lovely Hamilton girl – Georgiana wasn't it?"

I shrugged my shoulders, took a deep breath and began.

"Unfortunately Sir William Hamilton didn't approve of my interest in his only daughter. He didn't think me good enough. I am of 'insufficient means,' as he put it. He also didn't like the fact that I frequent clubs like Gordon's, and to make matters worse I think I upset one of his friends there."

"Tosh!" raged Aunt Violet. "The man is a rogue; an unscrupulous mercenary set on selling his daughters hand to the highest bidder."

I smiled. It felt good to still have the support of a family; I had missed that during my time in India. And it was in India where I had met Georgiana. She was accompanying her father as he attempted to involve himself in every possible way of making money. He did his level best to foster a lucrative arrangement with the East India Company, but they were completely unreceptive, judging him to be a 'chancer' who had little to offer in return. Being rebuffed in such a way rendered him even more sour than he already was and I felt the full force of his wrath as he, unfairly, held me partly responsible for his lack of success. He could not understand why anyone would not wish to enter into business with him and supposed that I had somehow poisoned his efforts with carefully constructed innuendos. Wide of the mark though he was, Sir William overlooked his own talent for irritating people which accounted entirely for his failings with the East India Company.

"He may have found few friends in India but I suspect that he may have influence at the Foreign Office, as it seems a strange coincidence that I no sooner expose a friend of his for cheating than I am summoned to a private meeting in St. James's with Lord Palmerston. I would have thought Sir William would have been just as unpalatable to His Lordship as he was to the East India Company, but who knows what goes on in the corridors of power?

Anyway, whether Sir William exercised any influence or not, I find myself having been ordered here ostensibly to look out for Russians, who have either just arrived here or are headed this way."

"Russians?" said my aunt.

"Yes, Russians. Our government is seemingly concerned about the Russians expanding their reach in Europe and perhaps taking the Istanbul strait which is vital to British shipping. That may or may not be fanciful but I do know from my own experiences in India that they are mischievously attempting to cultivate relations in Afghanistan."

My aunt nodded, although I doubted she knew that much about Anglo-Russian relations, which was probably just as well.

"Anyhow, because of all this plotting and scheming Lord Palmerston wants to know what every Russian in England is up to. Conveniently for His Lordship, nearly all the Russians residing in England are situated in London and he has them all under close observation. However, news reached him recently of a party of Russians based in the north of England who were on their way to Harrogate and essentially that is why I am here."

I paused, hoping that I hadn't said too much. I had to tell my aunt something by way of an explanation, as there was no telling where this errand might lead me. In truth, Lord Palmerston had gone into great detail and, in particular, mentioned Count Zadovich who it seems was expelled from England a year or two ago, yet still exercises considerable influence in the secret annals of Russia's foreign affairs. The concern is that the Russians based in the north of England are acting on orders from the Count.

I then added, "Old Palmerston thought I was less likely to attract attention than any other officer, as I could be seen visiting a relative. Either way I am very happy to be here."

Aunt Violet raised her eyebrows, took a sharp intake of breath and exclaimed, "Well that is a tale! I have to say that I find it hard to believe Harrogate is a likely venue for some great international conspiracy. Your Lord Palmerston is either overreacting or alternatively, he's dreamed this up to assist a friend to move you out of London. All the same, if there are any Russians here you should be able to determine that easily enough from the weekly visitor lists that are published."

This was indeed encouraging and I was about to ask more about these visitor lists when Aunt Violet continued, "How long are you to stay here?"

"That I can't say, but we need to make it clear to everyone including Benson and all the servants, that I am here solely to visit with you and regain my strength from the exertions of India. The Russian situation is for your ears only Aunt."

"I may enjoy gossiping from time to time, but you can be assured that I will not be mentioning Russian conspiracies and the like. At my time of life, I seem to be constantly proving that I am still of a sound mind and I would worry that any mention by me of a Russian conspiracy in Harrogate would seriously jeopardize that," she said, once more shuffling in her chair and stiffening her back.

"Nevertheless, we will endeavour to help you get as much rest as possible my dear boy; I hope it means you can stay for a long time. We will say no more of Lord Palmerston and his overworked paranoia for Russians. Harrogate is exceedingly pleasant this time of year and I am sure you will have an enjoyable stay and leave suitably refreshed," she added, now relaxing in her chair.

"We might even persuade you to take the waters," she smiled. "They can provide an invigorating tonic," and after a little thought continued, "that is, if you drink the right ones. The wrong ones are best not drunk at all."

"Thank you, Aunt, I will bear that in mind, but after India I reckon that I could pretty much drink anything and survive. Ghastly place! Death and disease everywhere."

I had momentarily forgotten that my aunt had her own unhappy and tragic memories of India in which a cholera epidemic had accounted for the death of my uncle. My insensitive remark prompted me to quickly change the subject.

"I wondered when the next horse race would be, Aunt? I thought it would be amusing to enter my horse Tribune," I said, thinking that this could help me meet more people and steer any suspicious minds away from the true purpose of my visit.

"You still love riding I see. Only you would choose to ride all the way from London on a horse when you could sit in the comfort of a mail coach," she said, completely ignoring my question. "I can't be certain but I think there could be a race this coming week. I will ask Benson to find out for certain. He knows about such things." Then after a brief and thoughtful pause added, "Do you think your Tribune would have a chance?"

I smiled and held my aunt's gaze for a full five minutes as I regaled Tribune's exploits and pedigree. Being a close relative of Touchstone, who won the St. Leger in '34, I was sure he would outrun anything Harrogate had to offer.

"I remember reading about Touchstone," said my aunt. "He went missing for months, did he not? As I recall, the stable boy charged with returning him to his home after winning a big race, lost him whilst under the influence of an excess of alcohol."

"That is to say, it was the stable boy under the influence of alcohol and not the horse," she laughed.

"That is true, Aunt and I dare say there are many horses now claimed to be sired by Touchstone."

With that I noticed it was time to ready myself for my return to the Queen Hotel and dinner with Miss Coutts. I was to take my aunt's carriage, which was to be at my disposal throughout my stay. I therefore retired to my room and then dressed myself in my uniform, which had been thoughtfully laid out for me. My boots had been polished along with my sword, giving me the distinct feeling that my aunt was keen to see I made a good impression. Suitably bathed, dressed and polished, I headed out of Holderness House and into the unknown of the night and dinner with Miss Angela Coutts.

Chapter 5

It was a beautiful summer's evening as we drove out of Holderness House and across the Stray towards the Queen Hotel. Although well past midsummer's day and despite being early evening, daylight still had plenty of life left in her. The surprisingly mild temperature ensured a plentiful supply of visitors embarking on an evening stroll. All the wells were now closed for the day and the visitors to Harrogate were turning their attention to more social pastimes. Many would go to concerts or balls and some would try their hand at cards, assuming they could find suitable opponents. I supposed that the cards played in Harrogate were likely to be more genteel and friendly than the intensity I used to witness at Gordon's.

The carriage drove past the elegant townhouses of Prospect Place and then the Brunswick Hotel, rattling effortlessly on towards the Queen Hotel. Peering through the carriage window, I witnessed the great and the good enjoying the August weather whereupon I returned my thoughts to the search for Russians.

My aunt confirmed that there were weekly lists printed of those visiting Harrogate and that seemed like a good place to start. In the meantime, I would need to keep my eyes and ears open. Gazing across the peaceful expanse of the Stray, I considered the words of my aunt concluding that it really did seem hard to comprehend there could be an international conspiracy developing here.

As that thought flashed across my mind, the carriage ran over something in the road and momentarily I was off my seat and my hair was grazing the silk lining of the carriage roof. I settled back down with a bump and instinctively let out a shout to the driver, "Steady on Cookson!"

"Sorry, Captain sir," came the apologetic response. Driving towards the race-course seemed to spur on Cookson and so once again I found myself bouncing uncomfortably.

"Damn it all man, have a care!" which was met with a repeat of the last apology. "I am in good time," I said leaning out the carriage window, "there is no need to hurry. Let the horses walk us in from here." Which he duly did and within a minute I could see the Queen Hotel through the left-hand window of the carriage.

We drove through the open gates of the hotel just behind a hansom cab, which delayed our journey momentarily. With its passenger safely alighted and heading into the hotel our carriage was able to pull up at the main entrance. A face appeared at the window of the carriage and in a fraction of a second the door opened, the step lowered and I was once again standing outside the famous hotel. On this occasion, however, I was not a semi-dishevelled traveller but a Captain of the 11th Light Dragoons, finely turned out with my boots, belts and sword gleaming in the evening sun. I stood proud and caught the eye of the boy holding the horses of our carriage; it was the same boy who held Tribune a few hours earlier.

I looked up at Cookson, who was no doubt relieved to be shot of me and said, "I should be ready to return around ten o'clock. I will meet you here and please ensure you're not late." I tried not to be too hard on the lad but his distant expression did nothing to inspire confidence. Gamefully he replied with a robust, "Yes, Captain," like as not to impress the boy holding the horses who would only be a couple of years younger than him. I then turned on my heel, took my shako from my head and walked into the hotel.

No sooner had I crossed the threshold than I was met by Jonathan Dearlove, who looked extremely pleased to see me. Then with a broad smile and outstretched hand said, "Captain Townsend, welcome back to the Queen Hotel. It's so good to see you again and looking simply splendid in your uniform."

"Thank you, sir," I replied as Mr Dearlove directed me through a reception area bustling with guests.

"Being so far from the capital we rarely get chance to see such magnificence. Generally we only see veterans and the poor wounded looking to restore their health following some ghastly campaign somewhere in the back of beyond. No sir, it is a privilege to see one of Her Majesty's Light Dragoons dining here and in such esteemed company too. We are indeed the most fortunate establishment in the entire county," added Mr Dearlove as we made our way along an impressively wide corridor.

His comments all sounded a bit too pretentious for me, but I nonetheless smiled politely accepting his compliment as graciously as possible. My aunt's insistence that I wear my uniform was appearing to have been a wise move. Happily there was no sign of Dawson, even though it may have proved enlightening for him to have seen me dressed like this. Mr Dearlove then personally escorted me to the private dining room.

He opened the door and announced my arrival as a footman stepped forward and relieved me of my shako and gloves. Mr Dearlove bowed to the room's occupants, wished us all a pleasant evening and politely took his leave.

The room was beautifully presented with swagged, golden curtains; walls lined with fluted silk, rich cut-glass chandeliers and handsomely carved furniture. A fire burned brightly in the hearth assisting the candles in illuminating the room. Although the sun wouldn't be setting for at least another hour the room faced east and was in much need of this additional light.

"Captain Townsend, we are so pleased to see you, I trust you are adequately rested after we inconvenienced you so greatly?" said Lord Redmayne as he crossed the room to greet me. Before I could reply, my hand was in his and he was shaking my arm most vigorously. His reddened face shone brightly against a handsome white cravat. By any account he was extremely well turned out and, save for the cravat, was dressed from head to toe in black.

I smiled and assured him that it was my pleasure to be of assistance at which point he led me to Lady Redmayne and Miss Coutts who were seated by the fire.

"Captain, how different you look in your splendid uniform!" remarked Lady Redmayne as she appeared to will a similar response from Miss Coutts. I wondered if Lady Redmayne harboured similar matchmaking ambitions to my aunt. Regardless of this, yet again Miss Coutts seemed a little ambivalent to my presence. Having probably repelled more advances from British officers than Napoleon himself, this was perhaps entirely understandable. Notwithstanding, I hoped that by the end of the evening I would make some improvement here.

"You are very kind, Lady Redmayne," I said, bowing to her in the process. I turned to greet Miss Coutts who smiled pleasantly enough and with the formalities over, Lord Redmayne beckoned me towards the table. The table was oblong in shape and around eight feet long and half as wide. It had been laid for four people, with Lord and Lady Redmayne seated at either end and I was to sit directly opposite Miss Coutts. Irrespective of there being just the four of us, almost every inch of the table was taken up with glasses, cutlery and adornments. This seemed to indicate that we were in for a long banquet. I was guided to my place and whilst endeavouring not to cause injury or damage with my sword, proceeded to sit down.

My efforts to keep my sword out of harm's way failed and I found the hilt wedged deep into my thigh. I began to cry out then quickly stopped myself, making a clumsy attempt to cover up my lack of elegance in the process.

"Are we expecting trouble tonight?" asked Miss Coutts mischievously, as a smile flickered across her face. It might sound strange but at that moment I suddenly warmed to her. She had appeared aloof and serious but it seemed that beneath it all lived a vibrant sense of humour.

"No, I must confess that I am in full military attire to please my aunt," I said smiling as if to suggest I had little choice in the matter.

"You have an aunt with you, Captain?" enquired Lord Redmayne. "You should have said; we would have been delighted to meet her."

Before I could answer His Lordship, Lady Redmayne asked if my aunt was in Harrogate for a daily dose of the waters. I then explained that she resided on a permanent basis at Holderness House, after having lost her husband in India to the cholera pandemic, ironically picked up from polluted water. "I am here to visit with her," I added after a brief pause.

"How awful," said Miss Coutts, speaking almost simultaneously. She had clearly chosen her words after hearing of my uncle's death and in the belief that I had finished speaking.

"My apologies, Captain, I don't mean that it is awful you are visiting her. I meant to say it is awful that she should lose her husband in such a way." Smiling, I reassured her that I knew what she intended.

"Does your aunt hail from Harrogate, Captain?" asked Lord Redmayne, who was now drinking wine with increasing enthusiasm.

"Not exactly," I replied. "Actually she was born near the New Forest. When she married my uncle she moved to his family home in Yorkshire and eventually to Dunsforth Hall which is only a few miles from Boroughbridge."

"Boroughbridge?" interjected Miss Coutts. "My father was formerly the Member of Parliament for Boroughbridge. That's where his political career really started." There was no mistaking the pride in her voice as she recounted her father's achievements to us all.

"Really? I had no idea," I said, feeling slightly embarrassed as to my ignorance of this fact. I had of course heard of her father but was not aware that he had represented Boroughbridge.

"Yes, my grandfather bought him the seat. It was a little ironic that my father joined Parliament in that way as he then spent the next thirty years campaigning for electoral reform," replied Miss Coutts.

"Yes, Captain, as I am sure you are aware, Sir Francis Burdett is one of our most notable politicians," interrupted Lord Redmayne. "A brave man whose sense of fair play has made him very popular with the public. We have been

31

friends since the time of that shameful Peterloo massacre almost twenty years ago, which sadly was not dissimilar to the recent and reprehensible Battle of Bossenden Wood."

The mention of, not only the Peterloo massacre, but also the Battle of Bossenden Wood, had me really wishing that I hadn't brought my sword as it was too graphic a reminder of the terrible events, where cavalry had charged demonstrators with swords drawn, killing many and injuring hundreds of others.

"I did hear of the Battle of Bossenden Wood," interjected a serious looking Miss Coutts. "But I have little knowledge of Peterloo, sir. I recall my father mentioning the name but I cannot recollect the exact details. Was it as bad as Bossenden Wood?"

"Unfortunately, miss, it was much worse. Peterloo was, in fact, St Peter's Field, Manchester where sixty thousand or more were demonstrating for the right to vote. Fifteen people died and hundreds more injured – a tragic day."

I inwardly cringed at the announcement of these daunting statistics.

"And what is your view on all this, Captain?" asked Lady Redmayne, sensing my unease.

"I think that any loss of life at these gatherings is regrettable," I replied as I quickly gathered my thoughts. "And whereas I know little of the incident in Manchester, I do know something of the Battle of Bossenden Wood. My understanding is that it all started as a former inmate of an asylum, called Tom Courtenay, murdered a constable who had been sent to arrest him. Courtenay, together with a group of followers then collided with soldiers from the 45th Foot, whereupon a young lieutenant and nine demonstrators were killed including Courtenay himself."

"So you would say that the events at Bossenden were not reprehensible?" enquired Lady Redmayne, prompting everyone else to look keenly towards me.

"It is very difficult for me to pass judgement, Lady Redmayne. I can't say whether or not either party should be censured. I know only too well that when two sides meet on a field, a wrong word or gesture can be as explosive as a spark on gunpowder. Only those who were there can say whether or not lives could have been spared," I replied as diplomatically as I could.

"I think it's time we changed the subject as this seems a little unfair on Captain Townsend who, after all, is our guest and I fear we may be embarrassing him," added Miss Coutts.

"Quite right," concurred Lord Redmayne as Lady Redmayne smiled apologetically.

All the while, the servants had effortlessly begun to serve dinner and we were soon moving through the courses. After several days on the road I was really enjoying the whole experience of good food, fine wines and the most interesting company one could find in England. Short of having Queen Victoria and perhaps the Duke of Wellington present, it was hard to imagine a more intriguing group.

In the meantime the wine flowed and most of it into the glass of Lord Redmayne, who as a result, became ever more demonstrative and progressively louder. His excited chattering was interrupted by the calm and measured Miss Coutts.

"How long are you planning on staying in Harrogate, Captain?" she enquired.

"That is hard to say," I replied. "I expect I will stay at least a couple of weeks. I haven't seen my aunt for several years and I am really looking forward to spending time with her. In any event, I find London can be quiet this time of year and the only thing I will miss is watching the odd game of cricket at Lords."

The absence of any nodding suggested that I was the sole cricket lover in the room and so I then returned the question to Miss Coutts only for her response to be equally non-committal. Lord Redmayne then turned to his young charge.

"I hope your father may yet join us?"

"Unfortunately, sir, I regret that is unlikely as now he's nearing seventy, he no longer finds travelling long distances agreeable. I did try to persuade him that a trip to Harrogate may prove beneficial as he is plagued by gout and is often in great pain. Under normal circumstances I would, of course, have remained by his side but I find myself in anything but normal circumstances and felt the need to retreat here to restore my own health."

Lord Redmayne nodded in acceptance of this, his cheeks glowing ever brighter. "I am sure Sir Francis understands the great responsibility that you now bear, and as soon as the Harrogate waters have restored your health, he will assuredly welcome your return."

Again, his dominance of the evening was interrupted by Miss Coutts who addressed another question to me.

"Did you ride that lovely horse of yours all the way from London?" she asked.

"I did actually," then after a moment's pause continued. "He is a fine horse and I was rather hoping that I might be able to enter him in one of Harrogate's horse races. He has a great pedigree having been sired by Touchstone, one of the best horses I have ever owned. Not Touchstone that is, but Tribune, which is his name." Everything came out rather clumsily, as I supposed I was still a little nervous at being in such august company.

"You clearly love horses, which I suppose is mandatory for a cavalry officer, but won't your horse be tired after such a long ride?" she said calmly, once again breaking into a smile.

"He is used to it, miss. He has a big heart and I am sure if he were to race, he would give a good account of himself."

"I too, like to ride, Captain, and have very fond memories of the ponies I've had over the years," she replied. It seemed that Miss Coutts was beginning to relax in my company and although shy, she demonstrated a pleasant and caring disposition. It was hard not to be impressed by her.

I offered to take her riding but she politely declined saying that her doctor required her to avoid over-exerting herself. Again I felt a trifle awkward. Another British officer successfully repelled, I thought to myself. Even though in truth, I had no business making social arrangements which, nonetheless, were borne out of a growing admiration for Miss Coutts and not some romantic notion.

"Anyhow, I do intend to take the waters and enjoy as much fresh air as possible," she added confidently, "I also wish to visit Bolton Abbey and skip across the stepping stones in the river. I have such happy memories of the time I spent there with my sisters."

"So this is not your first visit to Harrogate?" I replied, impressed by her undoubted knowledge of the area.

"Why no, Captain. I have been here many times. My late step-grandmama, the Duchess of St. Albans, brought me and my sisters here on more than one occasion. The Duchess loved everything about the town and its surroundings."

Under normal circumstances, I would have offered to escort Miss Coutts to Bolton Abbey or indeed anywhere else she chose to visit. But having already been rebuffed, and given I was on important business for Lord Palmerston, I thought better of it. Furthermore, she was clearly escaping the attention of young men intent on marrying her and I had no desire to be added to that infamous group. Consequently, I held back in the certain belief that if Miss Coutts welcomed my company at any time she would surely make that known to me.

The dinner progressed at a pleasant pace and the pattern of the evening continued with Lord Redmayne's excited conversation interspersed with moments of sobriety from Miss Coutts. Lady Redmayne barely spoke and seemed content enough to smile and nod in agreement with anything her husband said.

"That was a wonderful dinner, was it not Captain?" remarked Lord Redmayne cheerfully whilst nodding his head from side to side in time with the music which was now being played elsewhere in the hotel.

"It was as good as anything one would find in London," I replied with a genuine display of contentment.

"Indeed, sir, indeed!" said Lord Redmayne and then with some satisfaction added, "I am so glad we chose to reside here instead of the Granby. I may be alone in thinking this, but I can't abide the rigmarole they have at dinner."

"You're not alone, sir, although I expect that Mr. Benn will be disappointed at our decision," interjected Miss Coutts.

I took it that Mr. Benn was the owner of the Granby however I had no idea what this 'rigmarole' was that so displeased both Lord Redmayne and Miss Coutts. As the conversation unfolded it became apparent that it was a system by which the hotel avoided ranking its aristocratic guests. Apparently there was one long table at dinner and the most recent arrivals sat at the far end and the longer they remained in residence, the further they moved towards the top. The guest who sat at the top of the table was quite simply the one who had been in residence the longest and took no account of their rank in society.

"One has to say that it does avoid the host offending some earl or countess. However, when I was there, it made me feel like I was back at school," said Lady Redmayne receiving nods of agreement from her husband and Miss Coutts.

"How would such a system fare in the 11th Light Dragoons, Captain?" asked Miss Coutts. I could have laughed out loud at the prospect but restricted myself to a broad smile.

"Well it would certainly be interesting," I replied and after a brief pause added, "nonetheless, I suspect Earl Cardigan may not appreciate the spirit of equality as he seems completely at home with the present system of ranking. It is rumoured that he paid £40,000 for his regiment for that very purpose. When he is in the company of royalty then, perhaps, he may welcome the Granby's protocol!"

It seemed that the characteristics of the commander of the 11th Light Dragoons were well known to all those seated around the table, as everyone smiled in unison.

Lord Redmayne then suggested that he and I should partake of a cigar over a game of billiards. The ladies chose to head towards the ballroom and listen to the orchestra who sounded remarkably good. Had I closed my eyes, I could have fooled myself into believing that I was back in London.

As we parted from the ladies, His Lordship indicated that he might consider a small wager if I were to grant him odds. That seemed like a very bad idea. If he lost, I would be accused of taking advantage of an older man worse for the drink and if I lost, I would be well out of pocket. I therefore declined his kind offer with as much diplomacy as I could muster.

We wandered into the billiard room and His Lordship acquired two fine Cuban cigars from the attendant, which we promptly lit. I rested on my billiard cue and drew on the cigar which necessitated juggling with the glass of port which His Lordship had just passed me. Lord Redmayne attempted an ambitious pot, requiring him to stretch far across the table. He struggled manfully to reach the balls with his cue but found this manoeuvre difficult when all the while keeping one foot on the floor. As I continued smoking and drinking intermittently I couldn't help but think that life wasn't that bad after all. I had been packed off out of London on, perhaps, some wild goose chase, only to land on my feet dining in this fine establishment and with the richest woman in England.

"Now my boy, it's your shot," said Lord Redmayne as he stepped away from the table, having failed to get the balls to collide.

"Better with a pistol than a cue," said Lord Redmayne, "drunk or sober, I never miss."

I put my cigar down and as I moved towards the table His Lordship seemed to sober up and said in a friendly but equally serious tone. "You don't know how grateful we are that it was you who found us today and not some chancer or newspaper man, to say nothing of a band of villains or Chartists. Please keep the events of today to yourself. We are trying to keep something of a low profile. The whole country is aware of the good fortune that has passed the way of Miss Coutts but, sadly, at great loss to her of her grandmother. Although, if the truth be told, the Duchess of St. Albans was her step-grandmother. They were, nevertheless, very close."

"You can depend on my discretion, sir," I replied as I played my first shot.

"You may see me as too old to be taking charge of such a wealthy young woman," said Lord Redmayne provocatively.

"Absolutely not," I asserted as I prepared myself for another shot.

"I may be old when compared to the likes of you, Captain, but I assure you that I can still take care of myself."

"Of that I have no doubt, sir," I insisted.

"We will be staying as long as Miss Coutts needs us, having said that her companion, Miss Hannah Meredith will be coming up from London later this week, at which point they may feel our presence is no longer essential."

I continued to listen intently.

"I am sure you have a grasp of the situation, Captain, and also the need for secrecy. Therefore you can imagine my horror when I found out that some ambitious newspaper man circulates lists of who is staying at each hotel and boarding house in the area. Damn nuisance!"

He paused and I took the opportunity to play another shot, which was a good one.

"Excellent shot, my boy! Glad I didn't place a wager now. Anyway this fellow Pickersgill or Pickershill, or whatever his damn name is, will be endeavouring to publish our names and that of Miss Coutts in his weekly list. Mr Dearlove has assured us that the existence of the three of us in Harrogate will not be passed to him in the normal way but these things have a habit of getting out."

I nodded in agreement as I continued to play billiards. All the while Lord Redmayne took careful note of my progress.

"By God, you are quite the marksman! Now where was I? Oh yes, Pickey what's his name. Please do everything in your power to keep our names as secret as may be possible."

I stood up from the table and looked him straight in the eye and said, "You may rely on me, sir." With that he nodded in gratitude and picked up his cue to play another shot.

"I'm sorry, sir, but it's still my play."

"And so it is," said Lord Redmayne apologetically.

We played on, but the night's excesses took their toll on His Lordship, who suggested that we bring our game to a close and re-join the ladies. I happily gave up my cue but reluctantly parted company with my cigar. We then searched for the ladies and duly found them in the ballroom suitably reclined on a well-stuffed, red, damask sofa. Several chandeliers blazed away but the room still seemed dimly lit. Additionally, most of this light was concentrated around the musicians. A few couples were bravely attempting the waltz, drawing the attention of the less energetic guests away from myself and Lord Redmayne as we approached the ladies almost un-noticed.

"My dears, are you comfortable here?" said Lord Redmayne when we drew up alongside the sofa, taking them both by surprise.

"Most certainly, sir," said Lady Redmayne who politely enquired as to the outcome of the billiard game. His Lordship mumbled something inaudible relying on the music to drown out whatever he said. I was standing alongside him and couldn't decipher a single word. Lady Redmayne and Miss Coutts strained their hearing but, like myself, nodded as if they had heard and understood every syllable. The alternative was to ask him to repeat himself and no one appeared to think that would be a productive exercise.

Not wishing to dance and detecting that the ladies had encountered enough excitement for one day, I decided that I would take my leave. I waited until the music stopped along with the smattering of applause which followed and then addressed my hosts.

"Lady Redmayne, Miss Coutts," and then turning to my left added, "Lord Redmayne, I fear it is time for me to take my leave and allow you to rest after what has been a very trying day for you all. Please accept my most sincere thanks for a simply splendid evening. I could not imagine more convivial company," and with that I bowed my head as gracefully as possible.

"Think nothing of it, Captain. You did us all a great service and it has been our pleasure to repay you in some small way for your unselfish act on the Leeds Road," replied Lord Redmayne.

"We hope we will see you again, Captain, before we leave," said Lady Redmayne.

"I have been very pleased to make your acquaintance, Captain. I, too, hope that we may see you again," said Miss Coutts, smiling sincerely.

I again bowed my head acknowledging their kind words and with an exchange of good evenings and good nights, I headed out of the ballroom.

I was reunited with my shako and gloves, following which I left the hotel and went in search of my aunt's carriage. It wasn't hard to find, being only yards to my left with Cookson seemingly asleep with a blanket over his knees and the reins in his lap.

"Cookson!" I said, giving the lad a start.

"Yes, sir," came his belated response as he attempted to disguise the fact that I had disturbed him at a time when he was not completely in charge of his faculties.

"Home, Cookson. Nice and steady if you please," and with that I sat back in the carriage and reflected on an evening where I had really enjoyed myself far more than I had ever expected. All in all, an extraordinary day and fancy Angela Coutts's father being the Member of Parliament for Boroughbridge which is so close to Dunsforth where I had spent so much time in my youth! I momentarily contemplated going on to a club or a ball to see if I could find out anything which might assist me in locating Palmerston's Russians but I just didn't have the energy, as like the Redmayne's and Miss Coutts, I was decidedly tired.

In any event, with the help of the visitor lists which are apparently readily available, what could be simpler? Finding anyone here shouldn't be that hard. That is, of course, unless the Russians go to the same lengths as Lord Redmayne to keep their names out of the lists.

Chapter 6

I was down to breakfast at around eight o'clock, where I found my aunt sitting at the head of the table waiting for me and by the look on her face, she had been waiting for some time.

"Good morning, Aunt," I said, breezing into the room and heading straight for the breakfast which was elegantly laid out in silver salvers on the side table.

"And a very good morning to you too. Would you like some eggs to add to the bacon, ham and devilled kidneys which seem to have caught your eye?" she replied.

"Thank you, Aunt. That would be splendid."

"Splendid! Steady on George, it's a bit early for a splendid." She enjoyed teasing me and continued by saying, "The ways of the aristocracy seem to be rubbing off on you, and after just one dinner! The next thing you know, you will be saying 'ha ha' and 'how do'."

"Yes, very amusing," I replied. "Do you think I could I have two poached eggs please?"

My aunt passed on my request to Cookson, who seemed to have fully recovered from his efforts of the previous evening.

"Now you can tell me all about last night. I am most anxious to know whether or not my nephew will be rescuing the house of Coutts from their most miserable and impoverished existence."

I couldn't help but smile at the way my aunt had phrased the question which was an attempt to satisfy her extremely active curiosity. In due deference to my aunt's approach I responded by saying, "If only it were that easy. I fear that even I don't have enough money to restore health to the finances of Miss Coutts."

My aunt half smiled but was slightly irritated that I had followed her down the path of sarcasm. "Yes, very droll George and now, perhaps, you can give me a sensible account of last night's events," then leaning forward asked, "What is the young thing like?"

"She is simply charming. Quite shy really, but she is possessed of a sharp mind and wit to match. I liked her immensely. She can be a bit serious and solemn but that's hardly surprising, and before you go any further, I would suggest that there is more chance of Napoleon rising from the dead than Miss Coutts and I becoming romantically involved."

I could see a hint of disappointment dance across my aunt's face as I continued.

"She has left London to be away from all the fortune hunters and beggars and I am guessing that she would welcome friendship from someone rather than another marriage proposal."

"Alas, I fear you are right but you must forgive your old aunt for indulging in a little day dream."

My eggs arrived and they were perfectly cooked. With my aunt's hopes of a dramatic rise up the ranks in England's hierarchy well and truly dashed, I moved the conversation to the task for which Lord Palmerston had been so keen to have me travel to Harrogate.

"There is one thing you can help me with, Aunt, and that is to do with the visitor lists you mentioned yesterday."

Reluctantly, she accepted that her day dream had been short lived whereupon she returned to the present day and answered my question.

"Of course, George, how can I help you?"

I then recounted my conversation with Lord Redmayne whilst the two of us played billiards, explaining that the lists which she had first brought to my attention, although extremely inconvenient to Lord Redmayne and Miss Coutts, could be of great assistance to me.

My aunt then advised me that it was Mr Palliser who prepared the weekly lists, the same Pickersgill Palliser who had written the publication which she had left in my room. He also ran the post office in High Harrogate and that is where she suggested I should first look for him. She further cautioned me to be considerate with him as he had recently lost his son who was just three years old.

Following the conclusion of breakfast I excused myself, returned to my room, and then readied myself for the challenges of the day. I had no idea what those were to be, but upon remembering Lord Palmerston's words I picked up one of my regimental pistols leaving the other safely stowed in my trunk.

As was my custom I also picked up my folding pen knife made by Joseph Manning of Sheffield and tucked it into my boot. This little device had often been useful during the times I had been out on patrol in India, and even though

I couldn't see why I would need this, or indeed my pistol on a visit to the post office, I at least contented myself that I was taking my job seriously.

Thanks to my aunt, I had established that the post office was in High Harrogate, not far from the Granby Hotel. This represented either a healthy walk or a short ride and not wishing to waste time, I asked Benson if he could have Tribune saddled.

Tribune looked suitably recovered from our two hundred mile journey north and off we went once more in search of adventure. We walked through the gates of Holderness House and due to the large volume of people I could see milling about, I resisted the temptation to gallop. The paths and roads were filled with people making their way either to or from the wells. Many were walking with difficulty and some were being pushed in bath chairs. I was taken aback by their numbers and the scale of their infirmity. Harrogate was more popular than I had envisaged.

With Tribune proceeding at little more than walking pace, I found myself tipping my hat and exchanging a hearty 'good morning' with almost every step. Eventually it came to the point where I thought it more productive to leave these popular paths and gallop on the more sparsely used sections of the common grassland of the Stray. Pleasant though it was to be treated in such a friendly manner by complete strangers, some of which were young, female and attractive, I was by necessity anxious to progress.

Tribune seemed to welcome this opportunity to lengthen his stride and he was flying over the turf as we made our way past the Brunswick and Queen Hotels. We interrupted the odd sheep's peaceful grazing as we galloped across these two hundred acres of common ground and within minutes we were in High Harrogate, where I now set about looking for Mr Palliser.

I was meandering between Christchurch and the Granby Hotel and could not see any sign of a building which resembled a post office. All I could see was a row of smart town houses facing the green expanse of the Stray on a street named Park Parade. I followed the road until for some reason it changed its name to Regent's Parade and at the point where the row of properties ended, standing proudly on the opposite side of the thoroughfare I could see a white-washed building which looked promising. There were no signs visible to assist me in making this presumption; however the presence of a mail coach and a hive of activity outside seemed fairly conclusive.

The coach drawn by four large horses pulled slowly away as I dismounted Tribune and tied him to a rail. He immediately began to drink from the trough,

High Harrogate.

which moments earlier had been used by the horses pulling the mail coach. The smell of horses was quite profound. I straightened my coat, dusted myself down and stepped up to the entrance of the building. As I walked through the door I noticed a small brass sign on the left hand side announcing that I had indeed arrived at the post office managed by Mr Palliser. Once inside I saw two other people. One by one they handed over their letters for posting. I waited patiently as the scholarly looking gentleman attended to them. I took him to be Pickersgill Palliser, a man in his early thirties. He dealt with these customers quickly and efficiently, whereupon I stepped forward and introduced myself, adding that I was staying with my aunt at Holderness House.

"It is a pleasure to meet you, Captain," he replied. "Your aunt mentioned that she was expecting you, my name is Pickersgill Palliser," he said, taking my hand in his and shaking it enthusiastically. He then turned around and took a letter from a small pile of mail which rested on a table amongst many other neatly stacked piles.

"It is indeed fortuitous that you happened by, as only this morning I received a letter addressed to your good self and here it is. That will be three pence please." I was always irritated whenever I had to pay for letters, feeling that pleasure should belong to the sender. I didn't object to paying for good news but invariably I found myself paying for quite the opposite.

I knew the moment I held it in my hand that the letter would be one of Palmerston's coded missives. He could have prepaid the postage but obviously felt that privilege should belong to me, which hardly seemed fair. Mr Palliser seemed to detect my sense of dismay.

"Not bad news, I hope?" said Palliser in a rather enquiring manner.

"I expect not," I replied, dismissing it in an instant.

A notice on the wall behind him suddenly caught my eye. It was announcing the availability of a new edition of his popular publication.

"Mr Palliser, I see from your notice that a new edition of the *Harrogate Advertiser* is now on sale. Would this, by chance, incorporate an up to date list of visitors?" I said, almost reciting word for word the advertisement on the wall. "Having just arrived in Harrogate, it would be extremely useful to know if any of my friends or acquaintances are in residence."

"But of course, Captain. I have just published a new list today which should include everyone who is residing here as of yesterday," and with the air of a man pleased with himself for having initiated the publication, he duly handed me the paper. I thanked him and started to thumb through the pages, which were much more voluminous than I had bargained for. I didn't want Mr Palliser to gain any insight into the real reason I was interested in the weekly list and therefore prudently halted my search, folded the paper and then placed it under my arm.

After paying for his publication and bidding him a good day, I turned on my heels and walked regimentally out of the door. As I was leaving, I was stopped in my tracks by a pretty young girl who was heading into the post office carrying a letter. She looked familiar but I couldn't place where I had seen her before. I held the door open and bowed my head as she made her way over to Mr Palliser. She was dressed quite simply but there was no disguising her beauty. I considered inventing some question I could go back and ask Mr Palliser which would enable me to speak to the girl, but thought better of it, closed the door behind me and re-joined Tribune.

I decided to read the letter and Palliser's *Harrogate Advertiser* privately and consequently mounted Tribune and headed off towards the Stray to find somewhere appropriately secluded. There were odd benches dotted about the two hundred acre Stray and all I needed was to locate one which was empty. It was hard not to be slightly envious of the people of Harrogate at having such a large expanse of open grassland on their doorstep. And even more so due to the fact it could never be developed in any way whatsoever, preserving the integrity of the well water for everyone. For a small town such as this to have something akin to Hyde Park in its midst, was quite extraordinary.

After riding past three benches which were occupied, I came across a vacant one situated about as far from the hotels as was possible. I quickly dismounted and tied Tribune's reins to the back of the bench.

I sat down to some serious reading whilst Tribune took the opportunity to assist the sheep in keeping the grass well-trimmed.

I was torn between opening the letter and reading the list to search for Russians and in the end I opted for the latter. Palmerston's letter would be hard work as the true message was hidden in the second paragraph and in code. The date would identify the relevant words and this was a new code developed, supposedly, for my benefit. If the date was, say, the seventh of the month then the message would be every seventh word. If the date was the twenty third, then the message would be every fifth word, being the sum of the two and the three. The seventeenth would mean looking at every eighth word and so on. It was hard enough reading the code but extremely taxing on the brain when it came to replying as I had to send messages back using precisely the same method.

So, having parked Lord Palmerston's coded message to one side I started to read the *Harrogate Advertiser*. I found the list I needed at the back of the paper, set out in alphabetical order of the hotels. Following my discussion with Lord Redmayne regarding these lists I now had a certain scepticism as to their completeness. Surely any Russians residing in Harrogate would take care to keep their names out of any lists if their intentions were anything other than honourable? I pressed on regardless and could see no visitors with Russian sounding names at the Bay Horse Inn, Binn's Hotel, The Brunswick, Black Swan or the Commercial, but then I let out a stifled 'hallelujah' as I came to the Crown Hotel.

Residing there were Svetlana and Vladimir Von Benckendorff. Russian-sounding names if ever I heard any. "Well, well, old Palmy was right on the money," I said to myself, pleased that this whole thing suddenly looked more credible and was not just some fantasy dreamed up in order to get me out of London. Having said that, it still felt like Sir William Hamilton had a hand in all this. Anyway it was with a modicum of satisfaction that I opened the letter which read as follows:

29th July 1838

My dear George,

I trust this letter finds you well and suitably recovered from the ardours of your journey from London. We all miss you greatly but appreciate that your aunt's demands on your time are more pressing than ours. You will not be surprised to hear that we have a problem which we can ignore no longer.

(I doubted that – who writes these things, I wondered? And then came the important second paragraph. I noticed the date as being the twenty-ninth, which meant I needed to read every eleventh word being the sum of two and nine.)

*We are sorry to trouble you but we really do **need** your help as William is accumulating large debts. You must **know** that he's not himself and that your assistance is needed **urgently**. We suspect that he's losing most of his money gambling **as** he's rarely home of an evening. We believe he aims **to** risk his fortune regardless of advice he's receiving from us. **Whether** he is completely insane or not I couldn't say. Playing **Russian** roulette would seem to be all he hasn't attempted. He's **residing** in London but I suggest that were he to live **in** Cheltenham or Bath we would all be happier. Perhaps even **Harrogate**?*

George, we are at our wits end and extremely concerned at the behaviour of our cousin and would greatly appreciate your intervention.

Your humble servant,

Samuel

Having found two people I suspected of being Russian residing at the Crown, I knew I must reply quickly. I immediately wondered how on earth I was going to get the names of the Von Benckendorff's into a letter using this tricky code. This was going to take a while and so I headed back to Holderness House to think and create. I felt that, under the circumstances, I should also mention Miss Coutts was residing in Harrogate. With luck, and providing my intellect was up to snuff, I would catch the afternoon post.

Tribune soon had me back to my aunt's where I proceeded to the peaceful surroundings of the library. I repeatedly scratched my head as I made countless attempts to communicate using Lord Palmerston's code but failed miserably. A pile of aborted letters, screwed up into balls of paper, mounted by my side.

I eventually wrote as follows:

6th August 1838

My dear Samuel,

It was so good to receive your letter of the 29th July. Naturally I am vexed at my cousin's prolonged gambling problem. I do not believe relocating him to another town will prove useful as he is bound to find somewhere to gamble wherever he goes.

*William has been gambling for **two** years now. They say the **Russians** he met in Warsaw, whilst **staying** there, led him astray. I **hear** that they cruelly took him **in**, robbing him of his prized **Harrogate** town house. William has since **named** them, unfortunately having spoken to **Von Benckendorff**, I remain sceptical. I will **miss** seeing you this year as **Coutts** bank suggest that we should **also** limit our expenditure and remain **here** until William stops gambling.*

This sounds like good advice and I regret that I cannot be of more help at this time.

Your humble servant,

George

I couldn't say I was pleased with this work, but it was the best I could manage. It didn't make that much sense but the message was in there, which was the important thing. I felt sure that even if I had spent another week on its creation, I wouldn't have come up with anything much better. The moment I had finished writing, I rang for Benson and asked him to post the letter with all possible haste. I made a point of telling him not to prepay the postage as I did not wish to deprive His Lordship of the kindness he'd shown me. Benson obliged with his customary good grace and I hoped that within the next twenty four hours, Lord Palmerston would be aware of the confirmed Russian presence in Harrogate along with that of the richest woman in England.

With that out of the way, I felt I should track down the Von Benckendorff's and try and gain further information which would assist in establishing the true reason for them being here. According to lists in the *Harrogate Advertiser*, the Von Benckendorff's were staying at the Crown Hotel which was only a few hundred yards from Holderness House. Part of the hotel could even be seen from some of our north facing bedroom windows.

As the Crown was situated adjacent to, arguably, Harrogate's most popular sulphur well, it occurred to me that if I made my way in that general direction, I would likely as not attract little attention. I had contemplated limping or feigning some gastric complaint but abandoned that idea in case I happened across anyone from London who knew me. That could prove a trifle awkward and the masquerade seemed a little excessive. Having debated with myself long enough, I made my way out of Holderness House and down the hill towards the hotel.

The Crown appeared to be a much busier hotel than the Queen, with a constant procession of carriages collecting and dropping off passengers. Apparently, over the last few years it had grown in size and now had more bedrooms than any other hotel in Harrogate.

As I approached the line of carriages, I noticed a variety of shops on my right.

Low Harrogate.

There were milliners, shoemakers, hosiers, as well as a florist. The sight of the florist reminded me that in all the excitement of meeting the Redmayne's and Miss Coutts, I had completely forgotten to purchase a small gift for my aunt. It had been my intention to bring with me some small token of my affection in appreciation of her kindness, and flowers would do nicely. I was being presented with the perfect opportunity to remedy my oversight.

The florist was called 'Harrogate's House of Flowers.' I stepped inside and was immediately overwhelmed by the heady scent emanating from the colourful display of bouquets, sprays and arrangements.

"Good morning, sir," said the well-dressed lady I took to be the proprietress. There were two other girls at the rear of the shop who appeared to be her assistants. They could have been no more than eighteen and were busy assembling bouquets and sprays.

"And how may we be of assistance?" asked the proprietress warmly.

"Thank you. Yes, well, I would rather like an arrangement of flowers for my aunt," I replied, suddenly finding myself in unfamiliar territory and uncertain of my ground.

"Certainly, sir," she replied, leading me towards some splendid arrangements of roses, which had no doubt recently been assembled by the two young assistants.

"These roses look perfect," I said, which brought about a big smile from the proprietress.

"And which arrangement would you like, sir," she said, pointing to the various displays.

"I was thinking that I might like the large arrangement on the right."

"An excellent choice, sir," she replied looking extremely pleased.

"I wonder if you might also deliver the flowers to my aunt at Holderness House, which is but a short distance up the hill?" I said, pointing in the general direction.

I had been so taken with the scents and the colours of the flowers, I had barely given the proprietress a second glance. However, having now decided upon an arrangement for my aunt, I could see that she not only possessed a kindly disposition but also a beautiful face.

"What is your aunt's name and who shall I say they are from?" she said, continuing to smile broadly.

"Her name is Mrs Moore and my name is Captain Townsend," I replied.

"Is that Moore with an 'e'?" she enquired.

"It is indeed," I replied contemplating making some remark about the northern use of the letter 'e' as a word in itself.

"Well, Captain, I am sure your aunt will be as pleased as punch when she receives this arrangement," she said after carefully writing down my aunt's name and address.

49

I then paid for the flowers and touched my hat. As I turned to leave she added, "Thank you for calling. I hope we see you again, Captain."

I returned her smile and walked out of her shop with a renewed spring in my step. Yet again it was time to turn my attention to the Russians. I made my way past one or two more shops on the short walk to the Crown Hotel. The main door of the hotel was opened for me by a smartly dressed man standing ramrod straight and I instantly concluded he had served in Her Majesty's armed forces. Once through the door I saw a large reception area well furnished, with grand furniture and ornate decorations. There was a beautiful glass chandelier which reflected the light in an almost hypnotic way.

Due to the fact that I was effectively on reconnaissance, I felt that it might be more fruitful and less conspicuous to observe the comings and goings at the hotel whilst enjoying some refreshments. I therefore made my way to the main parlour where I was pleasantly surprised to see that it was furnished to a very high standard and noticed an unoccupied chair by the window. I headed for the vacant chair and en route I was asked by a servant if I required any assistance, to which I replied in the affirmative and duly ordered some tea.

I then sat quietly watching through the window as men and women walked to and from the sulphur well. They were of all ages, shapes and sizes. Some looked perfectly fit and healthy but, sadly, others looked as if they had been dead for a week. A number of these poor invalids were in bath chairs and several walked with the aid of sticks. Even the brightness and warmth of the sun failed to mask the discomfort of the most unfortunate ones.

I also saw army veterans who looked as if they had fought long and hard in the peninsular wars, as well as young army officers who were probably from the garrison at York and appeared to have only recently completed their training.

My beverage arrived and I turned my attention to the activity within the hotel. I had no idea what the Von Benckendorff's looked like and so, at first, I merely listened out for the hint of a Russian accent. I heard many accents all the while I drank my tea but none that sounded remotely east European. I picked up the papers which were available on the side table and glanced through them. I first read the *Yorkshire Gazette* followed by the *Leeds Mercury*. It would have been extremely fortunate to have found an article on the Von Benckendorff's but, unsurprisingly, there was nothing of the sort.

The refreshment was pleasant enough but other than acquainting myself with the interior of the Crown and some local news, I had learnt little else and so I paid for my tea and left.

I retraced my steps, passing the line of carriages and then the shops, which included Harrogate's House of Flowers. I then walked back up the hill and soon found myself heading back through the gates of Holderness House. As I walked through the door I was immediately set upon by my aunt.

"My dear George, there was no need to have flowers delivered, we have so many already but I am most grateful. It was kind of you." She leaned forward and kissed me on the cheek and then steered me into the privacy of a drawing room already adorned with a propensity of flowers. I immediately wished I had exercised greater imagination, for sending roses to my aunt now resembled sending coals to Newcastle.

"I noticed that the girl who delivered the roses was extremely pretty," she added with a degree of curiosity making its way into her expression.

"Indeed, Aunt, now that you mention it, the lady who sold me the flowers was charming but I must admit to having paid her little attention," I said, wondering if the flowers had been delivered by the lady I took to be the proprietress. Although likely as not, the flowers had been delivered by one of her young assistants.

"By the way, I saw Mr Pickersgill Palliser earlier and I obtained a copy of the weekly list of visitors," I quickly added.

"Excellent. Was he able to be of assistance?" she replied.

"Thankfully, yes. I obtained a copy of the *Harrogate Advertiser* from him and, sure enough, I came across two people named Von Benckendorff residing at the Crown who must surely be Russian. In any event, no other name looked even vaguely Russian."

"Tremendous," she replied sincerely. "So maybe you have not been sent on some spurious errand after all?"

"It seems that way, but I now need to find out more about Mr and Mrs Von Benckendorff, as it did occur to me that if they were in Harrogate for some sinister purpose, they would surely have taken steps to keep their names away from Mr Palliser's lists," I said, recalling my conversation of last night with Lord Redmayne.

"And then again, they may feel that by having their names published, they establish a degree of legitimacy to their presence here," she replied astutely.

"Quite so, Aunt," I replied. "Devilishly tricky, all things considered."

"I will ask Benson to make discreet enquiries. I'll tell him that I am thinking of inviting them to tea to see if they are acquainted with Count Brochevski who was an old friend of your uncle's. Also, I will ask my friends tactfully if any of them have come across your Russians."

"Thank you, Aunt. Is there really a Russian called Count Brochevski?" I asked, a trifle sceptically.

"Yes, although your uncle didn't know him that well. Nonetheless I have no intention of asking these Russians to tea, but I am guessing you would not want me to take Benson into my confidence as to the real purpose of your visit to Harrogate?"

"No, absolutely not! In the meantime, where do you suppose the Russians will spend their evenings?" I asked, as I continued to delve further.

"Well, there are a variety of places they could dine, but given that they are staying at the Crown, you might find it productive to attend the ball they are holding there tonight. Every Monday evening a ball is held there and there has to be a reasonable chance that they will make an appearance. It could present a good opportunity for you to catch sight of your Russians… you may also meet some nice girl who will capture your affections. It's high time you were married."

"Thank you, Aunt," I replied, wondering if she was still a little disappointed that I wasn't making an effort to progress a friendship with Miss Coutts.

Either way, she seemed pleased with the volume and quality of her advice and retired happily to the orangery whilst I returned to my room to contemplate my next move. It was beginning to feel as if I was caught up in a game of chess, but for the moment I was merely acquainting myself with the players.

Chapter 7

Emily returned to the Queen Hotel, having posted some letters for her mistress, to find her waiting in their private parlour suitably dressed for the day's activities, summer bonnet and all. Although the family carriage had already been restored to good health, it was Angela's intention to walk as much as possible. She had come to Harrogate to recuperate from the trials of the past year, to take the waters and enjoy the bracing air which blew in this corner of the north.

Previous experience had given her faith in the healing power of the waters and, to that end, vowed to drink from both the chalybeate and sulphur wells on a daily basis. The stresses of the last year had taken their toll on her health, rendering her pale and with a mild rash on her face. Whether it was the abundance of minerals and salts in the chalybeate water or the purging properties of the sulphur spring, she knew not, but one or the other, or both, had improved this condition in the past.

Angela and Emily walked slowly and in silence as they returned to the hotel from taking the waters for the first time. Both concentrated their minds on the effects the sulphur water was having on their insides. The waters seem to create havoc wherever they went, creating uncomfortable sounds and feelings along the way. It was with great relief that they reached the safe haven of their rooms where they would remain for the rest of the day.

Angela then busied herself in writing letters as promised to her parents, informing them of her progress. She had also accumulated a sizeable pile of letters that had been forwarded on from her house in Stratton Street, London which she was now intent on dealing with.

The first letter she opened was from someone who wanted her to invest in a calculating engine; next was a letter from a priest requesting the funds to build public baths in a school for the poor; another was from a man who needed finance to explore the far reaches of the Amazon. She arranged the opened letters into piles depending upon the content. Her thoughts were interrupted by Lord Redmayne who was shown into her private parlour and guided to a seat by Emily.

"And how are we today?" enquired the ever ebullient Lord Redmayne. "Did you manage to take the waters this morning?"

"I am well thank you, sir, and yes, I did manage to take the waters and can still feel their purging effects," she replied.

"Never tried the stuff myself, all the same Lady Redmayne continues to advocate that I am in need of a good purging!" he said, devilishly. Angela smiled and then looked at the pile of letters that awaited her attention.

"My dear, I never appreciated just what you have to endure. You must have twenty letters there," said Lord Redmayne sympathetically.

"Twenty-six actually and only two are from my family," she replied. "You might be able to help me deal with some of them, sir. Would you mind lending me some assistance for a short while?" asked Angela, sensing an opportunity to obtain some honest advice which would normally be provided by her father or a director of her bank.

"Certainly, only too pleased to help," he replied.

"Are you familiar with a country called 'Poyais'?" she asked.

"Oh no!" said Lord Redmayne in an exasperated tone. "Don't tell me that you have received a letter from Gregor McGregor?"

"Why yes," she replied, curious as to Lord Redmayne's reaction.

"Let me tell you the story about Poyais and Gregor McGregor which all started when you would be no more than seven years old," said Lord Redmayne.

"Gregor McGregor was a navy man who somehow became a colonel in the Venezuelan War of Independence. About sixteen years ago, he returned to London announcing he'd become Prince of the Principality of Poyais. Unsurprisingly no-one had heard of Poyais but it was apparently somewhere on the Bay of Honduras and the land had been allegedly bestowed upon him by the native chief.

"McGregor claimed that the country had miles of rich untapped land which could be farmed but there were also supposed to be vast quantities of gold and silver just waiting to be mined. All utter nonsense! The man even came up with a book written by some old captain, Strangeways, I think. Yes, that was it, Captain Strangeways. Well I suppose the clue was in the name. It seemed the truth was that McGregor obtained the land after getting the chief drunk, but no matter how he acquired it, the land was just a jungle. Many people, rich and famous ones at that, fell for his story. He became a very wealthy man at the expense of a lot of other people who lost a great deal of money. A couple of hundred Scots even sailed to the wretched place and most of them died of tropical disease.

Not unexpectedly, he has spent time in prison but the man keeps surfacing with new crackpot schemes for this Poyais place. What is it this time?" said Lord Redmayne.

"Oh my goodness!" said a quite startled Angela. "He has written requesting a meeting as he wishes to bring to my attention many exciting new developments. It seems there is a new constitution for Poyais and he is now President."

"Well, if you take my advice, that is one meeting I would avoid. He is quite a unique character though," concluded Lord Redmayne.

"Thank you, sir, that sounds like very good advice. May I ask you about another man who has written to me? His name is Sir William Hamilton. I have heard mention of him before but nothing particularly flattering."

Lord Redmayne considered his response to the mention of another name which he had little respect for.

"If you took Gregor McGregor and removed his soundness of mind and honesty you would be left with Sir William Hamilton. He is a remora," said Lord Redmayne with a look of a man who was digesting something unpleasant.

"Remora?" asked Angela.

"A remora is a fish that lives off other larger fish. A sucker fish!" he answered. "Rumour has it that, among other things, he was responsible for large sums of money collected for the starving people of Ireland failing to reach their intended destination."

"My goodness!" said Miss Coutts. "My step-grandmama told me that she had sent a good deal of money to Ireland which never arrived. But that is simply awful."

"Awful is about right but amazingly the man has a lovely daughter. Poor girl though is being hawked around for the best offer he can get. He knows she's a beauty. The man is a rogue and again I would suggest caution."

"Thank you once again, sir. Your help is most appreciated; I have much to learn and the more I see, the more I despair," reflected Angela as she discarded the letter from Sir William Hamilton.

Lord Redmayne left the room and Angela resumed dealing with her correspondence. By the end of the day she had managed to write several letters but was weary from her labours.

Following dinner and having finally recovered from the effects of the sulphur water, she contemplated attending the ball at the Crown Hotel. As few people were aware that she was in Harrogate, there was an outside chance she could mingle with the crowds without being recognised. However, with so many visitors up from London there was a strong possibility that someone would spot one of Europe's richest women. Whilst reflecting on this dilemma she again seemed to feel the presence of Harriot, Duchess of St. Albans.

As a result of the time she had spent with the Duchess, she was now well versed in the art of theatrical makeup and although she had never put her skills to the test outside her own home, a wild notion suddenly occurred to her. As Angela Coutts she may be recognised as the wealthiest woman in England but by transforming herself into someone else for the evening, she would be able to blend into a crowd without being the recipient of unwanted attention. Being fluent in French she had the idea of becoming a Parisian governess for the evening. It was outrageous and totally out of character, but why not, she reasoned? An opportunity to return to the less public life she previously enjoyed had presented itself and she was going to take it with both hands. Her maid Emily would take the part of the governess's charge, and given that their dress sizes were so similar, she was easily accommodated in her mistress's clothes. The two of them giggled like schoolgirls as they prepared for the evening.

By the time they had finished they were so unrecognisable that when they passed Lord Redmayne in the corridor, he had no inclination as to their true identities.

"Come Emily, let's find a carriage," and with that the two of them set off on an evening of carefree adventure. Both of them were playing roles. They were actresses for a night. When comfortably seated in the cab they agreed their new names. Angela was to be Madame Beaumont and Emily was to be Harriot Kent of St. Albans. They both trembled with excitement as the carriage made its way to the ball.

At first, they felt certain that someone would unmask them but the more they mingled with the other guests unnoticed, the more confident they became. At times they had to pinch themselves to stay in character as they found the entertainment of their play acting almost too much to bear. At any moment they could burst into fits of laughter. They found two unoccupied seats by the dance floor and looked at each other and smiled. They somehow felt invisible which, as Angela Coutts and Emily, they were.

Chapter 8

After dining with my aunt at Holderness House, I retired to my room to prepare for the ball at the Crown Hotel. I dressed myself in a black suit, silk waistcoat, thin shiny enamelled boots, a white neck cloth and white gloves. The only adornments were a set of shirt studs and a handsome watch chain left to me by my father.

Having given myself a final inspection in the mirror, I went in search of my aunt as I was keen to make certain that I was fully acquainted with the protocol at balls in Harrogate. The look on her face indicated that my attire met with approval, and in order to avoid soiling my boots by walking the few hundred yards to the hotel, I was instructed to take the carriage and arrive in style. This seemed a bit unnecessary to me but to raise an argument may have appeared ungrateful, and in any event unlikely to produce a positive outcome.

After being instructed in the conventions, or should I say lack of conventions, at balls in Harrogate, I wished my aunt a good evening and jumped into the carriage with Cookson, somewhat apprehensively in charge. I couldn't help but feel a little guilty at all the effort that would have been expended by Cookson and others, in order to transport me a few hundred yards. As always he carried himself with good grace, and on this occasion we arrived at our destination easily and without incident.

A footman at the Crown opened the door of the carriage and I stepped down to see a hive of activity. The ball was clearly very popular, evidenced by the hum of excitement and chatter in the air. The hotel looked magnificent with hundreds of candles burning brightly in the crystal chandeliers. It was a far cry from the atmosphere I had witnessed earlier in the day. Laughter and music could be heard emanating from the grand ballroom, which drew in hedonists like moths to a flame.

Theoretically it was necessary to provide the master of ceremonies with one's name, in order that he could affect introductions between the gentlemen and the ladies. All the same, my aunt told me that few people did that these days as informality was the order of the day in Harrogate. Nevertheless, I gave him my name as it felt like the appropriate thing for a British officer to do. He was a very officious looking gentleman, appearing more like the master of a hunt than the master of ceremonies; notwithstanding his appearance he set about his duties in an efficient manner. With probably two hundred people attending the ball I didn't envy him his task of remembering who was who. It did occur to me that he would be ideally placed to report the arrival of the Von Benckendorff's and so, with the help of a gold sovereign, the assistance of the master of ceremonies was duly secured.

I looked around the ballroom, surveying a scene where mothers were trotting out their daughters and young squires were doing their best to prize them away. Dancing was already in full flow as was, thankfully, the drinking which could be had from the bar at the far corner. Not surprisingly, this was the first port of call for many of the gentlemen, whereas most of the ladies sat around the room fanning themselves seemingly deep in conversation with each other. Many of them were dressed in white floating muslin and some wore almost transparent materials over coloured silk slips that just cleared the ground. Some wore flowers, though few wore much jewellery. I wondered how many had bought flowers from Harrogate's House of Flowers.

When safely at the male-dominated bar, I purchased a glass of the local punch which was tolerably good. I then stood and watched the performance of both the gentlemen and ladies alike, all the while keeping a close eye out for my Russians. There was a good chance they were here, but for the moment all I had heard was some intoxicated toff guffawing at some poor unfortunate's expense.

It was easy to resist asking the master of ceremonies to broker any introduc– tions on my behalf as I wasn't at all interested in dancing. Regardless of this I did enjoy watching others dance, especially the preceding rituals. I particularly enjoyed observing one young red haired toff in his early twenties stroll up to a young lady who was seated with either her mother or guardian. Having not been properly introduced, he was sent away sharply by her protector who was clearly intent on preserving proprieties despite Harrogate's efforts to do otherwise. The young man's cheeks turned the colour of his hair and he returned to his friends and yet more guffawing. Undaunted, he then approached the master of ceremonies to intercede on his behalf and minutes later they both returned to the young lady for a second attempt.

Much to his relief, on this occasion, the lady agreed to dance with him and they proceeded to move around the dance floor tolerably well in a lively round dance.

No mean feat, as the steps to a round dance are not easy and without practice, attempting such a dance would be foolhardy and reckless. At the conclusion of the dance the young gentleman bowed to his partner and escorted her safely back to her guardian.

Even though I was not dancing and was all alone, I couldn't help being uplifted by the atmosphere, generated by the sound of music and gaiety. My eyes moved around the room as I sipped my punch. I considered a cigar on the terrace may be in order and it seemed possible that I might find other like-minded gentlemen in need of a more masculine pastime. Perhaps even a Russian called Von Benckendorff.

As I made towards the terrace I was stopped in my tracks by the sight of the most beautiful creature. There was no mistaking the lady from whom I had bought the roses earlier in the day. I had clearly not been paying attention during my visit to her shop. She was dressed all in white making her look almost angelic in the light of the ballroom. My eyes followed her as she made her way around the room stopping where two other young ladies were already seated. They seemed very excited, talking quickly and laughing repeatedly. Not wishing to endure the same humiliation as the young red headed man and not wishing to trouble the master of ceremonies anytime soon, I walked onto the terrace and took out a cigar.

It was a warm evening and several others were already on the terrace. I found a quiet corner and lit my cigar. The smoke drifted away into the night and I looked up into the sky to see an abundance of stars. It took me back to India where I looked at the same stars, often on nights like these.

"I love the smell of a cigar," said a female voice which made me turn around in a hurry. To my very pleasant surprise it was the proprietress from the House of Flowers. This was a break with convention which made me look around almost like a thief surveying the scene whilst also committing a crime.

"Miss, are you not worried that we have not been introduced?" I remarked with a hint of surprise which bordered on shock.

"Of course not. In any event, Harrogate prides itself in the absence of tedious conventions," she said very assuredly. "Besides we met this afternoon or have you forgotten, Captain?"

"Most certainly not, miss," I replied. "My aunt was delighted with the flowers."

"I am glad. She has a lovely house, my favourite in all Harrogate. I watched it being built." She paused momentarily and then said, "My name is Virginia Hatherway but my sister calls me Ginny."

"Well, Miss Hatherway, I am very pleased to make your acquaintance," I said bowing my head.

"Likewise, Captain," came the reply together with a half curtsey. We both smiled at the way we handled the formalities of the day. I was starting to like the ways of Harrogate.

The more we talked, the more I liked her. She had a refreshing attitude which stemmed more from a love of life and only followed convention where it suited her. I wondered what her friends would make of all this and thought at any time she would make an excuse to re-join them but she stayed and we continued to talk. She was the daughter of a grocer who operated from nearby Parliament Street and explained that it was a love of flowers that prompted her to persuade her father to open the florist shop near the Crown Hotel.

She was clearly intelligent and aspired for a grander life, however she was irritated that all her hard work may ultimately lead to nought as her brother would likely as not inherit her father's shops. As we talked, I began to make a mental picture of her so that I could recall her beauty in minute detail when it came to parting. Her skin was flawless with a healthy glow. Her white teeth were perfection itself and her eyes were a hypnotic blend of blue and grey. With beautiful blonde hair, she was a most fetching creature. I chastised myself for my lack of perception earlier in the day.

"How long will you be staying in Harrogate, Captain?" she asked.

"That is hard to say at the moment."

Not having the remotest idea how long my assignment would take, there was little else I could say other than, "I am awaiting orders, nevertheless I would be surprised if I were called away before September."

She seemed interested in hearing that and then said, "So you are on leave! That is good to hear, Captain, as I am hoping to sell you more flowers."

I smiled at her and then felt perhaps the time was approaching when I might venture to raise the question of the Russians.

"I have heard that people are coming to Harrogate now from all over Europe, India and even China," I said, attempting to get the conversation around to Russia.

"Well, I don't know about that, but we do get a good deal of foreigners coming to take the waters these days," replied Miss Hatherway.

"My aunt seemed to think the waters were proving particularly popular with eastern Europeans which I find hard to comprehend," hoping to evoke news of the Russians.

"Indeed, your aunt is correct. Having said that I, too, am mystified as to why some of them come here. Some are royals too and I know that because I have spoken to quite a number of them – barons, counts, dukes and duchesses, I have met them all, Captain."

"Maybe they come here for the daring lack of convention or perhaps the girls?" I speculated, continuing to provoke a response.

"I shouldn't think so. I am sure they have pretty girls, even in eastern Europe," she replied assuredly.

"If there was an eastern European or even a Russian here tonight, we could ask him," I joked as I made an exaggerated attempt to cast an eye over the people standing on the terrace and those gathered in the ballroom.

"As I thought, there is never a Russian around when you need one," I said hoping to be contradicted.

"Well, there might just be one here tonight," she said as she glanced around the terrace and into the ballroom. I didn't like this pretence but the less she knew about the real reason for my interest the better. I was quickly acquiring a healthy respect for her and misleading her in any way felt wrong. I had growing hopes that, although we had only just met, she could be the girl I had been seeking all my life.

The evening was progressing nicely and just when it looked very much like I would have to wait until tomorrow to catch my first sight of Mr and Mrs Von Benckendorff, the master of ceremonies attracted my attention. He was waving one arm repeatedly towards a couple who had just entered the ballroom. His arm moved in much the same fashion as a conductor of an orchestra stuck on the same few bars of music. He was hardly discreet yet continued his bizarre performance until I indicated that I had indeed understood his message. All the while I was trying to maintain a conversation with Miss Hatherway, which was proving a little awkward.

Unfortunately Miss Hatherway noticed my nodding and turned around quick enough to see the master of ceremonies winking at me.

"Do you know the master of ceremonies?" she asked somewhat mystified. "He certainly seems very familiar with you."

"I only met him tonight when I gave him my name," I said, pleading ignorance.

"I'd be careful if I were you, Captain, as I have it on good authority that he has a liking for men," she said with a mischievous grin.

After all the master of ceremonies' unsubtle twitching and pointing, I took it that the couple who had just entered the room were the Von Benckendorff's.

They made their way over to the punch table where I was able to get a good look at them. The one I took to be Vladimir was a slightly built gentleman of medium height, aged around thirty, with a neat black beard and wearing spectacles. On his arm was a delicate looking lady with very pale skin who I presumed to be Mrs Svetlana Von Benckendorff. As they stood watching the dancing, they were joined by another man who was altogether more menacing in appearance. Judging by his actions, he could well have been their manservant. This man was older, taller and broad shouldered with a patch over one eye. A dangerous looking brute, not the type you want to find is fond of your latest sweetheart.

I made a quick mental note of their appearance and then turned my eyes back to Miss Hatherway. Unfortunately, the actions of the master of ceremonies, together with my own, had sparked her curiosity which now needed satisfying.

"What are you up to, Captain?" she asked.

"Nothing in particular. Harrogate intrigues me, that's all. I would never have believed that a small town so far north should attract visitors from all over the world," I said, then quickly suggested that Miss Hatherway might like to dance.

She didn't seem totally convinced by my response but the offer of a dance enabled me to guide her to the dance floor before she could question me further.

The evening was proving to be extremely productive and surprisingly enjoyable. Having now caught sight of the Russians, I made a conscious effort to temper my revelry as it was important that I kept my wits about me and my eyes firmly on them. Unfortunately, I now had to do this from the dance floor where I found myself in the middle of a quadrille. I hate dancing really, but the quadrille is tolerable given there are only four couples involved, making it quite a sociable dance which still allowed conversation to take place. Regrettably it also involves the frequent exchange of partners. Consequently, it was something of a relief when the exchanges were over and Miss Hatherway was returned to me. Most of the partners I gained in the exchanges were mature in age and body. It was eminently enjoyable barring one moment when a lady, who I later discovered to be a French governess, planted her large slipper on my left ankle causing me to let out a stifled cry of pain. This seemed to amuse her greatly. Not wishing to appear fragile, I disguised my pain and resisted any temptation to limp until later in the evening when I was alone, whereupon I limped like a one-legged peninsular war veteran.

Once the dance was over the French governess approached me and apologised most profusely. Even though I had paid some attention in French lessons at school I couldn't understand a word she said. In spite of this handicap, there was no mistaking the sincere remorse she expressed in a way only French people can.

"No harm done, madam," I said gritting my teeth. She smiled in a manner which had a degree of familiarity and then returned to sit with a young lady who I took to be her charge.

After a final glass of punch, Miss Hatherway advised me that she needed to leave, due to her father insisting that both his daughters returned home before eleven o'clock. Given that she lived only a short walk away, I offered to escort her safely back home however, despite seeming pleased that I had volunteered my services, she was insistent they were not required. Which, all in all, was just as well as it would have been reckless of me to leave the hotel having just identified the Russians.

We then walked towards the main entrance of the hotel where her sister and friend were waiting patiently. She then looked deep into my eyes and in a soft and gentle voice said, "Captain, I have had the most wonderful evening but alas I must take my leave and, given that it is unlikely that we will ever see each other again, I wish you a safe onward journey."

"But we will see each other again," I replied. "It could be months before I am posted elsewhere; please meet me tomorrow night."

I don't know whether or not she had been teasing me but with a little gentle persuasion she replied positively.

"Very well, tomorrow evening, seven o'clock outside the Montpellier Gardens and now I really must go. Good evening, Captain." No sooner had she finished speaking than she was walking out of the door, arm in arm with her two companions. I watched them gaily skip past the line of waiting carriages and then disappear into the darkness.

I was feeling a little disappointed at the loss of Miss Hatherway, and yet I was comforted in the knowledge that I would see her tomorrow – Russians permitting, of course. I really hoped that keeping an eye on the Von Benckendorff's would not interfere with this. From necessity I found myself having to push personal distractions from my mind in order to concentrate on the assignment given to me by Lord Palmerston. It still could prove to be a contrived mission but until I established that for certain, I was going to take my duties seriously and consequently, I headed straight back to the ballroom.

Conveniently, the Russians hadn't moved and so I worked my way around the room enabling me to get a much better look at them. I obtained another drink and stood alone ostensibly watching the dancing, just as I had done before meeting the lovely Miss Hatherway. I was close enough to hear the bearded Russian in conversation with the man standing just behind him. By the look of his attire I had taken this man to be his manservant but on closer inspection the patch over one eye and his build gave him the appearance of a fighting man. Either way I didn't relish meeting that one in a dark alley and fervently hoped that their presence in Harrogate was innocent.

Whilst trying to remain inconspicuous I endeavoured to listen to what they were saying but I could only make out the 'yes' and 'no's together with the odd other word here and there. They did, nonetheless, order their drinks from the steward in an east European version of English. I watched as the bespectacled Vladimir leaned forward and spoke to his wife who was now sitting quietly at the side of the room. I had already noticed that one or two unsuspecting dandies had tried to entice her onto the ballroom floor to dance, only to be growled at by the one-eyed manservant.

She looked to be a good few years younger than her husband. She was dressed in a very dark blue dress which, in poor light, would appear black. She had a handsome face but it was pale and lacked warmth, giving the impression that she had endured much in her short life.

I had no idea as to the name of the manservant as Mr Palliser's lists did not record the names of servants. Much like our electoral system – only people of property are recognised.

Interestingly though, Vladimir became engaged in conversation with a couple of middle aged gentlemen who, although not aristocratic in appearance, all the same looked richly attired. I strained my hearing but all I could make out was some mention of money, which in itself was not particularly helpful.

The later the hour, the livelier the dancing became. I continued to watch with amusement while simultaneously trying my damndest to pick up anything of interest from the Russian. I was contemplating leaving when I was tapped on the shoulder and, fearing the Russians had spotted me, I turned around with some trepidation.

"Captain Townsend! I never expected to see you here," said a surprised Duchess of Aldborough.

"Duchess!" I said in an equally surprised and also somewhat relieved manner.

"And what brings you to this northern outpost of society?" she asked.

"I'm merely visiting my aunt who has recently moved here," I replied.

"You have an aunt living in Harrogate? Is this some sort of code for a mistress?" she asked with a mischievous smile flitting across her face.

"No code. Just a regular aunt, my mother's sister," I said, still coming to terms with the unexpected sight of my former lover.

"And how is the Duke? Well, I trust?" I asked.

"He's shooting or about to go shooting… then again he could be hunting or about to go hunting," she replied adding, "Or possibly staying with one of his many 'aunts,'" at which she started to laugh.

"The truth is, George, I have absolutely no idea where he is. Quite probably at his shooting lodge on the other side of the Pennines. Anyway, I came here with some friends. You might know them. Lord and Lady Asenby and the Earl of Warkworth?"

I raised my eyebrows as I tried to recall a meeting but, before I could respond, the Duchess continued, "It's of no consequence." Then, taking me by the hand said, "Come, George, dance with me," and with a certain amount of apprehension I found myself attempting to avoid making a complete ass of myself for a second time.

"Don't you just love the lack of convention here?" she said, as she skipped her way around the room.

Dancing together brought back memories which I had thought were long since gone. I hadn't seen Mary, Duchess of Aldborough for at least five years and as I watched her move elegantly across the floor, I could see she was still an extremely handsome woman.

Somehow I managed to get through the dance unscathed, all the while taking care to keep half an eye open for the French governess with her free flowing feet. As we walked away from the ballroom I observed the Russians leaving, seemingly withdrawing to their rooms for the night. I wanted to follow them but that would have been difficult to achieve without raising suspicion. I therefore determined that, having seen them at first hand, I would resume my investigations in the morning.

We retreated to a quiet corner of the hotel where the Duchess happily advised me that she wished to rest a while. We sat down and she turned her captivating eyes on me and with a hint of sadness in her voice said, "I have missed you – you do know that don't you, George? I still think about you and what might have been if I had married you instead of William."

"I don't know what to say, Mary. Five years ago I would have done anything for you but you married William, became a Duchess and I joined the Light Dragoons. We are now different people," I said, completely taken aback by this revelation.

65

"Do you really believe that people change that much?" she asked.

"Time changes us all," I replied philosophically.

"And what did you get up to in the Dragoons that has changed you so much?" she probed.

"Well, I spent most of my time in India," I replied, "where I saw a completely different world. One where life can be precarious, where conspiracies and villainies are prevalent. That changes a man," I replied.

"I know little of India, but having said that, I couldn't help but notice that Clive of India stayed at our hotel, as they mention it repeatedly. Did you get chance to meet him when you were there?" she asked innocently.

"Hardly," I smiled, "he died quite some time ago. All the same I would very much have liked to have met him as his achievements were quite astonishing. Among other things he avenged the brutal murder of one hundred and twenty three people in the notorious Black Hole of Calcutta."

"I have heard of that. Was it quite shocking?" she enquired.

"Couldn't be worse," I said. "One hundred and forty six people thrown into a room a fraction of the size of this one and by morning only twenty three had survived."

I could see a look of horror appear on her face as she contemplated the bleak picture I had painted.

"So did you see any action?" she asked.

"Yes, although there were no major battles. But there were occasions when we were attacked, usually by one of the many rebel groups and invariably when we were out on patrol," I replied, letting my mind wander back to Calcutta for a moment. "The biggest threat to life came from disease. I saw more dead bodies than I would have liked and the majority were, unfortunately, children."

"You surprise me George, I was under the impression that India was all tiger shoots and polo," she said as she began to understand the reality of India.

"Well it's true that tiger shoots are commonplace but I only ever attended them if I was accompanying some diplomat or other. They are such magnificent animals, I rather admired them too much to want to kill them for sport. Unfortunately I did kill a tiger on one occasion, to stop it mauling a diplomat who had foolishly ventured far too close, but that was it for me."

"William would think nothing of killing a tiger, or an elephant, or anything in fact," she replied rather forlornly.

"Then William would enjoy India," I replied.

"We have a son…" she said.

Before either of us could say another word we were interrupted.

"There you are, my dear. Asenby and I have been looking everywhere for you," said a red-faced, red-haired Earl of Warkworth.

"I am sorry, Charles, but I ran into an old friend," at which point I stood up as Mary, Duchess of Aldborough introduced me to the Earl of Warkworth.

"Captain Townsend?" he said quizzically. "Aren't you the Dragoon that spotted Garraty cheating at Gordon's?"

This was news to the Duchess who seemed to sit up sharply on hearing this.

"George, you old fox!" she said. "Why didn't you mention this? When did this happen? You must tell me everything."

"There's nothing to tell, really," I responded, hoping that the subject would be quickly dropped as it seems that I made as many enemies as friends by exposing the young lord.

"Nonsense," said the Earl. "Young Garraty was busy fleecing all and sundry when the Captain challenged him and suggested changing the cards whereupon there was a fearful row and, sure enough, the Captain was proved right."

"My, my George, you never fail to surprise me," said Mary, Duchess of Aldborough looking decidedly impressed.

"Well you certainly saved me, Captain, as I would have been taken in by him sooner or later. Furthermore thanks to you he's banned from just about every gaming house in London," said the Earl of Warkworth emphatically.

I had tried to put that night at Gordon's to the back of my mind, however here it was being brought back with a vengeance. Lord Garraty had sworn to even the score with me and it occurred to me that if he was banned from his usual haunts in London, he might even be here in Harrogate. That was a chilling prospect. He was also a close friend of Sir William Hamilton, another man who bore me no love.

"Anyway, my dear, we are about to head back to the Granby," said the Earl addressing the Duchess.

"Then I shall come too," she replied and with that she took my arm and led me towards the row of carriages parked outside the Crown.

As we walked towards the door I spotted the French governess heading in my direction. A feeling of despair and trepidation instantly flowed through my body. She and her young charge came ever closer and it was only then that I noticed just how magnificent her green dress was. The detail and embroidery must have cost a small fortune.

I surmised that she wasn't on her way to kick my right ankle to sort of even things up but, nevertheless, felt it prudent to stay as far away from her as possible.

Despite my best efforts to avoid her she seemed intent on heading my way and another collision looked inevitable.

She drew alongside and ignoring the presence of the Duchess of Aldborough, spoke to me softly in an impeccable English accent. "I am ever so sorry I kicked your ankle Captain Townsend," and then, with a broad grin on her face, headed out to a waiting carriage.

Suddenly the familiarity of the smile all made sense. I had been kicked by none other than Miss Angela Coutts.

I wondered what else could possibly happen. To say that the evening had been full of surprises was like saying Waterloo was a minor scuffle. Perhaps the Earl of Cardigan will be driving one of the carriages? I could see by the look on the Duchess's face that she wanted to know what had been said to me, but the opportunity did not arise as the Earl of Warkworth was in close attendance. I was also intrigued by her saying that 'we' had a son; surely she meant her and the Duke?

We continued to walk out of the Crown and to the line of carriages where we found Lord and Lady Asenby waiting for the Earl and the Duchess. I was introduced to them and whereas Lady Asenby seemed pleasant, His Lordship was clearly very irritated at having to hang around for the errant members of his party. I looked for an opportunity to make my apologies and walk the short distance to Holderness House but the Duchess of Aldborough clung onto my arm.

"I would love to invite you to the Granby, George," she whispered and then looked deep into my eyes, "we did not finish our conversation, but we will," she said knowingly. I smiled and helped her into the carriage much to the dismay of the Earl of Warkworth. Lady Asenby, her husband and the Earl then quickly joined her.

I bowed my head to them all as the driver urged his horses forward and off they sped to the Granby. I was left standing alone outside the Crown to reflect on an evening I could have never predicted. Fortunately, I had now made contact with the Russians but I had also met the most angelic Miss Hatherway, whilst being reminded of a love that I lost to the lure of the aristocracy. To cap it all, I had seen the amazing Miss Coutts in a new light.

Somewhat baffled, I made my way back to the safety of Holderness House. It's hard to believe that only yesterday I thought my time in Harrogate would be sheer tedium.

Chapter 9

Early the next day Lord Palmerston put the finishing touches to a letter addressed to Captain Townsend. He had been concerned when he read the Captain's letter an hour earlier. Having received confirmation of the Russian presence in Harrogate, His Lordship had summoned Lieutenant Sinderby-Smythe together with 2nd Lieutenant Reeves to his offices in St. James's, as a matter of great urgency. The two young officers now waited patiently in the corridor outside.

Following one final read through, His Lordship declared himself satisfied with his work and placed it an envelope. He motioned to his private secretary to seal the letter and address it to Captain Townsend at Holderness House, Low Harrogate. He also added a letter of introduction he had written earlier for the Captain to present to Miss Angela Coutts.

Lord Palmerston then placed his pen back in its holder and, with a noticeable sense of urgency said, "Whitaker, are they both outside?" and his private secretary duly acknowledged that two officers of the 11th Light Dragoons were just a few yards away.

On hearing this Lord Palmerston stood up from his chair.

"Then show them in, man! And be quick about it, there is no time to lose."

Whitaker bowed his head, turned sharply towards the door and then opened it, revealing two young officers resplendent in their uniforms who appeared to be taken aback by this sudden flurry of activity.

"His Lordship will see you now," said Whitaker and the two Light Dragoons marched resolutely through the door towards the now seated Lord Palmerston. They saluted, whereupon they were asked to consider themselves at ease.

"Gentlemen, you will no doubt be wondering why you have been summoned to my offices at such short notice?" he said, not having the slightest interest in whether that was true or not. He then stood up and moved towards a large map of Europe which dominated the wall.

"It is a matter of national security and a delicate one at that. We live in dangerous times, gentlemen, with the Russian bear making advances throughout

Europe and making a nuisance of themselves in Afghanistan. They still occupy Krakow in contravention of the Treaty of Vienna, and if they make much more progress, not only will British trade will be jeopardised but a route to India may open up to them. What has this got to do with you and why are you here, you may be thinking?" he said, looking into the eyes of the two officers.

Both men signified by their expressions that they were predictably bemused and perplexed. Lord Palmerston walked over to his window where he paused for a moment. The two young officers took the opportunity to share a mystified look and then His Lordship turned and walked back to his desk.

"I am sure you are both acquainted with the existence of the Count and Countess Zadovich?" he said, looking to both men to confirm such knowledge, which they promptly did with a brisk nod of the head.

"They were based here in London until a year or two ago, but due to relations becoming strained between our two countries it was thought to be in everyone's interest that they returned to Russia," he then paused again. The young officers listened intently.

"I have it on good authority that the Count blames this country, and in particular myself, for being recalled to Russia. Make no mistake gentlemen, he is a very capable adversary, possessed of considerable guile and I have reason to believe that he has engaged a number of agents here in England.

"And this is where you come in, as it has just come to my notice that two Russians have recently moved to the northern spa town of Harrogate, which on the face of it may be innocent enough, as many different nationalities summer in our spa towns. However, these Russians possess the surname Von Benckendorff which as you may or may not know, is the maiden name of Countess Zadovich. There is also more than an even chance that these may be the same Russians who we know to have been active in northern England for the past ten days or so."

The potential seriousness of the situation was now being reflected across the faces of Lieutenant Sinderby-Smythe and 2nd Lieutenant Reeves. Lord Palmerston resumed with neither his features nor voice relaxing as he sought to impart the gravity of the situation onto the officers.

"Gentlemen, we must be on our guard. Count Zadovich is potentially very dangerous as he and his wife have succeeded in inspiring a confidence with prominent men throughout Europe and we believe from the reliable Captain Burnes that the Count has also visited Dost Mohamed in Cabul," he again paused, allowing the full effect of this information to be absorbed.

"At this moment in time, there are members of our own aristocracy as well as a number of prominent businessmen and politicians in Harrogate. It is therefore vital to find out what two Russians bearing the name Von Benckendorff are conspiring to achieve there. It may of course be entirely coincidental but I have been in politics too long to believe in such coincidences."

"Absolutely, my Lord," said Sinderby-Smythe.

"Yes, absolutely," concurred Reeves.

Lord Palmerston nodded, approving of their early grasp of the situation.

"After discussions with Lord Cardigan, I procured the services of Captain Townsend and promptly dispatched him to Harrogate. As luck would have it, he has an aunt residing there and now gentlemen you are to join him with all possible haste."

Lord Palmerston then considered precisely how he would divulge another prospect which disturbed him so. Deep lines on his brow betrayed his concern when all the while his mind disseminated his options. Having settled on a suitable course he continued. "The Foreign Office has, at times, to perform services of a delicate and confidential nature vital to preserving the well-being of Great Britain. Invariably these require an element of funding which, although no one likes to admit to, they are nonetheless a necessity. Whenever such matters arise we utilise the services of our bankers who, it goes without saying, must be beyond reproach.

"Now, gentleman, it may be entirely coincidental, but the new owner of our most valued bank is also in Harrogate at this time. Miss Angela Coutts is a lovely young lady who has much to bear, not only is she subjected to constant ludicrous proposals of marriage from idiotic young men, but she may also now be in real danger from these Russians. She could be kidnapped and held to ransom in order for them to obtain highly confidential and sensitive information. For example details of the business this government has conducted with her bank throughout Europe, which could reveal more than I would wish to contemplate.

"As a precaution we are making alternative arrangements to fund items of a delicate and confidential nature but there is still much damaging and revealing historical information which could be at risk. Then there is the prospect of them using her to gain access to one of the many people in this country working on advancing the capabilities of our armaments. Military inventions would prove useful to these land-grabbing Ruski's. Some of these inventors may bank with Coutts. We simply do not know, as there are many projects underway in this country at present and we cannot ascertain how they are all funded. I wish we could."

The two officers listened to every word as it was apparent that they were being entrusted with some of their nation's most delicate and vital secrets. The deep concern which had persisted in the voice of Lord Palmerston was then replaced with a sense of urgency as he became intent on positive action.

"I have arranged for a carriage to take you to St Martin's Le Grand where you will catch the fastest coach I could find, which will initially take you to York. Horses will be changed frequently which should mean that, following a change of carriage and a degree of luck, you will be in Harrogate sometime tomorrow morning. Your bags will be sent on separately. Once there, you will seek out Captain Townsend who I believe you are acquainted with and give him these letters. There is no time to lose as it is vital that he is made aware of this information as soon as possible," at which point the letters were handed to Lieutenant Sinderby-Smythe who clicked his heels and stood to attention. The 2nd Lieutenant Reeves followed suit.

"Captain Townsend is an experienced officer and you will take your orders from him. Needless to say, no one must be aware of the true reason behind your visit to Harrogate. If anyone asks, you are simply visiting a fellow officer. Now, good day gentlemen."

At that, Lord Palmerston lowered his head to turn his attention to some other pressing matter of state, when Lieutenant Sinderby-Smythe with more than a hint of trepidation in his voice asked, "Begging your pardon my Lord?"

"Yes, what is it, man?" said Lord Palmerston somewhat irritated that the two officers were delaying their departure by remaining in his office.

"May I ask why we were chosen for this assignment my Lord?"

"I would have thought it was obvious. It is precisely because you both speak Russian. Now make haste, you must not delay the coach!"

Sinderby-Smythe and Reeves both then saluted His Lordship and quickly left.

"Damn and blast!" said Sinderby-Smythe as they strode purposefully down the corridors of power and out into the London air where he continued to vent his displeasure on the unfortunate 2nd Lieutenant.

"I had been hoping to stay in London you know. Damn inconvenient, this. And to Harrogate of all places! Never been to the north. They say the weather there is damn chilly and the girls' even chillier, if you get my drift," finishing with an attempted wink aimed at his comrade.

The two young Light Dragoons then jumped into the carriage which had been laid on by Lord Palmerston and sped across London to St Martin's Le

Grand, the home of the General Post Office. As the coach bounced around, conversation became more difficult and Sinderby-Smythe had to restrict himself to the odd 'damn' and 'blast'. At one point, when the carriage was forced to slow down, he complained that joining the 11th Light Dragoons was not of his choosing. He confided in Reeves that he was there at the insistence of his father who aside from controlling his finances, was regarded as something of a hero having fought with the Duke of Wellington at Waterloo.

Reeves, who was from an altogether different background merely nodded politely. Arriving at St Martin's Le Grand, the two young officers were then guided to the waiting high speed coach to York.

The coach was resplendent in a shiny dark maroon colour fully laden with baggage and mail. The driver, fellow coachman and customary armed guard were in place and ready to travel. The horses waited patiently in the morning sun taking advantage of the unscheduled rest. As soon as the officers were on board and the door closed, they knew there would be a cacophony of noise; of men shouting and whips being cracked. In an instant the stillness would be broken and four horses would be straining forward, pulling the York-bound coach and its passengers with all possible haste.

With only two steps to go Sinderby-Smythe pulled up quickly, "Need a piss, old boy."

The marshal and Reeves rolled their eyes prompting Sinderby-Smythe to offer an excuse. "It's all that blasted bouncing about and I had no idea I would be on my way to the damn north this morning. Should have gone before I came out."

Reeves waited a few steps from the coach as Sinderby-Smythe was escorted by the marshal to relieve himself. Then much to the surprise of Reeves, a lady and her maid approached the coach.

"Good. It seems the two officers who have been delaying this coach have arrived at last," said the lady to her maid in clear earshot of 2nd Lieutenant Reeves. Regardless of her short stature she was nevertheless energetic and eloquent. Reeves took a step forward and moved to open the coach door much to the consternation of another marshal who would now be deprived of a tip.

"Allow me, madam," said the gallant Reeves.

"You're too kind, sir," replied the lady adding, "well, although you seem lacking in the concept of punctuality, it is indeed reassuring to see that Her Majesty's officers do at least possess some manners."

Reeves helped first the lady, then her maid into the carriage and returned to his former position where he waited for Lieutenant Sinderby-Smythe. Having relieved himself, the lieutenant strode forward with an altogether freer gait. With the marshal in tow he turned to his waiting comrade and as he made to climb into the waiting coach said, "By gad, I needed that! Now Reeves let's be on our way and get this damn journey over with."

The moment he finished speaking he was half into the coach and realised that his blaspheming had been clearly heard by a lady and her maid. Moving quickly to make amends he said, "Madam, I do beg your pardon. I had thought that 2nd Lieutenant Reeves and I were travelling alone."

He then rather sheepishly shuffled into one of the spare seats facing the lady. Reeves, acutely aware of Sinderby-Smythe's gaffe, boarded the coach endeavouring to add what little he could to the apology by rendering a polite smile.

"That is no excuse, sir, for such blasphemous language," replied the lady and with that there was the anticipated 'hurrah' of noise, the whip cracked and the coach lurched first forwards, then backwards before their journey to the north commenced.

Sinderby-Smythe after apologising a second time for his indiscretion ventured to ask the lady as to how far she was travelling. Her response did nothing to raise his spirits as she replied, "Harrogate," adding, "and yourselves?"

To which Sinderby-Smythe replied in a more resigned fashion, "Harrogate also," whereupon this information had the same effect on the lady as had occurred a moment earlier on the lieutenant.

Neither party was yet to realise the importance of their journey amidst the awkward silence, as the coach sped north to protect a lady and perhaps, a nation.

Chapter 10

Following a good night's sleep, I came down to breakfast to find my aunt waiting to hear the latest instalment of my adventures in Harrogate. I carefully edited events, leaving out Miss Coutts's theatricals, which I held back for some reason. Maybe it was because of Lord Redmayne's request for privacy or perhaps it was because she had given me the most almighty bruise on my ankle. Unsurprisingly, the events which most alarmed my aunt concerned the lovely Miss Hatherway, causing me to instantly regret not editing that too.

"Hardly appropriate behaviour, even at a public ball. I don't know what the world is coming to. I blame the Reform Act," said my aunt indignantly.

"The Reform Act is not to blame for anything other than making parliament less open to corruption, Aunt. And surely if Thomas Coutts can marry first a housemaid and then an actress, I can at least dance with a shopkeeper's daughter," I replied in defence of myself.

She seemed to accept that and so for the moment, at least, I was reprieved. I felt certain that had I been referring to Miss Coutts instead of Miss Hatherway, I would have received an altogether more positive response.

Other than my liaison with Miss Virginia Hatherway, my aunt seemed as much intrigued by the presence of the Duchess of Aldborough as she was about the Russians.

"Am I allowed to ask what you plan to do next? That is to say with the Russians, not your flock of admirers?" enquired my aunt.

"Quite frankly, Aunt, I have no idea. I am hoping that you or Benson may know someone who could affect an introduction to them whereby we may be able to get close enough to discreetly find out what they are doing here."

"I will talk to Benson directly and see what we can find out for you," she said reassuringly, after which she rose up from the table and headed off to the library.

I was starting to regret not making more of an effort to meet them at the ball last night. Perhaps I had made a mistake in letting myself become distracted by Miss Hatherway, all the same it was hard to see what more I could have done, short of striding up to them and asking them point blank what the devil they were doing here in Harrogate.

I was in need of inspiration and so decided that I would take a walk where I could exercise my mind as to how else I might get close to the Russians. What was blindly obvious was that I would achieve precious little if I remained within the confines of Holderness House. In any event, before leaving the house I rang for Benson who presented himself with his usual efficiency.

"Yes, Captain, how can I be of service?"

"Benson, my aunt advises me that you may be aware of the date of the next horse race here in Harrogate. Is that so?"

"Yes, Captain. If I am not mistaken, I believe there is one this coming Friday," he replied confidently.

"Excellent. Do you think you could possibly arrange for Tribune to be entered in, say, a two and a half or three mile event?" I asked.

"I don't see any reason why not. I will do my very best, Captain. Will that be all?"

"No Benson, one more thing. Where would you suggest that a Captain in her Majesty's 11th Light Dragoons should go for an evening's entertainment, assuming he is not that inclined to dance?"

Without being too obvious, I was attempting to find out about the less genteel side of Harrogate, where men could indulge themselves freely and where information might be bought and sold.

"I would suggest that you may find some amusement at the Dragon Hotel, Captain. That place is always popular, although they do have balls there as well."

"It sounds like Harrogate has a positive dance epidemic," I said with a hint of despair.

"Regrettably it's the main diversion in the evenings, sir. However, at the Dragon it is but one of many diversions," he replied.

I thanked him for the information but just as Benson was on his way out of the room, I called him back which must have irritated him. As usual he politely turned around and smiled. Somehow I needed to monitor the movements of the Russians in and out of the Crown Hotel which on my own was nigh on impossible. If I loitered outside their hotel I would soon be recognised, so consequently I needed another plan. In addition to the carriages and the new hansom cabs, Harrogate also benefited from a number of donkey carts driven by young boys. These carts came and went almost un-noticed and I wondered if one of them might be able to provide me with the assistance I needed. A young boy with a donkey could mingle un-detected. More people would look at the donkey than the boy.

"Do you know of a donkey boy that could be trusted to run some errands for me?" and to reinforce the point I said, "Someone you could trust with your last shilling."

I could see his mind trying to work out what possible use I could have for a donkey boy, which was a little worrying. I tried to steer him away from anything lurid by frowning at him which seemed to settle his thinking elsewhere.

"Yes, Captain, I am sure I can find one for you. Leave it with me," at which point he was finally able to make his way out of the room. He walked slowly, perhaps expecting a further question and was no doubt relieved when none came.

I then walked out of Holderness House and welcomed the fresh air filling my lungs. Before venturing out onto the Stray, I decided to visit Tribune in his stable. A young lad was busy grooming and I asked him to walk Tribune around as much as he could as I wasn't sure that I would get chance to exercise him that day. Tribune needed plenty of regular work to keep him fit for the race. I patted him on his neck, gave the lad a shilling and then headed towards the Stray.

Angela Coutts, having had the most enjoyable evening in the role of Madame Beaumont, awoke with renewed confidence and felt fully refreshed. Following a hearty breakfast, she took Emily with her to continue their daily ritual of drinking sulphurous water from the popular Low Harrogate well.

Despite the day being slightly cloudy and a little chilly, she decided to walk, much to the disapproval of Lord Redmayne. Still oblivious to the events of the previous evening, he expressed serious concern and suggested that he accompanied her.

"Please do not concern yourself, sir. I am confident we have nothing to fear in Harrogate. I have Emily, and thanks to you keeping our names out of the weekly visitor lists, few people are aware of our presence here," said Angela, reassuring Lord Redmayne as she made her way out of the Queen Hotel.

Lord Redmayne could see that further protests would be futile and resorted to urging her to take great care. His advice concluded that in spite of his best efforts to keep her name out of the visitor lists, there remained no telling who may know of her presence here.

Angela, turning to her maid Emily, said in a slightly hushed voice, "I wish Father had been well enough to come with us as, even though Lord Redmayne is a dear friend, he does fuss so."

Striding confidently away from the hotel, Angela walked towards the Brunswick Hotel and then past the line of carriages and cabs. She took a path running through the middle of the Stray which was the shortest route to the sulphur well. On either side of the path the green grass was entwined with heather, some of which was in flower. She had to watch where she placed her feet as the drawback to this shorter route was the endless scatterings of sheep droppings.

Angela felt herself unwinding as she was now far removed from the intensity of London, and the words of warning she'd received on her arrival seemed hard to believe. Her confidence was returning as the buildings which lay directly ahead came closer into view. She could now make out the Crown Hotel, which immediately brought a smile to her face as she recalled the events of the previous evening. She then looked to her left and saw a finely built stone villa which stood proudly in its splendid grounds. Angela strained her eyes as they came ever closer until she could just about make out its name.

"Emily, doesn't that say Holderness House?" she said turning to her maid, who was following close behind her.

"Yes, miss, I believe it does," replied Emily.

"That is where our Captain lives is it not? The house reminds me of Holly Lodge," she said, referring to the home of her step-grandmama where she and her sisters had spent so many happy hours.

"I wonder how the Captain's ankle is this morning?" added Angela, failing to prevent a slightly mischievous laugh. Emily followed suit and they both quietly giggled at the poor Captain's expense. Their amusement was abruptly ended when Miss Coutts looked down at the path only to see a collection of sheep droppings, which in order to avoid required urgent and deft footwork.

"It looks a very nice house, miss," continued Emily, after she too skipped to avoid the droppings.

"Yes it does, Emily. Very nice indeed. And isn't that the Captain's horse," she said pointing to a young boy walking Tribune.

"Yes, miss, I think it is," replied Emily.

Angela carried on walking but continued to look over her shoulder at every opportunity in the hope that she would catch sight of some activity at the Captain's residence. Her hopes were rewarded when much to her delight she saw the Captain striding out of the gates and without the aid of a stick!

I was deep in thought as I closed the gate to Holderness House. It seemed hard to believe that so much had happened in such a short space of time. I was content in the knowledge that I was making progress but was in desperate need of inspiration. Why, at this very moment the Russians could be committing some evil act.

"Good morning, Captain!" interrupted my thinking, causing me to raise my head only to see the delightful Miss Coutts with a welcoming smile flickering on her face.

"Good morning, Miss Coutts," I replied, then added, "or is it Madame…?" pausing to allow her to finish the name.

"Beaumont," she added and then started to laugh.

"Captain, you must forgive me. I am so sorry that my foot accidentally caught your ankle."

I smiled back, happily accepting the apology.

"And did you enjoy yourself last night?" I enquired.

"Most certainly," she replied. "I can't tell you how much fun it was to be someone other than Angela Coutts for a few hours. I have no wish to burden you with my problems, Captain, but I am sure you can imagine how it is hard for me to have a normal life since inheriting my grandfather's bank and my step-grandmama's fortune. Last night gave me a few hours of normal life again and I can't find the words to adequately express how good that felt," she said unashamedly.

"I do understand that you've been given an astonishing responsibility, which must have an enormous impact on your life," I said, in as reassuring manner as I could.

"It certainly has but I will do my duty and endeavour not to let anyone down," she said philosophically and then added, "Will you walk with us, Captain?"

At which point, I developed a pronounced limp and said, "I will do my utmost," whereupon she laughed unashamedly. It was a cloudier day than of late, making the temperature a little on the low side, even for Harrogate. We walked towards the bottom of Montpellier Hill and past Harrogate's House of Flowers. I was a little disappointed to observe that Miss Hatherway was nowhere in sight. I presumed that the lady I could see through the window was probably her sister. I continued to be amazed by the number of people heading to and from the wells. The streets were full of visitors as well as an abundance of street peddlers, many offering an array of cures and tonics.

Through an Act of Parliament, the water from the wells was free, but in order to drink the water in a civilised manner, drinking vessels were required and these were available from various enterprising peddlers as well as the hotels themselves. The Crown Hotel, which was now close by, offered weekly passes for the sum of one shilling and sixpence. Additionally this included the right to promenade in the adjacent pleasure grounds which were seemingly furnished with a great variety of beautiful shrubs and flowers. The sulphurous water had little appeal for me but as it appeared the pleasure gardens were extremely fashionable, I felt that I should at least obtain the right of access, if only for one week. Furthermore, the popularity of the gardens suggested that there was every chance the Russians would venture here at some point. Given that Miss Coutts was committed to a daily ritual of taking the waters, I volunteered to acquire passes for us all. Miss Coutts, having drunk the sulphurous water many times before, led the way to the well. We waited in a small queue and I took the opportunity to discreetly glance at the faces of those who had already taken the waters as they passed by us. As yet there was no sign of the Russians.

"Now, Captain, you first," said Miss Coutts, prompting me to reluctantly step forward.

"I wouldn't dream of it. Ladies first, please," I said, taking care not to call her by name in public.

She looked at me as if I lacked courage, and she was absolutely right. My nose was already rebelling against the pungent odour which was drifting our way. Drinking foul water was a stark reminder of the death and disease I had seen in India. With no honourable exit available, I forced a smile as the attendant gave us all glasses filled with the foul smelling stuff.

After emptying her glass, Angela concluded that its taste and smell had not improved. Then pulling a face, she turned to me.

"Villainous as ever!" she exclaimed whilst constantly moving her tongue around her mouth and across her lips in an attempt to remove the offending taste.

"It smells like rotten eggs and gunpowder and tastes even worse! Come now, Captain, drink up."

I winced at the request but proceeded to empty the glass in one big gulp, endeavouring to protect my nose from further invasions as I did so. I was not successful and Miss Coutts's description was more than accurate. The water tasted revolting.

Miss Coutts turned to her maid, "Emily let's find a confectioner's so that we may rid our mouths of that dreadful taste."

"Begging your pardon, miss, but shouldn't we also drink from the other well too? It will save us having to walk up to the Tewit Well later." Emily hoped that the information she was passing on to her mistress was reliable and the water did not taste as repugnant as the one they had just drunk.

"Very well, you're probably right."

This was not the news I was hoping for. With that, Angela Coutts asked the old lady in attendance for a glass of water from the other well.

The old lady was dressed plainly with a large white apron and matching bonnet. She quickly obliged us and handed over three glasses of water. "You drink that, my love, and it will do wonders for you," she said in a reassuring manner.

"Same for me, Betty," said the man standing behind me.

"Now you just hold your horses, young man, and wait your turn. Let me finish with these lovely people first."

I was quite prepared to let the man ahead of me, but Miss Coutts kept a careful eye on me as I was, yet again, encouraged to finish every last drop.

Miss Coutts finished her water last of all and concluded that it was indeed an improvement and would satisfy her routine for the day which came as a great relief. "Now for the confectioner's Emily," she said, thanking the old lady for the water and walking quickly away from the crowded scene. "Come along, Captain, let's try the pleasure gardens," and with that we all walked on.

As if in celebration of our arrival into the gardens, a band started to play, creating a most convivial atmosphere. It was a charming garden and there were quite a number of people enjoying a walk as many others sat listening to the music. As we walked towards the band stand, standing not twenty yards away on our right were the Russians. My heart rate increased as it seemed that the one-eyed manservant had been watching us before I had spotted him. All thoughts of foul tasting water vanished in an instant. I looked around to see if there was anyone behind us, hoping he was watching someone else, but there was no-one else close by.

Miss Coutts was unaware of my concerns but my instincts were to guide her away from the Russians and out of these gardens. I walked purposely slowly and showed no sign of concern even though my mind raced at the potential dangers and risks. I glanced around as we walked away from the Von Benckendorff's, and still their henchman's eye followed us. There was something unnerving about this, which prompted me to thinking that they knew precisely who I was escorting.

I needed to get Miss Coutts safely back to her hotel as soon as possible without causing her any alarm. In view of the number of people who were about, I quickly concluded that there was no immediate danger. Nonetheless, I chastised myself at having being lulled into a false sense of security as I was totally unarmed.

I had left both my pistols and knife in my trunk! A feeling of guilt ran through me as I had been given an important assignment and really hadn't taken it as seriously as I should. I took the notion of Russians connected to Count Zadovich being up to no good in Harrogate, as far-fetched. Lord Palmerston had impressed upon me the national importance of this matter, yet I had thought it more likely to be some tactic to get me out of London, probably at the request of Sir William Hamilton.

Somewhat spooked, I made every effort to hide my unease as I guided Miss Coutts towards Montpellier Baths.

"Will you be wanting a sulphur bath, miss?" enquired Emily, completely oblivious to my concerns.

"Certainly not!" came the reply, "drinking the foul stuff is bad enough. I have no wish to then lie in it!"

"Very good, miss," said a suitably chastened Emily.

Despite the crowded gardens, Miss Coutts didn't appear threatened in any way. As far as she was aware, her presence in Harrogate had been a well-kept secret and, as a consequence, she felt safe. Little did she know that she was being watched by the Russian.

We passed the Montpellier Baths which was a hive of activity, with a long queue of bath chairs waiting outside. We then headed towards the grandest of buildings, called the Cheltenham Pump Room. "Let's go inside, Captain," said Miss Coutts, staring at the six Doric columns which towered ahead of us. In view of the attention we had attracted from Von Benckendorff's manservant, this seemed like a prudent suggestion.

Consequently, we walked through the gates and up the handful of steps into a magnificent spa room. As appeared to be the local custom, for the use of the facilities we were required to pay a weekly subscription, although the price hardly seemed extortionate. In spite of being put on my guard by the Russians, I have to say that I was quite taken aback by the quality of the interior of this great salon. It had a superb barrel-vaulted roof which was hung with crystal chandeliers. There was a minstrels' gallery, a library, as well as several lounge areas. It seemed to be a popular meeting place and it crossed my mind that this would be a good place to bring Miss Hatherway when this assignment was over. I looked around and, happily, there was no sign of the Russians pursuing us.

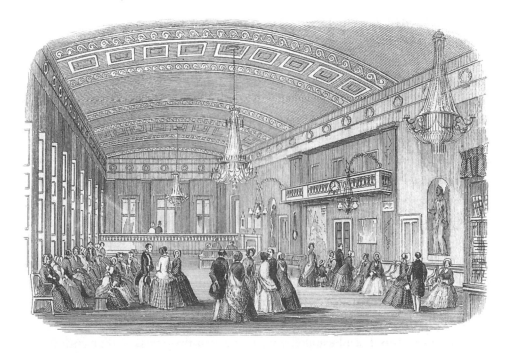

Cheltenham Pump Room, Harrogate.

We walked through the great hall towards the gardens at the rear and were soon back in the open air as the sun tried desperately to break through the clouds. Ahead of us lay two lines of walks, one on the upper slope and the other on the lower. Miss Coutts opted for the lower walk which was to the right of the lake separating the two paths. We could still hear the music which continued to be played in the pleasure gardens as we made our way along the tree-lined path. The scene was relatively quiet and it was apparent that Miss Coutts was revelling in this serene setting. I, on the other hand, kept looking over my shoulder for any sign that we were being followed.

"Do you know, Captain, this is the most relaxed I have been in the last twelve months," she said as we passed a mother pushing her disabled son in a bath chair, the unfortunate young man having sadly lost his left leg.

"When you look around it makes you realise just how lucky we all are," she said, empathising with the poor man.

"It certainly does," I replied. "Sadly the weak and vulnerable suffer whilst many of the strong and un-deserving prosper," I replied hoping that Miss Coutts hadn't taken that to mean that I thought she was undeserving of her good fortune.

"I totally agree, Captain. Can I take you into my confidence?"

"But of course," I replied.

"Playing the role of Madame Beaumont was the first time I had ever dressed up and masqueraded as someone else. It was on a whim, Captain, as if the spirit of my dear benefactor came to me in my hour of need. My step-grandmama, the Duchess of St. Albans, had been an actress, you know?" she said, pausing to look at my reaction which brought about a polite, "Oh really?" from me. Happy that I hadn't found this alarming, she continued.

"Well, she spent a great deal of time with my sisters and me and took great pleasure from teaching us how to transform ourselves into whoever we wanted. I never thought those things we did with her would prove so invaluable."

We continued to walk as she took me further into her confidence.

"When I inherited my grandfather's fortune, it seems I became a target for every single man in England and maybe Europe. I don't suppose it is much of a surprise that men are attracted to great wealth, but it makes it almost impossible for me to find someone who wants to be with me for the right reasons.

"Wherever I go, I am besieged with unwanted proposals and attention. The other evening I sat in my room looking out across the Stray and it was as if the Duchess spoke to me. I suddenly wondered what she would do in my position as she managed to combine the enjoyment of life with the serious business of managing great wealth. Despite all the parties and marrying a much younger man in the Duke of St. Albans, she fared admirably. Did you ever meet the Duchess of St. Albans?" she asked.

"Alas, no. Having said that, my aunt met her on at least one occasion when she stayed at the Granby," I replied.

"Then, like as not, I will have met your aunt too, as along with my sisters I invariably accompanied the Duchess on her travels," she said.

"Didn't the news of her marriage to the Duke alarm the other members of your family?" I asked, hoping for some insight, all the while praying that I wasn't being impertinent.

"Alarm!" she laughed. "More like hysterics. The Duke was in need of money and half her age but my step-grandmama was no fool. She still kept a firm grip on the bankers, the bank prospered and she always remained true to my grandfather's wishes.

"It would be an understatement to say that I now have difficulty in trusting people. The desire for wealth seems to bring out the worst in people. I am now totally cynical and find these proposals of marriage quite distasteful. Most only occur because their families have demanded it. Ludicrous, and quite insulting really."

She then stopped walking momentarily to ensure that there was no-one else within earshot.

"With the help of my companion, Miss Hannah Meredith, we have had to develop a system for dealing with them. When they arrive at the house, Miss Meredith and I sit with them in the drawing room. Then after about ten minutes of meaningless chatter she excuses herself to the next room. She leaves the door open just enough so that she can hear me cough, which is the sign that the proposal has duly been delivered and it's safe for her to return. One week I had three proposals," she said philosophically.

Looking straight at me, she said, "So what do you make of that, Captain?"

"You have my sympathy, miss; I had no idea that it would be that bad. But why let these men into your house at all?" I enquired.

"That's a very good question. I have been through this charade so many times that it has worn me out, which if the truth be known is why I am here."

She was the richest woman in England but was also intelligent and blessed with a good sense of humour. Nevertheless, there was sadness about her. The responsibility she had been given had irretrievably damaged her prospects of having the normal life of a woman.

I then added, "Fear not, Miss Coutts, and I hope this doesn't sound inappropriate, but you can always trust me."

"Thank you, Captain," she replied smiling, "I know I can and now let's walk back to the Spa rooms. Time is passing and I promised Lord and Lady Redmayne that I would lunch with them."

Chapter 11

We completed the pleasantly wooded circuit around the lake, or rather the swollen beck as it should more accurately be described. We then made our way out of the Cheltenham Spa, turned left and walked up the hill where many shops lined either side of the road. I wasn't sure whether or not this was Parliament Street; I hoped that it was as I was interested to see if there was indeed a certain grocer's shop bearing the name Hatherway. All the while I kept stealing a backward glance for signs of anyone following us.

We now found ourselves walking up a fairly steep incline where townsfolk and visitors busied themselves around the shops. Firstly we passed John Knowles Brazier's, then William Lawn Butcher's, Richardson's Chemist and Samuel Dearlove's Confectioner and Fruiterer, where Miss Coutts resisted the urge to enter now the foul taste in her mouth had gone. We then passed Nixon's Optometrist's and Morley's Grocery store, which had me wondering whether I was on Parliament Street after all, as it seemed improbable that there would be two grocers so close to each other. Then again, maybe Morley's was owned by the Hatherway family. The sight of Bainbridge of Parliament Street confirmed we were indeed on the street mentioned by Virginia. Before I could speculate any further we came to the last shop on the left at the top of the hill which bore the sign, 'Hatherway Grocer's and Tea Importer's.'

I was extremely pleased to see that at the very least the shop existed but I now had an urge to step inside and see if Miss Virginia was indeed there. Strictly speaking I should walk right by Hatherway's store and head straight to Holderness House, pick up my weapons and escort Miss Coutts back to the Queen Hotel. Nonetheless, curiosity had me behaving somewhat recklessly and walking towards Virginia's father's store.

I turned to Miss Coutts, attempting to give the impression that I had been struck by a moment of inspiration and that the sight of this grocer's shop had reminded me of something of great importance. "Please excuse me, Miss Coutts. I have suddenly remembered that I need to purchase some tea for my aunt and I would rather like to see if this shop has any for sale."

"Well, Captain, given that they claim to be tea importers, I suggest there is every chance. However, did you not notice that tea was on sale in at least two of the shops we passed earlier?" remarked Miss Coutts.

"I must confess that I did not, but it is of no matter as this store seems ideal," I replied, turning the handle on the door and stepping inside. As the door opened a small bell rang, announcing my arrival.

"Come along, Emily, we will join Captain Townsend," said the intrigued Miss Coutts.

Having allowed Miss Coutts and Emily through the door ahead of me, I slowly made my way across the store looking both right and left at the merchandise on display. There was an impressive range of produce which was obviously popular with residents, judging by the number of people in the store. Two ladies, having concluded their business, passed me on their way out allowing me a clear view of the counter which lay to my right. The bell rang once more as the ladies left. I could see another lady was now being served by none other than Miss Virginia Hatherway herself. My heart rate rose and, aware that I was being watched by Miss Coutts, my eyes frantically searched for tea. Happily it was easy to find, allowing me to turn around and say to her, "Perfect, Ceylon tea – just what I was looking for."

This was complete nonsense, of course, and Miss Coutts responded with a most unconvincing smile. My euphoria at that moment also caused Miss Hatherway to look up from the counter, where she had been tallying the lady's purchases, and break into the merest suggestion of a smile. I then waited patiently and, following completion of the accounting formalities, Miss Hatherway darted from behind the counter and helped her customer to the door.

"Goodbye Mrs Potter, don't forget to bring us two dozen of your lovely eggs tomorrow," she said, opening the door causing the bell to ring yet again. "Our customers love them," she added as Mrs Potter made her way back onto the street.

"And now, Captain, what brings you into our humble grocery store?" said Virginia quietly as she endeavoured not to be overheard by Miss Coutts.

"Tea," I replied handing her the tin of Ceylon tea I had just picked up together with a gold sovereign.

"Your aunt doesn't provide you with tea then?" she said quizzically looking past me glancing first at Miss Coutts and then her maid.

"Of course tea is provided, but ever since my tour of India I've developed a liking for Ceylon Tea. I happened by in the hope that someone in Harrogate would stock it, and as luck would have it, you did." I paused, feeling quite pleased with my spontaneous reasoning.

Unconvinced by my quick thinking, Virginia glanced suspiciously at Miss Coutts as she handed back my tea neatly packaged together with my change.

"And who is your lady friend?" she said continuing to speak softly.

"It is a long story, but her coach met with an accident just outside of Harrogate. I happened by and was able to ride for help," I said almost whispering as I certainly didn't want Miss Coutts to know that I was making reference to her.

Virginia's smile widened and she resisted the temptation to laugh out loud, at which moment another customer came in, prompting the bell to ring and our conversation to come to a premature end.

"I will see you at seven o'clock tonight as promised," she whispered and before she could say another word a silver haired gentleman, who I presumed to be her father, appeared through a door behind the counter.

"Good morning, sir," he said in a bright, cheerful voice. "Is my daughter attending to your requirements?"

Well that certainly took me back, requiring a conscious effort on my part not to say what immediately came to mind! After reassembling my thoughts into a more dignified order I replied in a very business-like manner.

"Absolutely, sir, first class."

On hearing this the proud father replied, "That is so good to hear, sir, please call again." He now turned to Miss Coutts and asked if he could be of any assistance, to which she replied "No thank you, sir, I was just browsing whilst my friend bought some tea."

I noticed that Virginia's ears pricked up when Miss Coutts described me as a friend. This surprised me too, in a very pleasant way.

We walked out of the store causing the bell above the door to ring for a final time. I immediately looked up and down the street for any sign of danger. The street was busy but nothing looked untoward.

"Wasn't that the girl you were dancing with last night, Captain?" said an inquisitive Miss Coutts with a knowing smile, as we resumed our walk up Parliament Street.

"Yes it was," I smiled. "I had forgotten that Madame Beaumont would have witnessed my dancing, dire though it was. And you being so close, as it were, to Madame Beaumont, she would have no doubt made you aware of that fact."

She laughed and then replied, "Actually she did say that you were a pretty dismal dancer."

"Of course she would be a fine judge, given the way she moved her feet around the floor and anything else she found in reach," at which point I feigned an extreme limp, demonstrating that I still bore the effects of the kick I had received on my ankle.

Both smiling freely, we walked past three tall poplar trees and soon noticed Holderness House coming into view on our right. It was no more than one hundred yards away, the rows of shops on our right had given way to the beginnings of the two hundred acre stretch of grass and heather of the Stray.

Miss Coutts, also spotting Holderness House said, "This is where we say goodbye, Captain. I trust you have been invigorated by the waters we have sampled this morning? Presumably you are no doubt keen to partake of a cup of Ceylon tea?" repeating her now familiar wry smile.

Despite the frivolity we had enjoyed together, I still retained a vivid impression of the one- eyed Russian watching our every move in the pleasure gardens. With a degree of trepidation, I looked around for any sign of him. Needless to say I felt duty bound to escort Miss Coutts back to her hotel. I began to wonder if she was, perhaps, the real reason for their presence in Harrogate.

"The tea will be most welcome, Miss Coutts, but it can wait as I confess that I would not be able to fully savour the taste knowing that you were walking all the way to the Queen unescorted," I said, hoping that would do the trick as I had no wish to alarm her by mentioning the earlier incident with the Russians.

"Fear not, Captain, we walked all the way here this morning without incident and I am sure we will return in the same vein," replied a confident Miss Coutts.

"Nevertheless I would be most grateful if you would indulge me on this occasion," I said and then in an effort to lighten the request added, "Perhaps all the villains were sleeping late this morning and it is only now that one must be careful."

Miss Coutts smiled and agreed to my request, which was something of a relief. We walked on and continued to chat about Harrogate whilst I regularly looked around for signs of anyone suspicious following us.

The streets were still quite busy and everyone we passed seemed very friendly. Again, there was almost a never ending dialogue of 'good morning' which was met by more of the same until we passed the Brunswick Hotel whereupon there were fewer people about.

I looked to my right and peered across the Stray. Perhaps one hundred and fifty yards away I could clearly see a man walking parallel to us. He was too far away for me to ascertain whether or not he was one of the Russians, but his behaviour was concerning. I said nothing but continued to follow the man out of the corner of my eye as we walked ever closer to the Queen Hotel. If we stopped to admire some flower in a garden or to rest on a bench the man also stopped. I was absolutely certain that we were being followed.

"Miss!" exclaimed Emily with an element of fear in her voice. "That man over there is following us," she said, pointing to the same man I had been watching.

We all stopped walking and Miss Coutts trained her eyes on the man, who seeing Emily pointing and the rest of us looking at him, turned and ran.

Before anything else could be said I pushed my recently purchased tea into Emily's hands and then ran as fast as my legs would carry me in pursuit of him. Turning to Miss Coutts, I shouted, "Go straight to the hotel. Talk to no one!"

Miss Coutts was understandably alarmed and set off to cover the remaining two hundred yards to the Queen as quickly as possible.

I ran hard but the ground was uneven and I nearly went over on my ankle a number of times. The 'Stray' is a deceptively glamorous name as it is really just a common heath laden with rabbit holes and heather. I was gaining on the man but still could not confirm that he was one of the Russians. I found myself running on the town's racecourse, making the ground marginally easy to cover. I continued to gain on the man who was now approximately fifty yards ahead of me. Running was not easy, as I continued to feel discomfort from the ankle Miss Coutts had so effectively bruised.

My quarry then turned off the Stray and headed down a lane towards a wood. My mind was turning over at a rapid rate. What if this man wasn't a Russian? Who was he and why was he following us? I had to catch him and continued to close in but he was now on the brink of reaching the wood and once in there, he would be much harder to find.

He was flagging but so was I, and one moment he was twenty five yards away and in the next, he had disappeared into the undergrowth of the wood and was gone.

I stood at the entrance to the wood breathing heavily. I peered in at the dark undergrowth and listened for the sound of footsteps. I was out of breath and all I could hear above the pounding of my chest was the sound of a pigeon landing on a tree branch. I walked alongside the small forest still listening for any movement. I saw a startled rabbit run out as if being chased by a fox or perhaps it had been disturbed by the man I was pursuing.

To venture unarmed into the darkness would be an unnecessary risk. For all I knew I could have been purposely lured to this place and there could be more than one person now lying in wait. But why would anyone want to do that, as surely no one knew the real purpose of my visit here? Even if anyone did know, what good would it do them to dispose of an officer in the 11th Light Dragoons as this would surely only invite more trouble? Perhaps this was a ruse by common criminals out to rob me. There were a number of unanswered questions circulating my mind but within the last hour or so my assignment here had become considerably more serious.

"Damn!" I said to myself as I continued to catch my breath. Being on patrol in India had taught me not to follow anyone I was chasing into a confined area. I walked slowly away from the woods, turning every five or ten paces to look back for any sign of movement. I was disappointed not to have caught the rogue but no matter how many times I looked back, nothing appeared. When I eventually reached the Queen Hotel I walked past the sneering Dawson who, for the sake of appearances, wished me a good morning. Before I could respond, Emily approached me. She had been waiting in the reception. She handed me the tea I had purchased from Hatherway's grocery.

"Captain, sir, would you please follow me?" As we walked she quietly enquired as to whether I had caught the culprit, to which I regrettably reported that I had not.

I was shown into a private parlour occupied by Lord and Lady Redmayne, in addition to Miss Coutts, who was sitting at a writing desk, piled high with letters. The instant she saw me she put down her pen and made her way over to me.

"Captain Townsend, did you catch the man?" she enquired pointedly.

"Alas, miss, I regret to report that I lost the blighter in some woods on the other side of the racecourse," and then in order to reassure her added, "I am sure there is nothing to be concerned about. If he had been dangerous, he would surely have taken the opportunity to shoot me."

At which point I heard the ladies gasp, indicating that my attempt to reassure them had failed miserably.

"What do you suppose he was up to?" asked a slightly un-nerved Miss Coutts.

"I have no idea but his interest could simply be that he has taken a shine to Emily and was too shy to make his feelings known," I replied trying to make light of the situation. The truth was that all the other reasons were too concerning to mention.

"Did you manage to get a look at him, Captain?" intervened Lord Redmayne.

"I regret not, sir. All I could say is that he was of medium height, medium build, modestly attired and, as I was unable to catch him, I would conclude that he must be reasonably fit and most probably less than thirty years of age. Until we find this person, I would strongly recommend that you allow me to accompany you whenever you venture outside the hotel."

It seemed the only sensible thing to say, which was heartily endorsed by Lord and Lady Redmayne. Miss Coutts assured me that she would not be heading out again today and so it was agreed that I would call on her tomorrow morning in order to escort her to the sulphur well.

Despite being of strong resolve, it was clear that the events of the morning had visibly unsettled Miss Coutts. Although satisfied with the protection all around her, she made it clear that she longed for her close companion, Miss Hannah Meredith, to arrive.

"My dearest friend has indicated in her last letter that she'd been hoping to book passage on a fast mail coach bound for York, otherwise she would use a private coach. Either way, with any luck, Hannah will arrive tomorrow," Miss Coutts confessed.

If it wasn't obvious before, it was blindingly apparent now that I needed to establish what the Russians were up to, and quickly. The manner in which the one-eyed manservant had looked at us in the pleasure gardens was a concern. I wondered if the man I chased had been sent by him, perhaps as a result of my having noticed him watching us. But why? There were a number of questions to answer which only grew the more I considered the morning's events.

Having arranged to arrive at the Queen early the following day, I took my leave and hurried back to my aunt's house.

Chapter 12

I arrived back at Holderness House to find my aunt reading in the orangery and immediately handed her the Ceylon tea.

"Thank you, George, but why are you giving me a tin of Ceylon tea?" holding the tin and examining it almost like an archaeologist surveying a recently unearthed artefact.

"Do you not like the tea we provide you?" she asked, continuing to question the purpose of the gift.

"Yes, Aunt, your tea is fine. I just caught sight of this particular brand on sale and thought you might like it," I replied, struggling to sound convincing.

"Anyway, following my endeavours this morning, I think you owe me more than a mere tin of Ceylon tea," she said teasingly.

"I detect you have some news for me," I said, bursting with anticipation.

"Indeed I have!" she replied, clearly anxious to tell me more.

"As promised, I made discreet enquiries with one or two friends about your Russians and they led me to my bank managers, Henry Payden and Gerald Beales."

"I have known Henry for some considerable time; he is a lawyer and a banker who lost his wife a few years ago. Very sad really, she was a lovely person. Since her death, Henry took in Gerald Beales as his partner in one or two ventures including the Bank of Harrogate, and they both seem to be very successful. I contacted Henry as there is little that happens in the area that escapes his attention, added to which I think he is quite fond of me. Anyway, by coincidence, he was apparently about to contact me as he had an investment proposition which he thought I would find had merit."

This was all well and good, but I was mentally urging my aunt to get to the point.

"You might find his proposal rather fascinating as it involves a railway project. On the other hand you might feel that this, in itself, is not terribly interesting as railways are springing up everywhere. However, I am sure you will be intrigued to learn that they have recently employed an expert to help them with the venture who hails from St Petersburg, Russia."

My aunt had exceeded all my expectations, but before I could thank her, Benson interrupted advising us that lunch was now being served.

"Aunt, what can I say? That is simply marvellous! You are the most remarkable of aunts. I dare say that if Lord Palmerston was aware of your talents he would have simply employed you and left me in London." Following which, I moved over to kiss her.

"I am so glad you are pleased, my boy, and now we must commence our lunch as at two o'clock we are to be visited by Mr Payden and Mr Beales, when you will be able to find out all you want to know about your Russian."

For the second time in as many minutes I was overwhelmed by my aunt's efforts.

"They are coming here to try and persuade us both to invest in their railway project," she added smiling broadly, "and now, George, the rest is up to you."

I simply smiled, remarking, "Aunt, you astonish me!" And with that, we headed to the dining room for a splendid game pie.

After lunch I sat with my aunt in the drawing room of Holderness House and looked out of the window, watching the world go by. My mind was very much on the events of the morning. I so wished that I'd been riding Tribune as I could have run the stalker to ground. The grandfather clock in the hall chimed twice just as two gentlemen walked through the gates and made the short distance along the path to the front door.

Benson greeted our visitors and escorted them into the house.

"Mr Beales and Mr Payden," said Benson, introducing them as they entered the drawing room. They were both elegantly dressed with sharply cut trousers and jackets. Mr Payden had a friendly manner and his grey hair suggested that he was quite a bit older than Mr Beales, whose friendly smile appeared less natural and somewhat contrived. Mr Beales' demeanour seemed to be in line with what I had always been told to expect from a northern business man, that is: dour, plain speaking and careful.

"My dear Mrs Moore," said Mr Payden, shaking her hand enthusiastically. The warmth in his smile betraying the fondness he had for my aunt which she had alluded to earlier.

"Mr Payden, it is a pleasure to see you again. Allow me to introduce my nephew, Captain George Townsend, who is recently returned from India with the 11th Light Dragoons," said Aunt Violet proudly.

"George, allow me to introduce Mr Gerald Beales and Mr Henry Payden," she added, whereupon we all nodded and then shook hands.

With the introductions out of the way, my aunt invited both gentlemen to take a seat and then instructed Benson to bring refreshments.

"Captain, might I ask what you make of our lovely town of Harrogate?" enquired Gerald Beales in a way which, although pleasant enough, seemed to lack sincerity. It felt as though the question he was now asking was not the question running through his mind. It was as if his mouth was asking one question and his eyes another. He reminded me of those rogues who ask you for the time of day when all the while they are picking your pocket.

"Very pleasant, sir," I replied. "It is not my first visit to the area but it's a number of years since I was last in Harrogate and in that time my aunt has built this magnificent house," I said demonstratively opening the palms of my hands as my eyes surveyed the room.

"Indeed!" said Henry Payden. "The envy of all Harrogate," he said, joining in the exchange and taking the opportunity to smile once more at my aunt.

"Thank you gentlemen, you are too kind. Now, I am intrigued to learn the nature of this proposal which you feel is so appealing," began my aunt, getting straight to the point. Her approach had me realise that she was far more accomplished in business matters than I had ever appreciated.

Henry Payden took it upon himself to respond.

"Mrs Moore, we are here today to invite you to partake in one of the most exciting business opportunities this town has ever seen. I am, of course, referring to the railways," he said with marked enthusiasm.

"And what interest do you think I would have in the railways?"

"Quite simply, the investment returns, madam," interjected Gerald Beales in his blunt northern manner, seizing the opportunity to re-enter the discussion.

After allowing a moment for his bold and direct statement to be fully absorbed by us all, he continued.

"A line from York to Harrogate will bring more visitors to the town; something which we all really need. Whereas Harrogate is unquestionably a fine town, it must continue to improve in every respect or it will be left behind in this modern age. Shortly there will be a railway running from London to Bath as well as one to Birmingham. A line is being constructed from Leeds to Manchester and I expect lines to be built joining the capital to York before too long. We must keep up in the great railway boom otherwise we lose out to the other spa towns such as Cheltenham and Bath," he paused and Henry Payden took up the story.

"We have formed the Yorkshire Railway Company and applied to parliament for government approval. We have already attracted investment from the majority of owners from the most prominent and prestigious hotels in Harrogate."

Even though this all made complete sense, I was questioning its viability. I could see the benefit to the hotel owners but I couldn't see the attraction for my aunt and so I took it upon myself to intervene.

"And pray tell me, gentlemen, where will the profit be to an investor who does not have the advantage of owning a hotel?" I said, gaining a nod of approval from my aunt who was well known for not suffering fools gladly.

"Why, in the dividends from the profits, Captain, and also from the increase in the value of the shares," replied a confident Gerald Beales. "Maybe you will be reassured to know that, in addition to having received support from the hotel owners we have also received substantial investments from many of our important visitors – some of whom I suspect you may know, such as Lord Redmayne."

That took me back somewhat, as how would this bank manager know that I was acquainted with His Lordship?

"Yes, His Lordship did mention something about the railway," I said, foolishly pretending that this conversation had taken place. I instantly regretted the lie.

"Additionally, we count ourselves fortunate to have Sir William Hamilton involved as well as the Duke of Aldborough, whose estate in Lancashire is so close to that of Lord Redmayne's."

A chill ran down my spine. My interest in Sir William's daughter had waned only because of his scurrilous actions, but my dislike of him had not. I wondered how he had become involved in a railway this far north. It must have been through the Duke of Aldborough, all the same I was not aware that the two of them knew each other. I looked at my aunt who knew that the mention of Sir William's name would have stirred my emotions. Whilst I came to terms with this revelation my aunt skilfully intervened.

"But how can any of us be certain that profits will be made, sir?" she asked.

"Our confidence is a reflection of our efforts and endeavours, madam. We have made thorough investigations into the costs of both building and managing the railway. Also, with the help of Mr Pickersgill Palliser, the newspaper publisher, we have carefully calculated the number of visitors expected to avail themselves of this more convenient mode of transportation. Additionally, we will be hauling coal and other merchandise into the town which also increases the railway's revenue. All in all, we expect to be every bit as successful as the line from Manchester to Liverpool which, as you probably know, is highly profitable. We have a full prospectus which we would be happy to share with yourself and your nephew, madam," replied Gerald Beales.

The thought of wading through reams of paperwork on some fool scheme filled me with terror. I was no bookkeeper and hated the prospect of being marooned indoors chained to a desk. All I was interested in was the Russians, and there had been no mention of them as yet. I hoped that my aunt was thinking along the same lines but before I could say anything else, she spoke.

"I am sure we would very much like to see a prospectus, gentlemen," she said, glancing in my direction, "but before we do, I would like to know what returns you expect an investor to receive."

Henry Payden was saying very little and seemed content for Gerald Beales to do most of the talking and the latter once again responded confidently.

"When the railway is fully operational in two to three years time we are predicting that it will generate an annual dividend of five percent, furthermore we expect that this performance will more than treble the value of the shares."

"That sounds excellent," said my aunt on hearing this news. "Almost too good to be true."

"Not at all, madam. It has been scientifically calculated using the Manchester to Liverpool railway line as an example to follow."

There was still no mention of the Russian and as I was fast becoming irritated, I intervened.

"Gentlemen, this sounds like a grand plan and you have impressive backers but have either of you built or operated a railway before?"

I then sat back hoping that I may yet prize some information from them regarding Von Benckendorff.

"You're absolutely right, Captain. Our own expertise is in banking which is why we have consulted with some of the best engineers in the country and, only recently, we managed to secure the services of one of Europe's most prominent authorities on railways. Someone who was largely responsible for building the Tsarskoye Selo Railway which, as you may or may not know, was the first public railway line in Russia. It ran for seventeen miles from Saint Petersburg to Pavlovsk."

"And who might that be?" I asked.

"Mr Vladimir Von Benckendorff," he replied.

Well at last we were getting somewhere!

"Who?" I exclaimed, in an attempt to disguise my interest, prompting Mr

Beales to repeat his name whilst also enquiring as to whether or not if I had heard of him.

"No, it's just an unusual name, Von Beck-ing-dorff," I said, deliberately struggling to pronounce the name properly.

"Von Benck-en-dorff," corrected Mr Beales adding, "Yes, it is an unusual name, but not if you are Russian," he laughed at his own witty remark.

Everyone, with the exception of yours truly politely tittered. I did my best to smile but I fear my expression may have more resembled that of a babe in arms struggling with a dose of wind. My first impression of Gerald Beales was somewhat questionable but nevertheless I was being handed the perfect opportunity to meet the Russian, which could go a long way to allaying Lord Palmerton's fears. It didn't explain the events of earlier this morning, but there could be many other explanations for that. For example, the Russian servant may have been simply admiring the good looks of the maid Emily, albeit impolitely. But who was the man who watched us walk back to the Queen Hotel and why did he run when he knew he had been spotted? Surely both events were not innocent.

"What do you think, George?" asked my aunt, turning to me, instantly ending my private speculations.

"Well, Aunt, I think it sounds like a good opportunity. Having said that, I do think we should meet with Vladimir Von Benckendorff and look at the costs if you are indeed interested in making an investment."

"I agree. Would that be possible?" my aunt asked, looking intently at Mr Beales and Mr Payden.

"But of course," said Mr Payden speaking for the first time in a while. "We are almost fully subscribed and so time is of the essence. Would tomorrow be convenient, Captain, at say eleven o'clock?"

My aunt looked to me to respond and I acknowledged that this time would suit, although having promised to escort Miss Coutts to the wells first thing in the morning, there would be little time to spare. We then agreed to meet at the bank's offices on Paradise Row which was next door to Smiths of New Bond Street, London, who apparently operated there during the season.

"One more thing, gentlemen," I asked. "If my memory serves me well, no railway can proceed without an Act of Parliament, so how can you be certain that parliament will approve this railway and might it not take forever to get the necessary act passed?"

Mr Beales and Mr Payden looked at each other and both seemed eager to answer my question. Yet again it was Mr Beales who spoke.

"That is an easy question to answer, Captain, as we have influence at the highest level within the government. We cannot go into details but we can safely assure you that the necessary Act of Parliament is as good as passed."

The meeting was drawing to a natural end but Mr Beales wasn't finished and wanted to make one last point.

"I am sure you will not regret making an investment, if indeed you decide to join us, Mrs Moore. The shares of the existing railway companies have performed handsomely over the last few years, returning substantial gains to their shareholders. If you do decide to invest, could I ask what size of investment you would contemplate?"

My aunt was not to be drawn on the point and forcibly said that she would advise him of that figure if, and only if, she was satisfied with my findings at tomorrow's meeting.

Mr Beales looked a little disappointed that his initial presentation had not made more tangible progress. At that point they both rose to their feet and after a deal of bowing and scraping, they collected their hats from Benson and, thankfully, left.

I was making good progress and it was very apparent that my aunt had an admirer.

Chapter 13

In spite of the fact that no further word had been received from Palmerston, I nevertheless felt that I should appraise him of today's events with all possible haste. I retired to my room, picked up my pen and started the arduous task of incorporating my message into his complicated code. After much head scratching I managed this and then rang for Benson, who assured me that the letter would be taken to the post office immediately. Again, I made sure that the honour of paying for the correspondence rightly fell to His Lordship.

Whilst he was in my room, I took the opportunity of asking Benson if he had managed to enter Tribune into Friday's race, in addition to finding me a trustworthy donkey boy. He assured me that Tribune would race on Friday, which was good news as it helped to disguise the real purpose behind my visit. However, he had less promising news regarding the donkey boy. Although he had someone in mind, despite all his best efforts he had not yet managed to make contact with him.

Having arranged to meet Vladimir Von Benckendorff tomorrow there seemed to be little more that could be achieved today, other than to look for any signs that the stalker may have left behind as he fled into the woods. With the horse race only a few days away, this would also present me with a good opportunity to take Tribune for some exercise around the nearby Harrogate racecourse.

The stable boy quickly prepared Tribune and it felt good to be in the saddle again. This time I took the precaution of picking up both my pistol and my knife. If I was to run into any additional surprises, I was going to be better prepared than I had been this morning. I dare say though, if I had shot the wretched stalker as I chased him, I might have found myself dangling from some rope or rowing a convict ship bound for Australia.

I walked Tribune onto the Stray and keeping him away from the paths being used by visitors, I spurred him on to a canter. A couple of sheep that had been grazing peacefully were sent running in opposite directions. I'd decided not to wear a hat, which allowed the wind to drive my hair backwards as Tribune moved from a canter to a gallop. We soon reached the racecourse and slowed down.

The legislation which protected access to the wells on the two hundred acre common prevented the erection of any permanent buildings. Consequently, unless you knew what you were looking for, you would never realise that a racecourse existed there. I wanted Tribune to get a feel for the course and so we trotted around letting him familiarize himself with the ground. As it was August, the ground was firm even though in parts, and maybe due to all the wells in the area, the ground was much softer. I had no idea whether on race days horses were expected to run around the course in a clockwise or anti-clockwise direction and so I did both. Tribune much preferred to run clockwise whereas my previous horse, Tiberius, always raced better when running anti-clockwise. Strange, but horses are like people and have peculiar likes and dislikes.

After a couple of steady laps, I allowed Tribune to gallop down the straights and he showed that the long journey from London had done nothing to diminish his speed. He would take some beating on Friday. I then guided him over towards the woods to the spot where I gave up the chase earlier in the day. The sun had broken through the clouds and we were bathed in sunshine but the woods still looked dark and uninviting. The trees were set too close together to allow anyone to ride through on horseback and so I decided to walk Tribune around the circumference. I was looking for any sign where our stalker may have made his escape. It turned out to be a relatively small wood and there were three possible paths which he could have reasonably taken. The first seemed to head in a round about way over towards the Granby, the next headed south towards Leeds and finally another which ran parallel to the road connecting the Brunswick to the Queen. The most likely escape route appeared to be the path heading south towards Leeds.

There was no one about, which kept the hairs on the back of my neck slightly elevated. The ground was so hard that there was no sign of any tracks which we could follow. In any event, even if there had been tracks I wouldn't have been able to ascertain if they belonged to the stalker or not. The exercise appeared futile but I continued to search as when people are running for their lives, they can easily drop things. A farmer walked by, leading a cow, which broke my concentration and after twenty minutes of unproductive searching, I decided to abandon the hunt, at least for today.

On returning to Holderness House, I handed Tribune back to the stable boy and went into the house to prepare for the evening. My thoughts then turned to Miss Hatherway. With some of the questions surrounding the Russians beginning to resolve themselves, the prospect of a few hours' relaxation was extremely appealing. And what better way to do that than with the beautiful Miss Virginia Hatherway? She had certainly captivated me, although I also found myself having to contend with emotions concerning the Duchess of Aldborough which I had thought long since dead. Maybe I was reading too much into this, but there was something in the way she said that 'we' had a son which was quite unnerving.

After dining with my aunt, I eagerly left Holderness House shortly before seven o'clock, the time I had arranged to meet Miss Virginia Hatherway. Despite my intention to relax a little, I nevertheless tucked my pistol into my belt. As the day was cooling down I wore a larger coat which easily disguised the fact that I was armed. Finally, I stowed my neat folding knife into my boot. As a consequence, I felt confident and full of hope as I walked through the gates of Holderness House and down towards the Montpelier Gardens.

As most of the balls didn't start until nine o'clock, I found the streets were still busy. Some people were heading to music recitals and others to dinners as well as those merely taking an evening stroll. I walked down Parliament Street and past Hatherway Grocer's until, at the bottom of the hill, I saw the magnificent Cheltenham Pump Room. There were a good number of visitors promenading around and the faint sound of a piano emanated from the building. All the while I was looking out for Miss Hatherway. Given my recent experiences of the fairer sex, the nearer I came to the Montpelier Gardens the more I started to think that perhaps she had been persuaded not to come.

Once in the gardens I looked around, all the while trying not to be conspicuous. Much to my dismay there was no sign of her but I couldn't help being drawn to the sight of a young couple seemingly caught up in a heated exchange. They were standing perhaps thirty yards away at the far side of the pleasure gardens. They were straining to keep their voices down when it looked as if they really wanted to shout very loudly at each other. It was making compelling viewing, however it was also a trifle distracting. I left them to their quarrel and continued to search for Miss Hatherway as my fears grew that she wasn't coming. All the same my eyes were repeatedly drawn back to the bickering couple. The lady involved in the altercation had her back to me and was neatly dressed wearing a yellow bonnet. The man she was arguing with faced me. He wore a long coat which appeared a shade too small and a hat which had seen better days. Although I had only met a handful of men since arriving in Harrogate, there was nevertheless something distinctly familiar about him. I ventured a little closer in order to get a clearer view of the man's face and as I did, it soon became clear that I had indeed seen him before. He was none other than the upstart Dawson from the Queen Hotel. Even though he was not wearing the livery of his employer, it was undoubtedly him. This reaffirmed my opinion that he was an ill-bred specimen and I immediately felt sympathy for the poor girl who was being subjected to his attentions. I resisted the temptation to listen to his argument and continued to peer through the crowded gardens for Miss Hatherway. There was no sign of her, prompting me to check my watch and put it to my ear to make sure it was in good working order.

I was beginning to feel a modicum of disappointment as I turned to see if the odious Dawson was still making an ass of himself with the lady in the yellow bonnet. The dispute showed no sign of ending; however their positions had changed full circle. Dawson now had his back to me and my jaw dropped when it became clear that the lady facing him was none other than Miss Virginia Hatherway!

I could scarcely believe my eyes and considered returning directly to Holderness House but thought better of it given that Miss Hatherway was far from happy and concluded that she may not be a willing participant in this conversation after all. Rightly or wrongly, I strode boldly into the fray and, whilst completely ignoring Dawson, addressed Miss Hatherway politely and confidently.

"Good evening, Miss Hatherway," I said as I raised my hat. "What a pleasant surprise to see you again," to which she seemed both relieved and concerned in the same instance.

"What in damnation do you want?" growled Dawson aggressively.

I continued to ignore him and before he could say another word I addressed Miss Hatherway for a second time.

"Is this person bothering you?"

Miss Hatherway was quite clearly looking to avoid escalating matters and consequently played down her obvious displeasure.

"Good evening to you too, Captain. Please do not be concerned, as everything is fine. Thomas and I merely had a difference of opinion in respect of a private matter which is now at an end and so I will bid you good night, Thomas," she said, turning to Dawson.

"No, we're bloody well not finished, missy. We have things to discuss and this Captain can piss off back to India or wherever else he came from and mind his own damn business," he said moving to grab Miss Hatherway by the arm.

I intervened and grabbed his wrist firmly which, much to his annoyance, stopped him from making contact with her. I held onto his wrist and then pushed it behind his back to the point where it would go no further without me dislocating his shoulder or breaking his arm.

"Please stop, Captain!" said a somewhat frantic Miss Hatherway. "There are people about."

Still holding Dawson with his arm behind his back, I looked around and it seemed that people were indeed taking note of what was happening, with a degree of concern etched on some of their faces. This was not what I had bargained for, and a public spectacle such as this was in danger of jeopardising my assignment.

I continued to press his arm into his back and moved my head towards his right ear. I smiled in a reassuring way to the onlookers and then spoke quietly in Dawson's ear.

"Now you take note of this, Dawson. I think you are a very unpleasant little man and if we were not amongst all these people here," I smiled reassuringly to the onlookers, "I would twist your damn arm off and beat you about the head with it. Now I strongly advise you to keep well out of my way in future and never swear in front of this lady again."

"She's no lady," said Dawson struggling to speak with his normal arrogance, as he was clearly in pain.

"Dawson don't push me, otherwise crowd or no crowd, I will snap your arm off."

As I spoke, I heard one onlooker mention alerting the constable and so I released Dawson who staggered back holding his right arm with his left.

"You haven't heard the last of this, Captain." Turning to Miss Hatherway he said, "I will talk to you later."

"No you won't, Dawson. You won't go within a mile of her," I snarled at him.

Despite my strong words it was abundantly clear that this man was unlikely to be appeased by words alone. Consequently I moved towards him to suggest that we go to some quiet corner of Harrogate where I could give him a lesson in manners when he threw a punch at me, which I just managed to evade.

"Stop it! Please, stop!" cried Miss Hatherway, becoming ever more distressed by the unfolding scene and so I resisted the temptation to return the compliment to Dawson. Undeterred he threw another punch, provoking an audible gasp from the onlookers. A growing number of people were clearly disconcerted by what they were witnessing. Most had come out for a pleasant walk or to step into the Cheltenham Pump Room for a music recital and here was a vulgar brawl taking place right in front of them.

I had dodged two punches and knew that the only thing Dawson would listen to was a strong blow to his chin, which is exactly what happened moments later when he attempted to hit me for a third time. He fell backwards into a bed of roses and was out cold.

I then dusted myself down, straightened my jacket and held my arm out for Miss Hatherway. It was time to take our leave and make a quick and relatively elegant withdrawal from the scene. As I looked around, I saw several outraged ladies as well as Lord and Lady Asenby, The Earl of Warkworth and the Duchess of Aldborough. The Earl looked as if he approved of my actions but both the Asenby's and the Duchess looked less enamoured.

I regretted my part in the proceedings but felt that, under the circumstances, I had been given little choice. I caught the eye of the Duchess and tried to communicate that to her with a look and a shrug of the shoulders. It seemed to appease her, as she gave me the suggestion of a smile. I then guided Miss Hatherway away from the garden towards Bogs Lane, leaving Dawson to enjoy a well-earned sleep. He stirred as we turned away and I heard a kindly old lady enquire as to whether he was still alive. He confirmed to the lady that he was and proceeded to play the role of the victim with aplomb, drawing a good dose of sympathy in the process.

Miss Hatherway and I walked briskly away and never looked back. After walking about one hundred yards along the unattractively named Bogs Lane, we reached a quiet spot near Cornwall House and then she stopped, turning to face me.

"What did you have to do that for?" she said in a stern voice.

"Would you rather I was the one laying prostrate in the flower bed?" I replied, somewhat taken aback at this apparent reprimand.

"Of course not. But there was no need for anyone to get hurt," she said calming herself.

"I couldn't agree more, but unfortunately Dawson was not of the same mind."

"Anyway, what on earth were you doing with him in the first place?" I said, pressing to bring some clarity to the situation.

"I don't think that is any of your business," she said defensively. "I have had a life before you came along."

It took a moment for me to join up the clues she had given me and then dawn broke in some corner of my mind.

"Good God! You're not telling me that Dawson has been part of your life?" I said, mystified that someone so beautiful could be in any way friendly with such an odious man.

"Well, what if he was? That is nothing to do with you is it?" she retorted.

"I suppose not," I said, rapidly resigning myself to this revelation. "It's just very hard to see you being 'friendly' with the likes of him."

"Well I was friendly with him, as you put it. But that was a long time ago. Tom hopes to become the next manager at the Queen and wants to marry me. I have told him repeatedly that I have no interest in being the wife of a hotel servant, albeit an important one. But every now and then he still tries to persuade me otherwise. Tonight was another one of those attempts. He seized upon our chance meeting and as you could see, he doesn't like it when he can't get his own way.

"Anyway, Captain, you are a fine one to question me! What about the lady who was with you when you came into the shop today, maid and all? You seemed to be very 'friendly' with her."

Smarting a little from this unexpected retaliation, I reassured Miss Hatherway that the lady in question was indeed just a friend and reminded her of the story I had recounted to her in the shop about the damaged coach wheel, Lord Redmayne and all. I only hesitated in revealing Miss Coutts's name as I was acutely aware of the sensitivity of this issue. However, by omitting this piece of information, I only raised her curiosity more.

She then looked me straight in the eye and asked, "So who is she?"

"I am afraid I cannot tell you," I said, trying to convey the seriousness of the situation to her.

"You mean, *will* not tell me?" she said curtly.

"I mean cannot. It's very complicated. Please trust me," I replied.

"You ask me to trust you when you won't trust me? That hardly seems fair," she remarked, adding in a soft voice whilst also looking into my eyes, in that way only ladies can when they are stealing a man's will, "Of course you can trust me. I will not let you down."

I knew that in telling her I was taking a risk but it seemed like a risk worth taking. I persuaded myself that being from a successful local family, Miss Hatherway hardly bore the characteristics of an international conspirator. Also, given that the likes of Dawson knew about Miss Coutts visiting Harrogate, it seemed that Lord Redmayne's hopes of keeping her presence secret was likely to prove a futile exercise in any event. And so I told her.

"Angela Coutts! Well I never! And she was in our shop," she said as her face lit up. I could see in her eyes that she was carefully assimilating this information and what it all meant to her.

"You should marry her, Captain. You would be the richest man in England," she added cheekily. I did not have to think too long before replying.

"Miss Coutts has had more marriage proposals than Harrogate has had balls," I said responding to the jest.

"And as much as I welcome her friendship I am not the man for her any more than she is the lady for me."

It seemed like the air was clearing and having reassured each other of our intentions we walked on a little further. We both began to notice that it was still a lovely evening and the unpleasantness with Dawson was rapidly evaporating from our memories.

We continued to stroll along Bogs Lane until we reached the four stones of Harlow Moor, which Miss Hatherway insisted on pointing out to me.

"They say they are like the Devil's Arrows at Boroughbridge."

"What are they?" I enquired.

"Well, they are like these stones only much bigger. Legend has it that if you walk anti-clockwise around the stones three times, you will raise the devil," she said squeezing my arm noticeably tighter.

"So you believe the legend?" I asked.

"Absolutely not," came her emphatic and yet unconvincing response. "Although plenty of people do. A young girl, newly married, came here many years ago and after walking anti-clockwise around the stones, was bewitched. She went home and murdered her husband." A gentle wind chilled the air causing her to squeeze my arm even tighter.

I had enough to worry about with the Russian and the man I chased across the racecourse without having the devil to contend with as well and so we walked on a little quicker.

She went on to tell me that she had lived in Harrogate all her life but she longed for pastures new. The thought of working in a shop all her life frightened her as she believed she was destined for higher things. In response, I told her something of my career in India, my love of horses and, in particular, Tribune who I hoped to race in Harrogate later in the week. I alluded to my own ambitions to improve my situation which in many ways mirrored hers, and also shared with her something of our family history which all started in Tullow, Ireland. After hearing that I had lost both my parents, she thoughtfully resisted any temptation to enquire further into my past. Even though my mother and father both passed away some years ago, I still feel a great sadness whenever they are mentioned. I miss them immensely and I don't think that will ever change.

The light started to fade as we turned around and headed back towards the sulphur well. All our cross words had been replaced by laughter and we were once more two people intoxicated in each other's company. Romance was yet again in the air as it had been at the ball on the previous night.

"Alas, Captain, I fear it is time for me to go home," said Miss Hatherway wistfully.

It was getting late and there was little point in my arguing, but I did request that I be allowed to walk her home and this time she readily agreed. She lived with her parents just off Cold Bath Road which was a walk of maybe three hundred yards if we cut through past the Bath Hospital. Having narrowly avoided falling into the black bog, we eventually joined Cold Bath Road just by the Binns Hotel. As we neared her house, we came across a young lady walking a black dog which looked like the spaniel I first encountered when I arrived in Harrogate a couple of days ago. Miss Hatherway clearly knew the lady and called to her. She looked familiar. I recognised her from the previous evening at the Granby and moments later I found myself being introduced to her sister, Grace. The dog was called Sam and he was as handsome a dog as you could wish to see. He was not only blessed with fine looks but also an admiral temperament.

"I am pleased to meet you, Grace. And what a simply splendid dog you have!" I said, now stroking Sam.

"He's a good dog but make no mistake, Captain, if he thinks we are being threatened, he makes an almighty row, don't you Sam?" said Grace, patting Sam on his haunches.

I bent down to stroke the dog who promptly rolled onto his back inviting me to tickle his tummy. In order to avoid disappointing my new found friend, I happily obliged.

"I can see you're soft on animals, Captain," said Grace.

"Yes, I am. Ever since I took in an injured bird and nursed him for two days. I must have only been around six or seven. I fed him and kept him supplied with water after which he recovered enough to walk and I thought he would simply fly away but the poor thing just fell onto one side struggling to right himself. I picked him up to try and help him but he died in my hands. I cried for two days after that."

"Aww, that's so sad," said Virginia, whereupon Grace tried to lift the melancholy air I had just unwittingly inflicted on the two ladies.

"Have you had a good evening, Ginny?" continued Grace, "Tom was around here earlier looking for you; he looked a bit worse for wear."

"I expect he was," replied Virginia. "Tom tried to hit the Captain and I suspect he now wishes he hadn't, given the ease with which he was knocked out."

Grace looked a little shocked at the news. I think that my story about the bird had given her the impression that I was a man of peace. Anyway, Virginia soon reassured her that all was well and there was nothing to worry about.

We all continued walking towards their home and within a minute or so we were standing outside their gate. The house looked very pleasant; built of stone, well maintained and with a neat and well stocked garden. Grace wished me goodnight and took Sam into the house leaving Virginia and myself alone, however it felt as if the eyes of the world were upon us. I didn't look at the windows of the house but I was certain we were being watched, and given the circumstances, it was only to be expected. I felt a little uncomfortable in a world which at times was almost devoid of convention.

"I have had a wonderful evening, George. I hope we can do this again sometime," said Virginia, readying herself to head into the house. I liked the fact that she had started to call me George.

"I thoroughly enjoyed myself too and I am sorry if I caused a bit of a stir by punching Dawson," I replied.

"Think nothing of it. He had it coming, but watch your back. He will not forget what you did to him," she said as she opened the gate.

"When will I see you again?" I asked.

"Do you want to?" came the teasing reply.

"Of course I do. Why would you think otherwise?"

"Well I wasn't sure whether the incident with Tom might have deterred you?"

"It would take more than that to deter me," I said, endeavouring to reassure her.

"Then I will speak to Father. Can I send you a note to Holderness House when I have spoken to him?" she replied.

"Absolutely," I replied.

After one last smile she headed for the house, opened the door and following one last glance in my direction, was gone.

Feeling remarkably content with life, I began the walk back towards Holderness House. The light was almost gone and by the time I reached the bottom of Montpelier Hill it was dark. I could see the lights of my aunt's house in front of me and the lights of the hotels behind me but other than that it was pitch black. There was no moon or stars and I was finding it hard to see where I should put my feet. I hoped that I would not put my foot in anything unpleasant after noting the number of sheep that had been frequenting this area recently.

Suddenly, out of the darkness I saw a figure directly ahead of me. It looked like a man with a hooded cloak, which made it very difficult to identify the person. I thought it may be Benson, but what would he be doing here and without a light? If it were Benson, he would surely be carrying a lantern to help me see where I was walking. Instinctively I felt that something was amiss. As the man closed to within a few feet I felt for my pistol and had just got my hand around the butt when I felt the most almighty pain in the back of my neck as someone brought down a club on me. I hit the ground, seeing several pairs of feet around me before I lost consciousness.

Chapter 14

I don't know how long I was out for, but when I came round I was lying awkwardly on a damp and cold floor nursing a splitting headache. I could feel a sticky patch on my scalp which I took to be blood. Slowly opening my eyes to the dim light from a solitary candle, I could sense that I was not alone and my hands were tied behind my back. As I struggled to sit up, a voice from across the room warned, "Now, Captain, don't you be making any sudden moves. I have your own pistol aimed right at your head."

I blinked a number of times trying my level best to accustom myself to these unfamiliar surroundings and then slowly sat up. I was in a corner of a dingy room with a fireplace on my left. Judging by the smell, I suspected that I was in some sort of farm building. A shepherd's hut perhaps.

"You're not welcome here, Cap'n! We want you out of Harrogate and a long way away at that! You've twenty four hours to be on your way, otherwise in twenty five hours you will be dead!" a different voice growled.

These words brought me back to my full senses rather quickly. Although I felt like making a remark about this not being in keeping with the much-vaunted northern hospitality, I decided to remain tight-lipped until I had the situation more under my control.

I tried to stand up only to feel the weight of a large club on my right shoulder. This was quickly followed by, "Stay right where you are," spoken aggressively by the second man who was now standing next to me. The light was behind them which made it very difficult to determine much about their appearance. Having said that, there was no mistaking their smell.

I then attempted to make myself more comfortable and manoeuvred my legs so that the boot housing my knife was within reach of my hand. I engaged my gaolers in conversation whilst my hands moved discreetly towards my boots. As my hands felt down the length of my right boot I was pleased to learn that I was still in possession of my Joseph Manning knife.

"Might I be told why you would like me out of Harrogate?" I enquired, squinting towards my captors only to receive another tap on my shoulder forcing me back into the corner.

"That's not your concern, nor ours. Our orders are to make sure that you move on. And quickly!" said the first man, who sounded a good deal more sensible than his club-prodding partner. I heard his chair squeak from across the room.

All the while we talked, my fingers edged the knife towards the top of my boot entirely out of sight to everyone else.

"Do you not realise that if you kill me you will have half the British army after your hides and when they catch you there will be hell to pay," I said now clutching the knife in the fingers of my right hand. The reason my blade often went undetected is because it's a new folding knife and easy to hide. However, due to the strength of the spring which kept it closed, this took several attempts to open.

"They will have to find you first," laughed the first man who continued to hold my pistol. "There's lots of bogs around here, Cap'n, and strangers like you can easily fall into them and never be heard of again."

The second man grunted his amusement to this. "Yeah, accidents 'appen."

I was now cutting the ropes that bound my hands and the razor sharp blade was making light work of them.

"That's all very well," I said, continuing to distract the two thugs, "but haven't you heard? I am no stranger to Harrogate."

"So people will assume you were drunk and lost your way – that's if anyone ever finds you. Many of the bogs round 'ere are really deep," responded the first man at the precise moment my bonds fell away. I kept my hands behind my back as if still tied and now gripped the knife tightly. It was just a question of waiting for the right moment to strike back.

"So what next?" I asked.

"Good question, Cap'n. You see, when the sun comes up we are going to take you back to your house and wait outside for you. There will be more than just the two of us watching and if you go anywhere except out of town we will grab you when you are least expecting it and then it'll be the bogs for you, my lad."

The two ruffians laughed at this and the second man then ventured towards me and prodded my shoulder with his club yet again.

He was about to speak when I grabbed the club with my left hand, ripping it away from him whilst pulling myself up and bringing my right arm around his neck and resting my knife under his bristled chin. In case the first man was tempted to fire at me, I swiftly turned the second man around to face him, turning my captive into a shield.

"You were going to say?" I said, pressing the razor sharp blade tight against the second man's throat, applying just enough pressure to convince him that I was in no mood to be trifled with.

"Cat got your tongue?" I said, suddenly picking up the stench from the man I was holding.

"Need a little air letting into your windpipe?" I added, stroking the blade along the line of his Adam's apple endeavouring not to draw blood.

Now that I was standing, I could see we were in a single room with one door and two windows. As I looked around I noticed that the fireplace on my left was directly opposite the door. The building was solidly built in stone but the walls were not plastered. Facing me was one small table, on which rested the solitary candle. In front of the table, the man sat holding my pistol. He was a rough looking brute aged around forty, unshaven and shabbily dressed. His nose looked like it had been broken more than once and I had seen horses with cleaner looking teeth. Not the sort of man you would want for a father-in-law.

"Now, you on the chair, I want you to hold the pistol by the barrel and then place it on the floor and kick it over here. Nice and easy. I am still a little dazed from that knock to my head and this blade could slip at any moment."

He paused and slowly considered his options.

"You've one shot with that pistol and the chances of you hitting me instead of your foul-smelling friend are pretty slim. Either way old 'smelly' here will be dead, for should you miss, I will slit his throat anyway. Then it's just the two of us and I have the knife."

"We 'aven't been paid enough for this!" bleated the foul-smelling man who was uncomfortably resting his throat on the blade of my knife.

"Put down the bloody pistol!" he pleaded to his accomplice.

The first man then carefully placed the pistol on the floor and kicked it towards me. I needed to pick it up but both my hands were full. After a moment's consideration, I resolved to use the club I had in my left hand to exact the same blow to this stinking thug that I myself had received outside Holderness House. I withdrew the blade from his throat and then brought down the club on his skull. There followed that all too familiar crunching noise resulting from the wood of the club coming into contact with flesh and bone. The man let out a groan and fell to the floor pole axed.

The instant I moved to pick up the pistol the first man overturned the table as he leapt from his chair and came at me. I slashed the blade at him and he swayed backwards. I slashed at him again. First to the right and then to the left, with as much menace as I could muster. The man avoided each thrust waiting for an opening to attack. He wanted the pistol which was now invitingly resting in the no man's land between us. His eyes widened and I knew that to be the sign that he had decided to lunge for the gun but my blade struck his arm causing him to cry out and back off, holding his arm. I followed this up with a swing of the club which I still held in my left hand. With him now in retreat, I picked up my pistol and placed my knife in my pocket. At this moment I felt an enormous debt to Joseph Manning and his wonderful folding knife.

"Now that was a stupid thing to try," I said with my confidence fully restored. I motioned the first man to get back to the chair which, regardless of all the excitement, hadn't moved. The table was near the door with its legs in the air resembling a dead horse. I decided to leave it where it was as it presented another obstacle for my captive to overcome if he was to attempt any form of escape. He sat back down still nursing his arm. Despite his injury, which can have been no more than a scratch, I kept the pistol aimed at his heart. At long last I was able to collect myself.

"Where the hell am I?" was the first thing that came to mind.

"On a farm," said the thug, still grimacing in pain.

"Very helpful, but which damn farm?" I said, snarling at his less than helpful response.

"Hill Top Farm," he replied.

"And where, might I ask, is Hill Top Farm?" I enquired.

"It's a short way south of Harrogate."

The second man lying prostrate on the ground moaned and it looked like he was coming round. This would have complicated matters and hence I thought it prudent to put him back to sleep. Another hefty blow with the club restored the status quo. I moved closer to the seated man.

"Why did you club him again? He couldn't harm a fly in his condition," he said disapproving of the blow I had just meted out.

"He looked tired to me and in need of a good sleep," I said with a wry smile. And now suppose you and I have a little talk about why you wanted me out of Harrogate."

"I can't tell you what I don't know," came the reply. The man was beaten and cut but still possessed a gritty determination.

"You don't expect me to believe that, do you?" I said as I took my knife from

114

my pocket and placed the club through my belt. I reckoned at that particular moment, I must have looked like one of Blackbeard's pirates.

"Do you know that a Joseph Manning newly sharpened knife can cut through bone?" I said and then paused, awaiting a response.

"Come on, don't be bashful. I think you know the answer, given that you've already felt the cut of this blade."

Still he remained tight lipped.

"Now, I am getting bored! I am tired and ache all over. It's the middle of the night and unless you start telling me what I need to know, parts of your body are going to start disappearing," and with that I moved menacingly closer to him.

"You don't scare me," came the defiant response.

"Very well. All I can say is that someone must have paid you a great deal of money or otherwise you are a complete idiot. Given that you don't seem to be a very good listener we will start with your ears."

I moved around the back of the chair still keeping my pistol aimed squarely at him. I then put the pistol in my belt and placed the knife against his right ear. I kept my left hand poised to take either the club or the pistol from the belt should the thug make an attempt to escape. Not an ideal situation, but if I was to perform minor ear surgery I would need my left hand free to maintain my balance.

"No, no, Cap'n. I can't tell you what I don't know," he said in genuine fear of his body parts as my blade started an incision.

"Don't take me for a fool," I growled, pushing the knife into the back of his ear. "Who paid you?"

I was getting angrier by the second. Someone had knocked me out, dragged me off into the night and threatened to kill me. I was tired and in no mood to prolong this interrogation any longer than necessary. A drop of blood slowly ran from his ear to his neck.

"All I know is that we were asked by the landlord of the Dragon if we wanted to earn a quick five sovereigns. All we had to do was to scare you into leaving Harrogate."

I relaxed the knife's pressure on his ear ever so slightly.

"Why would the landlord of the Dragon want me to leave?" I asked, still angry.

"I don't know, Cap'n. Maybe he's not the landlord, but he has something to do with the Dragon. I think he had been asked by someone else to put the frighteners on you," pleaded the thug.

"Then if you are telling the truth, you will have five sovereigns in your possession. Show me!" I demanded.

"And don't try anything stupid otherwise you can say goodbye to this ear."

The man went ever so carefully into his pockets then held out his hand, which did indeed contain five sovereigns and some change which I presumed he had taken from my pocket given that mine were empty.

"See, Cap'n, it's all there. I haven't even had chance to split it with Jack here," he said, nodding towards his sleeping comrade.

I took the money from his hand whilst removing the knife from his ear and stepped away from him.

"I will return this money to its rightful owner with interest," I said, putting the money into my coat pocket.

"But you still haven't told me why anyone would want me out of the way?" I said resuming my interrogation.

"In my business, Cap'n, you don't ask too many questions. It was just like I told you. Five sovereigns to make you leave and that's all I know."

It was evident that little more could be gleaned from this line of questioning, prompting me to turn my attention to finding my way back to Holderness House.

"So that in the corner is Jack. And who might you be?" I said, beckoning him to stand.

"Mick," came the reply, all fight having now left him.

"Well, Mick. Let's away and you can light that lantern which is lying on the floor. We're going to need that," I said prodding him firmly in the back with the club. He lit the lantern from the candle and held it in front of himself using his undamaged arm.

Lacking the defiance he had earlier and still wincing from the cut I'd given him, he led me outside. It was still dark but it looked as if dawn would be breaking soon. He told me that I had been brought here in the back of one of his friend's carts but he had long since gone. Consequently, we had no option but to walk.

I kept prodding Mick to remind him of my presence and after twenty five minutes or so of walking, it became appreciably lighter and I could just about make out some farm buildings on my left, shrouded in mist. The lantern was fast becoming ineffective.

"That's Moor Farm," said Mick. "If you keep straight on along Intake Lane, you'll come to the Queen Hotel."

"Where's Intake Lane?" I asked.

"It's what we've been walking on for the last twenty minutes," he replied.

We passed the farm away to our left and the Stray soon came into view. Despite it still being cloaked in mist, I was now in sight of the Queen Hotel and no longer required the services of Mick.

"This is where we part company," I said and pointed in the direction I expected him to leave.

"You and that foul smelling friend of yours would be well advised to keep well out of my way because if I catch sight of either of you, I will drag you to the constable and see that you are on the next convict ship to Australia."

I took one last look at him. His face and that of his partner were two faces I dare not forget. I walked across to the Queen Hotel and found an enterprising boy with a donkey carriage who took me safely back to Holderness House.

I walked through the front door looking very much the worse for wear. Benson saw me struggling to make my way to the stairs and nodded. The grandfather clock in the hall chimed six times.

"Good morning, sir," he said, looking somewhat concerned about my dishevelled appearance. My boots were soaking wet after walking through the early morning dew on my way to the Queen Hotel. "I will get those, sir," he added, just as I noticed the footprints I had left in the hallway.

I nodded by way of an apology and then sat in a reception chair whilst Benson removed my boots.

"Sorry about this, Benson," I said, suddenly feeling very sore and tired.

With boots safely removed I headed for the stairs at which point I then realised that I still had a club and a pistol tucked under my belt which made me stop on the first stair.

"Here Benson, a present for you," I said handing him the club. "Keep this safe, I may need it again when I visit the Dragon."

Benson looked perplexed and so I added, "A long story Benson, I will explain later. Wake me at eight o'clock, will you?" With that, I retired to the safety and comfort of my bedroom for the briefest of sleeps. With my head still spinning, my rest was anything but settled as I failed to find a position in which I could submit to the deep sleep I so badly needed. Eight o'clock arrived all too soon and after bathing, I felt a little more like my old self yet still very weary. I had a busy day in prospect, which would begin with me escorting Miss Coutts to take the waters followed by a meeting with the Russian on the railway venture at eleven. If that wasn't enough, I was also now determined to visit the Dragon Hotel. I was especially looking forward to returning the sum of five sovereigns to its rightful owner, whoever that might be. The usual breakfast interrogation by my aunt took on a more serious tone than usual as she prized from me details of my kidnapping. It seems that Benson, being somewhat concerned for my safety had mentioned the condition in which I returned earlier this morning. After reassuring her that all was well, I set off to meet Miss Coutts. In general a brisk morning walk would appeal to me but not today and so I had Cookson drive me around to the Queen Hotel. It was only a five minute ride, however it was an opportunity for a precious five more minutes with my eyes closed.

Somewhat reluctantly, I disembarked from the carriage, and was relieved that Dawson was nowhere to be seen. He was the last person I wanted to run into, although I did wonder if he had any part to play in my abduction last night. He certainly had the motive, and raising the sum of five sovereigns should not be beyond his reach.

When I met up with Miss Coutts, she seemed to have forgotten all about yesterday's incident with the stalker and looked well rested. I, on the other hand, looked the complete opposite.

"Another wild night dancing, Captain?" asked Miss Coutts, as she came into the reception area of the hotel.

"You might say that," I said bowing my head.

"Captain Townsend, we are so pleased to see you!" said Lord Redmayne, arriving to see Miss Coutts safely into my charge. I returned the greeting whereupon Miss Coutts took my arm and we walked through the door with Emily following on a yard or so behind. The temperature was once again subdued by the typically fresh breeze which blew through this part of the world. More often than not this would be an irritation, but after a night of little sleep it was a positive boon in keeping my wits about me. Happily there was still no sign of Dawson and I left the Queen Hotel in surprisingly good spirits.

I continued to look all around during our walk towards the wells but, thankfully there was no sign of anything untoward. By all accounts it was a normal morning in Harrogate with its usual number of visitors heading to take the waters. Additionally, there were the early risers who having already fulfilled their morning ritual were now walking towards us. After passing Holderness House, we approached the carriages outside the Crown Hotel and I looked towards the House of Flowers. I could just about make out the two young girls arranging sprays and bouquets but there was no sign of Virginia or her sister Grace. Our arrival at the well inflicted further punishment on my senses when the stench of the sulphur well blew into my nostrils.

Betty, the lady of the well awaited us in typically good humour.

"Here you are, sir. This will put some colour into those cheeks of yours," she said whilst handing me a glass of her purgative liquid.

I smiled politely but very much doubted the likelihood of a positive outcome as my top lip tried to avoid contact with the water.

Miss Coutts had drunk her water with typical good grace and smiled at my discomfort.

"It will do you good, Captain," she said and then we sampled the other spring which was an altogether much more pleasant experience. Yet again, I was humbled by some of the poor unfortunates who had made their way to these springs in the hope of regaining some or all of their health. Miss Coutts had made the same observation and I could sense a desire in her to help these people.

"It's awful is it not Captain, that some people have so much to endure?"

"Nature can be very cruel, miss," I said reflecting on the preponderance of misery I had seen in India. We walked away from the wells and thankfully straight back to the Queen Hotel. There was no sign of anyone watching or following us, and Dawson was still nowhere to be seen. All of which was just as well as my inners were now rebelling against the purging they had just received. This was no time for me to be called into action.

Once back at the hotel, Miss Coutts thanked me adding that she would more than likely remain indoors all day as she was sure that her companion, Miss Meredith, would be arriving shortly. Nevertheless I promised to look in on her later and then headed back to my aunt's to ready myself for the important meeting with the Russian.

The forthcoming meeting at the bank had taken on much greater significance following the events of yesterday. Was Vladimir Von Benckendorff really advising on the building of a railroad? If so, then why had his servant paid such close attention to Miss Coutts's movements in the pleasure gardens? Also, who had followed us back to the hotel and fled into the woods? Most importantly, who had paid a paltry five sovereigns to have me removed from Harrogate and why?

Chapter 15

My aunt had given clear instructions that she expected me to establish whether this plan to bring the railways to Harrogate was likely to be a good investment or not. Despite her fondness for Henry Payden, she was nobody's fool when it came to finance. I welcomed the faith she showed in my ability, but of more importance to me was whether or not the Russians really were here to work on the railways or for some altogether more sinister purpose.

After returning to my room, I gathered my pistol and knife but noticed that in all the events of the previous evening, I had lost my watch. I searched the room thoroughly but there was no sign of it. This really infuriated me as it had been given to me by my late father and was inscribed with my name. I was determined to retrieve it and vowed to retrace my steps from the previous evening the instant I had concluded these meetings. I kicked myself for not realising this last night, given the likelihood that the two thugs who had tried to abduct me, had stolen it.

Having resigned myself to the loss of my watch, albeit on a temporary basis, I then made my way down stairs where I found Benson waiting for me.

"Excuse me, Captain," he said. "May I ask if you met with some accident last night? You did not look yourself when you returned this morning and with you handing me a villain's club, I was concerned that some mishap might have occurred at a place I had recommended. I am thinking in particular that I had suggested you might find excitement at the Dragon Hotel."

I asked Benson to follow me into the empty library and, once inside, closed the door.

"No need to concern yourself, Benson. I did not meet with any problems at the Dragon, as I never made it there. Nevertheless, I do need to establish who the landlord is."

"Why, I believe it's William Beales, Captain. Mrs Frith owns the place, but with her husband dead and her son now a budding artist in London, I understand she is trying to sell it," Benson replied somewhat bemused.

"William Beales?" I repeated.

"I believe that is correct, sir," said Benson.

"Well, it would seem that he, or one of his minions, paid the sum of five sovereigns to have me relocated to the next county. At least, that is what I was told by the two thugs who had been recruited to give me the message. I don't suppose William Beales is any relation to the Gerald Beales we met with yesterday?"

"I think Gerald Beales is his brother and also banker to Mrs Frith, but I couldn't swear to that."

"How interesting!" I said, intrigued by the connection. I wondered why William Beales would have paid anyone to move me on, particularly when his brother was trying to attract investment from my aunt. It was hard to see a connection, unless the Russians were somehow involved. It was starting to become very confusing and my brain was foggy from lack of rest.

"By the way, Captain, Tribune is entered in the three o'clock race on Friday, just two days hence. The race is over two and a half miles which I hope is satisfactory. Your aunt paid the entry fee," said Benson and, after a brief pause added, "One last thing, sir, I am happy to say that I have at last found the boy I think you can trust. Coincidentally, he is the same boy who brought you home very early this morning."

"Excellent work, Benson. What would we do without you?" Whereupon I hurriedly left the library and then Holderness House, heading purposefully to the Bank of Harrogate for my eleven o'clock meeting.

Paradise Row was a little over one hundred yards away and was a typical bustling Harrogate street with many local people going about their business and a good number of visitors exploring the shops. During the short walk from Montpellier Hill into Paradise Row, I noticed with interest that there were several doctors operating there too. This made complete sense, being conveniently located close to the sulphur well and bathing facilities. The bank was easy to find, being prominently situated and grand in appearance. There was a group of four ladies standing outside Smiths of New Bond Street, happily chatting away. They stopped momentarily and turned towards me as I passed them on the way into the bank.

"Good morning, ladies," I said, raising my hat and acknowledging them as politely as I could. On opening the door to the bank, I could hear their chattering resume.

I walked into the main hall and announced my arrival to a clerk. Before he

121

could get word to either Mr Beales or Mr Payden, I was greeted by a more senior clerk who asked if I was Captain Townsend. Once I had confirmed that I was indeed one and the same, I was led up some stairs into the office of Mr Gerald Beales.

No sooner was I through the door bearing his name, than I was met by an ebullient Henry Payden.

"Good morning, Captain," he said, shaking my hand. "I trust both you and your aunt are well?"

"Indeed so, sir," I replied. "I trust you are in good health also?"

"Yes, thank you, Captain, and you will of course remember Mr Gerald Beales?" he said, beckoning his partner forward.

"But of course. How are you today, sir?" I enquired of Mr Beales, resisting the temptation to enquire after his brother.

"Very well, Captain, and can I introduce you to Vladimir Von Benckendorff of St Petersburg?"

The bespectacled Russian stepped forward and spoke in a heavy east European accent. "Dobraye ootro Kaptain – I am sorry, my English is not so good. I meant to say good morning, Captain, I am pleased to meet with you."

I shook his hand. "Good morning to you too, sir. How are you enjoying England?"

"Good. Very good," replied Vladimir Von Benckendorff.

"Now gentlemen, perhaps we could all sit down so that we may show the Captain here our exciting plans for the Harrogate Railways," said Gerald Beales, ushering us all towards the table which was situated at the far end of the room by the window.

Everyone took their seats while Gerald Beales remained standing at the head of the table ready to make his presentation.

"Captain, we have an unprecedented opportunity to bring rail travel to Harrogate. There is already five hundred miles of railway track in England, with more being built every day. Great North of England Railway is planning to link York to Darlington. Also, the York and Midland Railway are investing in a line from York to Normanton. Before long we will be able to travel from the capital all the way to this fine town and this will substantially increase the number of visitors coming to Harrogate. That in turn will increase the demand for coal, food and luxury goods; all of which will be cheaper if brought in by the railway.

"Did you know that the distance between Darlington and Stockton is just twelve miles and formerly there were barely enough travellers to support a coach three times a week? Yet after the railroad was completed, two hundred people daily make that journey. Neither Darlington nor Stockton are towns of any great merit, so just imagine how many travellers we may have using our railway. I have said enough and I do not want to go over the same messages we gave you yesterday, so let me show you our calculations."

At which point, he handed me a schedule showing estimated income from passengers each year in addition to the income they expected from transporting freight. I was no book keeper, but the figures looked impressive to me.

"Excuse me, Mr Beales, can I ask how many visitors currently come to Harrogate each year?" I enquired.

"Our best estimate is around twenty thousand, but that is based largely on the figures we received from Mr Palliser, who as you may know, keeps a weekly list of visitors. I must stress though that the numbers will be higher than he calculates as obviously servants are not included and not all visitors like to be recorded in the newspapers. We believe that the railways will at least treble the figure for visitors. You will see we have estimated that sixty thousand visitors each year will use rail transportation in preference to horse drawn coaches. However, we also believe that at least a further twenty thousand people each year will avail themselves of this new service and visit our town on a daily basis. Business people and the like," said Mr Beales in full swing.

"We have based our costs on advice from other railways such as the Liverpool to Manchester stretch and have estimated our costs at around thirty thousand pounds for each mile and so to finance the first eighteen miles of line to York, we will need to raise over half a million pounds. Quite a sum! I am not sure if you are familiar with the workings of shares and limited liability companies, Captain, but we plan to issue ten thousand shares of fifty five pounds each. The fifty five pounds is then called up in five instalments of eleven pounds each. Were your aunt to subscribe for, say, one hundred shares she would only make an initial payment of one thousand one hundred pounds. The shares will be traded on the local share exchanges in the north and we would expect them to start trading at a healthy premium. If the shares are sold, then so too is the obligation to make the further instalments. And to cap it all, everyone who subscribes for shares will be permitted to travel on the railway without charge!"

I read through the estimates and calculations whilst he spoke and, despite my lack of experience in such matters, I could see that the railway was predicted to make a healthy profit enabling good dividends to be paid. The assumptions looked sensible enough, nonetheless I had no idea whether it would cost thirty thousand or one hundred and thirty thousand pounds to lay one mile of railway. Having said that, thirty thousand pounds struck me as being a considerable price to pay for just one mile. This was my opportunity to talk to the Russian who, like Henry Payden, had sat quietly while Gerald Beales extolled the merits of his plans.

"Excuse me, Mr Von Benckendorff," I said, addressing the Russian sitting across from me. "Could you tell me how much it cost to build your railway in St Petersburg?"

"But certainly, Captain. From St Petersburg to Pavlovsk is perhaps twenty seven kilometres which I believe is a little shorter than Harrogate to York. The cost of this was, of course, in rubles not pounds but from the best of my knowledge, the cost would be very similar to the amount Mr Beales just mentioned," he replied confidently in his heavy Russian accent.

Without wishing to appear disrespectful, I couldn't help thinking that this was a bit of a coincidence.

"Excuse my ignorance on these matters, but I wondered if you could explain to me where you expect the major building costs to be incurred?" I was dredging the depths of my own knowledge in order to test Von Benckendorff.

He answered well. "Supporting the rail lines with long bearers, cross sleepers and iron rails will require much cost. Also we will need many workers and stone to keep the slope of the track within the limits of the steam engine."

"And what are those limits?" I replied.

"In my experience, no more than sixteen feet per mile," he replied, looking at Mr Beales and Mr Payden at which point they both nodded approvingly.

"And do you envisage any construction problems between York and Harrogate?" I asked, again looking to the Russian for a reply.

"No, Captain. There are a couple of small rivers to cross but we will be using a specialist bridge building company for them."

"Yes, the Great Yorkshire Bridge Company," interjected Mr Beales.

"But otherwise, Captain, the land is pretty flat and solid. It is good for a railway," concluded the Russian.

"Can I ask what you did before you became involved with the building of railways, sir?"

"Of course. I am engineer by training and before railways I worked with factory machines," replied Von Benckendorff.

"And will you be staying here, sir, until the railway is finished?"

He looked at Mr Beales and Mr Payden who both nodded to him prompting an answer.

"Yes," said Von Benckendorff. "This is my first visit to Harrogate and I must return to Russia very soon. But I will be back to help and advise wherever I am needed. It is a very exciting project."

All seemed surprisingly well thought out and organised. I didn't think I could find out much more at this meeting. It occurred to me that ideally I needed to get the Russian on his own, preferably with a drink in his hand. There is nothing quite like alcohol to break through any charade that is being performed.

Mr Beales then took the floor once more.

"Captain we are almost fully subscribed, and if your aunt and yourself would like to invest, we will need to know quickly." He then handed me a form and prospectus for the Yorkshire Railway Company.

"As I said yesterday, we already have applications from many prominent businessmen in the town but we also have some notable people investing including Lord Redmayne, Sir Charles Wadsworth, Sir William Hamilton, Lord and Lady Asenby to say nothing of his grace, the Duke of Aldborough."

I had no idea who Sir Charles Wadsworth was but it looked like the only people not investing at the moment were ourselves and Miss Angela Coutts. Although I did wonder to what extent these noblemen were actually investing. They could be subscribing for just one share and being paid extremely generously by the railway for the sake of appearances.

"If my aunt or I are inclined to invest, we will advise you of our intended investment within the next twenty four hours," I said, raising myself from my seat.

"Splendid, splendid!" said both Mr Beales and Mr Payden, almost in unison.

I shook hands with them all. Mr Payden made a point of insisting that I pass on his very best wishes to my aunt, after which I made my way out of the bank and back onto the street below. I momentarily stopped and looked up at the window of the room I had just left. It was just for a second but I noticed Von Benckendorff at the window looking down at me. Having caught my eye, he waved and I touched my hat in return. How odd, I thought, but he appeared genuine enough and so, suitably enlightened, I returned to Holderness House.

Chapter 16

I arrived back at the house to find Benson waiting to intercept me. "Excuse me, Captain, you have visitors."

"Visitors, Benson? Who do we have?" Judging by his demeanour, I surmised it was someone of great importance, prompting me to think that I may have been called upon by Miss Coutts.

"Well, Captain, you have two gentlemen of the Light Dragoons waiting for you in the drawing room."

"Light Dragoons?" I said, immediately thinking that Lord Palmerston was at last responding to those coded letters. Before I could say any more, Benson quickly added, apologetically.

"And there is the constable waiting for you in the library."

"What did you say? A constable?" I questioned, somewhat taken aback, presuming that he must have found my watch, seen the inscription on the back and traced me to Holderness House.

"Very well, Benson. Apologise to the constable, if you would and let him know I will be with him presently. First, I must see what news the Light Dragoons bring me from London." I then headed into the drawing room leaving Benson to deal with the constable.

The moment I stepped through the door the two young officers stood to attention.

"Lieutenant Sinderby-Smythe and 2nd Lieutenant Reeves, sir, with a message from Lord Palmerston," said the senior officer, handing me a letter from His Lordship in addition to what looked like a letter of introduction for Miss Coutts.

Thankfully, as the letter from Lord Palmerston was hand delivered, it wasn't in code.

"At ease gentlemen," I said, whilst I read my correspondence.

In essence, Palmerston made it clear in his note that he feared Angela Coutts could be a target for the Russians, and so their stated objectives in Harrogate may be spurious. This was more than likely because Countess Zadovich's brother is a Von Benckendorff and Palmerston strongly suspected that the Count was very active on Russia's behalf. He then spelled out the banking connection with Coutts, which he stressed could not be under-estimated and this was a concern to Her Majesty's government and, in particular, to His Lordship's office. He added that he had sent me the services of Sinderby-Smythe and Reeves because this situation merited the attention of more than one man acting alone. I was to make contact with Miss Coutts, hand her the letter of introduction and ensure that she remained safe at all costs.

"Gentlemen," I said, turning to the senior officer. "Sinderby-Smythe," to which he replied, "Yes, sir."

"Well man, which is it? Sinderby or Smythe?" To which he looked a good deal confused and with a puzzled look replied, "I am not sure I follow, sir. My name is Sinderby-Smythe."

"I am aware of that, sir, nevertheless should we get into a tight spot I will not have time to shout, 'Sinderby-Smythe, would you mind awfully shooting that villain?' It is your choice lieutenant however, all the while you are here, it's either Sinderby or Smythe."

He looked totally nonplussed but I couldn't do with this double barrelled nonsense at the best of times as I had come across too many officers with double barrelled names in India; many of whom were full of themselves until the bullets were flying, at which point they were the first to run for cover. I did not wish to be unduly hard on Sinderby-Smythe but I wanted him to see that I meant business.

"Then sir, I suppose it's Sinderby, if you please," he finally decided.

"And you, sir," I said, now turning to Reeves. "Do you possess any other names or are you content to be called Reeves?" He resisted the temptation to smile and replied simply, "Reeves is fine, sir. I have been called much worse."

"Well, now all that is out of the way, we have urgent business and we need to find billets for you both. As luck would have it, I have already made the acquaintance of Miss Coutts and can confirm that she is residing at the Queen Hotel along with Lord and Lady Redmayne. I think one of you should watch over her whilst the other stays at the Crown Hotel, keeping an eye on the Russians I have located there. Though for now, you may revive yourselves from your journey here. I have a local constable waiting to see me for some reason. I suspect it concerns a watch that I believe was stolen from me and so, gentlemen, perhaps we could all reconvene here in one hour's time? Benson will attend to your needs."

They thanked me and I rang for Benson who led the two officers to guest rooms on the first floor. I then marched into the library to find Harrogate's lone constable waiting a trifle impatiently.

He was about forty years old, with dark brown hair which showed no sign of ageing, about my height and sported rather a large waistband. In addition, he donned a considerable moustache which stretched from ear to ear. I resisted the temptation to make any comments regarding the standard of the cakes in Harrogate and proceeded to introduced myself.

"Now, sir," I said, addressing the constable. "I must apologise for keeping you waiting. My name is Captain George Townsend of the 11th Light Dragoons and I am told you wish to speak with me."

"Yes, Captain. My name is Samuel Hardisty and I am the appointed constable of High, Low and Central Harrogate and I regret to say that a complaint has been filed against you for inflicting bodily harm against a Thomas Dawson."

Before he could say another word I interjected. "Complaint? Are you serious, man? Is this some kind of a jest? I spent most of last night extricating myself from the thugs you have in this town. I was forcibly abducted, threatened with my life, and now you're telling me that Dawson has filed a complaint against me? It is laughable! It is I, sir, who should be making a complaint!"

I was incensed, although having just read Palmerston's letter, I knew I couldn't divulge the true purpose of my visit to Harrogate, meaning I would have to defend myself with one hand tied behind my back.

"It is certainly not a laughing matter, Captain. Witnesses confirm that you hit Mr Dawson with such severity, he was rendered unconscious. Do you deny this?" I fought back my anger and then carefully considered my response.

"No, constable, I do not deny it and yet your witnesses should have also told you that Dawson made several attempts to do the very same thing to me, only he failed. Were he successful, do I take it that you would be talking to him and not me?"

"Indeed, sir. Anyway, he was not successful and you were, which is why you will be charged to appear before the magistrates. We can't have people brawling in the streets of Harrogate, no matter who they are," said the constable in a most officious way.

"Now, constable," I said, attempting to be more conciliatory. "Have you spoken to Miss Virginia Hatherway about this incident?"

"No, sir, I have not," he replied.

"Are you acquainted with the lady?" I asked.

128

"Indeed, sir. Her father owns two of Harrogate's finest shops," he replied with a confident air.

"Then might I suggest that you talk to her before pressing any charges formally, as I am sure you would not wish to waste the magistrates' time." A thought which seemed to strike a chord with the constable, prompting me to speculate that he may have been guilty of such a folly in the past.

"She witnessed the whole event from close quarters and I am confident that she will confirm that I was acting in self-defence."

I contemplated mentioning that the Duchess of Aldborough had also been a spectator to the incident, but I didn't want to involve her until we had chance to speak. Regardless of this, the constable seemed to be weakening.

"Very well, Captain, I will do as you ask. Needless to say that if Miss Hatherway doesn't agree with your version of events, you can expect to be hauled in front of the magistrates."

I nodded as if accepting this fate, however I hadn't the slightest intention of appearing before some jumped up local magistrate. I had seen a number of them over the years and hadn't seen a competent one yet.

"And what are you going to do about my abduction?" I asked, reminding the constable of my earlier comment.

"Well – were there any witnesses?" he said thoughtfully.

"Of course not! It was the dead of night. The only witnesses were the thugs who abducted me and they are hardly going to present themselves as witnesses for the prosecution."

"Then I am sorry, Captain, there is nothing I can do. No witnesses means no case!"

Following this feeble attempt to administer law and order, the constable left and I cursed Dawson once more. Without a doubt, that man was trouble.

I began to feel very tired and desperately wanted to return to my bed, even though there was still so much that required my attention. I then went in search of my aunt to acquaint her with the events of the morning, and in particular the meeting regarding the railway proposition.

Predictably, she was in the orangery. My aunt was still concerned about my abduction and was outraged that the constable had made light of it. Eventually the conversation came around to the railway and I recounted everything I could recall, going on to explain to her the nature of the commitment she would be making. Regardless of the ongoing commitment to make further payments, she seemed to think that the railway venture amounted to a good investment and would subscribe for one hundred shares which meant handing over an initial investment of one thousand, one hundred pounds. A considerable sum, which is why I cautioned her to only invest if she completely trusted Gerald Beales and Henry Payden.

I also expressed the unease I felt at the involvement of the odious Sir William Hamilton. He was without any doubt a viper, and capable of destroying anything he touched. His knighthood must have been awarded for exceptional services to greed and corruption. Little wonder that so many people dismiss the value of knighthoods these days. On the other hand, if he had indeed invested his own money he would go to any lengths to ensure he made a profit. Having said that, had he really invested his own money, and if so, how much? My aunt thanked me for my help, insisting that she had every faith in Henry Payden and would take advantage of the opportunity presented. I fervently hoped that my aunt was not being swayed by her fondness for him.

Sinderby-Smythe and Reeves waited for me in the drawing room and I joined them the instant I had finished talking to my aunt.

"Well gentlemen, I trust you are suitably refreshed?" To which, Sinderby-Smythe piped up, "Rather," in a tone no doubt handed down by generations of double barrelled relatives. Reeves acknowledged with an altogether simpler, "Thank you, sir."

I wasted no time in bringing them up to date with what I had learned about Lord Palmerston's Russians, the stalker, in addition to all my meetings with Miss Coutts (although I purposely did not acquaint them with the time she portrayed a French Governess). I then moved on to more practical and immediate issues.

"I have been thinking about your billets and would like you, Lieutenant Sinderby, to reside at the Queen Hotel where you will keep a close eye on Miss Coutts. It goes without saying that this must be done tactfully, without interfering with her privacy. I am sure I have no need to tell you that she has had a very difficult twelve months and has come to Harrogate for a rest and to take the waters."

There was a blank look on Sinderby-Smythe's face. "You do know that people visit Harrogate to drink from its many wells in order to improve their health, don't you?"

"Absolutely," said Sinderby-Smythe confidently, but fooling no-one.

"And so to you, Reeves. I suggest we install you at the same hotel as the Russians, which happens to be situated only a couple of hundred yards from where we are now. Hopefully you will be able to catch them off their guard and establish whether they are really here for the railways or some other altogether more sinister purpose."

Having dealt with the main business of the Russians, I then described the events of last evening, carefully leaving out any mention of Miss Hatherway or Dawson.

"And that gentlemen, is why you find me a little weary. It is my fervent hope that after we get the two of you safely billeted, I will have the opportunity to catch up on my sleep. Needless to say you must stay armed at all times. Keep your pistols hidden yet within easy reach and carry a knife. If you don't own one, you should purchase one." I then drew mine from my boot. "Last night this knife saved my life."

I could see that the precarious nature of our assignment was now dawning on the two young officers.

"My word!" exclaimed Sinderby-Smythe. "So you have no idea who these blighters are, or why they wanted you to leave Harrogate?"

"All I can tell you is that following a little encouragement, one of my abductors revealed that someone at the Dragon Hotel had paid him five sovereigns to advise me to move on within twenty four hours or, after twenty five hours, I would be dead. Before I parted company with them both, I relieved them of the sovereigns and promised to return them to the rightful owner," then paused, "with interest."

"Absolutely!" piped up Sinderby-Smythe in his own distinctive way. A way which I was confident would soon irritate me enormously. Locating him across the other side of the Stray at the Queen would suit me well. Reeves seemed like an altogether different proposition who would do his duty with the minimum of fuss.

"Begging your pardon, sir, but doesn't it all sound rather too convenient? I mean to say, Russian railway advisers arriving just before the richest woman in England," continued Sinderby-Smythe

"Let's all hope that it is a coincidence, lieutenant. I got the distinct impression that Von Benckendorff really did know about building railways. Nevertheless, you are right to question everything. It is important that we always keep an open mind," I replied.

"Now gentlemen, it's time we visited Miss Coutts and appraised her of the situation, though we must take care not to alarm her unduly."

After which, I rang for Benson and led the officers into the hallway. My aunt appeared and seemed pleased to see that I would have support from two fellow

Light Dragoons. Whilst she made them welcome, Benson had the carriage brought to the front of the house with his customary efficiency.

Cookson brought the horses to a halt, while the three of us walked out of the house. It had just started to rain, which was a little unfortunate for Cookson. I looked up and saw him doing his level best to remain smart and elegant even though he was being soaked by this passing shower. He had my respect and I tried to communicate that with a nod, to which he politely doffed his hat.

Benson held the carriage door open and as I entered the coach, he quietly told me that the donkey boy he had enlisted at my request, would be at the house when we returned.

I took the opportunity of this short journey to point out certain landmarks to Sinderby-Smythe and Reeves. It was important that they learned the lay of the land, and quickly at that. Encouragingly, they keenly noted everything I said.

Once at the Queen Hotel, a commissioner came to our assistance with umbrellas. All the while the rain continued to fall heavily. Sinderby-Smythe looked at Reeves and in preparing himself to face the elements, said quietly. "I knew the weather here would be awful. It's just like I told you, Reeves."

Having done my best to avoid being soaked, I asked the commissioner to advise Miss Coutts that I was here to see her. Despite all the staff being well aware of my acquaintance with Miss Coutts, I still received a rather pompous, "I will enquire as to whether Miss Coutts is receiving visitors, please take a seat sir," and off he went. Dawson lurked in the background and I felt sure he had a hand in this treatment.

Much to the amusement of Dawson who had now recovered from his spell in the rose beds, we spent the next five minutes kicking our heels but eventually the commissioner returned with a positive response and asked us to follow him to the rooms of Miss Coutts.

When we reached her private rooms, he knocked on the door which was quickly opened by Emily and I was ushered in, followed by my entourage.

Miss Coutts was not alone, and in addition to Lord and Lady Redmayne, sat a lady slightly older than herself. Momentarily, Miss Coutts looked perplexed at the presence of my comrades and I probably looked equally taken aback at the presence of another lady. I wondered if this could this be the companion she had been awaiting.

"Captain Townsend, it is good to see you again. I trust you have had a good day?"

"Yes, thank you, miss," I replied. "I am sorry to have to impose on you in this way, however my plans for today were interrupted when I received urgent news from London brought to me by these two young officers. Allow me to introduce you all to Lieutenant Sinderby and…" before I could finish a voice said, "Sinderby-Smythe actually."

I continued. "Apologies, Lieutenant Sinderby-Smythe and 2nd Lieutenant Reeves." Reeves was his usual exemplary self and simply bowed when his name was mentioned. Miss Coutts then completed the introductions.

"Then, Captain, may I introduce you to my long standing companion, Miss Hannah Meredith," she said looking towards her friend. "And of course, Lord and Lady Redmayne, who you already know."

At which point, a good deal of bowing went on before Miss Meredith spoke tersely.

"I am very pleased to make your acquaintance, Captain. Miss Coutts has told me much of your gallantry in helping her, for which we are all very grateful. However, with regard to your companions," she paused looking straight at the two men in question, "we have already met, as I had the misfortune to spend the last twenty four hours crammed together in a mail coach with them both all the way from London." At which point, her face took on an altogether different expression for a fleeting moment while she recalled the journey in her mind.

This was, of course, news to me and when I turned to the two officers, I noticed their expressions had also changed whilst they, similarly, recalled their journey together. I had no idea as to what had transpired on the coach from London, but it had clearly made a lasting impression on them all.

I felt the best course of action was to move the conversation to the business at hand and hope that whatever had taken place on the road to Harrogate, would soon fade in the memories of those concerned.

Turning to Miss Coutts, I said, "I suspect that the urgent news these two young officers have brought me may also be contained within a letter of introduction from Lord Palmerston, who was obviously unaware of our chance meeting on the turnpike road to Harrogate."

I then handed her the letter and we all waited as she carefully acquainted herself with its contents.

"What does this all mean, Captain? Am I to assume that you have followed us all the way from London and that our meetings have not been a coincidence?" she asked.

"Absolutely not, miss. I was sent here by Lord Palmerston to investigate whether or not there were any Russians in Harrogate. I had no idea that you, too, were on your way to Harrogate, and I can assure you that our meetings were entirely coincidental," I replied.

"Well, I am relieved to hear that," said Miss Coutts who, whilst still holding Lord Palmerston's letter then added. "It would appear the Foreign Office have reason to believe that I may be at risk of being abducted and respectfully suggest that I return to London."

A hint of alarm crossed the face of Miss Meredith, who moved to hold the free hand of Miss Coutts.

"This is outrageous!" said Lord Redmayne. "Is there nowhere in England this poor child can go without fear?"

"Ladies, please do not be alarmed," I added quickly and confidently. "We believe we know the identities of those who pose this threat and with the help of these two officers we will be keeping them under close observation." I paused as I could see Miss Coutts was anxious to speak.

"Captain, I did receive a letter from my father warning me to be on my guard, although I supposed he was being over protective like most fathers. In any event, I felt that it would be easier to identify anyone who posed a threat to me in a small town like Harrogate, rather than in a large city like London. Nonetheless you said 'them' Captain. How many people are involved in this conspiracy?" said Miss Coutts probing for answers.

"Yes, Captain. Who are these people and how dangerous are they?" added Lord Redmayne.

"I regret that I cannot be precise as to how many people are involved. At this early stage in our investigations I would hazard a guess that there are just two or three people involved. Having said that, let me be very clear that we do not know for certain that anyone is plotting anything, let alone an abduction. We are merely taking sensible precautions against that possibility."

"I understand that Captain, but who are these people? Have we met them? Dear oh dear, it's not someone we know is it?" asked Miss Coutts now speculating wildly.

"Please do not alarm yourself, Miss Coutts. I very much doubt if you have met these people and, if you ever did come across them, I feel sure that they would not strike you as being particularly dangerous."

I was saying more than I wanted, yet it was clear from the look in Miss Coutts's eyes that she would not relent until I had answered all her questions. Despite which, it was her life that was at risk and in my book this gave her the right to know everything.

"And now Captain, their names if you please," urged Lord Redmayne.

"Very well," I said relenting. "The people we have been ordered to watch are a Russian couple called Von Benckendorff and their manservant. Mr Vladimir Von Benckendorff is ostensibly here to advise some Harrogate businessmen on the building of a railway from York to Harrogate."

"I know of that railway," said Lord Redmayne. "It's attracted quite a deal of interest. I've even bought a few shares in it myself."

Given that my aunt was investing in the self-same project, I was heartened to receive confirmation that Lord Redmayne was indeed an investor. Regardless of this being a minor point, it added credibility to the whole story of the railway which inevitably included Von Benckendorff.

"Captain, might I ask why your superiors feel that a Russian railroad adviser would be interested in me? And why would these Russians, or indeed anyone else, want to abduct me? To what purpose and to what gain?" insisted Miss Coutts, turning to Miss Meredith who was nodding in agreement.

"Well, miss, it would seem that an abductor may be looking to hold you for a sizeable ransom, or alternatively in exchange for confidential information known only to your bank." I could see the last comment puzzled her and she therefore enquired further of me.

"And what confidential information would that be, Captain?"

"Alas, miss, I know not. Due to its confidential nature, I am not privy to its content."

My comment, although obvious, nevertheless appeared evasive and brought with it a look of frustration from Miss Coutts.

"All I have been told is that Her Majesty's government wishes such information to remain private. They fear that under duress, vital national secrets could be revealed. We are here to ensure that this does not happen."

I felt it prudent not to go into any greater detail for fear of causing further unnecessary anxiety.

Miss Coutts was used to handling unwanted affections from overzealous suitors in search of her hand in marriage, but this was altogether more daunting. In spite of all she had heard, she remained calm and accepted the situation as if this was all part of everyday life and the price she must pay for being the richest woman in the country.

"Very well, Captain, yet in spite of these revelations we will not change any of our plans. We will continue to take the waters daily and we will not be deterred from making trips to the countryside. You and your fellow officers being close

135

at hand is reassuring, but please try to be invisible and allow us to enjoy our stay here in Harrogate. That is not to say that we object to your company, Captain. We welcome you as a friend, all the same we have no wish to be surrounded by armed guards in fear of our lives forever and a day. What sort of life would that be?" she said in a confident and matter of fact way.

"I understand entirely, Miss Coutts. However, can I ask that you keep us well informed of your plans? I also propose that one of these two officers takes a room in this hotel, preferably situated close to your own rooms. If you could perhaps tell the hotel's owner that Lieutenant Sinderby-Smythe is a distant cousin or similar, that might assist in him allocating a room nearby. Fear not ladies, between the three of us, we will ensure that you are kept safe at all times."

"Thank you, Captain, that is much appreciated but can't you simply apprehend these people before they act?" asked Miss Coutts.

"That would be ideal, however, at present we cannot prove our suspicions and without evidence we run the risk of a major international incident. Von Benckendorff is the maiden name of Countess Zadovich which means that these people in Harrogate could be related to Count Zadovich. The Count is a handful for even the most skilful politician such as Lord Palmerston, which is why we need to tread carefully. Anyway rest assured, we will search relentlessly for proof of anything untoward."

Miss Coutts and Miss Meredith, together with Lord and Lady Redmayne, seemed satisfied with all these explanations but before leaving, I attempted to lighten the moment.

"Before we take our leave, I wanted to invite you all to the races on Friday as I have entered my horse into the main race for which I am to receive a number of tickets to the grandstand. It would appear that the entire town will be attending and it should present an opportunity for you all to enjoy yourselves."

The ladies were delighted and readily accepted my invitation, however Lord Redmayne was more reserved in his response. After wishing them all a good afternoon we set about arranging a nearby room for Sinderby-Smythe. With the lieutenant's accommodation settled, all three of us made our way to the hotel's main door.

Dawson was attending to some old lady which distracted him long enough for us to pass by un-noticed. I looked out of the hotel to see if we would once again require the services of an umbrella but happily it had stopped raining.

"Lieutenant, you stay here and see that Miss Coutts remains safe. Reeves and I will head back to Holderness House and send on your things. We will book Reeves into the Crown Hotel. I am also lining up a donkey boy to relay messages between us. Having not yet met the young man, I cannot tell you his name. Irrespective of that, whoever comes to you with a message will give you a password which, let's say, is *banker*. Is that understood?"

Sinderby-Smythe nodded.

"Rest assured I will be back, but in the meantime keep your wits about you." With that, Reeves and I jumped into my aunt's waiting carriage which soon had us safely back at Holderness House.

Chapter 17

When we returned to Holderness House, Benson led me downstairs into the servants' quarters. Sitting at the kitchen table was a young boy who had just finished eating a piece of Mrs Parker's game pie. As was typically the case when I ventured downstairs, most of the staff went into the sort of panic I associated with Lord Cardigan making one of his rare and unannounced inspections.

"Good afternoon, Captain," said Mrs Parker whilst removing the plate from the young boy.

"Good afternoon, Mrs Parker," I replied and turning to Benson added, "Now, who do we have here?"

"His name is Horatio, sir, yet his friends all call him Harry," explained Benson before prompting the young lad to move, by nudging him in the back. "Stand up for the Captain, there's a good lad."

He looked very fit for his fourteen years, blessed with bright eyes and a handsome face. His hair was short and he was clean. His clothes were not his Sunday best, although that was only to be expected for someone working with donkeys every day. The boy stood up and faced me.

"Now Harry, what I need to know is – can I trust you?" I asked, looking down at him.

"Yes, Captain, sir," he replied confidently.

"Harry, I have some very important work for which you will be well paid, but you cannot tell anyone about it. You will be required to carry important messages between myself and my fellow officers all hours of the day which means that you will not be able to take on any other fares. Can you commit to that, Harry?" I said looking into his eyes, trying to establish his sincerity.

"Yes, Captain, sir," replied the boy.

"Very good lad. Then the first thing I want you to do is to go to Hatherway Grocer's on Parliament Street and hand a message to a Miss Virginia Hatherway. If she is not there, you should try the House of Flowers." Out of the corner of my eye, I could see a look of consternation on Benson's face. Through necessity

I had not been able to confide in Benson to the extent I would have liked, which was unfortunate as it now appeared that Harry was being employed primarily to assist me with my love life.

"Do you know where that is?" I asked.

"Yes, Captain. Everyone knows that," said Harry.

"Then wait here," I replied and promptly left the kitchen. I went back to my room and quickly wrote a note to Virginia telling her to expect a visit from the constable regarding last night's incident with Dawson. I also mentioned that a lot had happened since then, all of which would be revealed when we next met.

On my way back downstairs, I collected Reeves who had been waiting patiently in the library and asked him to follow me. I gave Harry the letter and also introduced him to Reeves, adding that there was someone else helping us with this important matter; that person being Lieutenant Sinderby-Smythe, who he would meet soon. I then handed him a gold sovereign – one of the five I had retrieved during my adventures from the previous evening. His face lit up and I told him he could expect more if he proved to be as capable and trustworthy as Benson had promised. With the sovereign safely in his pocket and clutching my note like his very life depended on it, he left the house through the back door.

Benson could see I was a little concerned at trusting someone I had only just met and who was so very young. We would be relying on him to be the vital link in a communication chain between the three of us and I felt a shade uneasy at the prospect.

"He will be fine, Captain," said Benson reassuringly. "I have known him since he was born. He's from a good family."

I took Reeves into the garden room and invited him to sit down. Even though he looked a decent enough chap, the nature of our assignment compelled me to learn more about him. From what I had read in Lord Palmerston's letter, he was a very intelligent and confident young man who, in addition to speaking Russian, was also fluent in French and Spanish.

Unlike the Dorset born Sinderby-Smythe, Reeves hailed from Lancashire; he was around five feet ten inches tall, clean shaven with brown hair, brown eyes and a fair complexion. He was from good stock, nevertheless, being a second son he was devoid of an inheritance requiring him to make his fortune in the Cavalry. I could relate to him in a way that I found difficult with Sinderby-Smythe who was from an altogether different set. Too many of his contemporaries were more concerned about breeding and dress sense than ability and courage. I may have been unfairly pre-judging Sinderby-Smythe yet his foppish blonde hair and his mannerisms had me feeling somewhat pessimistic.

I instructed Reeves to head down to the Crown Hotel and register as a guest. I had described the Russians to the best of my recollection and once he caught sight of them on the move, he was to get word back to me through Harry who was to be permanently based close by. I planned to visit the Dragon Hotel at some point that evening and it was my strong preference to have one of the two young officers watch my back. However, given that they had just arrived in Harrogate and were engaged on vitally important assignments, it seemed highly probable that I would be venturing into the Dragon alone. Maybe my abduction last night was connected to the Russians, or to Miss Coutts? Then again, perhaps this was something personal? Whichever it was, I was determined to establish who had paid those thugs to set upon me and invite me to leave Harrogate.

Meanwhile, given that my aunt appeared taken with Mr Henry Payden and his railway, I imposed upon her to invite him and the Russian to the house in order to put the finishing touches to her proposed investment. The closer we kept the Russians, the better. I also asked her to request that they brought with them a copy of the proposed route of the railway. I suspected that I may be riding out at some point, keeping a watchful eye on Miss Coutts and I was more than a little interested to see for myself just how viable this whole plan was.

Reeves headed down to the Crown Hotel and young Harry returned with a letter from Virginia which was exceedingly brief and to the point.

My dear Captain,

The constable came to see me. We need to talk urgently. Please come and see me at your first available moment.

Yours sincerely,
Virginia Hatherway

With everything that was happening, I drafted a response suggesting that she came to Holderness House on her way home from work. I hoped that she wouldn't feel uncomfortable about such a proposal; after all, she may have already been to the house when delivering roses to my aunt.

I was content that all was being done to safeguard Miss Coutts even though much was still to be resolved to determine whether or not the Russians posed a threat. Furthermore, I was still troubled by not knowing who had stalked Miss Coutts yesterday. Nonetheless, I had a feeling that I might find the answers to at least one of these questions at the Dragon Hotel, where I intended to seek out Mr William Beales.

Reeves sent me a message which was delivered efficiently by Harry. He had settled in at the Crown and was loitering in the reception area but had not caught sight of any Russians as yet. He had made discreet enquiries from one of the staff and established that the Russians were not in the hotel at that time and no-one seemed to know when they would be returning. This gave me a dilemma, however, after much soul searching I resolved that while Sinderby-Smythe kept a close eye on Miss Coutts, I needn't worry too much about the Von Benckendorff's.

At last, there was a lull in the day's proceedings which enabled me write a letter to Lord Palmerston bringing him up to date with events. More importantly, it allowed me to take back some of the sleep that had been so rudely stolen from me by Jack and Mick. Despite having so much on my mind, no sooner had my head hit the pillow than I was sleeping soundly. I was awakened by a knock on the door and Benson apologetically informing me that Virginia and her sister were waiting for me downstairs.

She was a welcome sight, although she arrived looking slightly uncomfortable given that she had come straight from work and had not been afforded an opportunity to dress in the way she would have favoured. Benson greeted the two sisters warmly and, having been told to expect Virginia, had rightly shown the ladies into the drawing room.

"What a beautiful house, George," said Virginia, marvelling at the furnishings and decorations as I walked into the room.

"It is indeed," I agreed.

I had hoped that the lack of convention in Harrogate might have allowed her to come alone thereby presenting me with the opportunity to do what I had wanted to do since I first set eyes on her, which was to take her in my arms and kiss her passionately. Thoughts of Georgiana and her deranged father together with the beguiling Duchess of Aldborough were fading fast, with the exception of the latter's comment that we had a son, which had me decidedly perplexed.

Virginia and Grace both took seats by the fire.

"Now, please tell me what is going on?" she said after settling herself into a chair.

"Where do I start?" I said, as the events of the last twenty four hours flashed through my mind.

"After I left you last night and when only fifty yards or so from this house,

I was knocked unconscious by some thugs and taken to some deserted farm house."

"Oh my God!" she exclaimed, bringing the palm of her hand to her mouth.

"When I came to, there were two of them. Ugly brutes. Foul smelling with teeth like rotting tree stumps. They called themselves Jack and Mick and advised me to leave town within twenty four hours otherwise I was likely to meet my maker earlier than expected," which brought another gasp from Virginia who again had her hand covering her mouth. Grace looked at her sister. Both ladies seemed equally taken aback whilst I continued.

"Despite relieving me of my pistol, they had failed to find my knife which I kept safely in my boot. The rogues also took my watch which I didn't realise until this morning but that's another story. Anyhow, with the aid of Joseph Manning's 'finely crafted Sheffield Steel' I cut myself loose and turned the tables on them. They told me that a man called William Beales had paid them five sovereigns to deal with me. I don't suppose you know of this man? Our butler tells me that he's the brother of the banker, Gerald Beales."

"William Beales is someone you shouldn't tangle with, George. He's nothing like his brother Gerald, who is a lovely man. You need to be most cautious," warned Virginia with a degree of trepidation affecting her voice. She was confirming what Benson had told me, however I was struck with the familiarity she expressed in her reference to Gerald Beales the banker. I wondered how she would have come to know him so well. Perhaps Beales was banker to her father? Or perhaps he visited their shops frequently? In any event, it was of no great importance and given that Harrogate was such a small town, doubtless everyone knew each other.

"Anyway, I have more news. Earlier today I received new orders which is why I had to send you a letter rather than visit you in person," I said trying to change the subject.

"Does that mean that your leave is over and that you will be returning to London?" she asked.

"Something like that, but I will be around for a few more days yet. After all, my horse, Tribune, is entered in the three o'clock race on Friday," I said, choosing my words carefully. Whereas Virginia was aware of my having met Miss Coutts, she was oblivious to the real reason behind my presence in Harrogate. To her, I was still a cavalry officer on leave.

"You are being very secretive, George. What are you up to?"

"I am just trying to stay out of trouble, having said that, at the moment it seems to be following me wherever I go. What else can you tell me about William Beales?" I asked.

"Not much I am afraid, although you should be aware that he is acquainted with Tom Dawson. I would let the matter rest if I were you George; you should enjoy your remaining days in Harrogate and stay away from these people," she replied, her eyes pleading with me not to pursue matters any further.

"Dawson!" I exclaimed. "Why doesn't that surprise me? Every time I lift a stone he crawls out. Which brings us around to the constable, what did you tell him?"

"The truth of course," she said adamantly. "I told him that Tom tried to hit you a couple of times and then you retaliated when he tried to hit you a third time. I suspect you won't hear any more about it, all the same, that constable can be a bit of an odd one and he has a high opinion of Tom. He seems to think that he will become the next manager at the Queen Hotel and so I suppose he doesn't want to get on the wrong side of him."

I expressed surprise at the last comment, nevertheless I thanked her for her support and at that point Grace reminded Virginia that their father would be wondering where they were and it was time they headed home.

I opened the door to the drawing room and Grace was first to pass me, quickly followed by Virginia. We were all walking towards the front door when Virginia suddenly stopped.

"Oh dear, I appear to have dropped a glove." At which, she retraced her steps down the corridor leaving us all standing in the hall with Benson readying himself to show the ladies out.

When Virginia didn't return straight away, I excused myself leaving Grace alone with Benson whilst I went to see what was delaying her. Virginia was waiting for me.

"Have you found it?" I asked.

"Yes," she replied, holding the glove in question. "I have been waiting for you, as I wanted a moment alone to…" and before she could say another word, I took the opportunity to steal a kiss. The surprise of it all made Virginia gasp and yet for a brief moment our lips touched as we kissed.

"George!" she said, somewhat surprised by my actions. "I was going to say that I wanted a moment alone to ask you what you are really doing in Harrogate! I thought if we were alone that you might tell me. I am concerned, what with you being abducted last night and all."

It appeared that I had wrongly assumed the reason behind her desire to be alone with me, however, I took encouragement from the fact that she didn't push me away when we kissed and that she was clearly worried about me. I took hold of her hands, looked deeply into those lovely eyes and spoke with deep sincerity.

"Virginia, I am very pleased that you care, and I can assure you that I have no intention of escalating matters with Dawson or anyone else. I know I sounded angry, but I was just letting off a little steam. I will do just as you suggest and enjoy my time in Harrogate and earnestly hope that will include the two of us spending more time together."

She smiled, although it was clear that, just like me, she was holding something back.

Even if I hadn't been here on an important assignment for the government, there was little prospect of me turning the other cheek after the events of last night. Someone, somewhere had crossed the line of decent behaviour and I would find out who and why, and then I would have my revenge.

Given the amount of time we had been alone, Grace would be wondering what had happened to us and I thought it appropriate to re-unite the two sisters without further delay. Grace looked a little confused when we reappeared in spite of Virginia's attempt to settle her curiosity by waving the missing glove and declaring, "Found it! Silly me, I'm always losing things, isn't that right Grace?" Whereupon Grace smiled in acknowledgement and we all made our way to the front door where we, unfortunately, collided with my aunt.

"Ah good afternoon, and who do we have here George?" asked my aunt, seemingly prepared for this moment.

"Aunt, allow me to introduce you to Miss Virginia Hatherway and her sister, Miss Grace," I said stoically.

"I am so pleased to meet you, madam," said Virginia sweetly.

"Likewise," added Grace.

"I have visited your shops many times and you are to be congratulated. It is my considered opinion that they are amongst the finest in Harrogate," complimented my aunt, warmly.

Both Virginia and Grace smiled in appreciation and even though this was a promising start, I was anxious to bring this impromptu meeting to a hasty conclusion.

"I regret that these ladies are needed elsewhere, Aunt, and we mustn't detain them any longer."

"That is indeed a pity," said my aunt, sounding genuinely disappointed. "Not to worry, I am sure we will have other opportunities to get to know each other."

She smiled, in spite of the fact that she would have undoubtedly preferred my female visitor to have been Angela Coutts.

"I shall look forward to that, madam," said Virginia sincerely, a sentiment which was echoed by Grace. "Goodbye, George," said Virginia finally and with one last smile, both sisters were gone.

With the evening now upon us and suitably refreshed after my much needed nap, I decided to head down to the Crown Hotel and dine with Reeves. As he was yet to cast eyes on the Russians, I was worried that they may pass undetected on their way to some mischief. I found him in the reception area doing his best to appear lost in the latest edition of the *Leeds Mercury*. On seeing me arrive, he put down the paper and joined me for a drink in the bar while we waited for a table to become available. The hotel was very busy, which proved to be to our advantage allowing us to mingle undetected amongst the multitude of guests. I left Reeves by himself whilst I wandered into the restaurant where I was able to satisfy myself that the Von Benckendorff's were not amongst the early diners. I re-joined Reeves where we continued to maintain our vigil. Given that I had already met Vladimir, the engineer, I kept a watchful eye from a quiet corner. Reeves faced me with his back to the centre of the room which allowed me to look over his shoulders with the minimum chance of being detected. Having the Russians catch sight of me was something I was anxious to avoid.

A short while later I spotted Mr and Mrs Von Benckendorff breeze through the reception area and out of the main doors. Once again, they were followed by their one-eyed manservant who looked around menacingly.

"Quick, Reeves!" I said quietly and with urgency as I forfeited the chance to finish what was left of my drink, placing the partly filled glass on a nearby table. "It's them!" Which was enough information for Reeves to follow suit and part company with his own drink.

They did not take a carriage but walked away from the hotel and up Montpelier Hill towards Prospect Place. I nodded to Harry who was waiting patiently around the corner with his donkey and cart. I held up my hand to indicate that I wished him to remain where he was for the time being. Reeves and I then gave chase on foot. It was still light which meant that we needed to follow carefully and from a safe distance. For one moment I thought that the manservant was about to turn around, prompting me to quickly drag Reeves into a nearby shop doorway.

"This is dangerous," I said to Reeves. "They have met me. If I am spotted, it will be awkward to explain. You will have to follow them by yourself and when they reach their destination send word to me with Harry. I will go back to the

Crown and send Harry up here to find you. In the meantime, I intend to go to the Dragon Hotel to find out why someone wants me out of town."

"Very good, sir," said Reeves. "Watch your back."

"I will and the same goes for you. If Lord Palmerston is right and these Russians are spies, they will be slippery… and dangerous."

Reeves now continued the pursuit alone. I stayed in the shop doorway and watched them all walk out of sight. I felt sure that they wouldn't be going too far given that they were on foot and had forgone the opportunity to take a carriage. I walked back to the Crown and spoke with Harry. I told him to head up towards Prospect Place and find the 2nd Lieutenant.

The instant Reeves had established where the Russians had gone for the evening, Harry was to bring the news to me at Holderness House and if I wasn't there, I would leave word with Benson as to where I could be found.

With that settled I couldn't help wondering how Sinderby-Smythe was progressing and so, after returning to Holderness House, I scribbled a message to him which Benson would give to Harry when he next appeared there. I stressed to Benson that he would first need to describe the lieutenant to Harry after which he would need to give Sinderby-Smythe the password so that there could be no doubting that the message came from me. Any reply from Sinderby-Smythe would then be delivered back to Benson at Holderness House who would know where to find me. In the note to Sinderby-Smythe, I advised him that Reeves had the Russians in his sights and suggested that if Miss Coutts was remaining at the Queen with Lord Redmayne for the evening then it would be safe for him to join me at the Dragon Hotel. I was confident that Miss Coutts would be out of harm's way whilst ever she was in the company of Lord Redmayne, with the proviso that, all the while, one of us was watching the Russians.

After writing the note, I tucked into some of Mrs Parker's lamb stew, feeling a little sympathy for Reeves who, unless he had eaten earlier, had unfortunately missed out on his dinner. With everything seemingly under control, I then readied myself for an evening at the Dragon Hotel, which promised to be very interesting indeed.

Chapter 18

Before I headed off for another night in Harrogate, Benson insisted on making me aware of everything he knew about the Dragon Hotel. My abduction from the previous evening had alarmed him and he was most concerned that I should be fully acquainted with all aspects of Harrogate's most lively establishment. I suspected that my aunt had encouraged this intervention.

Despite being a mere posting house, it appeared that the Dragon was the cornerstone of Harrogate social life. There were rooms available to play cards such as hazard, which instantly reminded me of Gordon's. Additionally, there was music, dancing and ladies' favours could be rented by the hour.

The Dragon, Harrogate.

It attracted the aristocracy, merchants and mill owners, in addition to retired military men; all looking for excitement in whatever form they could find it. He told me of an Indian nabob who lost a fortune at the Dragon's tables and a lady of some rank, who played cards throughout the night for one hundred guineas a game. Quite astonishing! Much more like Gordon's than I had imagined, although much larger sums were won and lost at their gaming tables. Mr Frith, the owner, died last year and his widow was searching for a buyer.

Regardless of all Benson's advice, there was only one thing in my mind when I approached the aforementioned hotel, and that was to find William Beales. Having been conveyed there by the ever improving Cookson in my aunt's carriage, I waited outside and surveyed the scene. I walked around the back, making a careful note of all the potential escape routes. The arrival of the two lieutenants and the events of the previous evening had heightened the importance of my endeavours. At last everything felt like a military campaign.

Just as Benson had predicted, the Dragon positively bounced with life. There was gaiety, music, laughter and dancing. It felt akin to walking into some grand party. To my left, the bar was busy with men buying drinks. Some, no doubt, for themselves and others, no doubt, for their ladies. Straight ahead, I could see a small dance floor with couples dancing and to my right was a throng of people all laughing loudly, presumably assisted by the various alcoholic beverages which were readily available. I saw ladies who were gaudily dressed with risqué plunging necklines, wearing an abundance of rouge. There were men drooling over them swaying back and forth, evidently overcome by drink, or perfume, or perhaps both. Past the bar on the left was a staircase and I could see two sharp suited gentlemen heading upstairs, most likely for a game of cards, given that they seemed an unlikely pair to be doing anything else.

I couldn't help being drawn to a man who looked very much like a retired general; well-set, grand posture, fine whiskers and all, who was enthusiastically talking to a young lady. He seemed to be perfectly content with his evening's assignment. Somewhat curiously, when I looked towards him, he turned his head to look past me leading me to wonder if, for some reason, he was watching me.

Undeterred, I confidently moved over to the bar where I found a large barman possessed of exceedingly strong and well-tattooed forearms.

"What can I get for you, sir?" he said, politely enough.

"A glass of your finest claret my man, together with some information if you please," I said assuredly.

The barman attended to the claret yet ignored my request for information. The glass was handed to me and, after I paid for the drink, I left my hand on the bar with several coins resting invitingly in my palm.

"I wondered if you could point out William Beales to me, my good man," I said hopefully, to which I received a blank look. "Then, perhaps you know Tom Dawson?" which was met with a further blank look. "How about Gerald Beales?" and once more the barman went about his work, oblivious to me and my requests.

"You don't know much do you?" I remarked, closing my hand around the sovereigns and returning them to my pocket.

"I know to mind my own business," he said, then turned and moved down the bar to serve someone else.

I took my claret and moved away from the bar. I was clearly going to have to work a little harder to find William Beales.

Few people seemed to be unaccompanied and moments later I found out why, as a pretty young girl, with striking black wavy hair and rich brown eyes sidled up to me.

"Hello handsome, what's a dashing man like you doing in the Dragon all on your lonesome?" she said, moving her body flirtatiously ensuring she made the most of her low cut, revealing dress.

"Waiting for you," I said, playing along and lifting my eyes to meet hers. "What's your name?"

"Maggie," she said.

"I am pleased to meet you Maggie. My name is Townsend, although you can call me George."

"Well, George, fancy a dance?" she added.

"Not really much of a dancer, Maggie. Can I buy you a drink?"

"Thank you, I will have a glass of champagne," she said in a somewhat automated fashion. Having spent too much time in the clubs of London, this came as no surprise. In any event, I was happy to supply her with whatever amount of champagne she desired in order to obtain the information I needed.

"What are you doing in Harrogate, George?" she said, sipping her champagne which arrived with spectacular speed.

"I am here for Friday's race meeting. I have a horse entered in the three o'clock," I answered, which was true enough.

"How exciting!" said Maggie. "What's your horse's name?"

"Tribune," I replied and then gave her a long winded account of how he was

149

related to Touchstone and three glasses of champagne later we found ourselves in a quieter corner. We sat down and I looked over to the dance floor to see yet another quadrille taking place. Maggie noticed me looking at the dancers and being eager to please, once again endeavoured to capture my attention using her natural attributes and asked if I had reconsidered my wish to dance. Despite being curious to see how she would co-ordinate her limbs on the dance floor following several glasses of champagne, I declined the offer for a second time.

The reason for my interest in the dancing was not just that the General had taken to the floor but that, amongst the dancers, were also the Duchess of Aldborough, the Earl of Warkworth and Lord and Lady Asenby. The Duchess looked radiant and the Earl appeared smitten by her every move. However, I needed to focus on Maggie, failing which, three glasses of champagne would have been wasted.

"I have every reason to believe that Tribune will win on Friday, in which case I intend to throw a large party."

"Wonderful," said Maggie clapping her hands. "I love parties, can I come?"

"The problem is Maggie, that I need somewhere to hold the party. I was told that if I wanted to arrange a private room here, I needed to speak to someone called William Beales. Do you know him?" I asked optimistically.

"Bill Beales? Of course I know him. I'm not sure if he's the best man for you to speak to though," she replied, taking another healthy sip of champagne. At the prices they were charging, I now wished that I had bought a full bottle of the stuff.

"Where do you suppose that I might find Bill?" I asked.

"He should be here somewhere, George. He usually is on an evening," said Maggie, turning around in her seat and craning her neck. "There he is," she said, stretching out her arm and, in the process, putting intense pressure on her low cut dress. The man she pointed out was tall and tough looking and, despite his more intimidating appearance, might conceivably be the brother of Gerald Beales.

All her arm waving caught his eye and moments later I was face to face with William Beales. Remembering the events of the previous evening, I suddenly felt a little exposed. I was taking on the unknown and was very much alone. I hoped that Sinderby-Smythe or Reeves would be arriving soon.

"Bill?" said Maggie. "Mr Townsend here wants to talk to you about having a private party after his horse has won at the races on Friday."

"Does he now?" questioned Bill, raising his eyebrows and speaking in a deep northern accent.

"Actually it's Captain George Townsend, sir. I am very pleased to make your acquaintance," I said, holding out my hand and rising to my feet, where I was relieved to find that he was no taller than myself.

He took my hand and squeezed hard. "William Beales," he said in response. "I believe that you have met my brother?"

"So, you are Gerald's brother?" I said, feigning surprise.

"That I am," he replied, quickly adding, "I know that your aunt is looking to invest in his railway venture, but I wasn't aware that you had a racehorse?"

"Yes, I have had him for some time. He goes with me everywhere."

"How can I be of assistance? What's this about a private party?" he added, frowning ever so slightly. His mannerisms mirrored his brother's, however the severity of his wrinkled brow together with his thinning, greying hair suggested he was Gerald's older brother.

"My horse is a fine animal and I am confident he will win, in which case I would wish to celebrate with the handful of friends I have here in the north," I replied, thinking on the spot.

"That includes me, doesn't it, George?" said Maggie anxious not to be overlooked.

"Well, perhaps I can help you," said Beales. "Let me show you a room which might suit your purpose."

Beales beckoned me to follow him and I rendered my apologies to Maggie who, surprisingly, seemed a trifle disappointed that I was leaving. I was then led upstairs into an amply sized private room which had a card table with six seats around it.

"This is the room I had in mind. It will comfortably cater for thirty guests. Please take a seat, sir," said Beales, ushering me to one of the chairs. He went over to a side table on which rested three decanters and asked me if I would like a drink. Needing my wits about me, I declined. He poured himself a glass of something red and sat down opposite me.

I was not entirely comfortable being alone with him, regardless of the fact that I had both my pistol and knife within reach and considered myself, at the very least, of equal strength. Consequently, I decided not to waste any further time on my fabricated interest in throwing a party.

"Last night I met two men who forcibly insisted that I leave Harrogate. As you can see, they were unsuccessful in their endeavours. However, they did say that someone from the Dragon had paid them five sovereigns for their trouble. All the same, I suspect you already know that?"

Suddenly, any friendliness that had existed between us, disappeared in an instant to be replaced by a chilling atmosphere. The expression on Beales's face changed and whilst keeping one hand on the table, I felt for my pistol with the other.

The initial anger he displayed suddenly changed and then he laughed loudly.

"Someone is messing with you," he said. "Why would I know anything about that?" adding, "Who were these ruffians? Have you told the constable?"

His laughter threw me and suddenly the information I had been given by my abductors looked less than reliable, but nevertheless I continued to challenge him.

"They were called Jack and Mick and no, we weren't properly introduced so I don't have their surnames. They also failed to give me their calling cards which I'm guessing is a big faux pas in this part of the world. Not only did they give me a fine bump to my head, but they also relieved me of my watch. I haven't told the constable anything, as from what I have seen of him, he couldn't spot a criminal if one sat in his lap with the word 'criminal' tattooed on his forehead," I replied robustly.

"And this Jack and Mick, what did they say? That I paid them to persuade you to leave Harrogate? Why would I do that? Isn't my brother negotiating with you and your aunt to invest thousands into his railway? It makes no sense."

I was forced to agree, even though I was sure that Beales was not the innocent victim he would have me believe. Beales could see that I was running out of ammunition and suggested that someone had deliberately misled me.

"Perhaps one of my brother's business rivals thinks he can damage the railway venture by scaring off investors. I will ask around. It's not good for my reputation to have such rumours circulating."

A smile returned to Beales's face, no doubt feeling he had won the argument. Nonetheless, his eyes betrayed a lingering bitterness. Either he was angry because someone had wrongly incriminated him or because someone had said more than they should.

We rose from the table and left the room. Beales slapped me on the back and said I should re-join the party and, if I wanted any of the girls for the evening, they were on the house. If he wasn't the manager of the Dragon, he certainly had a lot of influence.

Somewhat puzzled, I walked back to the top of the stairs and just as I was about to start my descent, I noticed a man disappearing almost frantically into one of the other rooms. Although I had seen little of the man before the door closed behind him, he still managed to give the impression that his haste was brought about by his desire not to be seen by me. Maybe I was suffering from paranoia, but I had an uneasy feeling that the man I had seen was Tom Dawson. If I was right, what was he doing here? Was he the reason I had been set upon last night? Were he and Beales in collusion? But why? Or was Dawson acting alone and where did the Russians fit into all this? Was the railway venture just an elaborate scheme to mask a heinous crime? This endless list of questions had my head spinning, increasing my concerns and despite the warmth of the Dragon, I felt a chill run down my spine.

Still trying to unravel all this, I soon found myself back in the thick of the party. Maggie had acquired another sponsor for her champagne business and the Duchess of Aldborough and her party seemed to have gained a few more followers, including a couple of ladies who looked at first glance to be French.

Rather than be set upon by one of Maggie's colleagues and instead of joining the Duchess of Aldborough, I decided to see if young Harry had arrived with any news. As a consequence, I made my way through the crowded room and headed outside for some fresh air.

Harry was waiting for me hidden away in the shadows. I walked over to join him.

"Now Harry, what news do you have for me?" I asked.

"Begging your pardon, Captain. I am afraid the lieutenant at the Queen didn't like it when I gave him your password. He hit me around the ear for being insolent. He said the password was banker. I am sorry Captain, I suppose I must have misheard Mr Benson," he half-smiled and I wasn't sure whether he had relayed the password wrongly on purpose or not. All the same, it was hard not to like the lad.

"No harm done Harry, and what does the lieutenant have to say for himself?"

Harry handed over a note which said that Miss Coutts was staying in for the evening along with Miss Meredith and Lord and Lady Redmayne. She was also planning to take an excursion to Bolton Abbey tomorrow. Once he was certain Miss Coutts had retired for the evening, he would head down to the Dragon to join me.

"And what news is there of Lieutenant Reeves?"

"I left him outside a house on Brunswick Place where there seems to be a dinner party in progress. The lieutenant says that the people you are interested in went there and he suspects that they will be there for some time."

"Good work, Harry. I now want you to head to the Queen and ask Lieutenant Sinderby-Smythe to report to me immediately."

With that, Harry moved out of the shadows and I could see by his face that he had been in a fight.

"Hold on there," I said, stopping Harry in his tracks. "What happened to you?"

"It's nothing, sir," said Harry, bravely.

"Nothing? It looks like you've done a few rounds with Tom Crib!" I said, likening his appearance to those unfortunate enough to have tangled with the great British boxing champion.

"Just a couple of the other donkey boys," said Harry quietly.

"What happened, Harry? You must tell me, it's important."

"Well, sir, I saw a couple of boys whipping their donkeys so hard, the poor beasts could barely stand. I went over and wrenched the whip from one of the boy's hands whilst some onlooker took the whip from the other. The onlooker gave the boys a piece of his mind, however, when he'd gone they swore that they'd have their revenge on me and that's what they did about an hour ago. The two of them came out of the darkness and set upon me."

"I'm so sorry to hear that, Harry. They sound like a really nasty pair, who I'm sure will get what they deserve in due course. In any event, for now you need to get my message to Lieutenant Sinderby-Smythe and then pop round to see Mrs Parker at Holderness House to get cleaned up. I expect to be here for some while and I want you to come back and look for me when Mrs Parker's finished with you. Oh and Harry, you'd better keep your face covered up when you get to the Queen, otherwise they won't let me in," I replied.

"Don't worry, sir. If they don't let me in the front door then I will just go around the back," he said, with a cheeky grin and with that, Harry headed back into the night. I watched the lanterns on his cart until I lost sight of them, hoping that the cowards who had set upon him were finished for the night.

I stepped back into the darkness created by the spread of a large horse chestnut tree, lit a cigar and waited for the lieutenant.

My solitude was continually interrupted by party goers coming in and out of the Dragon. Two young toffs came out bemoaning their luck, having apparently lost a good deal of money at cards. A couple came out with the lady complaining that her partner had spent the entire evening staring at the bosoms of a number of young girls. And so it went on until three fellows who looked decidedly menacing, came from around the back of the hotel, clearly looking for trouble.

Striding out first, a half yard in front of the other two, was the infamous Dawson. All three of them were armed with clubs. It was then I realised that I may be the trouble they were seeking. I continued to smoke my cigar as if I didn't have a care in the world whilst making sure my pistol was close at hand and loaded. With maybe three thugs to contend with, I now wished I had my other pistol with me too and so, in an attempt to fill the void, I reached into my boot and pulled out my knife. The knife went into my pocket and I continued to smoke. It was probably the smoke that gave away my location. All the while the three of them moved closer and I readied myself for action. I was far from calm and couldn't help myself thinking that now would be a good time for Sinderby-Smythe to arrive. Yet no one came; I was on my own. I sized up the three of them. I knew Dawson was a bully and safe in a crowd, although without that support I suspected he was a poor excuse for a man. The other two were an unknown quantity but were clearly involved at his request.

"Captain!" shouted Dawson, "We know you are here. Come out and face us like a man."

I took another draw on the cigar. The smouldering tobacco was giving me something of an advantage with the smoke hanging around in the still, night air like a morning mist.

From the darkness I could see Dawson and his companions much better than I suspected they could see me and so I decided to test their mettle.

"Let's see what sort of man you are, Dawson. Come over here and let you and I settle this like gentlemen."

"What sort of fool do you take me for?" he snapped back. "Come on lads, let's get 'im!"

With that, the three of them moved quickly towards my shaded space. My heart started to beat like a drum and my chest was pounding. My first thought was to isolate Dawson and, if that didn't work, I was in trouble. I moved out of the shadow to be within thirty feet of the gang of three. I drew my pistol with my right hand and gripped my knife firmly with the other. I stood side on to my attackers, extended my arm, cocked my pistol and then took careful aim at Dawson's head.

"Now Dawson, you can chose to live the rest of your miserable life by walking away or you can end it all by continuing to walk towards me."

"He's bluffing, Tom," said the thug on Dawson's left.

"That's easy for him to say, isn't it, Dawson, as he may still be alive? That is of course, if my blade hasn't slit his throat. In any event, whatever happens, you won't be around to see it."

Dawson was hesitating. He didn't look like a man desperate enough to die. His grievance involved his pride over a woman and I doubted if he was ready to risk his life for that cause.

Equally, I had no wish to escalate this situation, given the importance of the assignment entrusted to me by Lord Palmerston.

"Come on, Tom," interrupted the thug on the left once more.

"You don't see your friends volunteering to take a bullet for you, do you Dawson?" I replied, trying to unsettle him.

Dawson said nothing, all the same I could see him getting increasingly nervous.

"I beat you with my fists and I will beat you with pistols too. That's if you have the guts to go and get one," I said, throwing down a challenge.

Despite holding a pistol, I had no wish to fire it. I had one shot only and, once spent, I would almost certainly be overpowered.

"Are you challenging me to a duel?" asked Dawson, almost in disbelief.

"Yes. Does that scare you, Dawson? It makes no odds to me how I kill you, having said that, my regiment very much likes these things doing properly, you know. Even though duels are frowned upon these days, the Earl of Cardigan will not countenance death by brawling. It is just not gentlemanlike. So let's say I am giving you this chance for the honour of the regiment."

This was very irritating. Where the hell was Sinderby-Smythe? I really wanted this idiot Dawson, out of my way without any more scenes. He was making a noise which might be heard in the wrong places, making it harder for me to deal with the business at hand.

"Don't trust him, Tom," said the agitated thug on the left, and then addressing me added, "We don't fight duels up north. You're living in the Dark Ages, shithead."

"Yes, Dawson, you should listen to your friend. He's obviously a well-educated man and with such a command of the English language. An Oxford man, no doubt!" I said, ridiculing the insult.

However strong the initial threat of my pistol, it was now starting to recede and I could sense that the three of them were gaining in confidence.

"Come on Tom, he's bluffing," said the one on the right, speaking for the first time and then promptly swung his club striking the palm of his other hand in a display of aggression.

I had little choice but to take decisive action. I took a deep breath and a purposeful stride forward, still keeping far enough away to avoid any risk of them leaping for my weapons.

Then with an audacious display of venom and intent added, "I don't have time for this and you can either make a move, in which case you will almost certainly die, or you can bugger off," and after gauging their reaction continued, "Last chance Dawson, I am counting to ten and after that I am going to shoot you and be damned. So the nearer I am to you the easier you'll be to hit." I then began to count out loud.

I had taken control of events despite the fact that, if they called my bluff, I could be in desperate trouble. I stared fiercely at each one of them in turn to let them know that the time for talking was at an end.

"One," nobody moved, "two," still no-one moved, "three," not a twitch from anyone, "four," Dawson's leg twitched but otherwise nothing, "five," "six," then, "seven."

I could see in Dawson's eyes that he wanted to run, nonetheless, his friends seemed more confident, recognising that I would only have chance to fire one shot and that had been promised to Dawson. Both of them played with their clubs in readiness for a battle.

The palms of my hands were getting moist as the tension running throughout my body was threatening the strong grip I had on the pistol and knife. I was just about to shout out, "eight," when a voice from my left shouted, "That's enough… what the devil is going on here then?"

For the first time since this confrontation began, I took my eyes off Dawson and, with a feeling of relief, turned expecting to see Sinderby-Smythe or possibly Reeves. However my two lieutenants were nowhere to be seen. Yet, standing majestically tall and holding two pistols by his side, was the retired General who I had seen earlier charming the ladies on the dance floor.

My would-be assailants were stopped in their tracks and after sizing up the General, the thug on Dawson's left replied, "Piss off old man. This is none of your business."

"Yeah, bugger off, you fat bastard," added the thug on Dawson's right.

"Fat?" replied the General. "When I first saw you three, armed with clubs against one man armed with a single shot pistol, I was in something of a dilemma. Should I intervene and even up the odds or should I mind my own business and go back inside for another dance with the ever-enthusiastic, Mrs Barton? I must thank you – calling me fat has clarified my thinking." He raised both his arms and purposefully aimed his two pistols at my attackers. His chest seemed to expand as he took command of the situation. It was abundantly evident that he was no stranger to conflict and had done this many times before.

"Now you three louts! Unless you want to visit a surgeon or undertaker this night, you will slowly put your weapons on the ground and make your way over to that wall by the stables." The conviction in his words was too much for Dawson and his friends who meekly laid down their clubs and did what was asked of them.

The General's pistols followed every step they made in covering the short distance to the wall. I walked alongside him and was about to introduce myself when I saw Harry's cart returning. He was carrying Lieutenant Sinderby-Smythe.

Sinderby-Smythe had a worried look on his face. It was the look of a man who was in possession of bad news. His forehead shone with perspiration which matted his normally foppish blonde hair. Harry brought the cart up alongside me.

"Sinderby-Smythe reporting, sir," he said, hesitantly surveying the scene.

He then jumped off the cart and, leaning his head towards mine, added quietly, "I regret to say that I have lost Miss Coutts and Miss Meredith, sir."

"What?" I exclaimed. "How is that possible, you are jesting surely?"

"Unfortunately not, sir," he replied, apologetically.

"You're supposed to be helping me. Is this your idea of help?"

"I am sorry, sir. One minute they were there and then they were gone. It was just like they had disappeared into thin air. I searched the Queen Hotel from top to bottom and questioned all the staff but no one has seen hide nor hair of them."

I could barely bring myself to speak to him. I was simply aghast. I had no sooner extracted myself from a nasty situation, when I immediately found myself in another. Although this was far, far worse.

My outburst proved to be enough of a distraction for the General to momentarily take his eye off Dawson and his friends. They promptly jumped the short wall by the stable and ran off into the night.

"Hey, I know that man!" shouted Sinderby-Smythe pointing at the fleeing thugs. "He's always loitering around the hotel, I think he may work there."

"Do you think?" I said, despairing at Sinderby-Smythe.

"Blast it!" said the General.

"I am sorry, sir," I replied. "I fear my outburst presented them with an opportunity to abscond. Nevertheless, I am greatly indebted to you. That was a tricky situation," I said placing my pistol in my belt and holding out my hand.

"You are most welcome, sir" he replied, stowing his pistols then taking my hand and shaking it enthusiastically, all the while continuing to peer into the darkness for Dawson and his accomplices.

"Damn nuisance!" he exclaimed, at the loss of our captives. "I was only out here for a breath of fresh air and to get away from those damn women who only want to dance. Not as young as I was. I'm always concerned that if my feet consume so much valuable energy, there'll be nothing left for other appendages!" he said, grinning and twirling the end of his moustache with his right hand.

"Whilst I was conserving my energy, I noticed that you were a touch outnumbered. Allow me to introduce myself. Major Phillips, late of 47th Regiment of the Lancashire Foot."

"Well, Major, I am very pleased to make your acquaintance. Captain Townsend of the 11th Light Dragoons."

"Cavalry man, eh?" said the Major.

"Afraid so, sir," I replied adding, "If it is not too much trouble, Major, I would very much like to buy you a drink. However, I regret it will have to wait for another time as I have rather pressing business to attend to."

"Not to worry Captain, I will be happy to share a bottle or two with you when time allows. If you will excuse me, I have my own rather pressing business to attend to." Then, with a broad smile across his face added, "I wish you well, sir."

I stood with Sinderby-Smythe and watched Major Phillips walk into the entrance of the Dragon where he put the two pistols back on the wall, where they had been displayed. It had never occurred to me to look at his pistols in detail, yet they were clearly old and definitely not loaded. Having replaced the pistols he waved and I couldn't help smiling at how the old boy had out-foxed everyone.

Not for the first time, my father's old saying of 'never assume anything' sprang to mind.

Chapter 19

With the Major back in the Dragon, I turned to the shame-faced Sinderby-Smythe.

"She could be anywhere! She could have been abducted or she could have simply given you the slip. We need to search every hotel, every music recital and every ball in all of Harrogate!" Then addressing our young helper, I said, "Harry, please take the lieutenant here down to the main hotels in Low Harrogate; the Crown, the Swan and so on. You know the likely places."

"Sinderby, if you find the ladies, stay with them and send word back to me with Harry. I will head up to the Granby to see if they are there, after which, I will return here. If they have been taken by villains then there has to be a good chance that someone in this building will know about it.

"Harry, on the way to Low Harrogate, take a message to Lieutenant Reeves. Tell him to stick with the Russians and not to let them out of his sight…not at any cost! And now both of you, be gone! There is no time to lose."

Sinderby-Smythe left with Harry, urging every bit of speed he could out of his donkey. Time was of the essence. If Miss Coutts had been taken we needed to be on the track of her abductors without delay. Firstly though, it was essential for us to establish that they hadn't simply slipped past Sinderby-Smythe for the evening. The fact that no one else in the hotel had any notion to their whereabouts increased my concern and made Lord Palmerston's prediction of an abduction a worrying possibility.

I hailed a carriage and asked the driver to make all possible haste. It was only a short distance to the Granby and so, within minutes, I was dashing inside Harrogate's finest aristocratic hotel. I had told the driver to wait for me; with Harry gone I needed to have transportation at hand. Walking would cost me valuable time and also run the risk of another encounter with Dawson on the way. Under those circumstances, and in light of the urgency of the situation, I would probably just shoot him on sight. Even though it was a pleasurable thought, it was one which was unlikely to be all that helpful.

The Granby Hotel, Harrogate.

The door of the Granby was opened for me and I couldn't help but notice the calm and tranquillity of the place, in stark contrast to the revelry of the Dragon. My heart was still pounding from running into the hotel and with everywhere being so quiet, I wondered if anyone else could hear it thumping. I approached the uniformed man standing at reception. "It is imperative that I see Mr Benn on a matter of the utmost importance," I said.

"It's very late, sir. I am not certain that Mr Benn will be available," which was a reasonable statement given the lateness of the hour. The hotel was very quiet and I wondered if I would be rousing Mr Benn needlessly. The whereabouts of Miss Coutts was nevertheless of overriding importance and so I persevered.

"Please extend my apologies to Mr Benn and advise him that Captain Townsend of Her Majesty's 11th Light Dragoons has a pressing need to speak to him right away." Following which, he disappeared and I was left pacing around an almost deserted reception area. After a few minutes he returned to advise me that Mr Benn would see me shortly.

As promised Mr Benn arrived appearing concerned and looking very much like he had been dragged from his bed.

"Now, Captain. Who are you and what is so important that you need to speak to me in the middle of the night?"

I apologised profusely and stressed that I would not have disturbed him had the matter not been of the utmost urgency. I then proceeded to ask him as tactfully as possible if he had seen my friend, Miss Coutts, this evening.

"Might I enquire why you are searching for Miss Coutts at this time of night?" asked Mr Benn.

"I am sure you are well used to keeping confidences, sir, and can therefore appreciate that my orders prevent me from answering that question. You may however be assured that we only have the lady's best interest at heart."

Somewhat satisfied he went away to speak with his assistants and returned to advise me that no one had seen Miss Coutts and suggested that we try the Queen Hotel. He was clearly irritated that Miss Coutts was staying at another hotel, particularly as her grandmother, the Duchess of St. Albans, had always stayed at the Granby. To make matters worse, Mr Benn had been such an admirer of the Duchess that he named his own residence 'St. Albans House'.

This was indeed disappointing news given that this was one place in Harrogate I knew she would be safe, yet as I was preparing to leave, Mr Benn took hold of my arm.

"Captain, you should know that you are not the first person to have come looking for Miss Coutts," at which my ears pricked up.

"And who else, may I ask, has been enquiring after the good lady?"

"Some Irish barrister," he replied. "That's all I know and it was a couple of days ago now. He gave the impression that he was a close friend of Miss Coutts. But in view of his shabby appearance, we very much doubted that and consequently told him nothing and sent him on his way."

I thanked him for the information which gave me even more to think about. Not wishing to lose another minute, and before Mr Benn could probe further into my motives, I hastily apologised for a final time and sped away in the waiting carriage which returned me quickly to the Dragon.

I walked back into the hotel deep in thought and soon found myself in the company of Maggie who appeared to be in further need of male companionship.

"You're back, George!" said Maggie, placing an arm around my waist. I wasn't sure whether this was her normal approach at this time of night or whether I merely provided support for a lady slightly the worse for drink. Either way, I had no interest in anything that she had on offer. My eyes were looking everywhere. I searched everyone's face for any sign of guilt or stress that might betray an involvement with an audacious abduction.

Maggie dragged me to the table we had occupied earlier and I anxiously surveyed the scene, speculating all the while as to what might have happened to Miss Coutts. I also wondered what Lord Palmerston would make of it all. No doubt the Earl of Cardigan would take great pleasure in blaming me wherever possible. I then started to think about the next steps should we fail to find her in Harrogate. We would have to widen the search and probably involve the army garrisons based in Leeds and York. This was indeed an alarming prospect.

I nodded to Maggie not listening to a word she said, which mattered little as I felt sure she would not recall any of this tomorrow. At one point she threw her arms around my neck and suggested that we retire upstairs for some privacy. She insisted that she was formerly a professional dancer and wanted to give me a private demonstration of her talents. As I peeled her arms from my neck, I noticed Dawson looking in my direction and sneering. From the first time I set eyes on him I knew he was going to be trouble. I had hoped that he and his friends had gone elsewhere but it seemed Dawson's appetite for confrontation knew no bounds. I wondered if he was somehow involved in the disappearance of Miss Coutts. Perhaps the incident outside with his two cohorts was a 'ruse de guerre'? I looked around for Major Phillips as I felt sure he would still be here, but he was nowhere to be seen.

Casting aside all thoughts of Dawson, I suddenly recalled the night at the Crown when Miss Coutts attended the ball disguised as a French governess which caused me to instantly stand up and peer around the room. Maggie thought this was a cue for us to go upstairs, a presumption I quickly corrected.

"Excuse me, Maggie," I said, peeling one of her arms from my waist. "I think I have seen someone I know," which of course I hadn't but I needed to circulate amongst the guests in order to get a closer look at the ladies without appearing to be some perverted letch.

It occurred to me that I should have told Sinderby-Smythe about Miss Coutts and Madame Beaumont being one and the same. Anyhow that couldn't be helped right now. I was staring into the throngs of people dancing and felt a tug on my arm. It was Reeves and Sinderby-Smythe who were back with gloomy news. They had visited the main hotels and there was no sign of the ladies anywhere. Reeves had seen the Russians safely back to the Crown after sitting outside the house on Brunswick Place as a dinner party took place. He believed that the house belonged to the banker, Gerald Beales. The most intriguing part of his account was that after the Russians left, a young lady sneaked into the house taking great care not to be seen. A lover perhaps? Although given the clandestine nature of the meeting, not one for public display.

I relayed to Reeves and Sinderby-Smythe the details of my visit to the Granby, noting in particular the enquiries being made there a few days earlier by an Irish barrister. While I continued to look despairingly around the room, I spotted a lady dancing in a dress which seemed altogether familiar.

"One moment, gentlemen." The face of the lady was unfamiliar, but the dress drew me towards her.

"Come with me," I said to the two young officers.

"Lively place!" said Sinderby-Smythe to Reeves, absorbing the atmosphere of a party still in full swing.

I kept my eye on the dress and as the dance finished, the lady bowed to her partner and walked back to a sofa where another lady waited for her. I walked over and addressed the lady in the familiar dress.

"Parlez-vous Francais?" To which both ladies nodded and said, "Oui, Capitaine." I leaned close to the lady, remarking, "Miss Coutts, you have really given us rather a large fright this evening," and then in a conciliatory tone said, "Would you please let me know if you are intending on going out for the evening, in order that we may protect you? Otherwise I fear my career will be over before it has had chance to get going."

"I am sorry, Captain," she said. "I do appreciate that you have your orders but can't you see that I am much safer as Madame Beaumont or Miss Beaumont or whoever else I chose to be? The only person who is in danger is the real me and so it seems to make sense to hide that person away once in a while, particularly if it affords us an opportunity to amuse ourselves. Please don't be cross with us, Captain."

I took Reeves to one side. The sound of music, laughter and dancing made it hard to talk quietly but it also had the advantage of making it difficult for anyone to overhear what we were saying.

"Who are the two ladies you are speaking to, sir?" asked Reeves.

"Would you believe me if I told you that I was speaking to the two ladies we have been seeking this past hour or so?"

"Well blow me!" said Reeves looking at them a second time. "They look nothing like Miss Coutts and Miss Meredith. How did you know it was them?" he asked.

164

"It was the dress, Reeves. I noticed Miss Coutts had worn that dress on a previous occasion and it was so finely made that I remembered it. Now, let's get them back to their hotel with the minimum of fuss."

I asked Miss Coutts if she would allow me to see her home. Thankfully she agreed and headed for the door. In a way, I admired her actions this evening, nevertheless, I would much rather she had taken me into her confidence from the outset.

Sinderby-Smythe now drew alongside me. "See anyone you recognise?" I asked. Even though Miss Coutts and Miss Meredith were just a few yards away he was still unable to identify them. In fairness to the lieutenant, Miss Coutts seemed to have been very well coached in the art of theatrical make up by her thespian benefactor.

We all walked out of the Dragon and I beckoned to the next carriage in line and asked Reeves and Sinderby-Smythe to accompany the ladies to their hotel.

"Good night, Captain," said Miss Coutts, dropping the charade causing Sinderby Smythe's jaw to drop in the process.

"My God!" he blurted out, finally realising that he had been duped whereupon he instantly apologised for blaspheming.

I cast my eyes to the heavens, took a deep breath and exhaled hard whilst never taking my eyes off the carriage as it headed peacefully into the night.

I was about to ask Harry to return me to Holderness House when a familiar voice called to me. I was tired and having had so little rest the night before, I was in need of a long sleep. I turned round to see a smiling Mary, Duchess of Aldborough.

"I have been waiting for a chance to be alone with you all night but you seemed rather busy. What are you up to George?" she said taking my arm.

I smiled and answered in the only way I could, "It's a long and complicated story."

"Well you can tell me all about it on the way back to the Granby. You will escort me home, won't you George? I sent the Earl back there ages ago."

I looked at her face which had been transformed for that brief moment into that of an angel. How could I refuse? And so, for the second time in the space of less than an hour I was on my way to the Granby.

Yet again convention was being tested to the limits as she wanted me to escort her all the way to her rooms and whilst we walked along the wide corridors I cringed at the prospect of bumping into Jonathan Benn, the owner. Fortunately we went unnoticed, passing the odd servant who were rather used to looking the other way. As we stood outside her door, memories of our previous life together came charging back. She looked into my eyes and kissed me, then quickly opened the door and dragged me inside all in one movement.

She closed the door behind us and continued to kiss me passionately. The tempo of her kissing increased and her breathing became shorter. My body was responding almost independently of my will, which only encouraged her more. Every part of me wanted her but there was a voice in my head reminding me about a sweet young lady who sold me flowers and so I pulled away.

"I am sorry, Mary, but I can't do this."

She was undeterred and fixed her lips back to mine whereupon she threw her arms around my neck. For a second I tried to shut out the voice in my head but it was no good and I put my hands on hers and brought her arms away from my neck and down by her side.

"Oh George, please don't stop. I have missed you so much."

"I have missed you too, but you are married, Mary, and I have someone as well."

The intensity of the moment had subsided and it looked like we were both resolved to an unsatisfactory outcome.

"Who have you got George? It's not Georgiana Hamilton is it, because her father will never let you have his prize daughter? You know that don't you? That rogue is intent on selling her off to the highest bidder and he hates you with a vengeance."

"It's not that trollop who was hanging around you at the Dragon?" she then asked, speculating wildly.

"Of course not!" I said.

I had no wish to drag Virginia or Miss Coutts into this conversation either. I remembered that the Duchess had seen me with both of them and so I said nothing more other than to continue to refer Mary to her own marital status.

"My marital status!" she exclaimed. "What sort of marriage do I have? My husband philanders with anything and everything. I wish I was back at Drury Lane – we had some good times there didn't we, George?"

Moving away from me, she sat down at her dressing table looking unhappy and disappointed. I walked across the room to join her.

"There were good times, Mary, and in many ways I wish things were different but you chose to marry a duke. You'd met enough aristocrats at the theatre to know that most of them are arrogant wastrels."

"Perhaps," she said philosophically. "You really don't like aristocrats, do you George?"

"In general the answer is no, but there are one or two exceptions. Titles and knighthoods are generally bought, sold or inherited, so what sort of a system is that? If they were awarded solely for noble deeds then they would command my respect. Anything or anyone that can't be bought is always more highly prized."

"Does that include me then, George?" she said, clutching my hand as the fire in her eyes began to smoulder again.

I smiled, but it was no good. She was a beautiful woman and most men wouldn't think twice about bedding her, however, it no longer felt right for me to do so. Despite having just met Virginia, I had growing hopes that she may turn out to be the love of my life. To commit an indiscretion now would be to betray those hopes, and with that I stood up and prepared to leave.

"George, promise me that you will take care. The Duke knows that I don't really love him and that I really did love you. He lured me into his life with the promise of grand houses and fancy titles and you're right, at the end of the day, they count for nothing. He will never admit it, but I feel sure he is still jealous of you. He also suspects that you fathered our boy and that makes him dangerous. You should perhaps be aware that he is spending a good deal of time with Sir William Hamilton and Lord Garraty, which is particularly worrying as all three of them appear to thoroughly dislike you," she warned.

"Perhaps they are collaborating on what to buy me for my birthday," I said, making light of the warning. Having said that, the three of them working together against me was a daunting prospect. But I was well out of reach of them here in Harrogate, although I was slightly concerned that Sir William was investing in the same railway scheme which my aunt seemed so keen on. I headed for the door and Mary rose from her chair. She walked over to me and then kissed me tenderly.

She never failed to excite me, even when saying goodbye.

"Am I the father of your boy?" I asked softly.

"Of course not!" she replied. "But he was born very soon after I was married which makes the Duke suspicious."

I wasn't altogether convinced by her explanation and after a final exchange of goodbyes, I left her room. The instant her door closed behind me, I felt a degree of sadness. Maybe we could have had a good life together if only she hadn't been so obsessed with the things in life which didn't really matter. And maybe I was a father.

I came out of the Granby, happily avoiding a reunion with Jonathan Benn, the Granby's owner and much to my surprise found young Harry waiting patiently.

167

"My, you're a sight for tired eyes, young Harry. I see Mrs Parker has done a good job patching you up. What made you so certain that I would need a ride home before morning?"

"That was easy, Captain. I could see how knackered… I mean, tired you were. So I thought you would head for home as soon as you could."

I jumped into his cart and even though it was only a five minute ride to Holderness House, I still managed to fall asleep. Harry was right, I was absolutely exhausted.

Chapter 20

Following a good night's sleep, I woke refreshed. The previous day had been exhausting and I had slept like a Bengali opium dealer who'd over indulged on his own merchandise. Even a pistol being fired in the next room wouldn't have woken me.

Talking to William Beales at the Dragon about Friday's race reminded me that I needed to keep Tribune in peak fitness if he was to live up to my boasts. Consequently, I resolved to take him out for a ride immediately following the usual exchange of news with my aunt over breakfast. During this morning's discourse she advised me that she remained keen on investing in the railway project and had accordingly arranged for the Russian, her friend Henry Payden and his partner Gerald Beales to attend Holderness House at ten o'clock. This presented another excellent opportunity to enquire further into the bona fides of Vladimir Von Benckendorff. With that in mind I asked Benson to send word to Reeves, requesting his presence at this meeting. Given his fluency in Russian I hoped he would be able to assist in determining once and for all, whether Von Benckendorff was truly a Russian railway engineer or some imposter.

On my way to the stables, Benson advised me very diplomatically that he had managed to find a capable young rider who he felt may be more likely to ride Tribune to victory than myself. Much to Benson's relief, I smiled and thanked him. It made perfect sense to enlist a local rider as I would have my hands full and would need a good deal of instruction on the course rules governing the saddling enclosure, parade ring and such like.

With Sinderby-Smythe watching over Miss Coutts and no doubt escorting her to the wells, I felt a brief sense of calm returning. I was never happier than when riding Tribune, nothing else seemed to matter. It was just the two of us racing across the open common without a care in the world.

I galloped him across the Stray and out towards the racecourse. There was hardly anyone around save for a few sheep and the odd cow. We took a couple of turns around the track which had been softened by the previous day's rain, and then headed south. Two nights ago I had awoken from a blow to the head in a small farm building. It struck me that it could be useful to try and revisit that building, perhaps reuniting myself with my watch in the process. We were cantering as we headed away from the Stray along Intake Lane and, after a mile or so, I stopped to look for signs of something familiar. Tribune walked on slowly whilst I retraced my steps, testing my memory to the full. This was proving difficult, probably in no small way due to the clout I received to the back of the head, rendering my recollection of some details from that night sketchy at best. However, within a few minutes, I came across a series of fresh tracks made by two horses heading in the general direction I believe I walked early Wednesday morning. I left the main road and followed the path taken by these two horses. I was no great tracker but the soft ground made the tracks easy to see. We headed deeper into the countryside along this muddy path dotted with trees on either side. My eyes were now transfixed on the hoof prints left by the two horses and after a few minutes, I looked up to see a building barely one hundred yards ahead. Was this part of Hill Top Farm? It looked very much as I remembered it, although it was difficult to be absolutely certain, given that I never caught sight of it in the full light of day. The tracks of the two horses continued down a gentle slope towards the building and I kept my eyes glued to them until they stopped. It looked very much like the horses had been tied to a nearby tree as I could now see footprints leading straight into the stone built shelter. I dismounted and then, still holding Tribune by the reins, walked cautiously towards the building. A few yards from the doorway I spotted a half smoked cheroot lying in the dirt. I bent down and picked it up. Despite it appearing to be like any other cheroot, when I examined it more closely I noticed a very distinctive smell. The smell reminded me of India and the East.

I tied Tribune to a post, looked around one more time and with no-one in sight, moved towards the door and slowly pushed it open. The door's hinges creaked as I craned my neck to look inside. Even though the door was only half open I could clearly see that there was a man asleep on the floor. Everything looked innocent enough though, and given that his hands were not bound, I doubted that I was looking at another victim of abduction. I was also certain that I wasn't looking at either Jack or Mick, the thugs responsible for snaring me.

The sleeping man stirred at the sound of Tribune clearing his nostrils. He turned and partially opened his eyes, his hand shielding the light from his face.

"What the devil?" growled the man in an Irish accent.

"The devil indeed, and what business have you here, sir?" I blasted back.

"None of your business," said the Irishman still squinting in the light.

I stepped inside taking my pistol from my belt in the process.

"Now my bog-trotting friend, I will ask you just one more time what business do you have here?"

The sight of my pistol brought the Irishman to full consciousness quickly.

"No need for that, sir," he said in a much more conciliatory tone. "I am just a poor traveller, there is no need to threaten me with a pistol."

I lowered my pistol yet still held it firmly in my hand. The air was filled with a distinctive smell, identical to the one I noticed on the half smoked cheroot. Someone had smoked in here quite recently. I was sure this odour wasn't here two nights ago when I enjoyed an enforced sojourn and there was no doubt in my mind that I was indeed back in the same building. At first glance it was hardly surprising that there was no sign of my watch.

"Get up, man," I said and he responded by slowly standing and dusting himself down.

Now I was able to get a good look at him. He seemed somehow familiar, prompting me to quickly trawl through my memory banks for a flicker of recognition. But alas, nothing came to mind, causing me to now question just how much damage was caused by the blow I received to the head two nights earlier. I took careful note of the man in an attempt to return my memory back to normal. He was about my height, perhaps a year or two older, dark haired, unshaven, and unkempt.

"What's your name, Irishman?" I enquired.

"My name is Richard Dunn and who might you be?" he replied.

"I am Captain Townsend of the 11th Light Dragoons and now tell me Irishman, why are you sleeping in such a place as this?"

"I am keeping a low profile, as if it's any of your business," he replied, recovering his earlier arrogance.

"Low profile! Is that what you call it?" I said smiling, all the while looking around the hovel. "Well if that was your aim you've certainly succeeded, I don't expect that you will receive many dinner invitations here."

Then I slowly began to wonder if this Irishman was the same man I'd chased into the woods a couple of days ago. Added to which, Mr Benn of the Granby Hotel had told me only last night that a shabby Irishman had been enquiring after Miss Coutts.

"You wouldn't be the Irishman that has been making enquiries about a certain wealthy lady recently arrived in Harrogate would you?" I said leaning towards him.

"I don't know what you are talking about," he said, dismissing my question.

"You wouldn't by any chance be stalking this lady would you?" I asked speculatively.

"For the last time, I am a traveller. I know nothing of any lady. You only find me here because my purse is practically empty. However I can assure you that I do not intend to remain here a moment longer than is necessary."

He wasn't convincing at all. I wondered if he was spying on Miss Coutts for the Russians. On the other hand, if he was working for them, he would surely be in receipt of wages. In which case, why was he sleeping in a farm building? Maybe he really was out to keep a low profile.

"I don't believe you, Mr Dunn. But I haven't the inclination to waste any more time on you this morning. Nevertheless you may rest assured that I will be mentioning you to the constable. So I strongly suggest that you improve your circumstances immediately, failing which you must move out of the Harrogate area by nightfall. Simply put, if you don't move on you will be arrested for vagrancy," and with that I turned on my heels, leaving the Irishman mumbling curses under his breath.

"One more thing," I said, postponing my departure momentarily. "Do you smoke cheroots?"

He looked at me curiously and then replied, "No, what makes you ask?"

"No reason," I said, pushing my pistol back into my belt and leaving the Irishman with a puzzled expression.

I remounted Tribune and rode back to Holderness House, now exercising my poor head in addition to my horse. I was sure that the Irishman knew more than he was admitting. I suspected that he had met with two riders within the last twelve hours or so. The hoof prints were fresh and could only have been made after it had stopped raining. Also the smell of the cheroot would have dispersed in such a drafty stone building, had it been smoked more than twelve hours ago.

However there was no guarantee that the Irishman was in the building at the same time as the two riders. But judging by the unease he showed whilst answering my questions, I guessed that he was. In which case, who were the two riders he met and did that make him the man who has been watching Miss Coutts and making enquiries about her?

If he was met by the Russians, this could have only occurred during the time

Reeves was with me at the Dragon which, although possible, might not be that likely. But would they have left their hotel so late at night? Who were the two men who rode to the Irishman's lair if they were not the Russians?

Once again the sheep scattered at the sound of Tribune galloping across the Stray towards Holderness House. I had kept off the main roads in town due to the fact that they were alive with an abundance of visitors making their way to the sulphur well, signifying that another day in Harrogate was getting into full swing.

Reeves was the first to arrive at the house for the meeting with Von Benckendorff, leaving Harry to keep watch on the remaining Russians. Apparently young Harry had encountered another incident with the two boys who had set upon him after he'd chastised them for whipping their donkeys. It seems that in the night, they had taken Harry's donkey from its stable and hidden it. It took him well over an hour before eventually he found the poor beast.

"You know, we really should teach those two boys a lesson, sir," said Reeves leaping to support Harry.

"Oh we will, Reeves. Rest assured, we will! But for now, we have more pressing problems."

I then told him of my encounter with the Irishman and familiarised him with the potential railway investment. At ten o'clock, the bankers arrived with the Russian and met with myself, Reeves and of course my aunt. I noticed that Mr Beales had a large roll of plans under his arm which I hoped were the ones I asked my aunt to request.

Benson led our guests into the library. Conveniently, there was a large table on which we could lay out Mr Beales's plans.

I introduced Reeves as an old friend who had spent time in Russia and was particularly keen to practice his Russian on Vladimir Von Benckendorff and I hoped that no-one minded. We all sat around the large library table. My aunt, Reeves and myself down one side and the bankers and the Russian down the other.

"Nichevo strashnava," said Von Benckendorff with a big smile, which seemed to indicate that he had no objection.

"Spaseeb," said Reeves, acknowledging him.

"What did he say?" I asked discreetly.

"It is not a problem, sir," came the reply.

"Perhaps not, but what did he say?" I asked again.

"No sir, he said, 'It is not a problem' and I thanked him," answered Reeves.

I nodded, feeling a little foolish and immediately smiled at Von Benck-endorff.

"Ask him something else," I whispered to Reeves.

Reeves proceeded to ask him another couple of questions about the weather and so on and they both seemed pleased with their exchange. To the rest of us, it felt like we were watching the start of some foreign operatic performance. I nodded to Reeves that he had done enough to establish Von Benckendorff's bona fides as he appeared quite obviously Russian. Having said that, I wondered if there was anything else we could ask him to be certain that he was a railway engineer. Reeves evidently had more knowledge of Russia and its railways than I had appreciated and proceeded to ask a couple of searching questions about the very first Russian railway.

"How long did it take to build the Tsarskoye Selo railway, sir," asked Reeves in English.

"Good question," replied Von Benckendorff, also in English yet laced with a heavy Russian accent.

"We started construction in May 1836 and finished October last year and so about eighteen months."

"And is the gauge of the railway in Russia the same as used for example by George Stephenson, which seems to have become standard here?" probed Reeves.

"Another good question. The answer is that in Russia we use a wider gauge than used by your Mr Stephenson. Our gauge is around six feet and here you seem to use four feet eight inches," replied the Russian confidently.

I looked at Reeves who indicated that the Russian did in fact know something about the width of railways, which is what I had suspected from my own limited questioning when I first met with him.

"I see you have brought some plans for us, Mr Beales," I said, moving the focus of attention away from the Russian.

"Yes, Captain, may I show you the route for our railway?" he replied, resuming his customary control of proceedings. He laid out the plans in the centre of the table and pointed to the route being taken from Harrogate to Knaresborough and then across country to York.

"You can see that the railway cannot come any closer to Harrogate than this," he said, indicating an area on the map called Starbeck. "Many of the hotel owners are concerned that a steam locomotive will pollute the town and so, for the time being we will have to stop here, which is a trifle irritating."

Von Benckendorff then added, "We have looked at all options and this route is by far the best. We have a couple of small bridges to build over rivers but the rivers are very small. Otherwise the inclines of the railway line will be easily within the tolerances allowed."

"Very good," said my aunt reminding everyone of her presence and, with a smile for the benefit of the quiet Henry Payden, she continued.

"I do wonder however, gentlemen, what with the multitude of railways springing up all over the country, can you assure us that you will be able to obtain all the rails and equipment you need for your railway's construction?" once more gaining everyone's respect with the perceptive nature of her question.

"Indeed, madam," replied Mr Beales. "This is where we will have an advantage over our counterparts throughout England as Vladimir will be assisting us in locating the requisite supplies and equipment from Europe and at a much better price than we could obtain here."

I could see that as a northern businessman, Mr Beales took particular delight in telling us all this which inspired me to speak for the first time in a while.

"I realise that we have discussed this before, Mr Beales, nonetheless I would very much appreciate you reminding us of the approvals process. If I am not mistaken, an Act of Parliament is required for each and every railway before it can be constructed. Isn't that so?"

"You are quite right, Captain, and all I can say is that our application is, to all intents and purposes, approved," he replied smugly.

"With respect Mr Beales, that is easy to say. But how is it possible?"

Gerald Beales was clearly irritated by my question.

"Captain, I am sure you can appreciate that the workings of government are complex. If one doesn't know one's way around these intricacies then one can be waiting forever to progress. In order to avoid this, we have employed the services of The Railway Development Company who specialise in obtaining Acts of Parliament for railway lines and, what's more, they guarantee success."

"And who is The Railway Development Company?" I asked.

"It is a company who have contacts in government and, without being indiscreet, I can tell you that those are at the highest level."

The whole scheme survived every question we could think of and my aunt was so convinced that she handed over her payment for one hundred shares there and then. She also urged me to consider investing some of my own money because if I harboured ambitions to build an empire, I needed to start somewhere and this appeared to be as good an opportunity as any. Following a good deal of persuasion from my aunt, I subscribed for twenty five shares which she would pay on my behalf and I would repay when I could transfer the funds. My aunt exchanged a good number of smiles with Henry Payden, leading me to question whether she had any interest in him beyond assisting me and improving her own investment returns.

Nevertheless, everyone was happy enough and there proceeded to be a good deal of handshaking and smiles. Even I became quite excited at the prospect of making some money, enabling me to demonstrate to Sir William Hamilton that I would have been more than capable of looking after his daughter. The thought of that man brought to an end the pleasure of that particular day dream as I recalled Mary, Duchess of Aldborough warning me that her husband was now closely associated with Sir William in addition to Lord Garraty, the card cheat.

The bankers and the Russian were readying themselves to leave when Reeves asked Von Benckendorff one last question in Russian. I had no idea what he asked but the question seemed to receive a straight forward answer which satisfied Reeves.

When they left I asked him to translate the last exchange between the two of them. He'd asked the Russian how he had come to meet the bankers, to which he replied that they had met in Harrogate by chance just a few days ago when he and his wife came to take the waters. It appeared as if the Russians were genuine and Palmerston had little to fear, but all the same I asked Reeves to continue to follow them closely. There had to be a risk that the answers Von Benckendorff gave us would not have taken long for a charlatan to learn. Once they were safely out of sight, Reeves headed back to the Crown. Having now met Von Benckendorff in person, he would have to observe their movements from a more discreet distance. Despite contemplating switching the roles of my two officers, I opted to leave things unchanged, primarily because Sinderby-Smythe was yet to cast eyes on the Russians. This raised the possibility that we may lose sight of them, which was a risk I dare not take. I decided to write a letter to Palmerston updating him on the events of the day, including my meeting with Richard Dunn, the Irishman. After the usual head scratching, I eventually put together something which made some sort of sense but more importantly, included a coherent coded message.

With that out of the way, I headed round to the Queen on Tribune to see how Lieutenant Sinderby-Smythe was coping. I was sure that he would be more vigilant in his endeavours, given the events of the previous evening.

After leaving Tribune in the good care of a young boy, I went into the hotel in search of my lieutenant. Happily there was no sign of Dawson. Sinderby-Smythe was not hard to find as he was patrolling the corridors leading to the rooms occupied by the Coutts party, much like a palace guard. Up and down, up and down, which was proving rather annoying to Miss Coutts who advised me that his actions were making her feel somewhat like a prisoner.

Although she had taken the waters as part of her daily routine, she now wished to venture further afield and was glad that I had arrived at that moment as she wished me to reason with Lieutenant Sinderby-Smythe, which of course I did willingly. She was keen to embark on a trip to Bolton Abbey but I persuaded her to remain in Harrogate until we could be more certain that all potential dangers had been totally eliminated. I reassured her that things were looking promising but for now I begged that she remained cautious. She toyed with the idea of disguising herself in order to go to the abbey, until she caught sight of the look of horror on my face and in the end relented.

I took the lieutenant to one side and acquainted him with the notable highlights of our meeting with Von Benckendorff which led us to conclude that, for at least the time being the Russians appeared authentic, posing no apparent threat to Miss Coutts. The biggest threat Von Benckendorff posed at the moment was to my inheritance, having now become so heavily invested in the blasted railway. I desperately hoped that he really was good at building railways. I then ushered Sinderby-Smythe to a quiet corner in the corridor and told him how I had followed the tracks of two horses to the stone farm building where I had found the Irishman.

"You will recall, lieutenant, that when you first arrived in Harrogate I told you that I had spotted a man following Miss Coutts who I then chased across the Stray, only to lose him in some woods?"

"Yes, vaguely sir," he replied.

"Vaguely? What sort of answer is that?" I said, unable to contain my frustration with him.

"Well lieutenant, I suspect that the man I encountered this morning was the man I chased."

"Well I never! I wasn't aware there were any Irish in this part of the world," replied Sinderby-Smythe.

"The Irish are everywhere man! Haven't you heard? There was a massive potato famine and thousands of them flocked to the north of England."

"Why the north?" he asked. "Is it because there are more potatoes here?"

"What? Are you jesting with me, lieutenant? The Irish are everywhere. Who do you think dig the canals and lay the railway lines?" There was a faint chance that the lieutenant was revealing a sense of humour, then again he could be merely highlighting his shortcomings. I had to live in hope it was the former.

"Have you any other talents apart from being able to speak Russian?" I enquired somewhat exasperated.

"Why yes, sir. I am a crack shot!"

That was something I hoped would not be required. In any event, I felt that the best course of action was to try and simplify the position.

"Last night the owner of the Granby told me that an Irishman had recently been to his hotel asking about Miss Coutts. Naturally they chased him away and this morning I find an Irishman skulking in some nearby farm shed, having almost certainly met with two other altogether more affluent people. Doesn't that strike you as odd?"

"Absolutely, sir," concurred Sinderby-Smythe, seemingly oblivious to my concerns about him.

"Anyway, keep a sharp look out for him. He's about my height, around thirty years of age with a swarthy complexion. He was unkempt and unshaven when I saw him this morning, although he may have tidied himself up by now. Either way he was dressed pretty much all in black."

"Yes, sir. You can rely on me, sir. Will there be anything else?" he replied.

I left him with final instructions to continue to stay close to Miss Coutts but wherever possible, to remain out of sight. I promised that I would try and relieve him at some point in the afternoon to afford him a break. However, whilst I was retrieving Tribune, I received a message from Reeves delivered by young Harry. The Russians were on the move and Reeves had rented a mount and was following them at a safe distance.

Chapter 21

"Which way did they go, Harry?" I said, mounting my faithful horse.

"Road to Ripley, sir," he said, speaking and pointing simultaneously.

I brought my heels into Tribune's girth as we headed off to find Reeves and follow the Russians. I was desperate to move into a gallop as we rounded the Brunswick Hotel, straight into a strong breeze. I had to close my eyes for a moment when a cloud of dust blew up from the road. When the dust cleared, I could see that there were too many people walking towards Prospect Place for me to ride at speed. The nearer we came to the wells, the more people we encountered. By the time we reached Holderness House, I decided to exchange Tribune for one of my aunt's horses. This would take up valuable time but there was no telling how far I might have to ride and with Tribune being entered in the Harrogate Handicap Stakes on Friday, it seemed like a sensible course of action.

I quickly switched horses, sending the stable boy into a panic in the process. With so many people on the streets it was impossible to ride at more than walking pace and this continued all the way along to the shops on Parliament Street. Extremely frustrating as this was, and despite taking great care to keep out of everyone's way, I still received the odd complaint from those who had not seen me coming. I tried to look into Hatherway Grocer's for sight of Virginia but unfortunately the light reflecting off the window prevented that. We were still moving slowly until we reached the bottom of Parliament Street, passing the site of my first incident with Dawson. Quickly erasing that memory from my mind, I rode along the valley and up the other side of the hill where the buildings petered out, allowing me at long last to spur my aunt's mare into a gallop. The horse was unknown to me although she seemed game enough, which gave me confidence that we would be able to make up for any lost time. We had been riding hard for several miles when I thought that I should ease up to a canter, hoping I was close to catching up with Reeves. A stage coach from Ripon hurtled towards me which unsettled my horse, however she soon regained her composure. I was beginning to fear that perhaps Reeves had followed the Russians down some quiet farm track or footpath when, up ahead, I saw a rider on horseback. The posture of the rider was unmistakably cavalry and so I rode forward with increased optimism. The rider spotted me and waited which I took to be an encouraging sign. When only a hundred yards away, my hopes were confirmed as there was no doubting the rider up ahead was indeed 2nd Lieutenant Reeves.

"Hello again, sir," said Reeves.

"What's afoot, Reeves?" I enquired, peering ahead for sight of the Russians.

"They're way off in the distance, Captain, but they are travelling by coach and with the roads still a little damp, they're leaving tracks which are easy to follow. With few trees to provide cover I thought for the time being I should hang back and observe them through my telescope. Once we can find some denser cover, we will be able to get a bit closer."

This was a sound tactic given the situation. Reeves was proving to be a very competent officer. I just hoped their carriage didn't switch over to travelling on some road made of stone where it wouldn't leave tracks.

"So, what do you make of all this Reeves?" I asked, now we were riding side by side.

"Not sure, sir," he replied with a decidedly puzzled expression.

"I know what you mean. I can't make any sense of it either," I replied adding, "I can understand that Miss Coutts is a prize catch and Palmerston has issues with the Russians, yet why would someone want to intimidate me in order to get me to leave Harrogate? And where does that Irishman fit into all this? I am pretty certain the man I met this morning followed myself and Miss Coutts the other day. Surely it's inconceivable that a different Irishman was asking about Miss Coutts at the Granby, wouldn't you say, Reeves?"

"It does seem too much of a coincidence, sir," he replied.

"My point entirely. Nevertheless we need to ask ourselves, is there a connection with these Russians and the Irishman? He was hiding away in some semi-derelict farm building, which suggests that either he wanted to remain unseen or that he is simply without funds. From his manner I would hazard a guess that it is the former."

I paused for a moment and peered towards the horizon in search of the Russians' carriage.

"Do we really think these Russians would abduct Miss Coutts? I know Tsar Nicholas's palace burned down last year but even Miss Coutts's fortune would be a drop in the ocean for the rebuilding of that. They say it will cost over ten million pounds to restore it to its former glory. Therefore I don't believe that the Tsar would send over someone to kidnap her for money, there has to be more to it than that. Maybe this Count Zadovich is the one we should be more concerned with."

"Yes, sir, that does seem more likely. Furthermore, Lord Palmerston indicated that Coutts were the bankers to our own government and many embassies throughout Europe. Perhaps that is the connection we should be investigating?"

"That's right, Reeves. He did allude to that, and yet Miss Coutts is a mere slip of a girl and seems totally isolated from the daily workings of the bank. What information could she possibly have that would be of any interest to the Russians?"

We continued to travel slowly which allowed me ample opportunity to take further soundings from the astute young lieutenant.

"We know the Russians are itching for a fight over the Istanbul Straits or Afghanistan and maybe have their sights set on India, but where the hell is the link with Miss Coutts?" I asked.

"I must confess, sir, nothing springs to mind."

"Well, we need to find one, and with your knowledge of Russia you may be more likely to solve this mystery than I am," I replied.

"I will do my best, sir."

"Good man. If there isn't a connection, it looks very much like old Palmerston has sent us all on a wild goose chase. In any event, you put on a good show this morning with Von Benckendorff. Well done, Reeves."

We spurred our horses into a canter. Before reaching Ripley, we could see from the tracks in the road that the carriage had turned towards Knaresborough. We continued to follow ensuring that at all times we remained a safe distance behind. The land became more wooded enabling us to get much closer to the carriage without being seen. We cautiously continued our pursuit for about an hour as the carriage passed by Knaresborough and headed east towards York through a tiny hamlet named Ferrensby. Surprisingly, they were not taking the most commonly used roads, which led the sceptical part of me to speculate that they may be intentionally making it harder for anyone to follow. I eased my mount back as we reached the next woods.

"Good place for an ambush, Reeves," I said, prompting us both to bring our mounts to a stop. The road snaked its way into the trees and the carriage tracks were plain to see.

"Indeed it is, sir," said Reeves quietly. We both listened intently for any evidence of people, horses or a carriage, but apart from the sound of a few birds singing, the landscape was silent.

"Maybe they have stopped to see if they are being followed?" questioned Reeves.

"Or maybe they have stopped to attend to a call of nature? We will rest a while just in case," I said, feeling for my pistol which was nestled under my coat. I pulled it from my belt and prompted Reeves to do likewise.

"Let's watch our backs, Reeves, in case there is more to this than meets the eye. If these Russians are up to no good, I shouldn't be at all surprised if one of them hasn't left the carriage and is creeping up behind us as we speak."

That thought had us both looking in every direction and the slightest sound from the woods made us turn towards it. Moments later our tension was relieved with the familiar sound of a carriage up ahead banging and creaking as it wound its way along the makeshift road. Possibly they had stopped to allow someone to attend to a call of nature or perhaps someone had simply disembarked? Whatever the reason, we took no chances and kept our pistols handy.

We pressed on gingerly through the woods which turned out to be much longer than I had expected. Once back into open countryside we tracked the carriage through another couple of small villages and I began to recognise various landmarks as we neared my aunt's previous home of Dunsforth Hall. However, before we reached it, we could see that the Russians' carriage had come to a standstill outside a small country inn on the edge of the village of Upper Dunsforth. Memories flooded back as I recalled visiting this very inn many years ago after a hard day's fishing on the nearby river. The Plough Inn was a modest building with just two small rooms facing the main street.

Reeves and I stopped behind a small group of trees about fifty yards south of the village. The lack of cover between the trees and the inn rendered it impossible to get any closer without being seen. Regardless of that, it appeared the Russians had made their way inside, which now presented a challenge for us to establish what was so important as to warrant a fifteen mile journey to such a remote outpost? Were they simply surveying alternative routes for the railway or had they just stopped for refreshments? In order to learn the answers to these questions, we needed to eavesdrop on their conversation. For that, one of us would have to navigate the fifty yard stretch of land undetected. Given that there was a strong possibility they would be speaking in their native Russian, the honour of this exercise would naturally fall to Reeves, whilst I remained hidden by the trees, minding the horses.

Reeves accepted the challenge manfully, crouching down before slowly crawling his way, snake-like, through the long grass until he was alongside the inn. He moved around to the rear which is where I lost sight of him. I began the anxious wait for his return.

And I waited and I waited. There was no activity from the inn; no-one entered and no-one left. The carriage remained outside, the driver clearly enjoying his break with a tankard of beer. I envied him, as I was getting thirsty and hungry myself. The horses that pulled the carriage drank from buckets placed in front of them and that prompted me to lead our two horses back to a nearby beck, allowing them a well-earned drink. Fortunately I wasn't away for that long and when I returned to my original vantage point nothing appeared to have changed. I had no concept of how long Reeves had been gone, causing me to curse the loss of my watch. Irrespective of this handicap, I knew he had been gone long enough and I was beginning to worry that he may have been discovered.

Impatience got the better of me and I decided to leave the horses and make my way to the Plough Inn. Having sunk to my knees readying myself to crawl through the long grass, I heard a voice shout and the carriage driver leapt to his feet. Activity at last!

Moments later the one-eyed Russian manservant stepped out from the doorway of the inn with a man I had never seen before and the two of them walked away from us up a small slope into the heart of this tiny village. After walking about fifty yards they turned into a small cottage on the right and went inside. A few minutes later they reappeared on the main street and walked back towards the inn. As they were walking in my direction, I moved further behind the trees and hoped that the horses would remain quiet. I very much doubted that we could be seen, but as they were walking straight towards me I felt distinctly vulnerable. Once the two men had returned to the Plough Inn, the Russian manservant hailed his countrymen and Mr and Mrs Von Benckendorff came out into the daylight. All four of them climbed into the carriage which then headed along the main street, away from us and on towards Boroughbridge. Reeves scrambled his way over to where I was waiting, raising himself up to run the last few yards. "You won't believe what I have heard, Captain."

"Are you sure you were not seen?" I asked, initially more concerned that he hadn't been detected than what he had learned.

"Absolutely, sir," said Reeves confidently. "After crawling through the long grass, I worked my way to the back of the inn and then around the other side. I crouched down, hidden by a couple of old barrels which were next to an open window. Fortunately as the rooms are quite small I was close enough to where the four of them were seated. I got the impression that they were the only people in the establishment and whenever the landlord came over to serve them they stopped talking."

"My, that's damn caution for you. What's the chance of the landlord being able to understand Russian?"

"That's what I thought, sir," agreed Reeves.

With the carriage now out of sight, we mounted our horses and once more set off in pursuit whilst Reeves continued his report.

"In spite of the fact that I couldn't hear everything, sir, I was able to gather some important information."

We'd set off following far too quickly and I signalled Reeves to slow down, making sure we kept out of sight of the carriage. I also wanted to look at the cottage which the Russian manservant visited. I noticed it was called Homelands.

"Captain, I think they are planning to leave tomorrow which is nothing untoward in itself except they did talk about taking an extra passenger with them. They didn't mention the name of the passenger, but I am certain they were referring to a woman. They were also talking about sailing times of various ships."

"That could be innocent enough. Beales said that Von Benckendorff would be assisting in the purchase of equipment and steel from Europe. However, the mention of an extra passenger, and a woman at that, could mean that they are intent on kidnapping Miss Coutts and whisking her away before anyone can say 'Lord Byron'," I replied, immediately thinking damn and blast, maybe these bloody Russians are villains after all. And we have just invested a small fortune into the railway scheme which they could now be intent on deserting. I was beginning to feel more than a little foolish at this prospect.

"Kidnapping was going through my mind too, sir. Something else you might find of interest was that they talked about some valuable piece of merchandise which they needed to get back to Russia. This seemed to be integral to their plans and I also heard mention of a meeting with Count Zadovich," finished Reeves.

"Count Zadovich! So Lord Palmerston was right all along!" I said, continuing to digest this news.

"Could the valuable piece of merchandise be Miss Coutts?" I enquired.

"Yes, sir. That could be possible."

"Good job, Reeves," I said to the young officer. "Did you overhear which port they would be heading to?"

"They mentioned a couple of ports, sir," he replied, "Liverpool and Hull."

"Unfortunately that's not much help as they are at opposite sides of the country. Anything else, Reeves? Anything at all. No matter how insignificant it might sound, it could provide us with a vital clue as to what they are planning."

"Well they did mention a strange name – Theodore Botterill. Does that mean anything to you, sir? It seemed that he might have some financial problems given that they talked about an overdue loan."

"Did they talk much about this Botterill fellow?" I replied.

"Not really, sir. His name came up just before they mentioned the valuable merchandise and the ship. Nonetheless, I got the impression he had caused them a problem or two."

"Then clearly we must find out everything we can about Theodore Botterill. Just one last thing. Why did the manservant come out of the inn and go into that cottage we have just passed? The one called Homelands."

"Bit of a mystery, sir. I couldn't see what he was up to from my vantage point. Maybe they were inspecting it for some future use."

"Yet another mystery! The place is full of them! But what future use could they have for a house all the way out here if they are leaving tomorrow?" I asked, to which Reeves, like me, had no answer.

Deep in thought we followed the carriage, remaining a safe distance behind. After about four miles we came to the busy town of Boroughbridge. The town was a hive of activity, centred mainly on the Crown Inn which was a famous staging post in the north of England. This Crown couldn't have been more different to its namesake in Harrogate. It wasn't a large, elegant building constructed of stone and frequented by the well-to-do. Rather, it was a long, rambling inn with a vast number of stables to its rear. It had been a long time since I had seen so many carriages and horses all in one place. Not to mention the large number of travellers who were coming and going all the while. Being on the main coaching road connecting Scotland in the north with London in the south, a high level of activity was commonplace in Boroughbridge. All in all this made for a noisy place, and fortuitously, one where we could easily blend into the background without being noticed.

Once outside the inn, the Russians' carriage stopped and the man whom the Russians had met in Upper Dunsforth alighted. He waved to the coachman and walked into the Crown through the main entrance, whilst the carriage made its way amongst the crowded scene and headed back towards Harrogate.

Having watched from a distance, I ordered Reeves to continue following the carriage while I remained in Boroughbridge. I very much wanted to see if I could learn anything more about the man the Russians had just left.

Reeves rode out of Boroughbridge keeping well behind the carriage. Meanwhile I dismounted, handing my mount to a stable lad, and walked purposefully into the Crown Inn.

The inn was noisy and crowded with people. Some were travellers resting, taking advantage of the opportunity afforded to them as the horses on their stage coach were changed. Others looked like they were waiting to meet someone or gain passage on a coach bound either north or south. The man I had followed was seated as if waiting for such a coach, presenting me with an opportunity to partake of some liquid refreshment, together with a small amount of food. A delightful young girl quickly attended to me and even though there was only simple fayre on offer, it was in any event extremely welcome.

I found a seat close to the man I was keenly observing, without being so close that my interest in him would appear too obvious. He was reading what looked to be a timetable and also carried a copy of the London *Times*. I busied myself picking over my meal whilst watching his every move. Travellers continued to enter and leave the inn as the process of changing horses was carried out with remarkable speed. Every now and then some official from a Stage company shouted the name of a town, city or a coach, in response to which several people would gather their belongings and head to one of the many waiting carriages. This routine was repeated several times before the man I was observing was stirred into action. He was responding to a call for passengers heading south to Sheffield. I thought it imperative to find out more about him before he left and so, acting on an impulse, I clumsily crashed into him, causing him to drop the papers he clutched under his arm. He cursed me most harshly, forcing me to render my profuse apologies for the accident. I then annoyed him further by insisting that I pick up all the papers I had so recklessly knocked from his grasp. Continuing to apologise all the while, I went down onto the floor and laboured over the recovery of his papers. People continued to push past as I fumbled around, giving myself the maximum amount of time to read whatever I could. The man implored me to stop but I insisted on remedying my carelessness, providing me with just enough time to establish that he was indeed carrying timetables. There were two, one being a shipping timetable from Liverpool for the month of August 1838 and the other, a railway timetable from Manchester to Liverpool. Having gathered together the timetables along with his copy of the *Times*, I passed everything back to him with yet another apology. He was far from pleased, however his desire to make sure he caught the Sheffield stage coach ensured he spent little time noticing me. He frantically ran out of the Crown, panicking and waving his arms at the driver to wait, which he reluctantly did and, much to the relief of the man with the timetables, safely caught his stage.

It was impractical for me to follow him all the way to Sheffield and so I made my way back to Harrogate. I would catch up with Reeves in due course, but for now I wanted to reassure myself that Sinderby-Smythe hadn't allowed Miss Coutts to dupe him again and therefore I headed straight to the Queen.

Chapter 22

It was early afternoon by the time I returned to the Queen and, thankfully, all was well with Miss Coutts. After satisfying myself that Sinderby-Smythe had the ladies safety under control, I took him to one side to update him on what we had learned by following the Russians' carriage. It was pretty clear to us all that, just as Lord Palmerston had first thought, the Russians could pose a possible threat. The shipping timetables, the mention of important merchandise, Count Zadovich, in addition to the mysterious lady passenger, led me to conclude that I needed to revise the letter I had written earlier in the day to His Lordship. Somewhat fortuitously, I hadn't found time to pass it to Benson and so the letter remained available for amending in my room. I was also keen to mention the name, Theodore Botterill, as it might mean something to Lord Palmerston, and yet, if the Russians were planning to leave tomorrow, there was no time for him to respond either way. My letter would take at least twenty four hours to reach him and any response would take at least that again.

Before leaving, I told Sinderby-Smythe that I would revisit the Queen once I had posted my report. On my way out of the hotel I saw Dawson, who immediately turned away from me and rather shiftily headed down some stairs. Given the way events were unfolding, I began to wonder whether his role in all this was simply personal to me or something altogether more sinister.

I then headed back to the house and made my way to the library, armed with a pen and a stack of writing paper. Typically the exercise of writing in code proved extremely tedious, nevertheless, I managed to relay the rest of the day's events in something resembling a normal letter and finally passed it to Benson for the post. I also took the opportunity to borrow a map of northern England which I saw resting on the book shelves.

I had hoped to speak to my aunt and suggest that, if it wasn't too late, we should extricate ourselves from the railway investment or at least hold back until we knew for certain whether the Russians were in Harrogate for bona fide reasons. Unfortunately, the situation didn't look good in many ways as it transpired that my aunt was attending what appeared to be a celebratory tea party with Henry Payden, the banker.

I reflected that over the last few days we had gathered together a certain amount of information, but we didn't know how much of it was relevant and how much was entirely innocent. It was like having a few pieces of a dissected map and not knowing where they fitted or what it should finally look like.

Instinctively, I felt it was imperative to find the same timetables that were being carried by the man who I bumped into in Boroughbridge. I was convinced that clues lay within those documents which could point to what lay ahead. With that in mind, Pickersgill Palliser, the man who ran the Harrogate post office and author of the popular Harrogate Directory seemed to be a man worth talking to. After all, he was someone who thrived on lists and records and if anyone had railway and shipping timetables in Harrogate, it would surely be him. There was also a further possibility that he would know something of Theodore Botterill who, according to the Russians, may have financial problems.

When I arrived back at Holderness House, young Harry was waiting for orders. With the Russians on the move, there had been little point in him sitting outside the Crown all day twiddling his thumbs. He was now sporting two black eyes as a result of his beating, making him look much worse than he had last night. However, he was clearly on the mend and his spirits were undiminished. In recognition of his sterling efforts from the previous day, I gave him a further sovereign with the promise of more if he continued to impress. At the moment I was content to use the five sovereigns I'd taken from the two thugs who abducted me. Even so, if this assignment continued for much longer, I could see myself sending Lord Palmerston a rather large account of my expenses in the hope that he would settle it.

I envisaged the Russians' carriage was likely to return shortly, so I despatched Harry back to the Crown Hotel where he was to await the arrival of Reeves. If there was any more news regarding the Russians and their plans, he was to bring it to me without delay. I then left the house with a view to collecting Lieutenant Sinderby-Smythe on the way to the post office. Depriving Miss Coutts of her appointed protector for an hour or so was by no means ideal, but these were fast becoming desperate times. In any event, I felt sure that, provided she stayed within the hotel and with Miss Meredith also on hand, any risk would be minimal.

In the midst of all this intrigue and speculation, I invariably found myself thinking of Virginia Hatherway and resolved to call on her albeit for a few moments. I hadn't seen her for what seemed like an age and, despite having so many distractions in my life, she was never very far from my thoughts. At our last meeting she had made it clear that she was worried about me and so I felt it courteous to put her mind at rest on that score.

Consequently, before heading to the Queen, I took a brief detour to the top of Parliament Street and down to Hatherway Grocer's. I looked through the window to see Virginia happily attending to a number of customers. Given my natural preference to speak to her privately, I paced up and down for a few moments hoping her customers would soon leave.

This was proving to be most inconvenient as, depending on how things turned out, it might be my only chance to see her for a while. Thankfully my irritation was short lived and after most of the customers had left, I walked in. I was so pleased to see her but when our eyes met, I could see that the feeling was not entirely mutual.

"Virginia, it is so good to see you again," I said, smiling broadly.

"Well, I'm not sure why," she replied with a hint of hostility. Being a member of Her Majesty's armed forces, I was used to confrontation and had always been told to withdraw pending clarification when not in full knowledge of the opponent's strength. This seemed like one of those moments.

Obviously something must have happened, as less than twenty four hours ago this girl had been in my arms kissing me passionately.

"Has something happened? Is everything alright?" I foolishly asked.

"No, Captain, everything is not alright! You have quite a nerve coming in here, bold as brass, after cavorting all night with Maggie Simmonds."

"Is that what she's called?" I said at hearing the name Simmonds for the first time and then, half laughing, attempted to explain. "That was simply business."

I had barely finished speaking when her reply came hurtling towards me like a bullet from a baker rifle. "That's the problem Captain! Do you think me so stupid that I don't know what business she is in? Please do not contact me again. I truly hope you find what you are looking for but I for one am going to get on with my life," she turned on her heel and without allowing me chance to explain further, busied herself elsewhere in the shop.

I walked over to join her and said in a reassuring voice, "I don't know what you have heard, as I can assure you that nothing happened with Maggie what's her name. Unfortunately there is so much I'm not allowed to divulge at the present moment, Virginia. I beg of you to have faith in me and all will be well."

Under the circumstances, I felt the best thing to do was withdraw and let Virginia calm down. She would find out the truth sooner or later and then her trust in me would be restored. With so much to consider and plan for tomorrow, I had to leave this situation with Virginia for another time. I earnestly hoped that we would avoid any trouble with the Russians, Tribune would win the big race and I would charm Virginia at the regular Friday night ball at the Granby.

Deep in thought, I arrived at the Queen Hotel in time to see Miss Coutts and Miss Meredith returning from a short walk. Sinderby-Smythe was a discreet thirty yards behind. The ladies seemed genuinely pleased to see me. Anxious for them to feel safe and confident, I detained them in light hearted conversation for a minute or two, during which Miss Coutts passed on a message to me from Lord Redmayne who had been urgently called back to his main estate in Lancashire. He sent his apologies at this unavoidable turn of events, which had been brought about by a Chartist uprising involving many of the workers in his mills. He had also left one of his cards with Miss Coutts for my attention, together with an invitation to call on him whenever I was in his area.

The departure of Lord Redmayne was unfortunate as I was sure he would prove more than capable should a crisis arise. Of equal surprise was the compliment Miss Coutts then paid my lieutenant. Whilst walking towards the sulphur well, a man had approached the ladies clearly intent on engaging Miss Coutts in conversation, yet before he could get within a yard of them, Lieutenant Sinderby-Smythe intercepted him. It turned out that the man was none other than Jonathan Benn, the owner of the Granby Hotel. Rather than being upset by this, Miss Coutts took a good deal of comfort from the assertive actions of the lieutenant's together with his presence of mind. Mr Benn was rather shocked but apparently the lieutenant apologised for any alarm he may have caused, following which he retired to a discreet distance to allow Mr Benn to converse with Miss Coutts. This was welcome news, however without wishing to appear rude, the clock was ticking and I was acutely aware that somehow I must find these timetables in order to make sense of what Reeves overheard the Russians discussing.

Before making my apologies to leave, I cast my eyes across the Stray to see if there were any dangers present. This was fast becoming a habit. Once again, I could clearly see that we were being watched and, although he was some way off, I would have bet all my shares in the Yorkshire Railway Company that it was that wretched Irishman.

I did not wish to alarm the ladies and suggested they might like to head inside the hotel for a spot of afternoon tea. With them safely out of the way, Sinderby-Smythe and I would then intercept the blighter. Thankfully they accepted my suggestion. I was also reassured to hear that the ladies intended to remain at the Queen that evening, listening to a music recital in the hotel's ballroom. Whilst they walked into the hotel, I took Sinderby-Smythe to one side and asked him to casually walk across the Stray towards the Tewit well. Hopefully this would not appear to be a threat to the man who was watching this hotel, enabling the lieutenant to get close enough to capture him.

I was certain it was the Irishman and by apprehending him we would hopefully establish once and for all whether or not he was working for the Russians. Though if he wasn't working for them why else would he be watching Miss Coutts? Furthermore it was only to be expected that Miss Coutts would be the subject of some form of surveillance if Lord Palmerston's fears were correct. Even if we learned nothing from interrogating this man we could at least take the opportunity to have him locked up, which could only help us in our efforts to protect Miss Coutts.

Unfortunately before Sinderby-Smythe could give chase the man had disappeared and was no longer in sight.

"Damn!" I said to the lieutenant, "We could have done with running him to ground."

Without horses at hand, there was little point in wasting any more valuable time which was increasingly in short supply. The day was fast getting away from us and with the Russians planning on leaving Harrogate tomorrow, there was much to be done.

I was just about to hail a hansom cab to take us to the post office when Harry arrived with a message. Reeves reported that the Russians were back in their hotel, and nothing unusual had happened on the journey back to Harrogate. He added that he would continue to watch over them until ordered otherwise.

Decidedly frustrated at not being able to grab the Irishman, Sinderby-Smythe and I climbed onto Harry's cart which then set off towards the post office. As the afternoon was fading rapidly I was concerned that we may have left it too late. It was essential that the post office was still open and also that Mr Pickersgill Palliser remained there hard at work. Despite being bounced around in the cart, I still found time to reflect on the unfortunate departure of Lord Redmayne and wondered if events were starting to conspire against us. However, I was encouraged by the lieutenant's actions when Jonathan Benn approached Miss Coutts and thought I should share that with him.

"That was good work, lieutenant, protecting Miss Coutts in the way you did. Yes, very good work indeed," feeling that I had, perhaps, misjudged him earlier.

"Thank you, sir," he replied gracefully.

"Where did you say you were from?" I asked, seeking to learn more of the man.

"Wimborne in Dorset, sir."

"Somewhere near Southampton if I'm not mistaken," I replied.

"That's right, sir, not that far. Maybe twenty five miles or so."

"Anyway, keep up the good work, with there just being the three of us, we all need to be at our best."

Harry brought us safely to the white-washed post office and much to my relief, it had not yet closed. We entered and found Mr Palliser still labouring diligently. He seemed lost in his writings and oblivious to our arrival which necessitated my indulging in a spot of throat clearing. This achieved its purpose, causing Mr Palliser to look up from his work.

"Captain Townsend," he said, placing his pen carefully down on his desk. "It is good to see you again," adding, "I understand that you own a horse in tomorrow's crack race and as you may be able to see, I am busy compiling the race card."

I peered over his desk and could clearly see lists of runners and riders for the different races and felt compelled to compliment him on his presentation.

"I would give you a copy now, Captain, but alas it will not be finalised for at least another thirty minutes," he said apologetically.

"That is indeed kind of you, sir," I replied and then moving quickly to the purpose of my visit added, "Perhaps you could send one to Holderness House when it is completed? However, the reason for today's visit is to seek your assistance in acquiring various timetables. My aunt has told me that she would like to visit Europe and further afield at some point and I wanted to surprise her by helping to plan her trip. Accordingly, I wondered what information you may have regarding the timing of coaches and steam locomotives which could take her to the main ports?" I said, being deliberately vague in order to avoid giving him too much of an insight as to where my real interest lay. Despite Pickersgill Palliser being most probably the very pillar of the community, at this moment we could not afford to trust anyone.

"I am sure I have a number of timetables which will get you to the main ports of Liverpool and Kingston upon Hull, Captain. However, I am afraid you will need to look through the newspapers for a schedule of sailings. It is not something

I am often asked for," he replied, rifling through one of his drawers and placing a handful of timetables on his desk. They seemed to cover everything from north to south and east to west. He kept looking through the timetables as he spoke.

"Ha Captain! Here is the railway timetable for Manchester to Liverpool," said Mr Palliser expressing a moment's elation, "and here is one from Leeds to Selby."

Then after handing these to me he continued to sift through the pile of timetables in search of anything else which may be of assistance.

"And here are the stage coach timetables to get you to Manchester, and also Leeds."

"Thank you kindly, sir," I said. "My aunt was right. You are indeed the font of all knowledge in Harrogate."

Mr Palliser smiled, clearly pleased at the reputation he had gained for himself. He then handed me an assortment of steam packet timetables. There were several with strange names and yet for some reason I was drawn to the paddle steamer, Albatross and the wooden paddle steamer, Adelaide. Perhaps I was developing a sixth sense, nonetheless after sorting through piles of timetables, it was abundantly clear that getting to Kingston upon Hull from Harrogate was a lot easier than getting to Liverpool.

"I am sorry I can't provide you with the list of August sailings, but if you have time I can fetch you a number of old newspapers which I store in the stock room. Who knows, you may be lucky and find what you are looking for."

I accepted his kind offer and hoped that his collection would include more than just the local Leeds papers as I suspected that any advertisements for sailings were more likely to be found in the newspapers with the biggest circulation. Perhaps the *Times* or maybe even the *Guardian*, which although Manchester based, was extremely well read.

A customer came into the post office and I shouldn't have been surprised to see it was the same old Mrs Potter I had seen earlier at Virginia's grocery store. She had a basket of eggs and seemed to be exchanging them for some letters.

Mr Palliser then placed a large pile of newspapers on a chair in the corner which was generally reserved for customers awaiting a mail coach. I split the pile into two, sat down in one of the chairs and began to read. I passed the other pile to Sinderby-Smythe who did likewise. Some of the papers went back several months and so I decided to read through the more recent papers first. There were plenty to wade through including the *Times*, the *Morning Chronicle*, the

Morning Post and more locally, the Leeds papers including the infamous Chartist paper, the *Northern Star*.

News items kept distracting me, such as the terrible mining tragedy in Barnsley where so many young children lost their lives. I also spotted that the Marylebone Cricket Club had dominated Oxford University in a drawn game of cricket played over two days at Lords. How I missed cricket! Oxford only batted once and were all out for a mere 42 runs with only Borrer and Lord Ward reaching double figures. I'd seen Borrer bat before and he was an impressive fellow. This was all very interesting but not at all helpful. Curiosity then drew me to the *Northern Star*. I had never seen this paper before and the moment I opened it I couldn't help being drawn to an article relating to the flogging of soldiers from the 15th Hussars at the barracks in Leeds. The story did not portray the Hussars in a good light and drew the reader's attention to this being the sixth flogging in five months. This came as a stark reminder that Harrogate was an outpost for the aristocracy and mill owners to indulge themselves at will. One northern journalist compared the town to a lavish watering hole in a desert surrounded by the sands of discontent. Out of the corner of my eye, I could see that Mr Palliser was winding down for the day and so, in order to hasten the exercise I started to turn pages more quickly. People continued to come in, rushing to catch the post before Mr Palliser closed. One or two of these customers couldn't resist looking at us, no doubt curious to the purpose which lay behind our endeavours. I know we startled one lady when, after half an hour's reading, Sinderby-Smythe let out a cry of 'Hallelujah!'

A list of sailings appeared in the *Manchester Guardian* alongside an advertise-ment made by the Great Western Steamship Company. They were promoting the voyage of the SS *Great Western* which was leaving Liverpool in three days time and arriving in New York around 20th August. Helpfully, someone had drawn a ring around this notice which made it easy to spot.

"Were it not for the ring, sir, I might have missed it altogether," he said, feeling quite pleased with himself.

"Well done, Sinderby," I said and although equally pleased, I was also slightly surprised by his continued successes. Maybe my initial impressions of him were wide of the mark.

I walked over to Mr Palliser with the page containing the Great Western Steamship advertisement held firmly in my hand. He had finished serving the lady who had been startled by my lieutenant, affording me the opportunity to ask if we might retain this particular newspaper page.

"Not at all, Captain," he replied. "I suspected that you had found what you were looking for by your friend's enthusiastic exclamation."

"Yes, thank you Mr Palliser and please accept my friend's apologies for startling your customers," I said, looking at Sinderby-Smythe who nodded and smiled apologetically.

"You wouldn't happen to recall anyone else, perhaps a foreigner, showing any interest in the sailing of the SS Great Western from Liverpool? Someone has circled the listing," I asked pointing to the advertisement.

Mr Palliser considered my question carefully and then replied, "I am sorry, Captain, but I can't recall anyone being interested in that particular ship. Certainly no-one from foreign parts. From time to time some of the young labourers from the outlying villages look at these listings with a view to emigrating. More and more are seeking pastures new these days – perhaps one of them circled it."

That seemed to explain the circling to some extent. Obviously the advert had not been circled by the Russians as, if they were interested in that particular ship, they would hardly draw attention to it. Therefore, locals wishing to emigrate seemed the most logical explanation.

I then took a closer look at the advert which showed that the ship was destined for America. This made me question our theory that the Russians would be sailing from Liverpool. Why would they be kidnapping Miss Coutts and taking her across the Atlantic? This made no sense. There had to be a chance that we had drawn the wrong conclusion. Under normal circumstances you would expect the Russians to head east into Europe. The timetables carried by the man they met at the Plough Inn suggested otherwise and so maybe it was someone else and not the Russians planning to head west?

Mr Palliser looked at his watch. He clearly wanted to close up and head home. All the same and to his credit, he remained open allowing us to continue to read through the newspapers.

I noticed in the *Leeds Mercury* that a lot of wheat, oats and barley came into Kingston upon Hull from Russia. The same paper further reported that there were a number of ships leaving Kingston upon Hull bound for Hamburg and elsewhere in Europe. It occurred to me that the most logical course of action for the Russians was to simply travel home on a returning Russian ship. One which for example, had just delivered wheat, oats or barley. When I turned the page of the very last newspaper I resolved that there was nothing more to be gained by imposing further on Mr Palliser's goodwill. After all, in spite of Palmerston's speculation, these Russians might actually be who they say they are and be heading off to buy railway equipment in Europe. But then why the secret meeting at the Plough Inn? And why the mention of Count Zadovich, an extra woman passenger, valuable merchandise and, of course, Theodore Botterill? I had almost forgotten to ask about him.

"You have been so very kind and helpful, Mr Palliser, I am embarrassed to impose on you further. However, can you recall ever coming across the name Theodore Botterill?"

"Theodore Botterill. Yes I think I have heard of him. If I'm not mistaken he's some kind of engineer or inventor who lives in Sheffield. I believe he was in the news recently or perhaps I just imagined that. I read so much these days in my quest for newsworthy items."

My eyes widened at this. Sheffield was the destination of the coach caught by the man with the timetables. I was tempted to ask if we might read through all the recent newspapers for an article regarding Mr Botterill, however I was certain that we had imposed on Mr Palliser's good will for long enough. With the timetables firmly in my grasp, it was clearly time for us to leave when Mr Palliser called, "Captain, the race cards are now finished. You may have a copy if you wish."

I gratefully accepted the race card and once again thanked Mr Palliser. After what seemed like an age of reading newspapers, we walked out of the post office to be greeted by Harry. He had news. Reeves sent word that the Russians were visiting with Gerald Beales which seemed innocent enough and there was a message from Benson to say that the jockey he had hired for the race had been to the house to get to know Tribune. Apparently he was impressed with him and thought everything looked promising for tomorrow's big race. I couldn't help thinking that the race, instead of disguising the true purpose for my visit, was now something I could really have done without.

Before heading back to the house, I thought it sensible to visit the constable and make him aware of the potential danger facing Miss Coutts. I asked Harry to take me there and then return Sinderby-Smythe and all the various timetables to the Queen where he could resume his watch over the ladies.

I had no idea if the Russians would kidnap Miss Coutts themselves or hire cut-throats to carry out the evil deed. Perhaps I should also contact the army's garrison in York, but what if we had misconstrued what Reeves had overheard? If their travel plans were merely to Europe to acquire parts for the railway, I would look a complete imbecile and possibly create an international incident whilst doing terminal damage to my own career. It was clear that we still needed more information before calling out the garrison.

I wondered if my aunt had learned anything more from her meeting with her admirer, the banker. Perhaps Henry Payden had told her whether the Russians were planning to leave tomorrow? Maybe he had confirmed that they were intending to go to Europe or overseas in order to purchase the rail parts?

Whilst still trying to make sense of all this in my mind, we arrived outside the constable's house. We were now in central Harrogate which I supposed was ideally situated in order to attend disturbances in either the low or high parts of town. Harry continued on to the Queen with Sinderby-Smythe and would return to collect me once my business with the constable had been concluded.

I knocked on the door and a lady who I took to be the constable's wife answered. I asked if her husband was available as I had urgent business to discuss with him. She was a pleasant enough lady, plainly dressed with a round face and flushed cheeks. She showed me into a small parlour with four comfortable chairs placed around a roaring fire. The furnishings were modest but nevertheless well presented. A few moments later the constable came into the room.

"Good day, constable," I said. "We meet again."

"Good evening, Captain, and what can I do for you?" replied Constable Hardisty.

"I regret having to disturb you at this time of day but I need to warn you that I have reason to believe that there may be trouble at tomorrow's races."

Constable Hardisty's expression did not move.

"Together with two other officers of the 11th Light Dragoons, we have been keeping two Russians under close observation. Both my fellow officers speak Russian and after overhearing a conversation today at a clandestine meeting in Upper Dunsforth, it is our belief that they may be planning a heinous crime."

There was still no change of expression from the constable.

"You will, no doubt, be aware that residing at the Queen Hotel is one of the richest women in England? And we believe that she may be their target. I am sure you will understand that this is a delicate matter and with political relations between our two countries strained, we need to tread carefully, as for the moment we cannot prove any of it."

"Then why are you telling me?" enquired the constable.

"Because you need to have your wits about you, sir, and be ready to act at a moment's notice," I said authoritatively.

Constable Hardisty smiled but it was not a warm and friendly smile, being more of a mocking and arrogant sneer.

"You haven't been to any of our race meetings, have you Captain?" To which I acknowledged that was true.

"You see, if you had, you wouldn't make such an ill-informed statement. You cavalry toffs think you know it all," he said, displaying total contempt for my warning whilst trumpeting his own superior understanding of Harrogate's race meetings.

He then rocked back on his heels with the thumbs of both hands tucked inside his belt and continued to preach.

"Tomorrow morning the town will start filling up and those coming will be mainly what you would call your lower classes. They will head straight for the inns and any hostelry that will sell drink. Added to which, we will have every gambler, circus act and peddler arriving from all parts of Yorkshire. And you advise me to keep my wits about me. Do me a favour, Captain, stick to your Russians and keep out of my way. The sooner you get back to London, the better. Now, if you don't mind I have got a lot of tax collecting to account for," and with that the constable led me back to the door of his house.

"You would be wise to take heed of my warning, constable. If anything happens to Miss Coutts tomorrow, you will face some uncomfortable questions from the town's elders. The adverse publicity that such a crime will bring, could destroy Harrogate," I said, still standing in his doorway.

Again Constable Hardisty was unmoved. "Is that all?" he said with his hand on the door he was itching to close. "My dinner is ready and, if you don't mind, I'd like to eat it before it goes cold."

"No, I am afraid it's not all and I regret that your dinner may be waiting. However, last night the infamous Tom Dawson ambushed me with two others outside the Dragon and only the quick thinking of Major Phillips averted a serious situation."

"Doesn't sound like Tom Dawson, are you certain it was him?" he asked.

"Of course I am certain!" I snapped back, growing increasingly irritated at the constable's inane attempts at law enforcement.

"And before you close the door on me, there is another person you need to keep an eye out for and that is an Irishman called Richard Dunn. He's aged around thirty, about my height; dark haired, unshaven, dishevelled, dressed in black and seemingly penniless. Somehow I feel he is involved in a plot against Miss Coutts."

"Captain, I am the sole custodian of the law in Harrogate and there is not even a night watchman who can support me. This is a quiet town and I get the impression that you're a bit of a trouble maker. I have come across you military types before. Not happy unless you have a battle to fight and I am having none of it. The sooner you are out of this town the better. And now, if you'll excuse me, I am going to eat my dinner."

The constable commenced closing the door but before it was closed I shouted back one last thing.

"Just supposing we catch someone attempting to commit a crime against Miss Coutts, where would you detain him as I can see no prison cells?"

"You won't see any, Captain, because there aren't any. Like I said, this is a quiet town. On the rare occasion I have to arrest anyone, we have to hold them here in our out-building until we can get them to York."

"Thank you, constable," I replied, trying to rise above his surly attitude. Without anything more being said, the door to the constable's house slammed firmly shut.

"Cretin," I muttered to myself at his unhelpful behaviour.

It was clear that if we caught anyone attempting to abduct Miss Coutts, we would have to escort them all the way to York ourselves. As sure as night follows day, Harrogate's esteemed law enforcement official will be about as much use to us as a pair of spectacles on a blind man.

Chapter 23

I came away from the constable's house feeling more than a little aggrieved at his lack of co-operation. I resolved to dispatch his disparaging comments to the sewer, just where they belonged. It was bad enough that he had shown no interest in my own abduction, yet to ignore the threat of the same fate when it concerns the richest woman in England was incredulous. Harry had been waiting patiently outside and after driving me to the Queen, I asked him to take a message to Reeves requesting that he join Sinderby-Smythe and myself for an important meeting. Harry was to watch out for the Russians in place of Reeves. If we were going to avert a kidnapping, it was crucial we made some robust plans, and urgently.

Reeves arrived at the Queen in a hansom cab and I met him outside just where Harry had dropped me. I had preferred to wait in the invigorating Harrogate air, affording me the opportunity of smoking a cigar whilst marshalling my thoughts into some sort of order. Having successfully achieved the latter, I put out my cigar whereupon Reeves and I walked briskly into the hotel in search of Sinderby-Smythe. Happily there had been no sign of anyone watching the hotel and the odious Dawson was nowhere to be seen.

Our esteemed lieutenant was easy to find as he continued to patrol the corridors with a resolute determination.

"Gentleman, we need to make urgent plans for tomorrow, so let us withdraw to the lieutenant's room with haste," I asserted.

We took care to leave the door slightly ajar in order to keep an ear out for any sound of trouble. I reached for the timetables we had obtained from Mr Palliser and pulled out of my jacket the map of northern England which I had borrowed earlier from my aunt's library. I placed these down on the small dining table.

"It goes without saying that our first priority, gentlemen, is to make sure Miss Coutts is safe at all times. I will be with her whenever possible, although I am counting on you, Lieutenant Sinderby-Smythe, to remain with her no matter what, even if your bladder explodes."

Sinderby-Smythe winced at my remark, unwittingly crossing his legs in the process.

"Reeves, you and Harry will stick close to the Russians. Never, I repeat, never let them out of your sight. If we are to believe what we have been told, they will be on the move tomorrow and if you do see them leaving send Harry to find me, but wherever they go you must follow. Whilst you watch them, we will ensure Miss Coutts remains safe and unharmed at all times. It's hard to see how they could whisk her away with us by her side surrounded by thousands of race goers. However, if something goes wrong and they manage to snatch her from under our noses, then we need to catch them, and quickly! Which brings us to our dilemma should those unfortunate events occur. Where on earth are they planning on taking her?"

I walked over to the decanter on the side table and poured myself a glass of Sinderby-Smythe's red wine. I gestured to the other two to feel free to do likewise but they both declined.

We looked over the timetables and plotted the two most likely routes on the map. Whether they were heading east to Europe or west to the Americas and beyond, it seemed more than likely that they would firstly head to Leeds. If they left in the morning, they could catch a coach from either the Promenade or the Brunswick Hotel. There was also the Royal Mail coach which left from Gascoigne's Hotel. In the afternoon there was just the one coach to Leeds which was the Newcastle to Leeds line leaving at two o'clock, again from Gascoigne's. But surely they would only use a public coach if they were heading to Europe to buy rail parts, in which case there would be nothing for us to be concerned about. In any event, if their plan was to whisk away the richest woman in England then without doubt, they would take a private carriage.

We all poured over the map which looked very much like a foreign country to Sinderby-Smythe. He appeared to be greatly amused by some of the names given to northern towns especially, Ramsbottom and Hawes, guffawing loudly at the suggestion that the latter must be an ideal place to visit.

Were it not for the serious nature of our meeting, I may have smiled too. We then tried to envisage how the Russians would make their way to Liverpool should the unthinkable happen. I looked at the timetables for the North West and could see that the steam locomotive from Manchester to Liverpool, being a journey of little more than twenty miles, would take no time at all. If they made it to Liverpool, I reckoned that they would be as good as lost to us. Consequently it stood to reason that if the Russians escaped our clutches in Harrogate, we

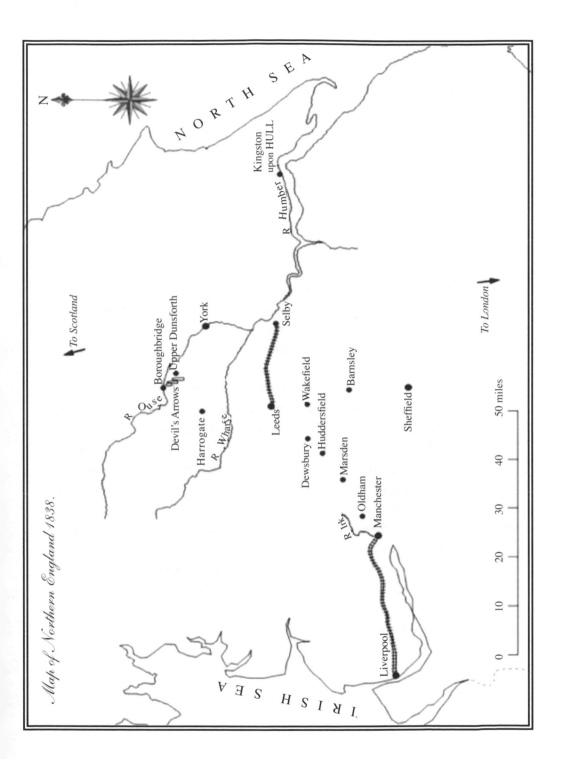

Map of Northern England 1838.

NORTH SEA

IRISH SEA

N

To Scotland

To London

Kingston upon HULL

R Humber

Selby

York

Boroughbridge

Devil's Arrows

Upper Dunsforth

R Ouse

R Wharfe

Harrogate

Leeds

Wakefield

Dewsbury

Huddersfield

Barnsley

Marsden

Sheffield

Oldham

Manchester

R Irk

Liverpool

0   10   20   30   40   50 miles

203

would need to apprehend them long before they reached that railway station in Manchester.

It was then that I recalled Lord Redmayne hailed from Lancashire and that he had furnished me with his card. "I seem to remember that Lord Redmayne has an estate over that way," I added.

"He does indeed, sir," said Reeves, "I know it well."

"You do?" I replied, pleasantly surprised.

"Yes sir, my father managed the Hopwood Hall Estate which is nearby and so I spent a lot of my formative years in that neck of the woods."

I trusted that I would not be in need of His Lordship's assistance. All the same, it was reassuring to know there was at least one person we could rely on should we ever be travelling that far west.

In the unlikely event that we needed to give chase, I decided to ask Benson to arrange for three mounts to be situated close at hand. The saddle bags would be fully stocked with provisions sufficient for us to travel all the way to Liverpool if necessary. Yet again, I reminded both officers to have their pistols with them at all times, and loaded.

"Not only will we have the Russians to deal with, but once we reach Leeds we may also have Chartists to contend with! Having glanced at their newspaper, it looks very much like they are spoiling for a fight. On the other hand the good news is that there are two troops of the 15th Hussars based at the Chapeltown barracks in Leeds and, although they have their hands full with the civil unrest, we should find some support there. Additionally, should Miss Coutts be abducted, letters will be dispatched to the garrison commander at York and more importantly, one to Lord Palmerston in London. I will write these overnight and leave them with Benson to post."

"Excuse me sir. If there are two troops of the 15th Hussars in Leeds why not write to them instead of the garrison at York?" said Reeves.

"Because it's almost certain that anyone fleeing Harrogate will initially head south, in which case we will arrive in Leeds faster than any letter. Additionally with the 15th Hussars battling Chartists between Leeds and Manchester, the garrison in York is more likely to be able to spare a greater number of men," I replied.

"These Chartists need dealing with sir, I hear there are thousands upon thousands of them in the industrial areas," remarked Sinderby-Smythe.

"I take it you have no sympathy for their cause?" I replied, probing the lieutenant's remark.

"Quite the contrary. I have sympathy for the fact that the voting system is still in need of reform. It can't be fair that only one in five men in this country are eligible to vote and it's equally wrong that six people can elect two members of parliament as is still the case in some areas. Equal votes and equal constituencies and secret ballots seem reasonable and will surely come sooner or later but I don't hold with some of the other Chartist demands. Paying elected members of parliament £500 a year, when at present they are content to serve without pay, seems ludicrous. So I suppose I do have some sympathy for Chartism and yet I have no sympathy for them when they resort to violence. After what happened in France at the end of the last century, I worry that we may be heading that way ourselves," preached Sinderby-Smythe, impressing us all with his grasp of politics.

"Your fears are shared by many in government, which I feel sure contributed to the massacre at Peterloo and more recently the battle of Bossenden Wood. The troops are called out the minute it looks like any sort of revolt is in the offing, to nip it in the bud," I replied.

"In which direction do the Chartists pose the greatest threat to us, sir, west to Manchester and Liverpool or east to Kingston upon Hull?" questioned Reeves.

"From what I understand I would say west to Manchester and Liverpool by some considerable margin. I read in the *Northern Star* that there is talk of a meeting at a place called Hartshead Moor where they are expecting over two hundred thousand people to gather! And unfortunately my instincts tell me that these Russians will head in whatever direction will present us with the most problems and so I fear they will head west. Why else would the man the Russians met at the Plough Inn have railway timetables from Manchester together with sailing times from Liverpool?"

"Yes, Captain, I can see your logic. But in the event that Miss Coutts is abducted, isn't there also a chance that they will hide somewhere locally whilst waiting for their ransom demands to be met before making their escape?"

"Yes, that is possible," I acknowledged.

"If Lord Palmerston is right, sir, the Russians will want to hold Miss Coutts in order to gain access to the British Embassy's banking records and the like, which will surely take time to obtain. And doesn't it follow that, under those circumstances, the Russians will need a safe hideaway whilst they wait?"

Reeves had a point. If that was the Russians' plan, the bank would be in a devil of a quandary, as in safeguarding the life of Miss Coutts, they could be endangering many others. A daunting prospect.

"Then there is Theodore Botterill," I added. "We established from Mr Palliser that he is an engineer from Sheffield. Some sort of inventor, I think he said. I wonder why the Russians mentioned him?"

"Didn't Reeves say that the Russians referred to a loan in the same breath as Mr Botterill?" enquired Sinderby-Smythe.

"That's right, I did," confirmed Reeves.

"Perhaps this Botterill fellow may be connected to the bank in some way?" suggested Sinderby-Smythe.

"That's possible, lieutenant. But the loan could be with any bank or any individual."

"How can we find out more about this engineer before tomorrow?" asked Reeves.

"Unfortunately, I suspect that nothing can be done in the time allowed," I said.

"Could this Botterill chap be providing the safe house in Sheffield?" asked Sinderby-Smythe.

"Again, that's possible, I suppose. In which case they could be heading not just east or west but possibly even south!"

"If Botterill is an engineer, he might simply be helping Von Benckendorff on some aspect of the railway," suggested Reeves intelligently.

"That would explain everything, in which case we are making a deal of fuss over nothing. All the same, the fact that there was mention of him having financial problems, leads me to be sceptical. There are just too many unanswered questions, not only concerning the Russians but also the Irishman, and Dawson too. We are just going to have to keep our wits about us, gentleman, and whatever happens tomorrow we must guard Miss Coutts with our lives. For us to allow the Russians to slip through our hands and make off with her is simply unthinkable."

The two officers acknowledged their responsibilities following which I brought our meeting to an end. I was content that we were taking precautions against every conceivable eventuality. Sinderby-Smythe returned to the corridors of the Queen and continued to keep a close watch on Miss Coutts. She would undoubtedly want to take the waters at the sulphur well in the morning, nonetheless barring the resurrection of Madame Beaumont, she should at least be safe for now. Happily the next ball in Harrogate would be at the Granby following tomorrow's race meeting, which hopefully reduced the opportunities or the temptation for Miss Coutts to assume another identity. At some point

I would have a private discussion with her in order to prepare her for all eventualities. All things considered, I decided to leave that conversation until the morning and by so doing, allow her a trouble free evening. There was no point everyone having a disturbed night at the prospect of foul play.

Reeves and I jumped into a waiting carriage outside the Queen and headed for the Crown whereupon Reeves would relieve Harry of the vital task of monitoring the Russians.

"If everything remains quiet tonight Reeves, Harry can take your place in the morning and I suggest you come to Holderness House for breakfast which will also allow us the opportunity of a final briefing. Please arrive early as I must also see Miss Coutts before the day gets fully underway."

"Thank you, sir," said Reeves. "By the way, good luck for tomorrow's race, Captain. Has Tribune a good chance?"

"I have no idea really," reflecting for the first time in a while on my trusted horse. What had seemed like a good idea at the outset was now anything but that.

"The race card doesn't tell us much about the opposition, but there aren't many horses that can beat Tribune over two and a half miles," I replied, attempting to show some enthusiasm.

We arrived at the Crown Hotel and Reeves smiled politely as he jumped out of the carriage and, in the fading light, went inside. The carriage then took me the short distance up the hill back to Holderness House with Harry following on. I looked through the window of the carriage to see the western sky glowing red. A good omen for a nice day ahead, or at least that's what I hoped.

I alighted by the gates of the house, paid the driver and went in search of my aunt whilst Harry went round to the kitchen to be attended to by Mrs Parker, the cook. I found my aunt in the orangery, where she had been waiting for some time.

"George, how are you?" she said. "It is so good to see you. I have missed you!" And then beckoned me to sit beside her.

"You look concerned, my boy. Is everything alright?"

"Everything is coming to a head, Aunt. I don't suppose you have any news for me?" I asked, more in hope than expectation.

My aunt obliged me by recounting the details of her meeting with Henry Payden which amounted to something of a tea party to celebrate the completion of the Yorkshire Railways share issue. Such was the appeal of this venture that they had apparently raised over two hundred thousand pounds. Despite the innocent nature of the tea party, I suspected that Mr Payden was hoping to spend a good deal more time with my aunt.

"Well, Mr Payden is a charming man don't you think?" she paused looking at me to nod in agreement, which I did, adding a robust, "absolutely," for good measure.

She seemed amused by this, which had me wondering about the possible plans that could be developing in her mind. Whatever those were I felt sure she would not be heading in any direction that she didn't want to.

"You will be pleased to know that my afternoon wasn't entirely wasted in idle gossip. Henry told me some news which I think will interest you. Vladimir Von Benckendorff and his wife can't abide horse racing. Strange I know, but they are foreigners. Consequently they are leaving Harrogate sometime tomorrow and sailing to Europe. Apparently Vladimir will be negotiating to buy steel and other such paraphernalia for the railway."

At which point I smiled. "I don't know all the technical terms, George, I have received no tutelage in the workings of a railway although I feel sure you get my point. I can tell by the smirk on your face." Her perception was right, for which I apologised.

"Apparently these items are required urgently as they anticipate receiving parliamentary approval for the railway very soon indeed."

My aunt had exceeded my expectations as usual, although I was puzzled by two things.

"Europe? Are you sure?" I said, being my first question.

"That's what he said," replied my aunt.

"And how on earth can they be getting parliamentary approval that quickly? I recall Mr Beales advising us that they had it well in hand, all the same I took that to be bluster. No-one gets anything through parliament so soon."

I was perplexed by this but did not want to alarm my aunt, particularly given the possibility that the conversation Reeves had overheard was innocent enough and we had leapt to the wrong conclusion. Nevertheless, there were too many things pointing to the Russians leaving with Miss Coutts. After all, if everything was so innocent why have a secret meeting in the middle of nowhere? Why did they mention the notorious Count Zadovich, valuable merchandise, Theodore Botterill and, most significantly, an additional lady passenger? To say nothing of the Irishman and Dawson.

"I don't suppose they mentioned an engineer from Sheffield called Theodore Botterill?" I asked speculatively.

"Actually," she said thinking hard, "That's not a name I recall. And now George, what news do you have for me? How is your flower girl? Blossoming I trust?" she said with a wicked grin.

"Very droll, Aunt," I said, smiling at her witticism. "However I regret to report that I am no longer in favour with the lady in question. My endeavours over the last few days have brought me into contact with certain people who did not meet with her approval. It seems that she would prefer no further contact with me."

"Oh dear," she replied with genuine feeling. "If I were you, my boy, I would forget about all these women. Miss Angela Coutts is the girl for you."

"I think it's time to ready myself for supper, Aunt," I said, changing the subject and rising from my seat.

I left my aunt with her provocative statement unanswered and headed back to my room. As I walked towards the main staircase I was stopped by Benson, who with his usual elegance handed me two letters on a silver salver.

The first was from my favourite Lord in the foreign office. After establishing whether I was reading every second, third or fourth word, I deciphered his instructions using our trusted code. It seemed Lord Palmerston did not believe that the Von Benckendorff's were rail experts. His enquiries failed to find any evidence to support their claims of having being involved on the Tsarskoye Selo Railway. It transpired that an Austrian called Franz Gertner advised the Russians on that one. His Lordship urged caution and ordered that we seek assistance from the local garrisons should any attempt be made to abduct Miss Coutts.

The second letter was in a lady's handwriting and from the Granby Hotel. It was from the Duchess of Aldborough. It simply read as follows:

My dearest George,

I have missed you and hope I shall see you at tomorrow's racing. Please be careful, not all is as it seems. I can't tell you any more, but please take great care.

With love,
Mary, Duchess of Aldborough

That was all I needed! Another dissected map. I had to trawl the depths of my memory to recollect what she told me that night in her room. If my memory served me right, she had said that her husband, the Duke, was spending time with Lord Garraty, the man I exposed for cheating at Gordon's club. Equally worrying was the fact that these two were seemingly friendly with Sir William

Hamilton, who hated me with a vengeance. Did she mean that the railway was just an elaborate hoax? What else could she mean? I read her letter repeatedly for answers but they were not forthcoming.

I went downstairs for supper with my aunt, but rather than raise concerns over our investments in the railway, I steered the conversation towards tomorrow's racing. We discussed her plans for the day which, unsurprisingly, included Mr Payden. I invited them both to join myself, Miss Coutts and Miss Meredith in the grandstand. As the owner of a horse in the top race, I had been sent tickets for admission to the grandstand sufficient for us all. Given that the grandstand was a temporary structure, I was not expecting anything overly grand.

Mrs Parker had once again excelled herself at supper, however I regrettably failed to do justice to her fine cooking. My stomach was starting to churn. I attempted to settle my inners with a brandy but in the end retired to my room. I looked out of my bedroom window and across the Stray to see a handful of hazy lights dotted randomly about the houses on Prospect Place.

It was a dark night causing these mellow lights to glow more brightly. I prayed that we would all stay safe and hoped the Russians would leave tomorrow without incident, before retiring to my bed and attempting to sleep.

Chapter 24

After some overnight rain, I rose to a remarkably fine day in Harrogate. The ground would be ideal for racing, not too firm and not too soft. I was out of bed the instant the sun came up, having lain awake most of the night mulling over all the various outcomes and possibilities, often leading to a grizzly end.

I cleaned my pistols and wrote letters to Palmerston and the garrison at York, which I would leave with Benson. I had also asked him to arrange for three mounts loaded with provisions, to be tethered near the racecourse and ready at a moment's notice. "Are you expecting trouble, Captain?" questioned Benson.

"Certainly not, Benson. It's just a precaution. That's what they teach us in the Light Dragoons. It's all in the planning," I said, dismissing the matter as if I hadn't a care in the world.

"Would you also make sure that these timetables and maps are placed in the saddle bags on one of the mounts?" I said, passing him the assortment of information I had acquired over the last couple of days.

"You might also consider packing a change of clothing, Captain. Mr Phillipson, the gardener, tells me that we can expect rain over the next few days."

"Thank you, Benson, I will do that," and then headed to the stables.

Tribune looked in fine shape and my aunt had dug out some old family colours for our jockey to wear, which were gold stars on a maroon background.

Reeves arrived early in order to finalise our plans for the day.

Apparently, the Russians visited the house of Gerald Beales again last night, presumably for dinner and most intriguingly, the same attractive girl who had visited Beales the previous evening sneaked in after the Russians had left.

"It would appear that our friend, Beales, has a secret lover after all," I said, expressing the surprise we both felt.

We then made our way to the dining room and breakfast with my aunt.

"I trust everyone is looking forward to seeing Tribune run as much as I am," she said, greeting our arrival.

"Absolutely," I lied.

"It should be the highlight of the day," suggested Reeves politely.

"The weather looks perfect for racing," enthused my aunt.

"It certainly does, although according to your gardener we can expect rain over the next few days," I added.

"What possessed you to discuss the weather with my gardener?" she enquired somewhat puzzled at the mention of her most prized aide.

"The information was given to me by Benson, Aunt."

"Well, if Mr Phillipson is predicting rain, then rain it will," she asserted.

The conversation between the three of us remained innocuous as we were all preoccupied with the day ahead. With no appetite for breakfast or to linger unnecessarily, we were soon heading our own separate ways.

Immediately after breakfast, I walked over to the Queen whilst Reeves headed back to the Crown and my aunt remained at Holderness House. It was essential that Reeves remained in close proximity to the Russians all the while they remained in Harrogate, and I needed one last meeting with Sinderby-Smythe to ensure we were all working to the same plan. Reeves was a very impressive young man but Sinderby-Smythe continued to worry me, as it appeared that half the time his mind was not in the same territory as his body. However, when he was in tune with the rest of us, he seemed extremely capable. Reeves told me that Sinderby-Smythe had been pressed into joining the cavalry by his father who'd served with Wellington at Waterloo. That probably accounted for his indifference at times, which I hoped would not be in evidence today of all days.

Even though the first race was still several hours away, the town was bustling with activity. Vehicles of all descriptions were arriving from every point of the compass, in addition to pedestrians and equestrians of every grade. The moment the course came into view I could see that it was in excellent condition. The overnight rain had breathed new life into the lush grass with each blade now standing upright and majestic, like a large green army of soldiers on parade.

The grandstand stood proud with brightly coloured flags flying on each corner, bolstered by the gentle morning breeze. There were countless booths and tents of all sizes and conditions from a spacious pavilion for the gentry to the tattered tents for the less affluent. Yet flags flew from them all. There was a gap between the tents and the pavilion which had been reserved for carriages. All in all, it presented a magnificent sight and a slight shiver of excitement ran through my body as my thoughts momentarily turned to Tribune. Having safely negotiated the busy streets, I arrived at the Queen and found Sinderby-Smythe in a chair in the corridor near the rooms of Miss Coutts.

"Good morning, Sinderby. All's well I trust?" prompting the lieutenant to stand to attention. His blonde foppish hair was looking slightly askew, something he tried to rectify as I put him at his ease.

"Yes, sir, absolutely, and a very good morning to you too, sir," came his almost excited response.

"Have you been here all night man?"

"Well, yes sir. Ever since Miss Coutts gave me the slip, I thought it best," he replied.

"Good man," I said, genuinely impressed with his commitment to the cause.

"But when do you sleep?"

"I get a bit in here and there, sir. It's not a problem, sir," he reasoned.

"Didn't sleep much myself either," I replied, empathising with him.

"Well, today's the big day, or at least that's what we suspect. Let's step outside. We can talk more privately there." We then walked out of the Queen and past the obnoxious Dawson who had the look of a man who knew something that we didn't. Could he be involved with Von Benckendorff? But if so, how? Nevertheless the presence of Dawson encouraged us to move well away from the hotel, with its ever growing queue of carriages and carts.

I went through all our plans one last time, stressing the need to keep our wits about us every step of the way.

"If the day proceeds without incident we will reconvene here after the last race by which time, hopefully, the Russians will have left Harrogate, taking all threats to Miss Coutts with them. Then we will celebrate in style at the Granby tonight. My treat!"

Sinderby-Smythe seemed pleased with this plan, which was designed to give us all something to look forward to. There was nothing more that we could usefully discuss and it was time for us both to press on, nonetheless, there was one last thing to say.

"Good luck today, lieutenant."

To which he replied with sincerity, "Thank you, sir and the same to you."

Before we went our separate ways, I looked across the Stray to where we had previously seen the stalker. He may have been there, but with so many people walking and riding towards the racecourse, it was impossible to see clearly. However, the mere thought that he could be watching us served as a timely warning.

"Remember that there may be someone across the Stray watching us. Mark him carefully, lieutenant. I do not know what his role is in all of this but whatever it is, I suspect it will not be to our liking."

With those parting words, Sinderby-Smythe resumed his guard duty in the corridors of the Queen and I took the opportunity to seek out Miss Coutts.

I was shown into her private parlour by Emily who seemed quite excited by the hive of activity in and around the hotel. Happily, I found Miss Coutts in surprisingly good humour. Having Miss Meredith, her companion, to keep her company in addition to taking the waters each day seemed to have lifted her spirits enormously. Due to the unfortunate threat the Russians posed, I sensed that my presence often darkened her mood, as I was continually the bearer of bad news.

I endeavoured to reassure her that we would keep her safe at all times and that, in all probability, nothing untoward would happen. However, I would be failing in my duty if I didn't take whatever precautions may be required in order to protect her.

"Lieutenant Sinderby-Smythe and I will be by your side throughout the day and 2nd Lieutenant Reeves will also be in close support. We will all be armed and ready to deal with any eventuality," I said confidently.

"That is good to know, Captain. Even though the thought of needing an armed guard simply to watch a horse race is disappointing in the extreme. Do you really expect someone to attempt something sinister at these races?"

Lying through my teeth I answered with a robust, "Of course not, but I have orders from Lord Palmerston and he'd have my guts for garters if I failed you in any way."

On a more trivial matter, I told her that she need not concern herself regarding entrance tickets to the grandstand and pavilion as I would bring those when I came for her, which would be shortly before the races commenced. With the course virtually on the doorstep, it seemed sensible for her to remain safely watching proceedings from her window until the last possible minute. Despite being a little disappointed at this suggestion, she gracefully submitted to my request.

"Very well, Captain, although I wondered if we might impose on you to allow us one more ticket in order to accommodate a friend of my father's who would very much like to join us."

"Certainly, Miss Coutts," I replied.

"I think you might have already met my friend," she said, which was a little unsettling given the dubious nature of some of the people I had met recently.

"His name is Major Phillips and he is here at the request of my father," she said.

"Ah yes, I have met the Major. Excellent!" I said, expressing relief whilst also wondering if it was purely a coincidence that he was on hand to assist me at the Dragon when Dawson and his cohorts sought to beat me to a pulp.

Miss Coutts then assured me, quite sensibly, that she would not be taking the waters this morning due to the large amount of additional visitors the race meeting had brought into town. Unsurprisingly, I was relieved to hear this. With everything settled I left Miss Coutts with Miss Meredith and made my way back to Holderness House. It was time for me to make my own last minute preparations for the races and anything else fate may decide to throw my way.

I was tempted to see Reeves again before going back to my aunt's but time was pressing and I had every confidence that he would have everything under control. The early morning chill of this August day had been replaced by warm sunshine and I could feel the temperature begin to rise on the short walk to Holderness House. This upturn in the weather would make it inappropriate for me to wear an overcoat, thereby making it much harder to conceal my pistols.

Back in my room, I repeatedly adjusted my jacket in order to hide the evidence of these weapons. However, for them to remain completely hidden, I would need to keep my arms down by my side wherever possible. This prompted me to contemplate wearing a cloak, which I rejected for being equally uncomfortable in the heat. Eventually I settled on wearing the largest jacket I had brought with me, which just about covered the pistols whilst also allowing me some freedom of movement. With my Joseph Manning knife tucked in my boot, I was as prepared as I was ever going to be.

I then went down to the stables where I found Tribune being groomed. He looked every inch the thoroughbred I believed him to be. His race wasn't until three o'clock, but the first race started at one and so we would take him across to the course around two, giving him just enough time to acclimatise to all the noise. I would meet the jockey at the course and give him his final instructions then.

Tribune had been entered into the top race of the day, being over two and a half miles and called the Harrogate Handicap Stakes. Although Tribune had not won any official races, he had won many a race in the Light Dragoons and so I took a voluntary penalty of eight pounds of extra weight which may prove too much for him. But if Tribune was to win without being handicapped, I ran the risk of being labelled a cheat and having caught Lord Garraty cheating at Gordon's in London, the last thing I needed was reputational damage. Entering a horse into these races was intended to be a pleasant diversion from the trials of late and in no way did I wish the race to be taken too seriously. Given the way events had unfolded, it was a decision I now regretted.

My aunt intended to travel to the racecourse in her carriage and I understood that Mr Payden would be joining her, confirming that the two of them appeared intent on spending more time in each other's company. I was going to walk across to the Queen and escort Miss Coutts to the grandstand along with Lieutenant Sinderby-Smythe. Reeves was to wait at the Crown until the Russians had left town and young Harry, much to his dismay, was to stay close to Reeves in order to pass messages to myself or Sinderby-Smythe if the need arose.

Before I knew it mid-day had arrived and it was time for me to move across to the Queen. I had heard nothing from Reeves or Harry, which implied that the Russians still remained in Harrogate. There were many ways they could leave and, should our fears of abductions be unfounded, I now suspected they would leave on the afternoon stage coach, scheduled to coincide with the start of the big race. If our fears were realised then I felt sure they would take a private carriage and also leave around this time. I marched across the Stray and the closer I came to the Queen, the more people I encountered. Harrogate was overflowing with persons of all classes making their way to the course. A number already walked in a manner resembling a sailor on the deck of a ship in rough seas. There were soldiers in uniform, farm workers in their Sunday best, to say nothing of the colourful spectacle of acrobats and jugglers. Many residents had chosen to walk to the course and it was a veritable sea of top hats and bonnets.

Once I arrived at the Queen, I looked across the Stray for any sign of the stalker. Maybe he was mingling with the crowds or perhaps he was conspiring with the Russians, as he was nowhere to be seen. Either way, I felt sure that we hadn't seen the last of him.

The hotel was even busier than it was this morning. I had never seen it so full of activity, which made it all the more surprising that Dawson was nowhere in sight. The more the day progressed, the more unease I felt, bringing back memories of patrolling bandit country in India. You knew something could happen at any moment, but all you could do was keep your wits about you and wait. It was the total lack of control which unnerved me the most.

I went in search of Sinderby-Smythe who had the look of a man riding alongside me on that same patrol in India. There were no formal greetings or exchanges – we both just nodded to each other.

I knocked on the door to Miss Coutts' room which was answered by her maid Emily. She too, was dressed for the occasion in her Sunday best. The lieutenant and I were shown into the parlour and asked to wait. Moments later Miss Coutts and Miss Meredith arrived looking captivating. Miss Coutts was dressed in cream whilst Miss Meredith wore golden yellow. Both dresses were heavily laced and both wore splendid summer bonnets.

I immediately felt that Sinderby-Smythe and I should have been in uniform, but that would have made hiding our pistols even more difficult, if not impossible. Anyway, we both sported top hats and, in truth, were still as well-dressed as anyone. And so, following an exchange of pleasantries, we were all ready to make our way to the racecourse.

Chapter 25

Sinderby-Smythe and I accompanied the ladies out of their rooms and down the stairs into the reception area of the hotel, which was now bustling with activity. Major Phillips was apparently meeting us at the course, prompting Miss Coutts to request that we left his tickets with Dawson. My adversary had now reappeared and proceeded to fuss around Miss Coutts whilst completely ignoring myself and Sinderby-Smythe. With the course less than one hundred yards away, we opted to walk. Given the threat of Miss Coutts being abducted, this was far from ideal. However, we made the journey in a matter of minutes and soon found ourselves in the comparative safety of the pavilion tent adjacent to the grandstand.

A good number of the local nobility were already gathered there, all splendidly dressed. Many others chose to stay in their own carriages, affording them the equivalent of a private box at the theatre, in addition to an excellent view of the finishing line. One carriage in particular caught my eye and that was the one occupied by the Earl of Warkworth, Lord and Lady Asenby and of course Mary, Duchess of Aldborough. Following the arrival of my aunt and Mr Payden, we found ourselves being introduced to a good number of the local dignitaries. Despite all Lord Redmayne's efforts to conceal Miss Coutts's presence in Harrogate, few of the people we encountered seemed surprised to meet her. Sinderby-Smythe and I stepped back from any further interaction and stayed by the entrance to the pavilion, both keeping a keen eye on Miss Coutts and all who came near her. It was good to see my aunt striking up a conversation with her, although I did cringe at the prospect of her matchmaking. Everyone seemed content with proceedings thus far and showed no sign of any sinister motives. I continually put my head outside the pavilion watching the comings and goings around all areas of the course. I saw a multitude of entertainers with crowds circling their makeshift arenas and countless race-goers drinking and discussing the day's racing.

There was the humming sound of excited chatter which grew as more and

more people arrived at the course. I asked Sinderby-Smythe to keep his eyes firmly on Miss Coutts whilst I kept searching for any signs of trouble. I couldn't help envying the city of Leeds with the army of constables they had to call on, whereas we had effectively none. With a crowd of this size we were hopelessly undermanned. Nevertheless, at that moment my spirits rose a notch when Major Phillips arrived looking positively splendid in the uniform of his Lancashire regiment.

"Captain Townsend," he said, thrusting his hand towards me, "how simply wonderful to see you again and thank you so much for gaining me access to these impressive facilities."

"It is the least I can do, sir. Without your help outside the Dragon, I suspect someone might have been seriously hurt, perhaps even me," prompting us to both laugh in unison.

"Who were those rascals, Captain, and what were they after?" he then asked.

"That's a good question, Major. One which I cannot answer with any great certainty. Although there is no doubting that the main protagonist was a chap called Dawson, who works at the Queen Hotel. Believe it or not, he was the person from whom you should have collected your tickets earlier today."

"You mean the chap at the Queen Hotel was amongst those three ruffians who accosted you outside the Dragon?"

"The ring leader, no less," I replied emphatically.

"You astound me, Captain! I would never have recognised him. So what possessed him to carry out such a cowardly act?" asked the Major.

"It would seem that he took exception to my striking up a friendship with a young lady of this parish."

"Oh, I see," said the Major with a knowing glance.

"In any event, Major, I am still indebted to you and, perhaps later today, I can buy you that drink I promised?"

"I shall look forward to that, Captain," he replied, whereupon he walked past me and moved over to where Miss Coutts and Miss Meredith were still talking to my aunt and Mr Payden. The mention of that evening at the Dragon reminded me of Virginia, and I so hoped that after the Russians had left I would see her again. I resumed my surveillance of the crowds from the safety of the pavilion and when I looked in the direction of the carriages, I caught sight of the Duchess of Aldborough laughing with the Earl of Warkworth. She didn't see me but the sight of her had me thinking about the letter she'd sent me last night. I took it out of my jacket and once again scrutinised the wording, 'not all is as it seems'. In other words, trust no-one. I looked back inside the pavilion and saw the Major had joined in the conversation with my aunt, Henry Payden, Miss Coutts and Miss Meredith. Could it be that the Duchess's message was warning me about the Major?

I stepped over to Lieutenant Sinderby-Smythe and said, "Keep a close eye on the Major, Sinderby. Even though he unquestionably did me a good turn the other evening, we know very little about him."

Time soon passed and most of those in the pavilion stepped outside to watch the runners and riders parade themselves ahead of the first race. This was the two year old stakes and there were some remarkably good horses on display, in spite of the fact that there were only three of them. The race was over three quarters of a mile and would amount to nothing more than a quick sprint which would be over in no time. There was much amusement amongst the ladies regarding the horses' names and their colours, which appeared crucial in determining their choice of horse. In the end my aunt plumped for a horse named Augusta, chosen not for its looks or form but because we were in the month of August. A good deal of betting was taking place with some of the men risking quite large amounts due to the low odds on offer.

The runners and riders moved their way onto the track and the crowd vied for the best vantage points. The pavilion emptied as everyone moved over to the grandstand and, all the while our ladies moved from one location to another, Sinderby-Smythe and I needed to be especially watchful. The race eventually started with the three young horses closely bunched throughout the short race. There was never much in it, however Augusta finally came out the winner, much to the delight of my aunt whose wager had been placed at odds of six to four. This added to the general level of excitement which threatened to distract us from the task in hand. I was forever reminding myself to keep a sharp eye open, for at any moment Miss Coutts could be snatched from our grasp. There was still no news from Reeves or Harry and the day's next race passed with my aunt picking the victor yet again. Her winning streak attracted no shortage of admiration from many of those enjoying the festivities in the pavilion, in particular Henry Payden.

Tribune was due to arrive at any moment, and after speaking to Sinderby-Smythe, I stepped out of the pavilion briefly. No sooner had I reached the stabling area when I was hit with an overwhelming fear that something dreadful was about to happen. I chastised myself for such pessimistic thoughts and pressed on to find Tribune looking absolutely splendid, being well cared for by my aunt's groom. I patted Tribune on his neck and spoke to him about the race which might sound like a strange thing to do, but I often did this. I asked the groom to make sure that the jockey sought me out when he arrived in order that I might personally give him his instructions.

Just then, the feeling of trepidation I had felt minutes earlier returned, after which I found myself running back to pavilion. I was being driven by a sixth sense which seemed to be vindicated when I caught sight of Richard Dunn, the Irishman I'd caught sleeping in the small farm building. I felt certain he had been spying on Miss Coutts and it was high time I found out why. I stopped running towards the pavilion and quickly took stock of the situation. If something untoward had happened to Miss Coutts, then surely there would be some sign of trouble. A noise, a shout or a scream. And yet, there was no such indication and all seemed well. The opportunity to interrogate the Irishman presented itself and I wasn't about to miss it. He could hold the key to everything.

The Irishman saw me coming for him and turned tail and ran. He darted through the crowds, around the booths and then out of the course area altogether. I was giving chase for the second time this week, only this time he would not evade me. I caught up with him about two hundred yards from the course as he made for some woods, whereupon I tackled him to the ground. I then sat on him, preventing his escape.

"Now, you have some explaining to do my lad!" I said, catching my breath.

The Irishman was struggling to shake me off, forcing me to lean on him all the harder, to the point where in the end he surrendered and accepted his fate.

"Perhaps you can start by explaining why you keep watching the Queen Hotel? And I want the truth."

"Don't know what you are talking about," grunted Richard Dunn in his strong Irish accent.

I kneeled on him harder and tried to force the words out of him yet, save for the occasional curse, he refused to open his mouth.

I was tempted to threaten him with my knife or my pistols, however, I could tell from the look on his face that he wasn't about to tell me anything. The man looked very determined with a madness in his eyes I had not seen since capturing a demented rebel in India, who later turned out to be much the worse for opium.

Still facing the threat from the Russians, I felt the best thing I could do was to take him back to the racecourse and then try and find the constable who, with luck, could hold him until at least the races were over. Undeterred, I pulled him up and yanked his arm behind his back and marched him towards the course. The ground we had covered in moments whilst we ran was now taking an age as the Irishman twisted and turned every step of the way. I heard the cheers, signalling that another race had been completed which meant that the next race would be the Harrogate Handicap Stakes – our race. Even though I kicked the Irishman hard, encouraging him to move faster, he still made hard work of walking. Finally we reached the stabling area where Tribune had already left for the saddling enclosure.

"Damn you!" I said to the Irishman. "If I miss this next race because of you, I will kick you all the way back to Ireland personally."

We headed for the saddling enclosure and, standing in the centre of the ring looking magnificent was Tribune, together with the jockey and my aunt's groom. I walked over to them still pushing and twisting the Irishman by his arm. I caught the eye of the groom who then led the horse to the edge of the ring and the jockey followed.

"Captain Townsend?" said the jockey looking uncertainly at me and altogether more strangely at the Irishman.

"Don't mind him. He's for the constable. You just worry about getting Tribune across the line first."

"We're up against some very good horses, Captain, and we are carrying an eight pound penalty," replied the jockey.

"Just keep him in touch first time round and aim to get in front about four furlongs from home. If you ask him for everything he's got, he won't let you down and whatever you do, don't use the whip or I'll take it to you."

After which, I wished him luck and pushed the Irishman onwards. I needed to offload him urgently and return to the side of Miss Coutts. I kept asking if anyone had seen Constable Hardisty but with no luck. Furthermore there was still no news from Reeves, which was a greater concern as surely the Russians would have left their hotel by now if they were to catch the afternoon stage coach to Leeds. I prayed I hadn't missed something. It looked increasingly likely that they were taking a private carriage, which would not bode well. Consequently, I kicked the Irishman again for good measure.

We walked past a series of tents on the way to the pavilion as I searched in vain for the constable. We passed a crowd gathered around a pair of jugglers from Spain calling themselves the Treco Brothers. Then there was a booth where some other games of chance were being played. There were tents offering all types of food: Mrs Potter was busy selling her eggs and a Gianni Bernardi was peddling his Italian ice cream. Despite all my searching, there was still no sign of the constable. I dragged the Irishman onwards passing Miss Meredith who was heading in the direction of the Queen. She had a look of distress on her face, as it appeared that punch or red wine had somehow been spilt over her beautiful golden yellow dress. I wanted to call to her to say that she should have someone to accompany her but the Irishman's constant wriggling prevented that. She looked straight past me, clearly concentrating on getting through the crowds with all possible haste. The Irishman almost twisted free at the precise moment we passed a rough looking tent full of even rougher looking race enthusiasts. One of them noticed me and seemed to take an instant dislike to a well-dressed gentleman leading away one of their own, against his will.

"What have we here?" he shouted, which immediately drew the attention of all the tent's occupants. My heart sank when I detected that he spoke with an Irish accent.

"I'm being taken away against my will," squirmed my prisoner. "I've dun nutt'n," he squealed, exaggerating his own Irish accent for all he was worth.

"He's one of us, lads," said one of the many, standing in the tent edging themselves closer.

Things were getting away from me. I needed to be by the side of Miss Coutts and my own horse was about to race. If I stayed and fought a tent full of Irishmen, I would certainly lose and it was no time to show anyone how adept I was with my pistols. It suddenly occurred to me that this whole incident could be a planned diversion intended to prevent me from protecting Miss Coutts. I pushed him towards the tent and said to the occupants, "Here, you have him!" and then ran as fast as my legs would carry me past the line of carriages on the way to the pavilion. Running so quickly necessitated me having to weave in and out of people, much to the amusement of two toffs watching from a carriage.

I arrived back at the pavilion and could see Sinderby-Smythe heave a sigh of relief. All seemed well; I could clearly see Miss Coutts still in conversation with my aunt. The Irishman had not been a planned diversion after all.

"Where have you been, sir?" asked Sinderby-Smythe, appearing concerned at my absence.

"I came across Richard Dunn, that blasted Irishman," I replied and then proceeded to acquaint him with all the relevant details. "Anyway, I am pleased to see that you appear to have everything under control lieutenant"

"Yes, sir," he replied, "although we have lost a couple of guests, as first Mr Payden left when he was called away by one of his staff from the bank. Then some blundering oaf barged into poor Miss Meredith, causing her to lose hold of a glass of fruit punch which ended up over her dress."

"Yes, I saw her heading back to the hotel and, were it not for that damn Irishman, I would have accompanied her. I tried to catch her attention once I was free of him, but, when I looked back for her, she was out of sight," I replied.

"I would have liked to have gone with her, sir, however, I felt it was more important to stay with Miss Coutts," he said with a note of concern in his voice.

"You did the right thing, lieutenant. It's my fault, if it is anyone's. I should have been here to help."

"Any news of Reeves?" I enquired.

"No, sir," said Sinderby-Smythe. We both looked at each other with growing concern.

The main race was almost ready to start and the ladies and gentlemen of the pavilion made their way to the grandstand. My aunt and Miss Coutts sat together, with the Major on their right, his girth providing a substantial shield. I then sat to the left of the ladies, establishing myself and the Major as something akin to two book ends, keeping them well protected. Sinderby-Smythe moved to the rear of the stand, thereby affording him the best view of both the race and the spectators sitting in front of him. I was satisfied that we were deployed in the best possible positions to detect and prevent any trouble.

Miss Coutts turned to my aunt and mentioned her disappointment that Miss

Meredith had not returned in time to see Tribune race, given that she had indicated she was particularly looking forward to it. She added that, such was her confidence in the horse, she had placed a small wager on him. I once again cursed the Irishman, but for chasing him, I would have been able to place a wager of my own.

Looking down towards the start, I could see that Tribune was hopping about a bit. His ears were pricked and his eyes were wide open absorbing all the noise and commotion that surrounds every race. There were five other horses competing in the Harrogate Handicap Stakes and, on listening to the gossip in the pavilion, the horse most likely to threaten Tribune seemed to be View Halloo. The starter then brought the horses under order and they were off. The excitement which prevailed was intoxicating. All five horses were well grouped as they made their way around the course for the first time. Tribune was lying third alongside View Halloo. They completed the first circuit to the intense cheering of the crowd with only one horse struggling to keep pace and he looked like being pulled up. They were now travelling well, and at the turn Tribune still lay third, about a length behind the leader, Little Davie.

The pace picked up and indeed, the back marker who had led at the start, was pulled up. The remaining four horses were all in contention as they reached the half way mark and started to round the course for the second and last time. The whips were now being used to urge on the challengers although Tribune's jockey stuck to his orders and allowed him to run his own race. With just four furlongs remaining Tribune's jockey was pushing him on. His arms moving like pistons, going back and forth like one of Robert Stephenson's steam powered machines. Unfortunately he did not move into the lead, with all the remaining horses still in contention for the sizeable first prize of some fifty sovereigns. Three furlongs out, one of the horses started to lose touch and with only two furlongs to go it was between the local favourite, View Halloo and Tribune. They were both now straining every vessel and searching for that extra strength to see off the other. They were neck and neck as they reached the last furlong and headed for home. The crowd was urging on both animals and View Halloo seemed to drift back a touch, only for a reminder from the jockey's whip to bring him back on level terms. It was going to be close and both my aunt and Miss Coutts were on their feet cheering as the winning post neared.

There was little to choose between them, but at the post Tribune just scraped home. He had done it! My amazing horse had pulled off the most glorious victory and we clapped and cheered him all the way to the winner's enclosure. Thankfully Sinderby-Smythe didn't seem much interested in all this which was fortuitous because had a Russian tried to abduct Miss Coutts during the race, he was all that stood between them. Suddenly everyone was my friend and my hand was shaken countless times on the way over to my victorious horse. What an incredible performance! I was bursting with pride when some Viscount presented me the winning trophy together with a note for fifty sovereigns which I passed to my aunt for safekeeping. Tribune was perspiring heavily, blowing hard with his muscles still twitching, while the groom walked him around to cool him off. A bucket of cold water was poured over him and steam continued to rise from his body. Whilst he was being cooled down, I accompanied Miss Coutts and my aunt to the winner's tent where my hand was shaken countless more times and the champagne flowed freely. Still feeling elated and given that I had Sinderby-Smythe in addition to Major Phillips in close support, I ventured a glass or two of rather fine champagne. I was starting to relax a little, even though I still hadn't had confirmation from Reeves that the Russians had left. I also kept half an eye open for Virginia, in the hope that she could provide the icing on the cake by joining us.

After the level of excitement returned to the more normal levels seen between races, Miss Coutts repeated her concern at Miss Meredith's prolonged absence. I had no wish to leave Sinderby-Smythe on his own for a second time, notwithstanding that he was performing his role admirably. Clearly, if anyone was to look for Miss Meredith, it should be me. I considered asking the Major to carry out the search but the Duchess of Aldborough's warning kept running through my head. Therefore somewhat reluctantly, I made my apologies to everyone, assured Miss Coutts all would be well and then headed back to the Queen Hotel.

Everyone's attention seemed to be on the next race as I walked away from the crowds. There was no sign of Miss Meredith returning to the racecourse and I was beginning to sense trouble.

There was no-one between myself and the Queen when I spotted a donkey cart travelling quickly towards the course. It didn't take me long to make out that it was being driven by young Harry, and Reeves was hanging on tightly as the little cart bounced from side to side.

The last remnants of the euphoria I had felt at Tribune's victory were now replaced by a dark sense of foreboding. The look on their faces gave me the distinct impression that something had gone horribly wrong. Harry spotted me and turned his cart to bring them both alongside me.

"What has happened?" I asked, dreading the answer.

"The Russians were onto us all along, sir. They waited until my back was turned and then two of them jumped me and left me trussed up in a linen cupboard at the Crown. I am sorry sir, I did manage to land a few blows but in end they got the better of me," said Reeves breathing heavily.

"Where have they gone? How did you escape? When did this happen?" the questions raced from my mind to my lips.

"It happened over an hour ago, sir. Young Harry saw the Russians leaving in a carriage together with their luggage and came looking for me. Eventually he stumbled across me in the cupboard," reported Reeves.

Harry then took up the story. "I would have found him earlier, sir, except I kept being thrown out of the hotel. They said I had no business being there. Anyway, I went around the back and sneaked in through the kitchen. They know me in there and they weren't about to stop me."

Even though I was pleased with Harry's presence of mind, it still came as a shock to know that whilst we had been watching the Russians, they had been watching us. "Good God, man! You don't suppose they have Miss Coutts? I left her to find Miss Meredith. Quickly, Harry, take us to that damn pavilion and fast!"

I jumped on the cart and Harry got us to the tented area in double quick time. Reeves and I then raced around to the front of the pavilion, our fears increased when we looked in and failed to see any sign of Miss Coutts or Sinderby-Smythe.

"Damn and blast!" I said. "We have been undone Reeves, quickly, let's try the winners' tent and hope that they are there."

We ran over to the winners' tent and to our immense relief saw Sinderby-Smythe leaning against the door looking bored and tired. I pushed passed him whereupon I discovered Miss Coutts deep in conversation with my aunt and Major Phillips.

"Thank God she is alright," I said looking at both Sinderby-Smythe and Reeves, the former looking most confused.

Reeves and I acquainted the lieutenant with the events at the Crown Hotel and we collectively breathed a sigh of relief as, contrary to our worst fears, Miss Coutts was safe. But why had they trussed up Reeves if they were not intent on taking Miss Coutts? To be on the safe side, I asked Harry to talk to the people at the various staging posts nearby in order to establish whether the carriage the three Russians left on, linked up with the afternoon stage to Leeds, or some private carriage. It was also conceivable that they had wandered out into the countryside for another clandestine meeting as they did yesterday. Harry left in a hurry as I think that, in spite of everything, he had aspirations of returning in time to watch the last race.

Miss Coutts, having seen us all return, came over and asked why Miss Meredith was not with me. I was forced to apologise and explain that I had received some unforeseen news from Reeves concerning the Russians. I then reassured her by adding, "It would, however, appear that the Russians have, thankfully, left Harrogate and, given that you are still safe and sound, it would seem that our fears were misplaced. I will now retrieve Miss Meredith and escort her back here in time for the final race," and with that, I turned around and made for the Queen, dragging Reeves alongside. Despite the threat to Miss Coutts appearing to be over, Sinderby-Smythe continued to remain close to her. Meanwhile, Reeves and I walked quickly towards the Queen. When only a few yards from the entrance, Harry arrived in his cart, his poor donkey looking almost spent.

"Captain!" he shouted, before bringing his donkey to a halt.

"What news have you Harry?"

"I found the driver of the carriage who picked the Russians up from the Crown Hotel and he said that they transferred to a private carriage."

"All three of them?" I questioned.

"No, Captain," and then after a moment's pause said, "All four of them! And they apparently headed south to Leeds. What's more they had armed guards to boot."

"Armed guards? And four people, you say? Who is the fourth?" I asked, turning to Reeves who seemed equally puzzled.

"Don't know, Captain. The man who dropped them off said there were just the three of them but the man who rented out the private carriage confirmed there were four people on board when it left Harrogate," explained Harry.

Seconds later, both Reeves and I looked at each other and then over to the Queen, and almost in unison, exclaimed, "Oh no... Miss Meredith!"

We raced into the Queen Hotel and pushed anyone aside who stood in our path. We carried on straight into the reception area and asked if Miss Meredith was in her room. The man behind the counter was well aware that Reeves and I had been regular visitors of hers and genuinely tried to be helpful. Regrettably, he knew nothing and hadn't seen Miss Meredith since she'd left for the races with us around mid-day.

In the absence of Mr Dearlove, we enlisted the support of the manager, who led us to Miss Meredith's room where he knocked boldly on the door. There was no answer and so, with the manager's help, we entered the room only to find it empty. Her clothes and belongings remained but there was otherwise no sign of her or the dress which had been stained with fruit punch. It looked very much like she had never returned to the hotel, and was now on a coach bound for Leeds having been kidnapped by the Russians.

I cursed myself for not thinking that Miss Meredith could be a target. Miss Coutts would obviously pay anything to see her returned unharmed. There was no time to lose, we needed to get the mounts Benson had secured for us and urgently give chase. Harry took Reeves to fetch our horses whilst I was left with the unenviable task of breaking the distressing news to Miss Coutts.

I headed past the tents and carriages as I worked my way through the crowds to the winners' enclosure, my mind still stunned by the news.

Walking towards me, I could see Constable Hardisty with a number of angry people. Where was he when I needed him? By the sound of them, a good many of their number appeared to be Irish and when they caught sight of me they shouted, "There he is, don't let him escape!"

I instantly looked around, certain in the knowledge that they were referring to someone behind me, but when I turned there was no-one else in sight. My first instinct, when seeing the mob moving in my direction, was to flee the scene and quickly at that, yet there was no time and it made no sense, so I did not move.

"What's the meaning of this, constable?" I said, as two burly fellows grabbed my arms. "What the devil is going on?"

"Don't give me all that," said Constable Hardisty, aggressively. "You know fine well what it's all about. Captain Townsend, I am arresting you for the murder of Thomas Dawson."

Chapter 26

My eyes were wide with shock. I spluttered to find any coherent words as I was quickly led away by the mob with my heart pounding.

"Are you all mad? I didn't even know Dawson was dead, you fool. You must release me!" I said, trying to break free. "Miss Meredith has been abducted and I must rescue her," but shout as I may, no-one was listening.

I was being dragged to the constable's house by the mob, who seemed so convinced of my guilt that I feared they may take the law into their own hands. I heard one of the Irishmen shouting, "String him up!" and that met with worrying agreement from many of the drunken rabble. By the sound of his voice, I would have made a large wager that particular cry came from Richard Dunn.

The last race had just finished and there was little doubt that I was now the main attraction. The mob grew ever more threatening and we had still not reached the constable's house. The calls to hang me there and then grew louder and I struggled to break free. No-one had thought to see if I was armed and my pistols were very much in reach. The two men holding me were ugly brutes. The one on my left was heavily tattooed whilst the one on my right looked like he had seen action in the army at some point. By the smell on their breath I guessed that they had been drinking all day. I continued to try and break free of the vice-like grip holding my arms. If I could just get my hands on one of my pistols I would have a chance of escaping. This was starting to look like my best option, given the frightening possibility that I may not otherwise get the opportunity to explain to these idiots that I hadn't been anywhere near Dawson, let alone killed him.

My fears grew and so did the size of the mob, causing our progress to slow to a worrying level. I was sure that once in the calm of Constable Hardisty's house, I could prove my innocence, but it was beginning to look like this rabble had other ideas. The expressions on some of the faces surrounding me were full of hate. They were encouraged by drink and incensed by the death of one of Harrogate's own. Reason and logic were nowhere to be seen. There were more cries of "String him up, we know he's guilty," and as I turned to appeal to the constable, I could see that he had lost complete control of proceedings. I continued to wriggle all the while, trying to work a hand onto a pistol, however every time I managed to get a hand close, it was forcibly dragged back. This was all starting to turn very ugly indeed and I was inwardly fighting my natural urge to panic. There were cries for unspeakable things to be done to me and the mob grew even larger, louder and more dangerous. I could see the constable's house approaching and attempted to march my captors towards it. The sooner I was inside that house the better, but when only a few steps away, the mob encircled me and I was trapped. Even if I could get a hand on a pistol or reach my knife, there were far too many of them to be able to orchestrate an escape. I was doomed. All my attempts to reason with them failed miserably. In fact, the more I tried to placate them, the more the cries went up for me to be silenced once and for all.

Just when everything was at its most daunting, a pistol shot fired and the crowd stopped in an instant. A horse charged the mob and it then reared up with its front legs clawing at the air. This was quickly followed by a second horse doing exactly the same. The mob retreated and they were forced into forming a line facing the horsemen with me in the centre. Handling the horses magnificently were Lieutenant Sinderby-Smythe and 2nd Lieutenant Reeves. They both had two pistols and were using their skills in horsemanship to great effect. I felt sure that even Sinderby-Smythe's father couldn't have failed to have been impressed with this display. As the smoke from the pistol shot cleared, they manoeuvred their horses first left and then right, keeping the crowd in line like dogs marshalling sheep.

"Now gentlemen, in case you haven't noticed, both of our pistols are double barrelled, so don't get any foolish ideas that we only have one shot left. Which, for those of you who struggle with arithmetic, means that having just fired the once, between the two of us we still have three shots left. I am sure no one wants to get themselves badly hurt and so you will oblige us by releasing our Captain," shouted Sinderby-Smythe, waving his pistol menacingly, taking me as much by surprise as it did the angry mob.

"He's a murderer," said the constable, angrily. "And you are interfering with the law!"

"Watch the bastards!" shouted a man in an Irish accent. "Remember what the cavalry did at Peterloo and Bossenden Wood," which was greeted by a chorus of approval from the mob.

"The Captain here is an officer in the 11th Light Dragoons and any charges against him will be heard by Lord Cardigan himself and not by any mob," shouted Sinderby-Smythe, confidently asserting himself.

"He is my prisoner and, until I get orders from Lord Cardigan telling me otherwise, he will be treated like any other murderer," countered Constable Hardisty, at which point I was led towards the door of his house.

"Hold there!" said Reeves, moving forward with his horse, once more intimidating the mob.

"What evidence is there to prove the Captain murdered this poor chap?" he demanded.

"His watch was found in the hand of the victim and it is well known that the Captain and young Tom were fighting over the Hatherway girl," said the constable.

Reeves was a little taken aback at this. With hindsight I should have informed my fellow officers about Virginia and the first altercation with Dawson. Somewhat speechless they both looked at me as much to say, 'what now?' I was not in a good position to help and attempted to communicate that by shrugging my shoulders which was nigh on impossible with the two thugs holding my arms. The only good news here was that my watch had turned up, which was small comfort. With the crowd still formed in a line facing my lieutenants, there was now a clear route to the constable's house. Constable Hardisty opened the door to his house and pointed the way towards it, signifying that it was time to take me indoors.

"Hold!" shouted Sinderby-Smythe, further advancing his mount, causing those who had edged forward to retreat a couple of paces.

"The Captain lost the watch a few days ago. Someone has obviously planted it in the dead man's hand. He is clearly being framed!" shouted the lieutenant, continuing to plead my cause.

"How do we know he lost his watch? You three could be in it together. Besides which, why is it that the Captain never mentioned his watch was lost or stolen when he came to see me last night? He had ample opportunity to do so, yet chose to spend the entire time harping on about some Russian nonsense," replied the constable placing both hands on his hips and puffing his chest out.

The mob collectively murmured in agreement.

"It's not nonsense about the Russians," I pleaded trying to make myself heard but no-one was interested in anything I had to say. For a second time, I exchanged a glance of 'what now?' with my lieutenants and a moment later we lost sight of each other as I was forced inside the house.

Constable Hardisty seemed to have recovered the situation and was more confident in his actions.

"You will stay overnight here, Captain, and tomorrow we will take you to York jail where you will be held until your trial."

He pointed to his outhouse which was to be my home for the night. The two brutes that had held me for the last twenty minutes or so finally let me go. The temptation to draw my pistols remained, although I needed to wait for the right time to make a move. I expected that would be soon, nevertheless the mob still hung around like a foul odour. It was clear that I needed to escape, and quickly. I was becoming increasingly convinced that these trumped up charges were a deliberate plan to prevent me from chasing after the Russians and rescuing Miss Meredith.

I did not resist when the constable pushed me towards the outhouse, but in doing so he brushed against the handle of one of my pistols. "Hello, what do we have here?" he said, reaching into my jacket to pull out the pistol and then fumbled around and found the other.

"Well, well. You do like to keep yourself well-armed don't you?" and with my pistols, went my hopes of an early escape. If that wasn't bad enough, the constable placed my wrists through a pair of handcuffs.

The door to the outhouse was unlocked and as it opened, I could see that I would not be alone this night. There were two men sitting in the far corners. They looked at me with great interest, raising themselves ever so slightly from the thin layer of straw which barely covered the stone floor. They then looked at each other as I was ushered in.

"Now Captain, meet your room mates. There's Pete the Cheat – I wouldn't play cards with him if I were you," at which point, the man in the left corner feigned doffing his cap. "Over there is the best pick pocket in Yorkshire, Benjamin Harris," to which the man in the right corner simply turned his head showing complete disinterest.

Being locked up like this for a crime I didn't commit was senseless and so I made one last effort to retrieve this seemingly lost cause.

"You're making a big mistake, constable. You have been fooled into believing that I killed Dawson in order to stop me chasing after the kidnappers of Miss Meredith. Do us all a favour, man, and take these damn irons off me or face charges of aiding and abetting the enemy."

Constable Hardisty was unmoved. My pleas had fallen on deaf ears and moments later I was pushed into the dark and dingy outhouse. The door slammed shut behind me and the key turned in the lock.

"You seemed to 'ave caused quite a fuss, Cap'n," said Pete the Cheat. "What you in for?"

"Those imbeciles seem to think I murdered someone as they found him clutching my watch," I said, rolling my eyes at the lunacy of the allegation.

"Watches," he replied, "Ben over there's yer man for watches." Ben smiled and with the formal introductions out of the way, I slowly regained my wits.

"It looks like we are all victims of misunderstandings, Cap'n," said Pete, "Ain't that right Ben?"

"Aye," replied Ben, adding, "Bastards!" after which, Pete regaled us with his complaint.

"I was only trying to teach t'Irish how t' play cards and some shit starts mouthing off that I'm cheating 'em all." This sounded all too familiar and I had a feeling that the Irishman he referred to could well have been one Richard Dunn. I nodded as if to sympathise and then Ben explained that he had tripped over a rope which supported one of the tents and then bumped into a doctor.

"So you were arrested for simply bumping into someone accidentally?" I asked.

"Not exactly, Cap'n. You see, in all t' confusion, doctor's money ended up in my pocket!" at which Ben laughed and Pete joined in.

These two were rogues, no mistake, but I thought I could be sharing a cell with much worse.

One way or another, I was breaking out of this place and quickly too. I was never going to clear my name rotting in a York jail and I needed to catch up with the Russians, fast, before they could flee the country. I felt sure that my incarceration was all down to them. They were onto Reeves and it follows that they were onto me, too. This could now explain what the Irishman was doing hanging around the Queen and why I was encouraged to leave Harrogate. My immediate concern was that they were already hours ahead and could be anywhere by now. Somehow we needed to quickly establish whether they had headed east to Kingston upon Hull or west to Liverpool. It was too daunting a prospect to think that they might have headed somewhere else.

I had to get out of this damn outhouse. Due to an exceptionally low ceiling in this make-shift jail, I wasn't able to fully stand up. Being unable to pace around only increased my frustration. After an hour or so I heard the sound of two people approaching the outhouse. The key turned in the lock and the door slowly opened to reveal the constable and Reeves.

"You've got five minutes, not a second more and I will be standing right here so don't try anything foolish," said Constable Hardisty as Reeves ducked his head on entering the dimly lit outhouse.

Reeves crouched down beside me whilst looking at my roommates. He skipped the formality of introducing himself but before he could say anything to me, I shook his hand and said, "Good work earlier, Reeves. You and Sinderby-Smythe were a credit to the regiment out there. I am proud to be serving with you both."

"Thank you, sir," he replied, and then in a hushed voice whispered, "The lieutenant asked me to tell you that Miss Coutts has received a ransom note. The Russians say they have Miss Meredith and will exchange her for the plans and specifications of a repeating rifle being developed by Theodore Botterill in Sheffield."

"My God," I said quietly. "I should have guessed that Miss Meredith was equally at risk and should never have ran after that damn Irishman. This is turning into a nightmare," I said digesting the news.

"Theodore Botterill is the fellow I heard the Russians talking about when they had their clandestine meeting in the Plough Inn at Upper Dunsforth. It seems that Botterill has been financed by Coutts Bank, and because of that, the Russians believe that Miss Coutts should be able to exert enough influence to persuade Mr Botterill to hand over his invention," said Reeves.

"Has Miss Coutts confirmed that?" I asked.

"Miss Coutts has no idea who deals with her late grandfather's bank. Apparently she leaves all the banking business and the like to the Directors. Nevertheless, she intends to travel to Sheffield first thing in the morning along with Major Phillips, to seek out Mr Botterill. The note from the Russians also said that if she involves the army or the constables they will kill Miss Meredith. That's why Miss Coutts hasn't come here herself. She's frightened of being seen talking to the constable. And if that's not bad enough the exchange must be made at half past seven on Monday morning, which doesn't give us enough time to involve Lord Palmerston. Even the fastest stage coach in the country wouldn't be able to get to London and back by then. Also the spot they've chosen for the hand over is a place called the Devil's Arrows, which I'm advised consists of three giant stones in the middle of nowhere, just a mile or so west of Boroughbridge. The stones are in open fields with only the odd tree in sight. It would be hard for a single man to hide close by, let alone an army or a troop of cavalry," he replied.

"That's right Reeves, it's a cleverly chosen spot. The Devil's Arrows must also be near to the Great North Road, which is one of the most well-used roads in England, providing the Russians with many alternative routes of escape," I said.

"But she can't hand over any plans to such an invention! Lord Palmerston would roast us all on an open fire. The first country to develop a repeating rifle will be unstoppable. No wonder the Russians want it. Instead of firing two or three shots a minute, a repeating rifle might be able to fire several times that amount. Damn it, man! If we have less than two and a half days to rescue Miss Meredith, you have to get me out of here," I insisted quietly.

"Don't worry, sir. One way or another, you will be out of here shortly. Constable Hardisty has been in a bit of a quandary since he heard that Miss Meredith is missing and the Russians have left too. He knows nothing of the ransom note, all the same, it starts to suggest that you could have been right about a kidnapping. Having said that, he still thinks the evidence points to you killing Dawson," replied Reeves speaking softly. All the while my roommates craned their necks to try and hear what was being said.

"What evidence? A watch! When and how was I supposed to have killed him?" I asked, keeping my voice really low on the last couple of words.

"The constable has found out that you went missing during the races and he thinks that was when you confronted Dawson and stabbed him in the chest," said Reeves, trying to lower his voice even further as he referred to the gruesome details. "But I wasn't the only one to go missing was I? Henry Payden left too. I wonder what he was doing whilst I was chasing after that damn Irish bastard?" I said, adding after a moment's thought, "Surely if I had stabbed Dawson, I would be covered in blood. It's all madness."

"Agreed Captain, someone has set you up really well and we need to find out who and why," replied Reeves.

"I don't think we have to look much further than the damn Russians. They knew we were onto them and so they trussed you up and framed me for Dawson's killing. They get us both out of the way, allowing them to take Miss Meredith and head off unchallenged. With half the town at the races, that made it even easier for them," to which Reeves nodded in agreement.

"The important thing is to get me out of here and to get after those villains without further delay."

"Time's up," said Constable Hardisty, putting his head around the door. "Come on, sir. Time to leave if you please."

Reeves raised himself from the floor whispering, "I will be back," and after a pause added, "one way or another." Then, after ducking his head, he disappeared through the doorway and was gone. The now familiar sound of the door closing and the key turning in the lock soon followed. I suddenly thought that I should simply order Reeves and Sinderby-Smythe to waste no more time and pursue the Russians without me. Although with three of us, we stood a much better chance and so I fervently hoped that my two lieutenants would secure my release quickly.

I had completely forgotten about eating with all the traumas of the day and was pleasantly surprised when Mrs Hardisty brought through some food and water for us all. Her cooking was actually very good and went a long way to explain the extra-large girth sported by the constable. My digestion was interrupted by another visitor. The door opened and Constable Hardisty asked me to step outside, raising my hopes of an early release.

"You've a lady visitor and I can't bring her here," said the constable.

At last, something a little positive. I hoped it was Virginia, but rather suspected it would be my aunt.

The evening shadows lengthened as I walked across the small yard between the makeshift jail and the house. Constable Hardisty followed behind me with a pistol in his belt. I walked up a couple of steps, back into the house and was then guided into the room where I had tried to enlist the support of the constable only the day before. I must have looked a sorry state, having been man-handled by a large angry mob, handcuffed and then made to lie down on a stone floor covered in straw. When the Duchess caught sight of me she took a sharp intake of breath quickly followed by a smile.

"Duchess," I said, moving towards her, only to be held back by Constable Hardisty.

"George, what on earth is going on? Has the world gone mad? It's the talk of the town that a young man has been killed and that you are charged with his murder! The fact that you are standing here in chains suggests that it is true. Surely not?" she asked with disbelief written across her face.

"Of course it's not true," I said, ridiculing the allegation and then turning to the constable. "I have been framed. Someone stole my watch and put it in the victim's hand after they'd killed him. As Constable Hardisty knows only too well, I warned him only yesterday that I believed that two Russians, masquerading as a railway engineer and his manservant, were planning a heinous crime. Now Miss Coutts's companion, Miss Meredith, is missing and the Russians are nowhere to be seen. And you, Mr Hardisty, by holding me captive, are actually helping them get away with this. If you don't let me go free now, I may not be able to retrieve the situation which could have dire consequences. More than you could ever imagine. I expect our government will reward your interference with passage on a convict ship bound for Australia and you will never be heard of again."

The Duchess listened intently, raising her eyebrows at the mention of Angela Coutts's name. Meanwhile the constable bridled at my remarks.

"Is this true George? You didn't tell me any of this. What's going on, I thought you were just visiting with your aunt?"

"I couldn't tell you, Duchess, because I was ordered to Harrogate on a matter of national importance. Nonetheless, I did warn the constable, yet for reasons best known to him he didn't take me seriously. He was more concerned with the races and now we have a murder and Lord knows what else to deal with!"

Irrespective of the fact that the Duchess looked convinced, Constable Hardisty could not resist countermanding my story.

"It is true Your Grace, the Captain did tell me about a possible crime. But if I acted on every rumour I heard, I would never get any work done. More importantly, there is no evidence to support any of the Captain's claims about Miss Meredith being kidnapped. I spoke to Mr Payden and he says that the Russians have left for Europe to buy equipment for their railway project. As to the Captain's claim that he lost his watch prior to the murder, why is it then that he never reported it to me when he had chance?" At which point the constable took my watch from his pocket. He then swung the watch chain back and forth to prove that he did indeed have the incriminating evidence which bore my name.

"And what would you have done if I had reported it missing, you imbecile?" I said, getting increasingly angry. "I warned you that something could happen today and you did nothing about that, so what chance is there that you would do anything about a mere watch? With respect to Mr Payden, what else can he say? He's never going to admit that the Russian he employed as an authority on railways, was actually only in Harrogate to kidnap someone. I ask you man, engage your brain!"

"Now, Captain. I will not have you talking to me like that. It's back to the cell for you," said Constable Hardisty, taking me by the arm.

"Hold on there!" said the Duchess, stopping the constable in his tracks.

I could see that my frustrations had got the better of me and, if I was to get out of here quickly, I would need to mellow. Before the constable could lead me back to his poor excuse for a jail, I attempted a more conciliatory tone.

"Duchess, if I am supposed to have killed Dawson with a knife, why I am not covered in blood? I ask you to look at me. I may be a little dishevelled, thanks to the way Constable Hardisty and his ruffians treated me, but I guarantee you will find no traces of blood anywhere on me. And given that I was carrying two pistols, don't you think that if I was going to murder someone that I would simply shoot them?"

The constable thought for a moment and then responded.

"A knife makes a lot less noise than a pistol and so the fact that you carried pistols proves nothing. Also the fact that you are not covered in blood can be simply explained, you could have worn gloves and a coat and then thrown them away," at which I laughed.

"Constable, are you seriously suggesting that I went to the trouble of wearing different clothes and gloves which then magically disappear. And yet by the same token, I am careless enough to leave my watch in Dawson's hand?" I said, ridiculing the allegation.

Despite Constable Hardisty having no answer for this, he nevertheless continued to argue my guilt.

"The Captain may have an answer for most things, Your Grace, however more importantly, he does not have an alibi for the time Dawson was killed."

"In the first place, I have no idea as to when Dawson was killed and the only time I was away from my friends was when I was chasing after a damn Irishman who had been stalking Miss Coutts. No doubt just as whoever framed me, hoped I would," I said, endeavouring to contain my anger. Then, after calming myself completely, I continued, "I apologise for my language, Duchess. It has been a trying day to say the very least."

She nodded as a Duchess should, still every inch the actress she once was.

"Which Irishman?" mocked the constable. "We have had hundreds of them here today."

"The one who has been watching the Queen from across the other side of the Stray these last few days. The one I mentioned to you last night! And if you were doing your job properly, instead of gorging yourself at the dinner table training for a pie eating contest, you too would have seen him."

Constable Hardisty bristled again, causing me to instantly regret that remark. He tugged at my arm in an attempt to return me to the outbuilding. I resisted, and tensing my muscles, I stood my ground.

"I apologise, constable, but can't you see, the longer you hold me here, the less chance we have of finding Miss Meredith? The Irishman was the bait and I took it. I had seen him watching Miss Coutts and Miss Meredith, which was probably intentional. In any event, I never managed to catch the blighter in the act and so when he came within range of me at the races, I had to chase after him."

"Then what happened?" asked both the Duchess and Constable Hardisty almost in unison.

"Why, I caught him and despite all my powers of persuasion, he refused to tell me anything. So I marched him back to the racecourse, ironically to look for you," I said, looking at the constable.

"I grant you that was probably a fool thing to do, given there being such a large number of people in town, and so unsurprisingly, I couldn't find you. Then I had the misfortune to run into a number of drunken Irishmen who took exception to me holding one of their countrymen and there I lost him."

There was a pause whilst Constable Hardisty and the Duchess considered my story.

"Don't worry, George, I believe you. It sounds to me like you are right and that your watch was planted on the dead man to implicate you and allow some villains to make off with Miss Meredith. I don't believe for one moment that you killed him," said the Duchess assertively, which caused me to smile in appreciation.

"Well, Your Grace, that will be for a jury to decide, as I still feel there is a case to answer. No-one else saw the Captain chasing any Irishman and yet we do have witnesses who saw the Captain threaten Tom Dawson in the Montpelier Gardens and again outside the Dragon Hotel a couple of nights ago."

By the expression on her face, the incident outside the Dragon was yet more unwelcome news, but thankfully she let it pass without comment.

"Dawson had been goading me ever since I arrived in Harrogate. He was obviously employed by someone to drive me out of town. What better man could any villain have watching Miss Coutts and her companion, than someone who worked inside the hotel where she was staying?"

"Now, Captain, there is no call for that. The poor man's only been dead a few hours and you're here making slanderous remarks he can't defend," said the constable indignantly.

"Well, I will apologise if I am wrong, however, you must admit that it doesn't look good, does it? I mean to say, Dawson was no choir boy was he?"

"How do you know that he wasn't killed trying to prevent Miss Meredith being abducted?" argued Constable Hardisty, adding, "The man could be a hero and here's you running him down."

"That's a very good point, constable, and if he was killed by someone abducting Miss Meredith then that rules me out of the reckoning," I said, seizing on the opportunity I had just been presented.

"The Captain would seem to be making a very good point, constable," said the Duchess, adding her support.

"But there are still doubts," said Constable Hardisty, who was definitely weakening.

"And doesn't our legal system decree that for someone to be convicted, they must be found guilty beyond all reasonable doubt?" I added quickly.

"Constable," intervened the Duchess. "I suggest that you let the Captain go. If you find more evidence you can present it to the Earl of Cardigan. The Captain will not be fleeing the country. He is an officer and a gentleman and I will vouch for him as I am sure others will."

The expression on his face suggested that the constable was coming around to the Duchess's proposal. Even though he had been pushed into a corner, she cleverly offered him a way out.

"Whatever else you say, I couldn't let the Captain go until after dark, Your Grace. Feelings are still running high and a lot of spirits have been consumed which makes for a dangerous situation. If certain members of the public saw the Captain walking around free as a bird, there is no telling what they might do."

"That sounds very sensible," replied the Duchess. "What say you, Captain?"

At last, we were getting somewhere.

"Absolutely, very sensible, constable," I answered. "And have no fear, I will return and if you can make a case, I will happily answer to it. However for now, finding Miss Meredith is all I am concerned with."

I smiled at the Duchess in appreciation. I then held out my hands which were still bound by the handcuffs. Constable Hardisty sighed and then with great reluctance, unlocked my bonds.

The constable suggested that it was time for the Duchess to leave, which surprisingly resulted in her eyes filling up ever so slightly.

"Thank you so much, Duchess," I said bowing to her. "Might I ask one last favour?" to which she nodded in the affirmative.

"It would be of enormous assistance if you could get a message to Lieutenant Sinderby-Smythe, who you should find at the Queen Hotel."

"Certainly Captain, and what would you have me tell him?"

"Could you tell him it is my wish that he and 2nd Lieutenant Reeves be ready to travel as soon as it's dark and to meet me at the rear of the constable's house?

I trust that is satisfactory to you, sir," I said, showing respect towards Constable Hardisty, who signified his agreement with a short nod of the head.

The Duchess wished us all a very good evening and left in the carriage that had been patiently waiting for her. Without her assistance I would surely have remained in chains, destined to spend the night kicking my heels in a small outhouse. I would have liked a few moments alone with her but didn't want to unsettle the constable, having taken so long to talk him around. I also wanted to know what she meant by the warning in her letter. From all she had said this evening, it looked very much like she knew nothing of the Russians' planned kidnapping. Therefore what had she been warning me about?

"You'd better wait in the back, Captain. It wouldn't do for someone to catch sight of you in our front parlour," said a tired looking constable.

I accepted his point and followed him into a snug little room at the back of his house. It was very small yet warm, comfortable and a good place to wait for Sinderby-Smythe and Reeves. Before I was left alone to my thoughts, I asked Constable Hardisty for the use of pen and paper and then added, "Excuse me, constable, would you be so kind as to return to me my pistols and my watch?"

"The watch is evidence, Captain," he replied officiously.

Not wishing to start another argument I simply smiled and said, "I do understand your point, constable, nevertheless I presume that you have many witnesses who can testify that Dawson was found clutching my watch. That is not disputed, even I am happy to confirm in writing that the watch is indeed mine. What is most definitely denied is that he took it from me whilst I was stabbing him. I think we can rule out me placing it in his hand to incriminate myself, don't you?"

Constable Hardisty appeared to have been partially, if not totally convinced by my story and duly handed me back my pistols and watch. I think the man was just worn out by the events of the day. There was little doubt that he would not have seen their like before. I placed my pistols back through my belt and wound my watch, setting the time with the constable's help. The time was half past seven and the sun should set in one hour's time. I then made myself comfortable in the constable's little room and moments later I was handed a pen and some paper.

I wanted to write to my aunt to let her know that I was alright and that she was not to worry but I also had an idea which I wanted to pass on to Major Phillips. It seemed to me that Vladimir's arrival in Harrogate was no coincidence, which meant that somehow they had been keeping Miss Coutts under close observation, probably from the time she left London. They had also been carefully monitoring our movements and so it seemed logical that they would also follow Miss Coutts and the Major on their trip to Sheffield. This created the possibility that, should Miss Coutts be able to acquire the plans to the repeating rifle, the Russians could simply take these away from her as she travelled back to Harrogate. In order to prevent this, I suggested to the Major that he should recruit a further two well-armed guards and also carry a package with him, to look as though it contained a set of plans. This was to be addressed to Miss Coutts at the Queen Hotel and posted from Sheffield. My hope was, if the Russians could be convinced that the plans had been posted back from Sheffield using the mail service, they would be less inclined to attack Miss Coutts on her return journey. If nothing else, it would confuse them and perhaps buy more time for us to rescue Miss Meredith. Pleased that I was starting to fight back, I put the pen down and allowed myself a moment to let out some of the tension which had been gripping me all day.

Whilst reflecting on the challenges that still lay ahead, I felt my eyelids growing heavy and despite my best efforts, I drifted off to sleep.

Chapter 27

Angela Coutts sat in her private parlour at the Queen, fighting back the tears whilst being comforted by Captain Townsend's aunt. She held the ransom demand firmly in her hand. The note was most insistent that no harm would come to her close companion, provided the plans to Mr Botterill's invention were handed over in precisely the manner instructed. The moment the plans were received, Miss Meredith would be released unharmed. However, the warning about involving the constables or the army was harrowing.

She had re-read those words many times.

It appeared that Captain Townsend had been correct all along, only the target had in fact been Miss Meredith and not herself. She surmised that this could have only happened because of the comprehensive protection she herself had received. She now very much regretted not accompanying Miss Meredith to the hotel when she left the racecourse to change her dress. The preposterous notion that Captain Townsend had murdered a local man over a girl only added to her despair. Yet it was his incarceration preventing him from giving chase, which distressed her most.

"Surely the constable will soon realise that the Captain has been framed, and allow him to pursue these villains," said Angela to Mrs Moore, the Captain's aunt.

"One would hope so dear. Nonetheless, Constable Hardisty is not a man blessed with clarity of thought. He has largely been employed to collect taxes where his physical presence and his simple approach have been put to good use," replied Mrs Moore philosophically.

"I would speak to the constable myself, though I fear there may be people watching the hotel and I can't risk doing anything which would endanger poor Hannah. What good is it doing anyone holding the Captain for some crime he most certainly did not commit? It is sheer folly!" retorted Angela.

"I do agree, dear," said Mrs Moore. "I should have thought it obvious to even Constable Hardisty that someone who is cool enough to leave the racecourse, stab a man to death, and then return to cheer on his horse, all without the slightest hint of anything untoward, would hardly leave his own watch in the dead man's hand! Preposterous!"

"Yes, Mrs Moore, I am in total agreement. Clearly the evidence was fabricated in order to divert the Captain's attention long enough to allow these villains to make off with poor Miss Meredith. And whoever abducted her almost certainly murdered the young man."

The reference to the murder brought with it a realisation that, if the abductors would kill to get the Captain out of the way, they may not hesitate to kill Miss Meredith too. This resulted in a look of deep concern across her face which did not go un-noticed by Mrs Moore.

"Please do not alarm yourself, Miss Coutts," reassured Mrs Moore as she leant forward to take hold of her hand. "If George is not released within the hour, I will box the constable about the ears until the man sees sense." Despite her positive words, the Captain's aunt was also troubled by the day's events, as not only was there the murder for which her nephew had been incarcerated, but also the perpetrators of the abduction were seemingly the same Russians who were working for The Yorkshire Railway Company, one of which had been introduced to her by Henry Payden. Mr Payden, having himself mysteriously disappeared during the races, also gave rise to the possibility that he too could somehow be involved in all this.

With the ransom warning of the consequences of involving the constable, and in the absence of anyone else, Angela had sought assistance from Major Phillips. The Major came to Harrogate at the request of her father, Sir Francis Burdett, and being a seasoned military campaigner he had the necessary skills for almost any eventuality. He had been discreetly watching over Miss Coutts ever since he arrived in town a few days previously. After making enquiries about the town, the Major arrived at Angela's rooms to be greeted by Emily who showed him into the parlour.

"What news do you have for us, Major?" asked Angela, anxiously.

"I have good news for you both. I have just left Lieutenant Sinderby-Smythe who has assured me that Constable Hardisty will shortly be releasing Captain Townsend, for which we have the intervention of the Duchess of Aldborough to thank," replied the Major, resulting in both ladies immediately clapping their hands in an expression of relief.

"Under the cover of darkness, he and his two fellow officers will be permitted to make their way out of Harrogate where they can at last give chase to these abominable wretches."

"All the same, why wait until its dark? Surely they need to commence their pursuit of the Russians whilst it's still light," enquired Angela impatiently.

"Indeed, that would be ideal, however the constable felt that with feelings in the town still running high, it would be prudent to slip away after the sun has set."

"So, Major, where do you suppose my nephew will be heading?" asked Mrs Moore.

"The very same question I asked the lieutenant, madam. It would seem that they will try and pick up the trail of the Russians in Leeds, which is where the carriage carrying the Russians and Miss Meredith headed when it left Harrogate this afternoon. The Captain had initially believed that if the Russians were to succeed in an abduction, they would seek to board a ship at either the eastern port of Kingston upon Hull or the western port of Liverpool. And then, quite by chance, he discovered that the Russians had been pouring over railway timetables for locomotives leaving Manchester bound for Liverpool. Consequently he is now of the opinion that they will more than likely escape to the west. He also learned that they had been looking at sailing times of ships from Liverpool and, significantly, there was no evidence to suggest they were contemplating a route to the east," answered the Major.

"But surely they will not go anywhere until they have collected the ransom at the Devil's Arrows?" asked Miss Coutts.

"I agree, providing they do as they say. In which case they could be holding Miss Meredith virtually anywhere. My fear is that these rogues will only hand over poor Miss Meredith when we have given them the plans and they are safely on board a ship bound for Russia. In which case they may have no intention of meeting us at the Devil's Arrows," said the Major.

As the reality of the situation unfolded, so the tempo of the conversation increased.

"I think we need to hope that the Captain can pick up their trail quickly, Major, as we have so little time," asserted Angela.

"Indeed, the time they have allowed us is sufficient for us to travel to Sheffield and obtain the plans, yet insufficient for us to enlist the support of Lord Palmerston," said the Major.

"That may be true Major," said Mrs Moore, immediately gaining everyone's attention.

"Nevertheless, George, that is, Captain Townsend left two letters with my butler Benson, to be dispatched in the event of trouble. One of those letters was addressed to Lord Palmerston and so there is a chance, albeit a slim one, that His Lordship will be able to come to our assistance."

"That is good news. Isn't it Major?" enquired Angela.

"I should say so," said the Major, pleased at this small piece of good news. It remained unlikely that His Lordship would be able to do much by Monday morning, nevertheless, with the fast horses and carriages at his disposal, there stood an outside chance he could help.

"And what of the other letter, Mrs Moore?" asked Miss Coutts.

"Ah, not quite so good news, as I am afraid to say it went to the garrison at York," she said with a touch of remorse in her voice.

"Major, you must do something! The Russians said they would kill Miss Meredith if we sought help from the army," said Angela, instantly fraught with concern.

"Then we must make sure they don't see them," replied the Major.

"I pray that is possible, sir, although I suspect they have eyes everywhere. How else would they have known that we had travelled to Harrogate? A fact which they must have learned shortly after we left London," she replied, her fears still unresolved.

"Spies, I shouldn't wonder," he replied, "they're everywhere these days."

"And what's more, how can I be certain that even if we give them these wretched plans that I will ever see poor Hannah again?" said Angela, beginning to fight back a tear.

"Precisely why we must outwit these villains, and we will! Please do not fret, Miss Coutts as without doubt, you will see Miss Meredith again," added the Major.

"Amen to that," said both ladies.

"And tomorrow, Miss Coutts, we must travel to Sheffield," said the Major, moving the conversation forward, readying himself to leave.

Angela quickly composed herself, recognising the vital role she now had to play in securing her companion's safe return.

"Yes Major, I have given instructions that my carriage is made ready to depart first thing in the morning. I am advised by Mr Dearlove, that if we leave early enough, we can make the sixteen mile journey to Leeds in time for a late breakfast or an early lunch, where we can either rest or change our horses. Thereafter, Sheffield is a further thirty six miles or so beyond Leeds. Still a long way to travel, however, with luck we should be there sometime tomorrow afternoon," said Angela.

"Never fear, we will get there in good time, miss," replied the Major.

"Major, I cannot help but wonder that if these plans are so valuable, why the Russians didn't simply travel to Sheffield and acquire them? Why do they need to involve Miss Meredith and my grandfather's bank in this matter?" reflected Angela.

"The same thing occurred to me, miss. One is forced to assume that they have tried to get hold of the invention and failed. After which, they resorted to this evil plan. We must hope that we have the success the Russians believe is possible," he replied.

Weary and desperate, Angela then suggested that everyone should retire for the evening as tomorrow was set to be a long and tiring day. Mrs Moore would not be travelling to Sheffield, only the Major, Miss Coutts and Emily her maid would be making that trip.

The Major headed back to his room in the hotel and Mrs Moore went in search of Lieutenant Sinderby-Smythe, after which she took her carriage back to Holderness House where, instead of celebrating Tribune's victory, she remained alone, worried and deep in thought.

Chapter 28

The sun had set in Harrogate whilst I slept briefly in the back room of the constable's house. My fitful rest had been unfortunately curtailed, mainly due to a harrowing dream involving the Russians, Miss Coutts and a large gun shooting at me over and over again, which had me opening my eyes sharply to check if any of it was real.

I then heard some faint noises outside and a voice at the back door of the house.

"Captain, Captain? Are you there?"

The noise caught the attention of the constable and he put his head into the snug and said, "Captain, your men are here."

"Thank you, constable," I said, handing him two letters.

"Can you please make sure that my aunt at Holderness House and Major Phillips at the Queen Hotel receive these letters without delay?"

"I'm not a post man you know," he replied, reluctantly taking them from me.

"I appreciate that, constable, but we both know that I can't deliver these letters, can I?"

"Very well, Captain," he said reluctantly.

"Just one more thing before I go," I added.

"Don't push your luck, Captain," replied Constable Hardisty, warily.

"Fear not constable, you will thank me for this one. I want you to let it be known that you still have me in custody, at least until Monday morning. That will not only keep the mob happy but it could also give me a slight advantage over the villains who have kidnapped Miss Meredith."

"Very well, Captain. I can say that," said the constable, after which I walked to his back door, once more a free man.

I felt a chill as the night air eased its way into the constable's house. Whether it was this sharp change in temperature or whether it was being shot in my dream, I couldn't say. Either way, it suddenly occurred to me that it may not be Sinderby-Smythe and Reeves who had come for me.

249

I lingered in the doorway for a moment, remembering the Duchess's words that everything was not all it seemed.

"Sinderby-Smythe, Reeves? Are you there?" I called a little hesitantly as faces began to appear, illuminated by the light shining from the constable's house.

"Yes, Captain," came their familiar responses.

I walked further out of Constable Hardisty's house and into the back yard that led to the outbuilding, enabling me to clearly see my two officers.

My two former cell mates stirred as I was happily reunited with Reeves and Sinderby-Smythe. They made all manner of strange noises and I refused to allow my mind to speculate on the nature of these and walked slowly away from the constable's house with the two lieutenants in close support.

"Here Captain, put this on," said Reeves, handing me my coat. "A present from your aunt, sir. There are more clothes in your saddle bag."

"Thank you, Reeves. How is my aunt? Did either of you see her?"

"Yes, sir, she sought me out before we left and I was also with her when news of your arrest broke," interjected Sinderby-Smythe.

"How did she take it?" I asked hesitantly.

"Didn't believe it, sir. I think she felt you had been framed from the outset. She only showed concern when it became clear that you were at the mercy of a drunken mob. That's when Reeves and I ran for the mounts."

"Then who stayed with Miss Coutts?"

"Major Phillips was there, sir, and both he and Miss Coutts insisted that we prioritised your safety," replied Sinderby-Smythe.

"After we left you with the constable, we returned to the Queen. We initially spoke to Major Phillips and then to your aunt. It seems that she was all set to head to the constable's house and free you herself, when the Duchess of Aldborough returned with news of your impending release."

I quietly put on the coat and smiled at the actions of my aunt. I looked around. It was a dark night with the moon hiding behind some heavy clouds. We were in a quiet area of Harrogate, away from all the hotels and inns. Even though there was no-one to be seen, we were still too close to Constable Hardisty's house to light a torch and so we stumbled through the night slowly and carefully.

"Bloody cold, sir," said Sinderby-Smythe, flapping his arms around to keep warm.

"Keep it down, lieutenant," I replied. "This is nothing; you should come here in January."

"If it's all the same to you, sir, I will give that a miss."

"I'm guessing it's warmer in Wimborne?"

"Absolutely, sir," he replied.

We moved quietly and stealthily out of Harrogate, when out of the darkness we could see two eyes staring straight at us.

"Fox, Captain," said Reeves, still whispering and when I looked again those eyes were gone. There was the odd house that still had a light burning and although we welcomed the limited assistance these lights gave us, it added to our tension, reminding us that there were still people very much awake. We headed away from the town and towards the common grassland of the Stray.

"Where are we going, Reeves?" I asked.

"Not far now, Captain. I have our mounts tethered a short way ahead."

"Good job, Reeves," I said.

"Thank you, sir, but Lieutenant Sinderby-Smythe deserves the credit more than I do. Someone certainly went to a good deal of trouble to frame you," he replied, our voices getting progressively louder as we moved further and further away from any form of human habitation.

"Thank you, lieutenant. You did well," I said, turning to Sinderby-Smythe.

"Thank you, sir," said Sinderby-Smythe.

I had never really warmed to him as I had to Reeves, and yet the way he kept watch over Miss Coutts was first class and his actions outside the constable's house were exemplary.

"Nearly there, sir," said Reeves reassuringly as he led our small force across the Stray.

Up ahead through the darkness, I could just about make out a small copse of trees where our three horses had been hidden. I would have very much liked one of the mounts to have been Tribune, however that was clearly impossible given his Herculean efforts earlier in the day. In any event, at first sight it looked like Benson had secured sturdy working animals. At last we could set about rescuing Miss Meredith and clearing my own name in the process. The horses whinnied fretfully on hearing us approaching but, once we were in view, they calmed themselves. We untied them and slowly walked them away from Harrogate. I was fearful of the horses being injured by walking into a rabbit hole and so we led, and the horses followed. If anyone fell into a hole it would be one of us.

Navigation at night and a cloudy one at that, was tricky. The only thing we could do was keep to the road south with the lights of Harrogate at our rear. We eventually found our way onto the turnpike road to Leeds where we were able to travel with a little more confidence, endeavouring to make up as much ground as possible before daylight. Once the lights of the town disappeared, we lit three torches and walked on much easier.

We travelled slowly but surely. Travelling at night always made me nervous. I didn't believe, as many still did, that this was the time the dead walked. Nevertheless, my mind worried about what my eyes couldn't see. After an hour or so we reached a small stream which looked like a good place to stop. Happily it was the same stream I encountered on my way into Harrogate just before I came across the broken down carriage belonging to Miss Coutts. That seemed like a lifetime ago. We let the horses drink when an owl hooted, reminding us that under the cover of darkness another world prospered. We walked them over to a small wooded area, tied their reins to a sturdy tree and then found a dry place to sit down. The three of us rested, leaving the remainder of the night to the spirits and the owls.

Chapter 29

None of us had slept very well. The night air was cold and the nocturnal creatures active, nevertheless the rest we did achieve was welcome. Sinderby-Smythe constantly complained about the cold and frequently disappeared behind a tree to relieve himself. The sounds of the night were now replaced with the singing of small birds welcoming the arrival of a new day. With dawn breaking, we mounted our horses for the start of what we all expected to be a very long day in the saddle.

We continued to head south and were soon close to Leeds. Breakfast had been bread and cheese, which had been kindly made for us by my aunt's cook, Mrs Parker and neatly stored with all manner of other supplies in our saddle bags. Benson had added the timetables and maps I had requested.

"I could kill for a cup of hot tea," I said to Lieutenant Reeves as we rode through a wood just beyond Harewood House.

"That would be nice," agreed Reeves. "Did someone say hot tea?" added Sinderby-Smythe.

"Yes, lieutenant, although don't get your hopes up, it may be a day or two before we get chance of one."

I then reflected on the events of the previous day, "I ask you gentlemen, who but Constable Hardisty would believe that anyone would leave his own watch in the hands of the man he'd just murdered?" I said, continuing to express disbelief.

"Someone clearly knew the constable's limited powers of thought," added Sinderby-Smythe.

"You don't think the constable is somehow involved in this conspiracy do you?" asked Reeves.

"Unlikely," I said. "All the same, I would guess for a few pies he would do anything for anyone."

We all laughed, which boosted our spirits and took our minds off the uncertainties that lay ahead.

As the sun rose over the hills to the east, we rode down into the industrial heartland of Leeds. We began to see more and more people commencing their daily labours, providing us with a sharp reminder that we needed to get to Leeds' main coaching inn quickly.

"What's the plan, sir?" enquired Sinderby-Smythe.

"The plan, lieutenant, is to see if anyone remembers seeing the Russians' carriage yesterday evening and take it from there."

A good starting place would be one of the main coaching inns and the only one I had heard mention of was the Bull and Mouth which is on the east side of Briggate near the centre of town. I remembered from the various timetables that stages left every morning at ten o'clock bound for Manchester. I was hoping that someone at the Bull and Mouth would know something. Even though the Russians were travelling in a private carriage, they would almost certainly stick to the best roads which would be those used by the mail coaches. They may also need to arrange changes of horses or simply stop for a rest. I hoped it would be the latter as that would make them much easier to catch. If they change horses regularly, it will be a devil of a job to make up the time we've lost.

We had already given them over twelve hours' start although I was hoping that they would have spent a good deal of those hours sleeping. With a renewed sense of urgency we spurred on our horses to the east side of Briggate, in the heart of Leeds. We were now riding through streets lined with workers' cottages with smoke rising out of almost every chimney. We slowed to a walk as we approached the Bull and Mouth Inn and, despite the fact that it was still early, there was a great deal of activity with horses and coaches alike being prepared for their daily journeys. I could clearly see the 'True Briton' stage which would be heading to Manchester at ten o'clock. Coaches went from Leeds to all parts of England and so now we needed a deal of help and a lot of luck.

There was a small post office next to the inn where tickets for travel could be purchased and also mail and parcels could be left for posting. I motioned to Reeves and Sinderby-Smythe to tie our horses up outside the office. Irrespective of the time of day I hoped there would be someone around who would be able to assist us. We all dismounted and then were instantly stopped in our tracks. At our feet by the right hand side of the door was a parcel of newspapers. Our eyes couldn't help being drawn to the headline on the front page of Saturday's *Leeds Mercury* which read, 'Horrific Killing in Harrogate – Captain in 11th Light Dragoons Charged with Murder.'

We all looked at each other, speechless. That was uncomfortably quick reporting and probably due to journalists covering the race meeting finding more to write about than they had bargained for. The ink on the paper could have barely had chance to dry. In view of this unfortunate newspaper headline, we needed to be extremely circumspect in what we said for fear of being overheard. Regardless of the fact that the newspaper headline had been superseded by my release from custody, there were around thirty constables in Leeds and I daren't risk being arrested again. This came as a sharp reminder that yesterday's events in Harrogate would place many obstacles in the way of our efforts to rescue Miss Meredith. No doubt exactly the way her abductors had intended.

We walked through the door and thanks to a night in the countryside, I looked nothing like a Captain in the Light Dragoons. In a strange sort of way, the fact that the newspaper believed I was still in custody made it unlikely that anyone would make any connection between me and the Captain referred to in the paper. Nevertheless, no matter how hard I tried to hide it, I still possessed a guilty look.

There was a portly middle-aged man, bespectacled and bald, standing in the office behind a counter. At first I wasn't sure whether his role was clerical or not, until I spotted a pen in his hand which suggested he almost certainly was. We needed to find out whatever we could without raising any alarm bells. Meanwhile I was conscious that in all probability, this place was being watched.

"Mornin' gents, 'ow can I 'elp thee?" asked the man cheerfully.

"Good morning to you too, sir," I said, removing my hat.

"We all work for The Yorkshire Railway Company and a couple of our engineers and two ladies may have passed this way last night. They were in a private carriage. You didn't happen to see them by any chance?"

The man thought about my question and then replied, "Aye, we get a lot o' carriages through 'ere each day, lad. Where d' tha say they'd cum from?"

"I didn't say. But I am pretty sure they travelled down from Harrogate," I said.

"Last neet, tha sez?" he asked as he deliberated. "Arrigate. Posh then," he reflected.

"That's right, should have got in around five o'clock," I said, turning to Reeves and Sinderby-Smythe who both nodded all the while, straining to understand the man's accent.

"Aye, I do remember now tha cums to mention it. There warra private carriage, an' it 'ad two armed guards. Tha' wouldn't a' thought they needed guards for railway engineers, would tha?"

"No, that will be them. The engineers are Russian. Nervous sorts, the Ruski's," I said, trying to play down the importance of the guards. The last thing I wanted was a hue and cry spooking the Russians whilst they had Miss Meredith in their grasp. "I don't suppose you saw which way they went? I have an urgent message for them," I added hopefully.

"Well, if I'm not mistaken they split up, ant forrin gentleman an' his wife 'edded for t' railway station at Marsh Lane. An' when I say forrin, I dunt mean a Lancastrian or owt like that. I mean a proper forinner, so cud a' been Russian."

I looked at my fellow officers who seemed amused at the definition of a 'proper foreigner'.

"Could you describe the man and wife who headed for the railway station? I need to be certain that he is our man," I then asked, trying to firmly establish who had gone where.

"E 'ad a black beard, an' wore glasses an' all, 'is misses were a gud looker, bit peeky looking though."

There was no mistake, this was Vladimir and Svetlana Von Benckendorff.

"That's them," I said, adding, "So what can you tell us about the others?"

"The others stayed in t' carriage an' 'edded west. Can't a' gone much futher though, as there werra big Chartist meetin' planned last neet," said the manager.

"You mean they couldn't have gone too far for safety reasons?" I enquired.

"Dead right, lad," he replied. "Even wi' armed guards, it can be very dangerous at them there Chartist meetins. I'm told that summ'at troops from barracks went ower there to keep t'peace."

"I don't suppose you could describe the two who remained in the private carriage?"

"Sorry, lad," replied the old man. "They nivver got art, so I couldn't gerra a gud look at 'em. It worra a man and a woman though, reet enough. An' it looked like they won'id sum privacy cos cuttens ont' carriage wur partly drawn."

That had to be the one-eyed Russian and Miss Meredith. That would explain the guards and the need for privacy. At last, we were on their trail! They were headed west but their reasoning for this still puzzled me.

There was nothing more to be learned here, so we thanked the manager by giving him a few shillings for his trouble and then led our mounts away from the Bull and Mouth.

We stopped a few hundred yards away near a blacksmith's forge. It looked like the blacksmith was just firing up his forge for the day, so we walked a little further in order to be out of ear shot.

"Well, gentlemen, there we have it. They have split up and it looks like Miss Meredith has gone west with the one-eyed manservant whilst Vladimir and Svetlana are heading east and home," I said.

"I'm glad you understood what that man said, sir, for the life of me I couldn't understand a word he was saying. Do I take it that since they have split up, we will be splitting up too?" asked Sinderby-Smythe.

"Unfortunately, yes," I replied. "I will take Reeves and head west. He's a Lancastrian, a 'forriner', which might come in handy," I said, lightening the moment. "Also, depending on where we end up, we may be able to seek assistance from Lord Redmayne."

"And you will head east and try and catch Vladimir and Svetlana before they can board a ship. You are going to need help though, if you were on your own you would have an almighty job to get them under lock and key before nightfall. I wouldn't want them escaping because you'd fallen asleep. No disrespect to you lieutenant, but we must head directly to the barracks in Chapeltown and co-opt support."

We all mounted and rode through yet more rows of workers' terraced houses, interspersed with factories, until we reached the home of the 15th Hussars. The barracks were surrounded by a high brick wall and had two large wooden gates facing Chapeltown road. We dismounted and I banged on the side door.

A sentry opened the door.

"Take me to your commanding officer, my name is Captain Townsend," I said exerting sufficient authority to compensate for my lack of uniform.

"Captain Upton is not here, sir. He has taken most of the troop to Hartshead Moor," said the sentry saluting.

He reluctantly pushed the gates open allowing the three of us to walk our horses into the barracks.

"Then who's in charge?" I asked as the sentry closed the door behind us.

"Lieutenant Atkinson is the officer in charge, sir."

"Then, take me to him," I replied.

The sentry took our horses and led us across the parade ground towards the main building. He then handed over our horses to a private and told him to find Lieutenant Atkinson 'sharpish'. After which the sentry promptly returned to his post by the main gate.

The private scurried off, returning a minute or so later with Lieutenant Atkinson.

"I'm Lieutenant Atkinson," said the fresh faced young officer.

"Lieutenant, my name is Captain Townsend of the 11th Light Dragoons," I said, which immediately brought a salute that I quickly returned.

"And these two officers are Lieutenant Sinderby-Smythe and 2nd Lieutenant Reeves," whereupon both of my officers stood to attention.

"At ease gentlemen," I said to them all.

"Now lieutenant, you may be wondering what we three officers from the 11th Light Dragoons are doing here in Leeds? Well, not to waste too much time on this, I will be brief. We are in pursuit of three Russian spies who, yesterday, kidnapped a young woman in Harrogate. They fled this way and arrived in Leeds yesterday evening. Having made enquiries at the Bull and Mouth, we now understand that two of them have headed east and the other, together with the kidnapped lady, appear to have headed west in a private and well-armed carriage. As I am sure you can understand, this now makes pursuit of these villains very difficult for the three of us without additional support."

"I see," said Lieutenant Atkinson thoughtfully. "But I regret that there are only a few of us left here, sir, and with all these Chartist meetings, I cannot spare anyone."

"Well, like it or not lieutenant, our need is greater than yours. I will take full responsibility, nonetheless, I will be leaving here with at least one of your men," I said, pressing the young officer hard.

"I fully understand, sir. However, I regret to report that all we have here are the injured and a couple of men who I feel sure you will not want."

"And who might these unwanted men be?" I asked, growing increasingly impatient as my mind conjured up a picture of the Russians' carriage moving further away from us with every passing minute.

"Private Bates and Private Roylance, sir."

"Didn't I read about those two being flogged in the newspaper?" I asked, recalling an article I had read whilst trawling through a pile of newspapers at Pickersgill Palliser's post office.

"That is correct, sir, although strictly speaking they weren't actually flogged," replied the lieutenant sheepishly.

"And what does that mean?" I asked impatiently.

"Well, sir, with the masses being a bit hostile towards the military at present, they like to hear of our men being punished if they have misbehaved. Having said that, if they had their way we would be whipping men for the most minor of indiscretions and we would have no men left. Anyway, given that the sentences are carried out behind these high walls, the masses are none the wiser if we chose to exercise leniency. But having told the public that the men have been thrashed, we tend to keep them hidden away for a few days, saying they are not fit for service."

"And what did Private Bates and Private Roylance do to warrant a flogging in the first place?" I asked.

"Private Roylance got involved in a misunderstanding over a saddle and Private Bates had an altercation with a landlord who served him beer in a tankard that he had moments earlier been using as a spittoon."

"How did Private Bates react to that?" I asked.

"He made the landlord drink the beer. The landlord spat out the beer at Bates and then Bates laid him out with one blow."

"He'll do. Ask Bates to be ready to travel in ten minutes. Get him a horse, provisions and also have him take his uniform off. No-one around here will see him if he's accompanying Lieutenant Sinderby-Smythe east to Kingston upon Hull."

"Very good, sir," said a somewhat reluctant Lieutenant Atkinson.

I then walked out of the building, back into the parade ground and went straight for my horse. Reeves and Sinderby-Smythe followed suit.

"We cannot afford to wait to meet Private Bates. In spite of his record, he sounds like a capable man. Nevertheless, I would caution you against drinking beer with him," I said, a little mischievously to Lieutenant Sinderby-Smythe.

"I suggest that, whether we catch our respective quarry or not, we all meet back at the Bull and Mouth late Sunday afternoon, which will give us enough time to get back to Harrogate and prepare for the hand-over on Monday morning at half past seven. I pray that at least one of us succeeds."

"Very good, sir," said Sinderby-Smythe. "I presume that Mr and Mrs Von Benckendorff have travelled on the railway to Selby and then some barge to Kingston upon Hull?"

"That would be my guess," I replied adding, "Good luck lieutenant, I am counting on you to bring those Russians back. If we are not successful in rescuing Miss Meredith, having Vladimir and Svetlana will at least give us something to bargain with. If either of us are not at the Bull and Mouth by six o'clock on Sunday evening, the other should head for Harrogate and seek out Miss Coutts and Major Phillips."

I then took the eastbound timetables out of the saddle bags and handed them to the lieutenant, who promptly placed them in his own saddle bags. We all wished each other good speed and vowed to meet back in Leeds at the earliest possible moment.

Reeves and I mounted our horses, rode across the parade ground and out through the large gates. We would be chasing the carriage west. It was heavily armed and now there were just the two of us in pursuit.

Chapter 30

Angela Coutts woke early, the events of the previous day having replayed themselves many times in her head during the night.

Her maid, Emily, helped her prepare for the long journey to Sheffield, which was likely to be hectic and stressful. Emily had already loaded onto the family carriage additional provisions and clothing for all eventualities. With all the preparations complete, Miss Coutts made her way down to the hotel's entrance to find Major Phillips already waiting.

They walked towards the carriage and noticed several sprays of flowers which had been laid in memory of Thomas Dawson. Once again, she was provided with an unwelcome reminder of the dangers which may lie ahead. A point which was underlined when Angela spotted four armed coachmen sitting on the top of the carriage, two at the front and two at the rear. With everyone safely on board, the carriage made its way onto the popular turnpike road to Leeds, after which it would head into the industrial heartland of South Yorkshire to find Mr Botterill.

The Major sat facing Angela Coutts, with Emily alongside her mistress. The Major poured over a map of Sheffield which he had obtained earlier from Mr Dearlove, the concerned owner of the Queen. The abduction of one of his guests could have far reaching repercussions for the hotels of Harrogate. Consequently, he was happy to provide assistance in any way he could.

"You will not be surprised to hear, Major, that I had a very troubled night," and then with her emotions trying to get the better of her added, "Poor Hannah. This is simply awful. We must find her before it's too late."

"I know this is very difficult for you, Miss Coutts, but please don't upset yourself. Everything that can be done is being done," said Major Phillips confidently as he put the map of Sheffield away.

After composing herself, Angela continued, "Have you managed to find out anything more about Theodore Botterill?" she asked.

"I am afraid not, miss, we only know what was in the ransom note and that

Mr Botterill can be found in the area of Ecclesfield in Sheffield," replied the Major.

"And the garrison at York? Have you managed to get word to them to keep their distance so as not to alarm the Russians?"

"Most certainly, I made sure a despatch was sent first thing this morning," he replied.

"Thank you, Major, let us hope they follow your instructions," reflected Angela.

"I am sure they will, but Lord Palmerston is another matter, although I would be very surprised if he can get additional support to us by half past seven on Monday morning," said the Major.

"I share your concerns, nevertheless we have done all that can be expected of us, have we not Major?" enquired Angela. "Perhaps by acquiring the plans for the repeating rifle we are at least buying time for Captain Townsend to find Hannah and rescue her."

"Quite right, miss. That is how I see it, too. We need to hold our nerve and look to outwit these devils," said Major Phillips, pulling a parcel from his travelling bag.

"And what have you there, Major?" asked Angela.

"Late last night I received a letter from Captain Townsend, obviously written whilst he was being held at the constable's house. In the letter he made a couple of suggestions which I acted upon. I think we all agree that we are being watched and so there has to be a chance that if we succeed in obtaining the plans from Mr Botterill, the Russians will not wait until the Devil's Arrows on Monday morning to get their hands on them."

"You mean that they might attack us en route?" said Angela, clearly shocked.

"Well, I am afraid that has to be a possibility, which is why the Captain suggested we do two things. One was to bring extra coachmen and make sure that they were all armed. That may be enough to discourage an attack, but in the event it is not, he also recommended that we appear to post the plans to ourselves at the Queen."

"And why should we do that?" asked Angela, a trifle confused.

"To avoid the Russians being tempted to dispossess us of the plans without handing over Miss Meredith in exchange. Clearly, if we do not have the plans there is no point in attacking us, particularly as we are so well defended. The Captain feels that they are unlikely to risk their lives without being certain that at the end of it all they will capture the plans."

"Won't they think posting the plans odd? Surely there is not sufficient time for the plans to arrive by post?" asked Angela.

"The post takes less than twenty four hours from Sheffield and so anything posted later today should arrive in Harrogate well before the handover. We want the Russians to believe that we have posted the plans to discourage an attack against our carriage. We hope they see the use of an armed mail coach to transport the plans to Harrogate as a prudent measure on our part. They may suspect that it is merely a diversionary tactic, however, by the time they have established that, ourselves and the real plans will be long gone."

"Interesting plan, Major. Let us hope it works," said Angela.

"My sentiments entirely. If nothing else, it will give these rogues something to think about. At least some good came from the Captain's enforced incarceration. However, I fervently hope that the Captain and his men can rescue Miss Meredith before the appointed hour. Failing which, we will just have to pray that he can come up with another scheme to outwit these scoundrels and wrestle the plans back. After all, it's a long way back to Russia from here."

The Major's remarks, although comforting to Angela, were nevertheless without guarantees and extremely daunting. She remained deeply concerned, not only for the safety of her companion, but for her travelling party too.

The carriage travelled to Leeds with all possible haste. Angela had told the coachmen that even though they must travel quickly, they must also take care to avoid a repetition of the broken wheel they experienced a week earlier on their journey to Harrogate.

All the while the coach sped on and Angela found herself constantly looking out of the window thinking deeply about Miss Meredith and the challenges they faced in getting the plans safely to the Devil's Arrows. The road was badly rutted in parts and in their quest for speed, the passengers regularly found themselves buffeted about. The carriage slowed as the horses struggled up the hill at Harewood and then came to a complete stop near the gates to Harewood House, allowing the horses a chance to drink. Emily took advantage of this to obtain liquid refreshment for both her mistress and Major Phillips from the Harewood Arms.

The break was all too brief for time was precious. The carriage lurched forward and then backwards as it resumed its journey south towards Leeds. The road became increasingly congested as they made their way into the centre of town. Eventually, the carriage arrived at the Bull and Mouth Inn in Leeds, enabling everyone to take a well-earned rest. Miss Coutts disembarked with Emily and they both walked into the inn. The Major looked around carefully to ensure there were no more surprises lying in wait. If they were being watched by yet more spies, they were not in evidence. Everything was quiet save for the activity surrounding the 'True Briton' stage, which was being prepared for its journey to Manchester. They were now a third of the way to Sheffield and had less than two days to acquire Mr Botterill's plans and return in time for the handover at the Devil's Arrows at half past seven on Monday morning.

Chapter 31

The more I thought about the abduction, the more convinced I became that everything had been carefully planned and very well executed. We were obviously dealing with experienced professionals who were extremely cunning and expert in the art of deception. Dividing themselves into two groups in Leeds was something I should have considered.

Reeves and I galloped out of the Chapeltown barracks in Leeds and followed the coach roads to Dewsbury, which provided us with a fairly uneventful ten mile ride. We were now in the heavy woollen district of West Yorkshire. Smoke billowed from the tall mill chimneys and by the appearance of its townsfolk, this was a tough place to live. We both dismounted and left our horses at the livery stables whilst we made enquiries at Dewsbury's various inns. I hoped that by stopping at all the regular coaching inns on the way to Manchester, I would hear more news of the Russians' carriage fleeing with Miss Meredith on board.

We were met by a wall of suspicion because anyone asking questions was immediately thought to be working for the authorities looking to root out Chartist agitators. Whether we were being deliberately misled or not, it was hard to determine. Nevertheless, no-one could recollect any heavily armed private carriage stopping in Dewsbury last night. With all the talk of a Chartist meeting and the 15th Hussars out on patrol, I was hoping that the Russians' carriage would have resisted the temptation to continue travelling too much further and opted for safety by spending the night nearby. Having retrieved our horses from Dewsbury's livery stable, we rode hard in the direction of Huddersfield.

On we rode through the heart of the woollen mills of Yorkshire, where the elegant hotels and wells of Harrogate were replaced by large factories and endless rows of terraced houses. In another lifetime the surrounding hills and countryside would have been picturesque, but for now it was very much over shadowed by the industrial footprint of wool production.

"I say, Reeves, when you listened in to the Russians talking at the Plough Inn, did you mention something about a meeting with Count Zadovich?" I said.

"That's right, sir. They definitely talked about Count Zadovich and meeting up with him," he replied.

"I don't suppose you formed an opinion as to where that meeting was set to take place?" I continued.

"I just assumed they were talking about meeting the Count back in Russia when they had successfully completed their mission."

"But could they have been talking about a meeting in England?" I asked.

"Well yes, I suppose so. I just presumed the meeting was set to take place in Russia."

"All the same, it could be here in England?"

"Well, yes, I suppose so, sir."

"Then that might explain why they are headed west and why they needed timetables for Manchester and Liverpool. We assumed these timetables were to help the Russians navigate their way out of the country, however isn't it just as likely they were to be used in assisting someone to navigate their way into the country?"

"Yes, that would make sense, sir," said Reeves.

"Suppose that Count Zadovich came into Liverpool and boards a locomotive to Manchester? He could meet up with the one-eyed manservant and Miss Meredith anywhere between here and Manchester. It does make sense! It does! Meeting right in the middle of the most volatile part of England where Chartists outnumber the military by at least a hundred to one. That makes it really tricky for us and beats just holing up somewhere until Monday, where they are at risk of being discovered."

It felt like a light was at last being shone in the darkest corners of my mind.

"What odds will you give me that they never contemplated handing over Miss Meredith at the Devil's Arrows and always intended snatching the plans from Miss Coutts on her way back from Sheffield before cutting across country to rendezvous with Count Zadovich somewhere near Manchester? Then, once he has satisfied himself that he has everything he needs to build a repeating rifle, they all set sail from Liverpool, maybe even in the Count's own boat?"

"If that's right, sir, Miss Coutts is in grave danger," said Reeves, at which I reassured him that I had at least anticipated one move they might have made and taken steps to avert it. We rode on with our spirits lifted, more certain of the rationale for heading west.

It was late morning by the time we arrived at the next coaching inn, with our horses white with sweat. Again we rested them at the local livery stable whilst we continued to make enquiries. Keeping these animals fit was essential for us to have any chance of rescuing Miss Meredith and returning to Harrogate in time to stop the rifle plans being handed over.

Reeves and I then walked into the Waterloo Inn which, happily, had news of the carriage we were following. At first, the landlord was typically reluctant to say anything, forcing me to line up some gold coins on the bar. These had the desired effect and he started to talk. He informed me that the occupants of the carriage had wanted to press on towards Manchester, but the threat posed by the Chartist meeting made them rethink their plans. They spent the night at the Waterloo Inn and left around eight o'clock this morning. I looked at my watch and noted that they were a little over three hours ahead. The race was on and we were gaining on them. We were about thirty miles from Manchester and we needed to make haste.

I couldn't be certain whether they were heading for the steam locomotive to Liverpool or rendezvousing with Count Zadovich in some hidden corner of the Lancashire/Yorkshire border. Either way our best chance of intercepting them was on the open road and although we were well behind, two single riders should be able to travel considerably faster than a heavy carriage. Added to which, the roads were tricky to negotiate, mountainous and congested in places with carts taking wool from the mills to the railway station in Manchester. Carriages often became stuck behind these carts for miles until they found a safe place to pass.

Lifted by the news from the Waterloo Inn, we rode out of Huddersfield with renewed purpose. Then, six miles later, we reached Marsden. However, due to the steep inclines on parts of the road, this stage of our journey took much longer than we'd hoped. We could no longer spare the time to stop at every inn and ask if anyone had seen the private carriage we chased. Wherever possible, we asked carriages coming towards us if they had seen a heavily armed coach, but without success. We had to hope that they hadn't turned off this road and were continuing to head for Manchester.

On we sped with little being said between myself and Reeves as we hung on to our mounts for dear life. Riding was becoming increasingly difficult as muscles ached and joints creaked. Every so often we would stop for a short while to allow the horses a rest and a drink, yet we kept the stops brief. We covered the nine miles from Marsden to Oldham a little easier as we came over the top of the hills and down the other side into Lancashire. The most welcome benefit of this was that it afforded us a panoramic view of the landscape and the road ahead. We stopped, took out our telescopes and whilst still in our saddles, we searched the terrain for signs of the Russians' carriage. A few miles further on, we could see a carriage but it was too far away for us to determine if it was armed and carrying Miss Meredith.

Oldham was the penultimate stop on the stage coach route from Leeds to Manchester and if they were planning to meet Count Zadovich in this border region between Yorkshire and Lancashire, this would represent our last chance to intercept them on the open road. If, on the other hand, they were planning to board the locomotive from Manchester then they would be in Liverpool in next to no time. Although Liverpool was a fine port, over the years it had attracted many individuals of dubious character, which would make finding anyone there almost impossible. Both Reeves and I were tiring and we were forced to stop again to water the horses and catch our breath. The horses were now permanently white with sweat and on the brink of being played out. Meanwhile, we continued to keep ourselves fed, thanks to the packages in our saddle bags prepared by my aunt's cook.

Occasionally we met carriages coming towards us and also passed several carts laden with products from the mills. On these narrow highways, I hoped that all of these would have caused delays to the carriage we chased. In spite of the fact that we were riding for all we were worth, there were no further sightings of the carriage we pursued. Then, a few miles from Manchester, Reeves spoke up.

"Sir, that's Lord Redmayne's estate up ahead," he said pointing to a considerable expanse of land on our right. I could just about make out a large house which gave the appearance of a grander version of Holderness House in Harrogate. So, this was where Lord Redmayne lived! I was torn between continuing and visiting His Lordship and swopping our horses. To stop now would almost certainly end our chances of catching the carriage before it reached Manchester. To continue risked losing our mounts through exhaustion. In the end I resolved to ride on for another mile, after which, if there was still no sign of the carriage, we would turn back and then pray that Lord Redmayne was in residence. When it looked like we had no alternative but to turn back, a carriage travelling west came into view, and now only a few hundred yards ahead.

"Do you see what I see Reeves?" I said to the 2nd Lieutenant.

"Yes, sir. There's the carriage," at which we both stopped our horses and delved into our saddle bags for our telescopes. I trained mine far ahead and focused in on the road.

"My God, that must be them!" I cried. "Come on, man. We must intercept that carriage before they can catch that damn steam engine to Liverpool." I was starting to think that if my theory of a meeting with Count Zadovich was still possible, then the location must be in either Manchester or Liverpool.

Our horses continued on bravely, even though they must have been exhausted. There was no doubting that we were pushing their endurance to the limit. On we rode and the carriage grew in size as we closed in on our quarry. Armed guards were now clearly visible riding up top which was a timely reminder of the dangers which lay ahead. They then rounded a bend, heavily wooded on both sides where for a moment we lost sight of them. Less than a minute later we rounded the same bend and as the road straightened out, we fully expected to be right behind them. And yet, much to our surprise, the road was deserted.

We both brought our horses to a stop and frantically retrieved our telescopes, however wherever we looked, there was no sign of them.

"A carriage can't just disappear," I said to Reeves, turning in my saddle to look behind us.

"Maybe they spotted us and pulled into those trees?" Reeves replied.

That appeared to be the only logical explanation and so we turned around and walked the horses back into the wooded area of the road searching for signs of our missing carriage. Unhelpfully, there were many wheel marks on the road, making it impossible to determine which had been made by the carriage we followed. We continued to retrace our steps until we came to the bend in the road at the start of the wooded area and there we noticed a narrow road leading off to the left. On closer inspection we could see deep channels in the soft ground which were clearly made recently by a heavily laden carriage. This had to be the carriage we sought and so we followed the tracks deep into the woods travelling carefully, anticipating trouble around every bend, but none appeared. The road looked hardly used; it was overgrown and in semi-darkness caused by a canopy of trees blocking out the light.

"Sir, I have a feeling that we are close to the shooting lodge of the Duke of Aldborough," said Reeves. "I used to live not far from here myself," he added.

"The Duke of Aldborough?" I replied. "I didn't realise that he had a house in this area," I said, suddenly recalling Mary, Duchess of Aldborough mentioning a shooting lodge in Lancashire. It never occurred to me that this would be sited so close to Lord Redmayne's, after all, Lancashire is a very large county.

"Yes, sir, the Duke and Lord Redmayne are neighbours," he replied.

"It's hard to see those two co-existing happily," I said, after having recently met Lord Redmayne, he appeared an altogether much more likeable fellow than the Duke of Aldborough. The Duke was a rake, a gambler and a rogue.

We came through the woods and brought our horses to a stop, as about two hundred yards ahead lay a shooting lodge. It was a fine brick built house with a long drive leading up to the front entrance. There was a turning circle for coaches and a road winding its way to a small coach house on the left. The coach we were seeking was parked there with two men fussing around the horses.

"There's a river to the back of the house. Good fishing there, sir," said Reeves, describing the landscape.

"Well, let's see if we can catch something ourselves, Reeves," I said, quickly dismounting. We then hid our mounts deep in the woods and tied them to a tree. Despite there being no water for them, there was plenty of grass and at least they could get a well-deserved rest. We took our pistols from the saddle bags and loaded them. I also took out my telescope. We walked stealthily towards the house and I wondered how on earth the Duke of Aldborough had become mixed up in all of this. Was he being paid by Count Zadovich for the use of his lodge? I tried to hazard a guess as to where the two might have met. I knew the Duke was a wastrel, although I never suspected him of what amounted to treason. We worked our way around to the right under the cover of the trees until we were level with the house which was now little more than one hundred yards away. All that lay between the house and ourselves was open grassland. I crouched down, brought the telescope to my eye and then focused on the windows of the house. Even though I could see men through the downstairs window, I couldn't get close enough to make out who they were. I was hoping to see the Russian servant with the patch over his eye, but despite all my best efforts, I couldn't get a good enough sighting. I moved the telescope to the top windows and briefly caught sight of a woman. Miss Meredith? I couldn't make out any of her features and yet I was certain it was her.

"Reeves, top window on the left. Tell me if you see anything," I said, passing him the telescope.

"I see a woman, sir. She looks familiar, but I can't be certain as we are too far away," he replied.

"And how many men can you see through the downstairs window?" I asked.

"I count four, sir," he replied, handing the telescope back to me.

"And now we need a plan to rescue her. So, Reeves tell me, how do two officers from the 11th Light Dragoons take on two or maybe three armed guards, one Russian and all the staff of the Duke of Aldborough?"

Reeves thought for a moment and then said, "We need help, sir. Might I suggest we call on your good friend, Lord Redmayne?"

"If he's in residence, I am sure he will help. After all, Miss Coutts is a very close friend of his. What's the quickest way to his house from here?" I asked, all the while retreating further back into the woods.

"I can show you, sir," he replied.

"No, Reeves, you're going to have to remain here on watch. It is still possible that they have not come here to meet anyone and could have stopped merely to rest a while. They could be back on the move at any time, and if they do move, you need to follow them and leave me a trail."

"Very good, sir. Lord Redmayne's house should be easy enough to find. Just follow the river east for about two miles."

"Then this is the plan, Reeves. I will try and get to Lord Redmayne whilst you keep watch from here. If you see the carriage leaving with Miss Meredith on board, fire two shots in the air and I will return just as fast as I can. Hopefully the sound of the shots won't spook them and they will think it's just some poacher, shooting game. I will also see if His Lordship will lend us two fresh mounts."

"Very good, sir," replied Reeves.

I then retrieved my game horse and slowly led him through the woods in search of the river. I could hear the sound of running water quite a while before I saw anything and then once I reached the river, I headed east. It seemed further than Reeves had suggested. So much so, that I began to think I must have gone wrong somewhere. Before I could question the directions again, I saw the house we had seen earlier from the Manchester coach road. It was undoubtedly grand and elegant, nevertheless, that was all I could take in as my mind worked excitedly at the prospect of rescuing Miss Meredith. I rode up to the front door and was greeted by a young man who took the reins of my horse, allowing me to dismount with ease. I walked up the dozen or so steps to the front door, and while trying to locate some form of bell to ring, the door opened.

"Can I help you, sir?" enquired the man I took to be Lord Redmayne's butler.

"Yes, could you please inform Lord Redmayne that Captain Townsend is here to see him?"

"Do you have an appointment, sir?" asked the butler.

"I regret not, nonetheless, if you could tell His Lordship that I am here on a matter of life and death and seek his most urgent attention, I would be very grateful," I said, endeavouring to convey a degree of calm authority.

"Please wait in the library, sir," said the butler, who was completely unmoved by my mention of a life and death matter.

I was shown into a very large and handsome library where I waited. Mercifully,

I did not have to wait long and within a minute or so, Lord Redmayne marched purposefully through the door.

"My dear boy, how are you? What brings you to this neck of the woods?" he enquired, extending his hand and shaking mine warmly.

"I'm well, sir, thank you, but sadly I bring grave news," at which point I relayed the events of the last two days. I spoke quickly, even though there was much to tell.

"My God!" he exclaimed. "I can't believe that Aldborough would work with the Russians on something like this! I knew he was a loose cannon, yet betraying one's own country is the worst crime a man can commit. We must stop them all, Captain!" and with that he called for his butler and told him to assemble all his men, fully armed and ready to ride in ten minutes.

"Come, Captain. We have a lady to save. I should have stayed in Harrogate and helped you. Damn Chartists stirring up trouble. If they had behaved themselves, I would never have left that poor girl," said Lord Redmayne, grabbing his pistols and coat from his butler as we walked out of the front door where horses and men were being assembled.

"Fortunately, Captain, in order to protect ourselves from these Chartist riots, we have been forced to keep our men well trained, well armed and ready for battle." All the while, men readied themselves to ride.

At this point, I mentioned that our horses were played out and ventured to ask if Reeves and I might exchange our horses for two fresh ones of his.

"Certainly, Captain," he said and after barking orders to his groom, two fine horses quickly appeared, being led by one of Lord Redmayne's armed riders.

"They should do you, Captain. Not quite up to the standard of that thoroughbred of yours. All the same, they're good stayers."

I quickly took my saddle bags from my exhausted horse and threw them over the back of my new mount. I patted the horse on the neck and asked the stable boy to take good care of him. He had worked so hard and deserved good treatment. Lord Redmayne and I then mounted and readied ourselves for a battle. There were now eight of us, all armed and ready to catch a traitor and retrieve Miss Meredith from the Russians. There had been no shots fired from the Duke's hunting lodge, so off we sped to join Reeves, knowing that Miss Meredith was now only a short distance away.

Chapter 32

Earlier in the day, Angela Coutts and Major Phillips, having breakfasted at the Bull and Mouth in Leeds, headed south to find Mr Theodore Botterill. The coach first travelled through Wakefield and then onto Barnsley, where they stopped to water the horses and rest for a short while at the White Bear. They didn't stay there long and were soon back on the road, continuing to travel south to Sheffield. Despite the coach bouncing around on the uneven roads no-one showed any sign of discomfort. Major Phillips used the time productively by constantly reassuring Angela that a positive outcome would be achieved and that Miss Meredith would be rescued by Captain Townsend. Yet in spite of this apparent confidence, he persisted in prompting the coachmen to keep a sharp look out for signs of anyone following. They neared Sheffield in the early afternoon of Saturday.

"How do you propose we find Mr Theodore Botterill?" asked Angela.

"I would suggest that we first make enquiries at the post office," replied the Major, who was once again studying the map of Sheffield with great care.

"There should be a turning to Ecclesfield shortly. It ought to be on our right, given that we are travelling south," he added, as he looked hopefully through the carriage window.

There were no signs marking the way to Ecclesfield and so the carriage remained on the main road. Before too long they had entered the city of Sheffield through an area called Brightside.

"Looking around at all these factories and steel works, how does anyone come up with such a name?" observed the Major, acutely aware that they had travelled too far and had plainly missed the road to Ecclesfield.

The carriage drove towards the centre of Sheffield, passing more and more factories on the way. Huge clouds of smoke billowed from the countless chimneys and then slowly drifted away. The air became increasingly polluted and the passengers on the coach soon found difficulty in breathing. All the while the sounds of machinery and men working in tandem could be heard rising above the clatter of horses' hooves and carriage wheels on the cobblestones lining the road.

"How on earth do people survive here?" asked Angela, covering her mouth with a handkerchief, passed to her by Emily.

"With great difficulty, I shouldn't wonder," replied the Major, wafting the air with his outstretched hand.

The coach made its way past a cart laden with steel, pulled by extremely large horses.

"Those poor animals," noted Angela, wincing at the sight of one of the horses being whipped whilst pulling the overloaded cart.

The coach progressed slowly through this heartland of heavy industry. The Sheffield to Rotherham Railway was nearing completion and the Major pointed out what he thought looked like a station being built.

"Railways are popping up everywhere. Soon we will be able to travel in comfort from London to almost anywhere," said the Major.

"That can't happen a moment too soon," said Angela, still holding her handkerchief close to her mouth.

The carriage was passing a very large factory when the Major shouted for the coachman to stop. They were now outside the factory of Joseph Manning, manufacturers of knives and cutlery.

"Wait here a moment, Miss Coutts. I have an idea that someone at this place will know where we might find the road to Ecclesfield and the premises of Mr Botterill."

The Major descended the steps of the carriage and walked through the front entrance of the factory, which was the most impressive Angela had ever seen. It was three storeys high with a grand façade and ten large windows on each floor. All things considered it appeared to be a surprisingly elegant building.

Angela and Emily waited patiently and after a few minutes the Major returned, instructing the coachman to turn the coach around.

"Mr Botterill is well known here and I soon found someone who was able to direct us to his house," said the Major, looking very concerned as he resumed his seat in the carriage.

"What's wrong, Major?" asked Angela, sensing a problem.

"I don't quite know how to put this, but I regret to say that Mr Botterill is dead."

"Dead?" exclaimed Angela. "Why, that's simply awful! How can that be? What in the world are we going to do?" she asked anxiously.

"I agree that this makes everything devilishly difficult. However, I am advised that his death is very recent. Therefore, we can only hope that his widow or issue will be amenable to helping us," replied the Major.

The carriage duly turned around and, after about a mile, bore left by a large oak tree and along an unmarked road which apparently led to Ecclesfield. Retracing their steps necessitated returning through the smoke filled streets surrounding the foundries. Angela appeared oblivious to this inconvenience, having now found herself concerned with far greater problems. News of the death of Mr Botterill came as a shock, although it certainly went some way to explaining why the Russians had not found his invention easy to come by.

Despite the distance to Ecclesfield being a relatively short one, the road was in an increasingly poor condition. Frustratingly, it took a long time to arrive at their destination as they left the factories and workers' cottages of Sheffield well behind them. When they reached Ecclesfield, the Major looked out of the window and tried to match the view in front of him with the picture which had been planted in his mind at the Joseph Manning factory. He struggled to match the two and once again asked the coachman to stop. Whilst the horses had another breather, the Major walked around the carriage looking in all directions for the house described to him at the Joseph Manning works.

"I think it's over there," the Major said to the coachman, pointing to a modest detached house which was at the far side of a park. Although much smaller, this park was not dissimilar to the common grassland of the Harrogate Stray. The Major climbed back into the carriage and they drove to the house. The moment they arrived there, Angela straightened her clothing and then followed the Major in stepping down from the carriage. Emily watched on as her mistress and the Major stood for a brief moment surveying the Botterills' house. The Major repeated his instructions to the coachman to remain vigilant and watch closely for anyone paying an unhealthy interest in them. Then, following a reassuring glance to Angela, they made their way to the front door. The Major knocked on the door and a maid answered.

"Would it be possible to see Mrs Botterill?" enquired the Major. "We have come a great distance to meet with her on the most urgent business."

Before she could answer, a lady's voice could be heard from inside the house. "Who is it, Judy?"

"There is a lady and a gentleman here to see you, ma'am," replied the maid.

"Then show them in, girl," said the voice from within.

The maid opened the door fully and stepped to one side, allowing Angela and the Major to enter. The entrance hall was panelled in oak which seemed to extend throughout the house. They couldn't have progressed by more than two paces when they were met by a small middle-aged lady with greying hair, dressed from head to toe in black.

"Mrs Botterill, I presume?" enquired the Major, and the lady dressed in black nodded her head in affirmation.

"Allow me to introduce myself. I am Major Phillips, formerly of the 47th Regiment of the Lancashire Foot and this great lady is Miss Angela Coutts."

Mrs Botterill, on hearing the last name, immediately curtsied.

"Miss Coutts, I am very pleased to make your acquaintance…and yours too, Major," she said politely.

"And we are very pleased to meet you too, Mrs Botterill. May we say how sorry we were to hear of the passing of your husband," said Angela sympathetically.

"Thank you, miss," said Mrs Botterill. "It came as a great shock. Very sudden it was. He fell in the woods and broke his neck. A freak accident, they say."

"How awful for you, madam," added Angela.

"Please also accept my condolences, madam. We realise that this is a very difficult time for you and have no wish to impose on your grief, however, we would really appreciate a few minutes of your time to discuss a delicate matter," said the Major.

"Certainly, Major. Please follow me into the parlour. Judy, bring some tea," said Mrs Botterill, guiding the Major and Angela into a neat and charming room, warmed by a roaring fire.

"It's nice and warm in here," noted Angela, welcoming the fire after a long day on the road.

"I have felt ever so cold since we lost our Theo and so every fire in the house burns all day," replied Mrs Botterill, folding her arms as if to illustrate the chills she felt.

The three of them sat down around the impressive blaze which spat and roared at them while its flames reached ever higher. Both the Major and Angela took a moment to cast their eyes around the room. Aside from a few portraits and the odd landscape painting, there was nothing unusual to be seen, other than a display of pistols and rifles. Mrs Botterill observed her guests looking at these.

"Theo was obsessed with guns. He designed all the ones you can see. There is something special about each and every one of them; single barrelled, double barrelled and that strange looking thing on the right has three barrels."

"Actually, that is why we are here, Mrs Botterill. I am in desperate need of your help," said Angela.

"And I will be happy to help, miss, if I possibly can. But how can I help such a great lady as yourself? Is it something to do with the amount we owe the bank?" she enquired apprehensively.

"Not at all, Mrs Botterill, in fact quite the opposite. I would very much like to settle the loan on your behalf."

Mrs Botterill was puzzled by this, yet before she could say any more, Judy entered the room with the tea. Once the tea was poured, Judy left and the conversation resumed.

"I have travelled all the way from Harrogate to talk to you because we have been led to believe that your husband has developed a repeating rifle."

"That is true, miss. I told him to be careful and that no good would come from it, but he went ahead anyway," said Mrs Botterill, with a degree of sadness in her voice.

"Well, Mrs Botterill, I am in a dreadful situation. A close friend of mine has been kidnapped and the only thing that can save her are the plans to your husband's rifle. Consequently, I would very much like to purchase them from you," said Angela, her eyes pleading with Mrs Botterill.

Mrs Botterill looked lost for words and so Major Phillips attempted to further explain the desperate situation which had brought them to Ecclesfield.

"Mrs Botterill, what Miss Coutts has told you is unfortunately true. The villains responsible for kidnapping her close companion have murdered one man already and we believe that they will not hesitate to kill again. We have been given until half past seven on Monday morning to produce your late husband's plans, failing which, they assure us that we will never see our friend again."

Mrs Botterill gasped at the news.

"But that's simply awful!" she said. "Theodore was certain that he had perfected the repeating rifle, all the same, he only had his scribblings. He didn't have a completed rifle. He had made the odd piece of it and that was all."

"Might I enquire as to who else might have known of your late husband's work?" asked Major Phillips.

"Why, lots of people," replied Mrs Botterill, a little taken aback by the question, which in turn, surprised the Major.

"I would have thought that being of such importance to the country, secrecy would have been the order of the day," said the Major.

"Yes, you're right, Major, but I don't think anyone really believed that Theodore would succeed. A lot of people have tried to invent a repeating rifle and no-one has ever overcome the technical challenges. Even now, I don't think anyone believes his invention will work," replied Mrs Botterill.

"Well, madam, the Russians certainly believe it, as it is they who are threatening the life of my friend," said Miss Coutts.

"Russians, you say?" enquired an intrigued Mrs Botterill.

"Yes, that's right," replied Major Phillips.

"Now, that is strange," said Mrs Botterill. "Theodore told me that a Russian with a patch over one eye had been pestering him for work. Frightening he was, and very persistent. He wanted to know everything about his inventions. Anyway, Theo didn't like the man and wouldn't tell him anything. Judy thinks that it was him who broke into this house whilst we were all at the funeral."

"What is the world coming to? Only a sewer rat would do such a thing!" said Major Phillips adding, "Was anything stolen?"

"No, Major, that was the strange thing. In spite of the house being a mess, with drawers pulled out in every room, nothing appeared to have been taken," replied Mrs Botterill.

"Thank heaven for that!" said a relieved Major Phillips. "However, from what you say Mrs Botterill, the Russian could have heard about the repeating rifle from almost anyone?"

"Yes, I suppose that's right," answered Mrs Botterill.

"Do you think that you might allow us to purchase the plans to your husband's repeating rifle, Mrs Botterill?" implored Angela. "As I said before, it is a matter of life and death and rest assured that I will purchase them from you and only on terms to your liking."

"Miss Coutts, that is very generous of you, but there is no guarantee that my husband's invention will work. He was a good talker and when people said he couldn't design a repeating rifle, he told them that he already had." After a moment's reflection, she added wistfully, "I thought he was just saying that to shut people up."

"Would you happen to know if your late husband filed anything with the patent office?" added Major Phillips. If a patent had been filed there would have been drawings of the repeating mechanism sitting in London.

"No, Major, he didn't trust them at the patent office. He said inventions just pile up there and many are lost and never seen again."

"Did anyone else work on the rifle with him? Someone who could continue from where he left off?" asked Major Phillips, persisting to try and establish whether or not the rifle could still be built in England even if these plans fell into the hands of the Russians.

"No, Major. He wouldn't let anyone near his plans and drawings. He kept the details hidden. He didn't want anyone to know how he had solved the problems of the repeating mechanism until the time was right," replied Mrs Botterill.

Angela finished her tea and looked at the time. She was keen to conclude this business and commence their return journey before nightfall. It would be dangerous continuing in the dark and after damaging a wheel on the way to Harrogate, she didn't want to take any risks on such an important matter as this. There was the added worry of being intercepted by the Russians.

"I really am very sorry to press you, Mrs Botterill, nevertheless we have such a distance to travel and with time so very much against us, would it be possible for you to let us see your husband's plans to the repeating rifle?" asked Angela. "While you retrieve them, I will write you a promissory note for whatever sum you deem fair."

Mrs Botterill agreed and went in search of the repeating rifle plans whilst Angela, having been provided with a pen and paper commenced writing. Meanwhile Major Phillips was rapidly coming to the conclusion that Mr Botterill had perhaps exaggerated his claims. And unfortunately for him these claims, on reaching the ears of the Russians, had probably resulted in his early demise. He now anxiously awaited the plans, fearing that they could just reflect the ravings of a man pressured by his friends into saying more than he should. Either way, whatever Mrs Botterill handed them was what they would be taking to the Devil's Arrows on Monday morning. The longer they waited for Mrs Botterill to return, the more agitated Major Phillips became. Eventually his patience evaporated and he rose emphatically from his chair and paced up and down the room. The flames in the fire weakened, no longer spitting venom and radiating heat. Angela began to wonder whether Mrs Botterill had fled, as it seemed unlikely that she would let her fire die like this. Maybe, whoever broke in on the day of the funeral had taken the plans and it was only now that Mrs Botterill was realising that.

The fire weakened further and the house was quiet. Major Phillips looked outside and could see Emily waiting patiently in their carriage guarded by four armed coachmen. The room grew ever darker as daylight began to fade. A clock somewhere chimed seven times.

"I think we need to go in search of her, Major," said a concerned Angela.

Before he could respond, the door flew open and in walked Mrs Botterill. It had taken an age, but she had found her husband's drawings and notes to his treasured repeating rifle.

"I am sorry it has taken me so long. I couldn't bear to look at Theo's things and so I had Judy move all his belongings into the attic. He had a lot of drawings and it took me a while to find these," said Mrs Botterill, handing to the Major two sheets of paper which amounted to the plans.

The Major looked at what he had been given. He had learnt how to strip and rebuild any gun during his many years of fighting battles with the 47th Regiment of the Lancashire foot. He studied the drawings hard and after a few moments he found himself understanding them. Whether this invention would work or not was debatable, but at least they had secured the ransom demanded by the Russians. Either way, he prayed that Captain Townsend would return with Miss Meredith before the appointed time on Monday morning. For now though, it was a race against the clock, with their next objective being to return quickly to Harrogate whilst still in possession of the plans. By the time Angela and Major Phillips had concluded the formalities with Mrs Botterill, the sun was signalling that the end of another day was drawing near. They asked Mrs Botterill where they might find the nearest post office on the road north and then thanked her for all her assistance. When they eventually reached the post office it was well after its usual closing time. However, Major Phillips managed to persuade the post master to accept the bogus package they had brought with them from Harrogate, enabling them to turn their attentions towards finding an inn or hotel where they could safely spend the night.

They soon found such a suitable place conveniently located within a few hundred yards of the post office and a much fatigued and yet partially relieved Angela eventually retired for the evening. Major Phillips guarded Botterill's plans while he himself was guarded by the armed coachmen who took shifts during the night. They had acquired the plans that would procure the release of Miss Meredith at the Devil's Arrows on Monday morning. They were, however, only a few miles north of Sheffield, almost certainly being watched and now faced the challenge of securing safe passage for themselves and the plans on the long, precarious road north.

Chapter 33

Daylight was in the process of saying farewell to another day, as we headed for the Duke of Aldborough's shooting lodge. Riding west we found ourselves constantly shading the setting sun from our eyes. We were working our way through the trees on the southern bank of the river which conveniently marked our route. The eight of us travelled quietly with only Lord Redmayne occasionally breaking the silence.

"I hope you can shoot with a gun as well as you can with a billiard cue," said Lord Redmayne, seeking to lighten the mood.

No-one knew what awaited us at the Duke's lodge, other than trouble. Having gone to such extreme lengths and murdered one person already, the Russians were not going to give up Miss Meredith easily. There was a feeling of unease amongst us all at the involvement of the Duke of Aldborough. As we neared the lodge we dismounted, secured the horses and then moved cautiously forward. We walked side by side between the trees with weapons at the ready. Most of the men carried rifles, with just one or two preferring pistols. His Lordship was in the centre of the line sporting two pistols, both double barrelled. Recalling that Sinderby-Smythe and Reeves both used similar weapons outside the constable's house made me feel like a new fashion in armaments had been born, which had passed me by. I kept one of my pistols in my belt and my Joseph Manning knife in my boot. Up ahead there was the sound of movement in the woods and Lord Redmayne signalled everyone to stop. Someone was walking towards us. Lord Redmayne directed us all to lie low and hide behind whatever cover we could find. His Lordship went to ground carefully, muttering that he was too old to be doing this sort of thing. The sound of footsteps became louder although it seemed that whoever was heading for us had slowed their pace. Then there was silence. The only sounds to be heard were that of the river running free and the occasional squawk of a lone crow. Everything was so quiet that I could hear my own breathing. Then in the next instant I nearly leapt out of my skin as I felt a tap on my shoulder.

"All's well here, sir," said Reeves, who had outflanked us all and crept up behind me with worrying ease.

"Christ almighty, Reeves! Don't ever do that again!" I said, my heart pounding in my chest like a base drum.

Lord Redmayne and his men turned when they heard me speak and their fingers twitched on their weapons.

"It's alright, he's with us," I said, attempting to make myself heard without speaking too loudly. Lord Redmayne immediately gestured to his men to lower their weapons.

"What the blazes, Reeves? Why did you sneak up on me?" I said, feeling my heart rate beginning to slow.

"Sorry, sir. I heard you approaching but didn't recognise anyone and so I thought I'd better play it safe."

"No harm done. I might have done the same thing in your shoes. Lord Redmayne, I am not sure if you've met 2nd Lieutenant Reeves, he is the man who's just frightened the life out of us all," I said, effecting an introduction whilst we all remained crouched down in the woods.

"Pleased to meet you, Reeves," said His Lordship. "Nice work in sneaking up on us. Nearly gave me a bloody heart attack! Nevertheless, I am sure that such cunning will come in handy before this night is over," reflected Lord Redmayne.

"What can you tell us, Reeves?" I asked with my heart now functioning normally.

"Nothing much has happened since you left, sir, save that I lost sight of the girl when she was taken out of the upstairs room and unfortunately she didn't reappear in any of the other rooms visible from here," he replied.

"Any sign of the menacing looking brute with the patch over one eye?" I asked.

"Not sure, sir. I saw someone who resembled him from behind but I couldn't get a good enough look to see if he was wearing a patch," Reeves replied.

"Let's get closer," said Lord Redmayne, at which we all slowly stood up and, stooping ever so slightly, walked forward. The start we had been given by Reeves seemed to have heightened everyone's sensitivity to noise and movement. We reached the spot where Reeves and I had watched the lodge through my telescope and stopped. We peered through the undergrowth at the house which was now in the shade of the setting sun. The lodge cast a large shadow which almost reached the spot where we were hiding. In a few minutes the shadow would disappear completely as the sun set behind the trees protecting the western aspect of the lodge.

"Gentlemen, we need a plan," said Lord Redmayne while myself, Reeves and his senior staff closed around him.

"I have been to the house a few times and I suggest our best chance of surprising them is to go in through the kitchens. There are generally only a small number of servants at any one time because the Duke only comes here once or twice a year. With the element of surprise on our side we should easily be able to overpower them and prevent the alarm from being raised."

We all nodded as we listened intently while Lord Redmayne continued.

"I suggest that two of my men go around to the other side of the house and watch for anyone trying to escape on horseback or in a carriage. Ayres, you take Andrews with you and only charge into the house if I shout for you."

With that, two of his men armed with rifles, crept through the woods making their way around to the western side of the lodge, close to the coach house and stable block. They would have the cover of the woods all the way around apart from when they crossed the drive from the main road to the lodge.

"I want two men to remain here and apprehend anyone trying to escape east. Forsythe, you take Hartley with you and mind you don't fall asleep like you did two nights ago," making some obscure reference to an incident which presumably involved Chartists.

That left five of us to make the assault, which I hoped would be enough.

"The rest of us will steal our way into the kitchens where we will overpower the staff and have them restrained. You have brought some rope haven't you, Scholes?" asked Lord Redmayne, turning to the tallest of his men.

"Yes, my Lord," replied Scholes.

"I will go in first with the Captain and Reeves here, whilst Scholes and Davies follow on, watching our backs. We will hold the staff at gunpoint and then you two," he said, looking at Scholes and Davies, "will enter the kitchen and tie them up. Davies can stay guarding them whilst the rest of us go upstairs and, all being well, give the Russians and their thugs a nice surprise. With luck, we will rescue Miss Meredith but make no mistake gentlemen, when fighting indoors, if you have to shoot, shoot to kill. I regret it's a case of kill or be killed. Hopefully with surprise on our side it won't come to that."

Everyone nodded, all having understood the grim possibilities that lay ahead.

"Right then, gentlemen, let's pay a call on the Duke of Aldborough," finished Lord Redmayne and we then moved to the very edge of the wood.

We manoeuvred ourselves to the position where we would have the shortest distance to travel to the lodge. This was important as we would be out in the open and could be easily spotted. The shorter the distance, the less chance there was to be seen. The absence of any lights suggested there was no-one in the rooms on the side of the lodge facing us. A further look through the telescope confirmed this. With luck we would get to the kitchen undetected.

"You first, Reeves," said Lord Redmayne. Reeves never flinched and while stooping low, he ran across the clearing to the eastern side of the dwelling. He ran quickly and once he reached the lodge he pressed his back against the wall so he couldn't be observed by any of its inhabitants. One by one we followed, with Lord Redmayne bringing up the rear. His stoop was not that pronounced and his movement not that swift, causing a few anxious looks from the rest of us. Nevertheless, he too crossed the clearing safely, albeit a little out of breath. We all then inched our way to the corner of the lodge nearest the river. The door to the kitchen was a few yards around the corner and then down a handful of steps. When we reached the top of them we could hear the sound of activity in the kitchens, reminding us all to keep quiet. Half way down the steps was a window which meant that for a brief moment we would be in full view to anyone looking our way. It was crucial that we moved so quickly that even if we were seen, no-one would have time to react.

"Who's going first?" whispered Lord Redmayne looking at Reeves and me, prompting me to push myself forward, with Reeves following right behind me. We edged our way to the start of the steps when suddenly, there was the sound of someone opening the kitchen door. In the next instant we all pushed back quickly, struggling to avoid tripping as our feet moved back in an uncoordinated panic. Somehow we managed to avoid colliding with one another as we withdrew back around the corner and waited. No-one moved and we all held our breath as we listened to the sound of a man climbing up the kitchen steps. When he reached the top, he appeared to stop. Moments later the unmistakable smell of tobacco smoke filled the air, as smoke drifted past us. The footsteps once again resumed, getting ever nearer to us. They were slow and small steps, suggesting the man was simply enjoying a smoke but the steps continued to come closer. Any moment he would be upon us, and so I brought my pistol up to my own chin. If he walked around the corner I would push my gun into his head which would hopefully prevent him from crying out. He stopped at the corner and didn't come any further. I could tell by the density of the smoke that he was only a few feet away.

There seemed little point in not taking advantage of this situation and in the next breath I moved effortlessly and silently around the corner and put my pistol to the man's head. His eyes widened in horror and he nearly swallowed his pipe.

"Do not move, friend, and you will survive this night," I said, pushing the barrel of the pistol into his temple. Reeves then crept around the corner and took up a position on the other side of our prisoner. The man was armed with a pistol and Reeves promptly relieved him of it.

I pulled our prisoner around the corner and handed him over to Lord Redmayne's men. They set about tying his hands and were about to gag him when His Lordship asked, "How many men and women are in the house, including servants?"

"Four upstairs and three downstairs," he said reluctantly and before he could utter another sound, Scholes had pushed a scarf into his mouth and tied it around the back of his head.

"Did you hear that, Captain? Three downstairs and four upstairs," said Lord Redmayne quietly.

"Yes, my Lord, assuming the man's telling the truth," I replied and then crept stealthily down the steps, closely followed by Reeves. I quickened my decent as I passed the window and found myself outside the back door ready to enter. Reeves joined me and he was followed by Lord Redmayne, who seemingly felt that it was futile for him to make any attempt at avoiding detection. He appeared to believe that whatever he did, he could not move quickly enough and so why bother making some bizarre attempt, which in any event was more likely to draw attention to us than not.

"Are we ready gentlemen?" I said, once again bringing my pistol barrel to my chin. With my free hand I took hold of the door handle and then quickly and quietly marched into the kitchen.

The first thing I saw was a plump lady putting the finishing touches to a pudding and a young girl helping. I then noticed a man sitting by the fire, who was dressed like a footman. Before a word could be spoken by anyone, I had taken a few steps forward and had my pistol aimed directly at the footman. At the same time, Lord Redmayne covered the cook and her assistant.

"Do not be alarmed, ladies. As some of you may already know, my name is Lord Redmayne and I am here to surprise my neighbour. Nobody will be hurt unless someone does something stupid." Scholes and Davies then walked in with the man we had already taken prisoner, which increased the look of distress on the faces of the women.

"As I was saying, there is nothing to be alarmed about," repeated Lord Redmayne in a composed and reassuring manner. His calming influence was having a profoundly positive effect, not only on the servants but also on the rest of us. One by one, all the servants were bound to chairs and had scarves tied around their mouths, for which the women received an apology from Lord Redmayne. Keeping everyone's nerves steady was essential for us to retain the element of surprise. When people panic, anything can happen. Then, in a quite bizarre moment, Lord Redmayne took a spoon and tasted the pudding being made by the servants.

"Quite splendid!" he said, looking at the horrified female servants. "You must come and make this for me."

Having done his utmost to put everyone at their ease, Lord Redmayne turned his attentions to the serious business at hand.

"Now gentlemen, let's head upstairs and rescue Miss Meredith from these Russian rogues."

We had started to head for the stairs when we heard the sound of voices, which stopped us all in our tracks. After a few moments it was clear that the voices were not, in fact, coming towards us, but were travelling down into the kitchen through some passageway. I had never seen anything like this before. It was a passage resembling a chimney, which connected the kitchen to a room immediately above. There were ropes and pulleys enabling food to be transported safely and quickly. Lord Redmayne said he had seen them before on his travels and that Americans referred to them as 'dumb waiters'. By looking at the plates on the tray, whoever was upstairs had just finished their main course and were now awaiting their dessert. More significantly this provided us with a heaven sent opportunity to listen to what was happening above which could only help in determining the timing of our attack. We stopped what we were doing, given that sounds would travel both ways through this passage.

Lord Redmayne, Reeves and I remained motionless, listening intently to what was happening above us whilst Scholes and Davies watched over the servants.

"Where the hell is the Duke?" said a man in the room above. "We need to settle up and get out of here. It's bad enough that we had to stay in some mill town last night and I don't want to stay there again."

This was followed by a mumbled reply from someone who was too far away from the opening for us to hear what was said.

"Shouldn't really have to give these bastards twenty five thousand," said another voice.

"Just as well we managed to appropriate the equivalent amount from our famous Bridge Building Company," said the first voice again, inducing a deal of laughter from the others in the room.

Then there was the sound of more activity with doors opening and a number of footsteps.

"Where the hell are my servants?" said a man, bursting into the room.

"Probably run out on you, old boy. You don't pay them enough," joked another, who seemed to have arrived at the same time. This man sounded horribly like Sir William Hamilton and my heart sank at the prospect of a reunion with him. But what was he doing here? We listened on.

"It is good to see you again and, of course, yourself too, Sir William," said the first man, confirming my suspicions.

"Your footman was here a moment ago," said another.

"We have been waiting here for some time and would like to conclude this business and be on our way," he added hesitantly.

"Would you now?" said Sir William. "Well, have you brought the money?" At which point Lord Redmayne and I looked at each other. What on earth was going on?

"We have brought the twenty five thousand pounds you requested," said the first man, whose voice was increasing in familiarity. Again, Lord Redmayne and I exchanged puzzled looks.

"And when can we expect the parliamentary approval for our railway?" continued the first man, who was starting to sound a lot like Gerald Beales. What was he doing here? Were they all involved in the kidnapping? Surely not! My mind was trying to make sense of all of this. Maybe this is what Mary, Duchess of Aldborough meant when she said nothing was as it seems? Quite worryingly, we heard no Russian accents or any mention of Count Zadovich.

"Approval will be granted the instant I am back in London, consider it done," said Sir William.

"But how do we know that you won't just keep the money and do nothing?" nervously enquired the man who sounded like Gerald Beales.

"Now look here," snarled Sir William Hamilton. "We do this all the time. Every railway company in this country has paid us. Those that haven't paid have not received approval and as a consequence remain a figment of someone's imagination. You will just have to take my word that once we receive twenty five thousand pounds, your Act of Parliament will follow shortly thereafter."

There followed a good deal of mumbling and it then sounded like the money was being handed over.

"And what about the woman?" asked Sir William. "Has everything gone to plan?"

"Yes," replied Gerald Beales. "She's here."

At the mention of a woman, Lord Redmayne listened ever more intently. This is why we were here. We all readied ourselves to storm upstairs and rescue Miss Meredith.

"I would like to see her," said Sir William.

"She's upstairs, Sir William," said Gerald Beales.

"Enough of this!" barked the Duke of Aldborough. "Where are my damn servants? I want some food."

The sound of a door slamming was heard and we all looked at each other. It sounded very much like the Duke was heading in our direction, in search of his footman. Rather than risk the Duke raising the alarm we all moved forward towards the stairs. It was time to break up this den of corruption, find the Russian and rescue Miss Meredith. I was first onto the stairs with Reeves following closely. Behind him came Lord Redmayne and bringing up the rear was Scholes.

Once at the top of the stairs, I ran straight into the Duke of Aldborough, who was extremely shocked to see me. "Townsend!" he spluttered, but before he could do or say anything else he was surrounded by us all and had my pistol barrel pressed up under his chin. The Duke was a few years older than me and, despite all his aristocratic breeding, there was still terror and fear in his eyes.

Lord Redmayne then signalled me to turn the Duke around and march him back into the room he had just left. The Duke walked down the hallway with Lord Redmayne and Reeves either side of him whilst I kept my pistol firmly held against his jaw. Scholes all the while covered our backs in case someone should attack us from behind. The Duke's eyes continued to search everywhere for help, but there was none to be had. When we reached the room, Reeves opened the door and I pushed the Duke inside and we quickly followed, all pointing our pistols.

The four of us stood together. Our entrance caused a gasp from the inhabitants of the room, followed by a series of, "What the hell?" and worse. We were in the dining room and facing us, sitting at a table fifteen feet away, were William Beales and Sir William Hamilton. Gerald Beales sat opposite his brother, with his back to us. There was another man standing in the far right hand corner and one more in the left. As they both carried two pistols each, I presumed them to be the guards. They looked very different from each other, suggesting that probably one of them was with Beales and the other with the Duke. We moved further into the room with our backs to a side board on which a buffet would generally be laid out.

"What the devil?" added a very shocked Sir William Hamilton. His eyes quickly settling on me, adding spitefully, "It's you, Townsend! What in damnation are you doing here? I hoped I'd seen the last of you," he added, with his top lip curling in disgust, all the while trying to cover up the pile of money which lay on the table.

"My sentiments entirely, Sir William. And now gentlemen, I would ask you to very carefully drop your weapons on the floor and keep your hands in the air," I replied. The guards dropped their pistols and Sir William and the Beales brothers raised their hands suggesting that they were not armed.

The first man we captured said that there were four people upstairs which was immediately before the Duke and Sir William arrived. It occurred to me that at least one of the guards would have come with the Duke and Sir William and, if they had arrived by carriage, there would be further servants unaccounted for. This was all based on the servant we captured having told the truth. With all this money, there was bound to be more than just the two guards standing in the dining room. But how many more and where were they?

"Reeves, secure the house and see if you can find the lady and the one-eyed Russian. And be on your guard, as likely as not there will be more of them lurking somewhere," I said, then turning to Lord Redmayne, added, "Would it be in order for Scholes to assist Reeves?"

"Absolutely. We have these villains covered."

Reeves and Scholes left and I then took my pistol away from the Duke's chin. The Duke sneered at me and edged his way towards the guard in the right hand corner of the room.

"Well, well," said Lord Redmayne. "What a scurrilous bunch you all are! Sir William, selling parliamentary approvals with the Duke here. Dear, oh dear. I have to admit to being disappointed in you both and yet you'll pardon me for not being surprised. Mr Beales, from what we overheard, you are certainly not fit to run a company. I believe you will be making full restitution to all those people you have taken money from, starting with me. You can forget the Yorkshire Railway Company and your Bridge Building Company, which was obviously another subterfuge for you to embezzle from the investors. Consider them both closed for business."

Gerald Beales turned in his chair to protest his innocence but was met with a stern look and a quick rebuke from Lord Redmayne.

"What I find hard to understand though, is why you would turn against your own country and work with the Russians to abduct Miss Meredith? It will mean the gallows for you all!"

"Russians? Miss Meredith? What are you prattling on about, Redmayne?" said a very unhappy Sir William Hamilton. "Have you gone completely mad?"

"Von Benckendorff was just helping us attract investors. We only met him just over a week ago when he came and offered us his services. We dropped them off in Leeds last night and that's the last we've seen of them," said Gerald Beales, once again straining himself as he turned in his chair to face us.

Before I could ask another question, a gun went off elsewhere in the house which made us all turn our heads. That was all the time needed for William Beales to reach for his own weapon, which he had hidden under the dining table. He was first to fire and his shot narrowly missed both Lord Redmayne and myself as we ducked, shattering a vase somewhere behind us. More shots were heard outside and I then fired at William Beales preventing him firing again. The noise was deafening and the room soon filled with the smell of gunpowder and smoke. Sir William pulled out a tiny pistol from his waistcoat and fired at us, hitting Lord Redmayne in the arm. I fired my other pistol, hitting Sir William and then took a bullet in the arm from the guard in the corner who'd retrieved one of his pistols from the floor. All the while, shots were being fired outside. William Beales found another pistol from somewhere and again fired in our direction, causing Lord Redmayne to take evasive action and he went down like he was mortally wounded. His double barrelled pistol fell from his hand which I was able to grab. There was still one shot left and I was in desperate need of it. Through the smoke I could see that the Duke had grabbed a pistol from somewhere and took a step towards us shouting, "B.a.s.t.a.r.d.s!!" I had no idea as to whether his anger was at the loss of some priceless vase or whether it was just the hatred he had for me. Safe to say that he showed no fear and was intent on shooting Lord Redmayne or myself. Without thinking, I lifted Lord Redmayne's pistol up with my good arm, aimed at the Duke and fired. The Duke also fired and a bullet flew past, narrowly missing my head. As the smoke cleared, I could see that I had hit the Duke and he fell to floor where he lay doubled up.

In through the door burst Reeves with Scholes. The sight of these two, together with that of the Duke of Aldborough twitching on the floor, had the rest of them shouting that they wished to surrender. It was all over in a matter of seconds. I raised myself up from the floor and helped Lord Redmayne to his feet. We had both taken bullets to the arm but were otherwise safe. His wound appeared more serious than my own, as fortunately for me the bullet had passed straight through me. Sir William looked quite badly hurt, having been shot in the chest by either Lord Redmayne or myself although it was the Duke who had come off worst, looking close to death. Miraculously, everyone else was unhurt: Gerald Beales coming off best of all, having hid throughout the entire exchange under the table. Scholes kept his pistol trained on the Beales brothers and their guard, whilst Reeves removed all their pistols from the room.

"Reeves, what on earth went off outside?" I asked, once he had gathered in all the pistols. "And where is Miss Meredith?"

Reeves told me that the gunfire started when one of the Duke's men had fired at him. After that the man fled, only to be captured by Lord Redmayne's men who were waiting in the woods. More shots were fired and one of the Duke's men was hit in the exchange, however none of Lord Redmayne's men were hurt.

"As to Miss Meredith, you'd better come with me, sir," said Reeves ominously. More of Lord Redmayne's men appeared and, with them assisting Lord Redmayne, I followed Reeves away from the dining room.

We walked down the hallway into the drawing room and there, sitting by the fire was a lady with her back to us. My first reaction was one of immense relief.

"This is the lady I saw leaving the house of Gerald Beales late at night," said Reeves, stopping me dead in my tracks and then I saw her face. The lady in question was, in fact, Virginia Hatherway.

Chapter 34

Having asked Reeves to assist Lord Redmayne in tidying up the mess, I sat down opposite Virginia with my head swimming in confusion.

"Have you any idea how much trouble you have caused, Miss Hatherway?" I said, speaking to her for the first time in days. She buried her head in her hands and just cried. I immediately felt a certain sympathy for her, yet resisted the temptation to say so. Nevertheless, I handed her my handkerchief with which to dry her eyes.

"So it was you we saw running into Gerald Beales' house night after night?" I added, which also failed to gain a response as she continued to weep.

"How deeply are you involved in all this, Virginia? You know that sooner or later I will find out. I suggest you tell me your version because as we speak, your friend Beales will be telling Lord Redmayne his."

She lowered her hands and looked at me through reddened eyes, her cheeks still glistening with the trails of her tears.

"I don't know what you mean, I just wanted to get away and live the life of a lady. I was tired of seeing rich women strutting around Harrogate whilst I was working all those hours in the shop. It wasn't fair! Then Gerald Beales offered me the future I had long since craved. He promised to establish me in a grand house in London and Sir William was about to take me, then you arrived and that's all I know," she said, still sniffling.

"What about the time we spent together and everything you said to me?" I asked.

"I enjoyed meeting you, and who knows? Things might have been different had Gerald Beales not offered me everything I had ever dreamed of. I am ashamed to say that I took advantage of the feelings he had for me," she said, steadily regaining her composure.

"Gerald became aware that we had met and was a little jealous. That is the main reason I had to go to his house late at night. I had to reassure him that I still wanted a life in London and to finalise our travelling arrangements. Tom

Dawson told his brother, William, that he had seen the two of us together. Anyway, Gerald asked me to keep you busy and report everything I learned back to him. I think he was testing my loyalty. I only found out in the carriage coming over here that Sir William was behind that request as he had already asked Gerald to do everything he could to make your life uncomfortable," and then looking up added, "Sir William really doesn't like you, does he?"

"No, he doesn't and I can honestly say that his dislike of me is only exceeded by my dislike of him."

"Why does he hate you so?" asked Virginia.

"When I was in India, I wanted to marry his daughter and she wanted to marry me, however Sir William had other ideas and the last I heard, he had sold her off to the highest bidder."

"I see, so now his daughter hates him and he blames you for that?" she suggested, now having partially recovered her composure.

"Perhaps. So you agreed to spy on me?" I asked hesitantly.

"No. At first I told him everything I knew but when I learned of the attacks on you, I told Gerald that I wasn't prepared to help him. I, therefore, pushed you away as I really didn't want any part of it."

Suddenly I felt a fool. This is what the Duchess of Aldborough had warned me about. But how did the Russians and Miss Meredith fit into all this? There was a seemingly endless list of unanswered questions.

"Tell me about the Russians, Virginia. How involved have they been with Beales?"

"Russians? I don't know much about them. Even though I only met them a couple of times, there was something frightening about them. Especially the one with a patch over his eye. He didn't act like a servant to me, it looked much more like he was the one giving the orders. Anyway, Gerald liked them."

I nodded as I listened intently.

"And when did they first come to Harrogate?" I asked, all the while continuing to try and unravel this mystery.

"Just before you did. They sought out Gerald and told him that they knew how to build railways and were keen to help. Gerald loved the idea of having an expert who'd worked on the railway in St Petersburg and so did investors."

"But didn't Beales think it strange to be approached by a Russian rail expert?" I asked, a little sceptical of all this.

"Not at all. The entire county knew about the project and Gerald was constantly approached by all manner of individuals. Masses of people wanted to be involved. It's the greatest thing ever to come to Harrogate and hundreds of jobs are being created."

"Not any more," I replied, interrupting Virginia's explanation.

"Well, Vladimir seemed very excited by the plan and said he would return to Russia and bring back some of the best men he'd worked with on the railway he built for the Tsar. And when they heard that we were leaving Harrogate and heading for Manchester, they asked if they could ride with us as far as Leeds. They told us they were heading east to Hull where they were to board a ship bound for Russia. That's it! That's all I know."

"So, did the Russians know that you would be travelling with Beales?" I asked.

"Yes, what's wrong with that?" After a short pause she added, "They liked the idea that I was joining them."

"Am I right in assuming that the Russian with the patch over his eye never got on your carriage in Harrogate?"

"That's right. They said they had left him with some unfinished business to attend to and he would follow on later."

It was beginning to look very much like I hadn't given the Russians the credit they deserved. They had set me up. They must have known that we would follow the coach with the lady on it. Maybe even Beales didn't know he was helping them do that.

"With four of you in the carriage to Leeds, I presume that William Beales was one of the armed guards riding up top?" I asked, trying to piece everything together.

"That's right. Since we were carrying so much money, Gerald wanted his brother along as I'm not sure if he entirely trusted the other guard."

"And what about Tom Dawson? Was he your lover? How does he fit into all this?" I asked, somewhat apprehensively.

"Tom? No, absolutely not. He courted me and I had stepped out with him a long time ago but that was it. He may still have harboured hopes that I would marry him one day, however they were not shared by me."

"So who killed him? William Beales? Gerald Beales?" I asked.

"Tom's dead?" she said, looking totally shocked. "My God! When did that happen?"

"Just about the time you left Harrogate with Beales and the Russians," I said.

"It's more likely that the Russian with the patch over his eye killed him," she asserted.

"Why would you say that?" I asked.

"Because Tom was reckless at times and would do anything to better his circumstances. He was far too easily seduced by the promise of money. He often involved himself with the wrong sorts," she said philosophically.

"Well the courts will decide who killed him. Nonetheless, your friends Gerald and William Beales can't be ruled out. Whatever else they are, they're certainly not honest and upright citizens. They're liars, cheats and corrupt as hell. They most certainly qualify as wrong sorts. Anyway, I have to leave now but Lord Redmayne is a good man and will deal with you fairly."

Walking to the door of the room, I paused and turned round to look at her for what I expected would be the final time. She was just another very beautiful girl who had her head turned by the prospect of riches. In the end, she was probably no different to Mary, Duchess of Aldborough, although considerably less successful.

"Virginia, I hope everything works out for you. But let me tell you this, the ladies you see parading themselves in Harrogate shouldn't be envied. I bet many, if not all of them, would have traded places with you any day of the week. I hope that one day you will know what I mean."

As I turned towards the door she called to me.

"George?"

"Yes?" I answered, facing her again.

"I am sorry for all the trouble I have caused. Thank you for your handkerchief, you've been most kind to me."

With a heavy heart, I walked into the hall where two of Lord Redmayne's men were standing guard. I had forgotten all their names but they nevertheless responded positively when I asked them to look after Virginia until Lord Redmayne was ready to see her.

I returned to the library to find that the Beales brothers had been tied up and Lord Redmayne and Sir William were both seated, receiving medical attention from the Duke's female servants. Once the fighting had finished, the women had been released on Lord Redmayne's orders. It was only then that a sharp pain in my arm reminded me that I, too, had been hit. I instinctively held my injured left arm with my right.

"I will get this lovely lady to attend to you in a moment," said Lord Redmayne, smiling at the Duke's cook who still looked quite disturbed by the events of the evening, despite her master's body having been mercifully taken out of the room. By all accounts he was still alive, although it transpired that my bullet had hit him in his nether regions.

"We've sent for a doctor for Sir William and the Duke. Blasted crooks don't deserve one but they are supposed to be one of us. Unfortunate about the Duke, eh?" said Lord Redmayne philosophically.

"Absolutely," I replied, somewhat concerned as to the extent of his injury as well as my part in all this, mainly because we had entered his house on a false premise.

"Don't worry, Captain. The man is a rogue and deserves to have his tackle shot off. If you hadn't gelded him, some irate husband would have done so sooner or later. Might have been more merciful to have killed him though, as the scandal of this railway business will do for him anyway."

The servant attending to Lord Redmayne finished bandaging his arm and then started to look at the wound I had received.

"She will take good care of you, Captain," said Lord Redmayne admiring the bandage he had just received.

"I understand from Reeves that the lady this lot brought with them from Harrogate was not Miss Meredith. Which presumably means that, after you have had your arm fixed, you need to head back to Yorkshire to find her?"

"Yes, sir," I replied. "But what of all this?" I asked, looking at the carnage we had made in the battle scarred dining room.

"Don't you worry about this, my boy. I will see to it that these rogues get what they deserve. After my men have tidied up, I will bring the banker and his brother back to Harrogate, together with the twenty five thousand pounds and make sure that this is returned to investors. Someone else will build that railway, but it won't be these crooks."

I thanked Lord Redmayne for all his help and, after having a simple bandage applied to my arm, Reeves and I left on the two fresh horses given to us by His Lordship. We had learned little about the kidnapping of Miss Meredith and had lost a valuable twenty four hours in the process. We were a long way from being of any assistance and I had neutered the husband of my former lover, for which I was certain he would seek revenge. There was a hollow feeling in my stomach and I felt sick. We had followed the wrong trail and I felt very responsible and extremely foolish. I had drawn all the wrong conclusions from the Manchester to Liverpool timetable. These timetables remained a puzzle, since it now looked certain that the Russians were always intending on heading east and meeting Count Zadovich in Russia. We rode back to the main road in silence, deep in thought and then turned left towards Leeds. I had no idea how far we would get in the dark, but I was determined to make as much progress as we could before stopping for the night.

With the benefit of torches and a bright moon, we managed to retrace our journey along the main coach road to Oldham. To have attempted to cross the Pennine hills in the dark was asking for trouble and so we made our way to the nearest coaching inn and rested up for the night.

Chapter 35

It was around ten o'clock at night when we arrived at the Black Bull Inn which lay on the outskirts of Oldham. We found someone to take care of our horses and went inside. Following the most trying of days, we were very much looking forward to a good meal and a warm bed for the night. Sleeping in the forest, after being released from jail, only increased our anticipation of some welcome rest. Yet the moment we stepped into that inn, I knew we had picked the wrong place to stay. The gaiety we had heard when outside suddenly stopped and everyone in the room turned to stare as Reeves and I walked through the door. While we drifted in, smoke drifted out. There were, perhaps, forty men and twenty women within and they all looked menacingly towards us. The fiddler stopped playing whilst I forced a smile, looked at Reeves and then nonchalantly walked through the crowded room to the bar.

"Yes, sir?" quizzed the man I presumed to be the landlord, clearly seeking to establish who we were and what we wanted.

"We would like two rooms for the night, ale and food if you please, landlord," I replied, as soft murmurings replaced the silence.

"It's late in the day to look for a room," he replied suspiciously.

"It is that," I replied. "And we are exhausted. We left Leeds this morning to visit Lord Redmayne and were hoping to return home before nightfall, but everything has taken longer than we expected."

The sympathetic response I expected was not forthcoming as it seemed that Lord Redmayne was not universally popular in this particular hostelry. It soon became clear that we had walked into the same Chartists that Lord Redmayne had left Harrogate to deal with.

Ale, food and a bed did not appear and instead we found ourselves encircled by a crowd who were looking increasingly hostile. Reeves and I looked at each other in dismay. Everything was going from bad to worse.

One man stepped forward from the crowd. He appeared to hold some rank, was just short of six feet tall, aged around forty years, and had dark skin with a leathery texture.

"I can see you've been injured. Would you mind telling me how you came by such a wound on a social visit to Lord Redmayne?" he asked, which brought a murmur of approval from his followers.

"Oh this? It's nothing!" I said, dismissing the injury to my arm.

"Humour me," said the spokesman.

"It was an accident, just an accident. I caught my arm in the woods," I said, attempting to dismiss my wound as an irrelevance.

"Do you work for Lord Redmayne?" I was then asked, prompting another murmuring of approval.

"No, absolutely not!" I replied awkwardly. I could see where the questioning was leading. If I said I was working for Lord Redmayne, I would be in trouble. Worse, if I said he was a friend and the consequences of admitting to being a Captain in the 11th Light Dragoons could have been fatal.

"I am working for the Yorkshire Railway Company in which Lord Redmayne is an investor. He had asked for an update on the progress we had made on the railway line to Harrogate and that is it. Now, may we have a room, ale and some food?" I said, breathing something of a sigh that I had come up with such a plausible story.

"Then why do you both carry two pistols," the spokesman asked.

"These are difficult times and the roads have many dangers," I said, becoming increasingly confident.

"What are your names?" he asked.

"George Townsend and …" I hesitated as I didn't know Reeves' Christian name.

"Jack Reeves, sir," said Reeves, covering for me.

"And who do we have the honour of addressing?" I then asked.

"Names are dangerous things, Mr Townsend. Now suppose you were not Mr Townsend but say your name was William Lamb, then what reception do you think you would get then?" he replied, referring to our Prime Minister.

I shrugged my shoulders and someone close by shouted, "We'd roast your balls!"

The spokesman smiled and said, "That's my point. With one name you are safe and with another you can be…in trouble …Best you don't know my name, Mr Townsend. Leastways, not for the present."

After I had answered a few railway questions successfully, ale and food appeared. Attention now turned away from us and the fiddler started to play again. Whilst we ate our supper, the spokesman sat down alongside Reeves and continued to press me for answers. Two of his followers towered behind him watching our every move. His manner was perfectly friendly but his eyes still drilled into every part of us, searching for more information. I wondered who he was.

"You will understand, gentlemen, that we can't be too careful these days. Our honest struggles to right the wrongs done to the poor are met with the force of the militia and the constables. Spies are everywhere and it's hard for us to know who to trust. You appear to be who you say you are, however I regret that before you can leave you will need to convince our leader of that, too. And of course, you must give me your pistols to look after while you are here," said the spokesman.

In a room full of Chartists, we had little choice but do as we were asked. Being reduced to the Joseph Manning knife which rested in my boot, was little comfort.

"Leader?" I said. "I had assumed that you were the leader?"

"The Irishman is the leader, not I," he replied.

My heart sank. Not another Irishman!

"Approval of the Irishman? Why do we need to convince him of anything? Surely you can see that we pose no threat?" I asked, praying that this was a different Irishman to the one who had plagued us in Harrogate.

"You will meet him soon enough, but for now you just enjoy your ale and with luck he will be here in the morning. He is returning from important business near Leeds and if he agrees with my assessment, you will then be free to resume your journey," he said standing up to re-join his friends, leaving the two large Chartists to watch over us.

There was nothing more to say and we could not make a break for freedom in the middle of the night across wild moorland, so we asked to be shown to our rooms upstairs where we would rest and make our escape at first light. It was hard to see how this day could have gone more awry and for the second time in two days, I was once again a prisoner.

On our way into the bedrooms, I exchanged a knowing glance with Reeves. This was picked up by the spokesman.

"I know that you wouldn't be reckless enough to attempt to escape during the night. That would be disappointing and also very dangerous. So merely as a precaution and for your safety, these two selfless men will sleep outside your doors tonight. There are also many more of us staying overnight, and so I will wish you both a very good night."

The door to the very basic room then closed and I was left alone with my thoughts, my wounded arm and the light of a solitary candle. Exhausted and despondent I lay on the bed and fell asleep, resigned in the knowledge that the day couldn't get any worse.

The instant that dawn broke on that Sunday morning, I was up and about and looking to leave. I could not afford to waste any more time here in Oldham. I glanced out of the window across to the stables, where our horses were waiting. The window was far too small to climb through, leaving the door as the only way to freedom. I decided not to put on my boots, for fear of making too much noise. I crept out of my room, past the sleeping guards and into Reeves' room next door. He, too, was readying himself to leave. I put my finger to my lips to indicate that we mustn't make a sound if we were to successfully make our way out of the inn and around to the stables. We crept along the corridor. Even though the floorboards creaked with almost every step, the noise failed to rouse the guards. We made it down the stairs and back into the room where we had received such a stony reception the previous night. There were, perhaps, half a dozen men scattered around the floor, but mainly near the fire, all sleeping. Fortunately, no-one stirred. We walked across the room to the door, still carrying our boots. The smell of stale tobacco smoke and ale filled the air. With luck we would be back on our horses and riding hard for Leeds within a few more minutes. Still, there was no sound of any activity from anywhere else in the inn. It appeared as if, at last, our fortunes were changing. I attempted to open the door, only to find it was locked! I pushed again and the door rattled.

"Good morning, gentlemen," said the spokesman, coming from behind the bar with the same two burly men who watched over us last night. Despite appearing to be asleep only moments earlier, they were now most definitely awake.

"Oh no," I said to myself and then I turned around.

I sat down in the closest chair and put my boots on, as there was no longer anything to be gained by creeping around in my stocking feet. Reeves did likewise.

"Good morning to you," I said, attempting to cover up our failed attempt at escaping. "Just fancied a breath of fresh air," causing one or two of those sleeping on the floor to stir.

"Did you now? And without your boots?" questioned the spokesman.

"Didn't want to wake anyone," I replied, looking at the bodies littering the floor.

"Very thoughtful, I am sure," he said with a large smile on his face. "You may stay where you are gentlemen. Rest assured the Irishman will be with us shortly. If it's fresh air you want, we can open a window."

I had never before felt so helpless. I had allowed the Russians to abduct Miss Meredith, been duped into following a corrupt banker and his misguided lover and was trapped without my pistols some thirty miles from where I was due to rendezvous with Lieutenant Sinderby-Smythe. To make matters worse, my freedom was now dependent on an Irishman who, for all I knew, was the same one that had plagued me throughout the last week in Harrogate. After all, they said that he had been on some business near Leeds, and Harrogate qualified on that score. There were now just twenty four hours to retrieve the situation and I had lost patience. If I was going to fail, I was going to go down fighting.

I nodded to Reeves who seemed to have read my mind and we both ran at our captors. Our sudden move caught them unawares. I wrestled one of the burly men to the ground, prompting a large stabbing pain in my arm as my wound opened up again. Reeves was trading blows with the other man and I felt certain we would prevail. For good measure, I pulled out my Joseph Manning knife only to have it kicked from my hand by someone new joining in the fray.

"Stop this!" shouted a man with an Irish accent. I looked up and towering over us was a tall, clean shaven man along with six others in support. The fighting stopped and Reeves and I stood up dusting ourselves down in the process. The tall man with the Irish accent must have been surprised to see me smiling, but I smiled for no other reason than he was not Richard Dunn.

"So who are these two?" he said to the man we had assumed to have been the leader.

"They claim to be called Townsend and Reeves."

The Irishman nodded and we all moved to stand around the bar.

"Duncan here is not keen on our names being bandied about. In any event, my name is Patrick O'Shaughnessy and who might you be?" he said whilst we were guided to a table surrounded by four chairs.

"My name is George Townsend and this is Jack Reeves. We work for the Yorkshire Railway Company who are building the railway to Harrogate."

"And what are you doing so far from home?" he enquired.

"We were visiting with one of the investors and providing him with a report on the railway's progress," I said. "And although it's a pleasure to meet you, I am afraid we are needed back there most urgently," I said hopefully.

"Well, Mr Townsend, I will see if that is possible," he said in a soft Irish accent.

"As I am sure both you gentlemen are aware, we are in the struggle of our lives. We are fighting for the oppressed. For the poor. For the rights of everyday men to have a say in how their country is run. Yet there are those, like Lord Redmayne, who would have the poor stay poor and downtrodden, remaining forever in the gutter. And you are a business associate of his, so what does that make you?"

"Mr O'Shaughnessy, let me tell you that I detest mistreatment of men and women every bit as you do. I even support the right to vote and abhor the corruption that exists in some areas of government, but from what I have seen, Lord Redmayne is a good man. If we are to have a fairer society, then shouldn't we be able to form our own opinions of people or policies and not have other opinions thrust upon us?" I replied. "Isn't that what you're fighting for.... liberty?"

"You speak well, Mr Townsend, nevertheless you have presented me with a problem."

"And why is that?" I asked.

"Because if you are not who you say you are and we allow you to leave, the lives of many of our followers will be put at risk. You admit to being an admirer of Lord Redmayne, who only a few days ago was suppressing our peaceful demonstration for the six demands of Chartism. How do we know that you are not spying on his behalf?" he replied assertively.

"The honest answer is that you don't. But what sort of spy would walk into an inn, completely oblivious to it being occupied by Chartists? Regardless of what you may think, I can assure you that you have nothing to worry about. However, despite being outnumbered and out-gunned, one way or another we are leaving. We have business which is just as important to us as your cause is to you and if we are further delayed in returning to Harrogate then many people could suffer. Much more than Peterloo or Bossenden Wood." When I finished speaking, I stood up and the two men who had guarded us all night immediately pointed pistols at me.

"Brave words, Mr Townsend, you must have some of the Irish in you," said Patrick O'Shaughnessy.

"I do. My father came from Tullow," I said confidently, all the while continuing to stare down the barrels of two pistols.

"Tullow? I know it well. What was your father called?" he asked.

"Henry Townsend," I replied.

"Well, believe it or not, I knew your father and he was a good and kind man. I was sorry to learn of his death. So perhaps you might tell me the real reason you are in such a blasted hurry to get to Leeds and why I should trust you, particularly when, if I am not very much mistaken, Henry Townsend's son joined the Light Dragoons and went to India?"

The game was up and there was no point in lying any further and so I had to tell him much more than I would have liked. The alternative was to be trapped here for an indeterminate amount of time, which was something we simply could not afford. He listened intently and seemed to believe me although I was unable to change his opinion of Lord Redmayne. Nevertheless, we achieved a mutual respect, enough for us to be allowed to leave without further delay. I think Patrick O'Shaughnessy was intelligent enough to realise that holding a Captain and a 2nd Lieutenant from the 11th Light Dragoons might cause him even more problems. Particularly as I had told him that we were expected back soon and if we failed to appear, a great many more troops would come looking for us.

"These two will travel with you to Leeds and make sure that none of our Chartist comrades cause you any problems along the way. You have your father and your Irish blood to thank for your release," at which point he shook my hand and wished us a safe journey back.

I reckoned that the two guards were more for his protection than ours. I supposed that he didn't want to risk us heading straight to the nearest barracks and alerting them of his presence at the Black Bull Inn. Our pistols and my knife were to be returned when we reached Leeds. Following a quick breakfast, we retrieved our horses and the four of us then rode across the Pennines towards Yorkshire. And then the rain came!

Chapter 36

Unsurprisingly, Angela woke early on Sunday morning and with a long journey ahead of her, wasted little time on the usual formalities of breakfast. At precisely seven o'clock Angela, Emily, the coachmen and the Major were back on board the carriage which headed north. Twenty four hours remained for Angela to return to Harrogate and then on to the Devil's Arrows. With no delays or interruptions, there should be little difficulty in meeting this deadline, however with Miss Meredith's life in their hands, the journey was bound to be stressful.

There was still the threat that the carriage could be intercepted by the Russians, and to make matters worse it had started to rain. The carriage went through Barnsley, where they resisted the temptation to stop. The roads were much quieter, which was not unusual for a Sunday, although the weather must have deterred many from venturing outside. The only people to be seen out and about were those heading for church which prompted Miss Coutts to consider stopping and saying a prayer for Miss Meredith. Yet with so much at stake, she felt it would make more sense to get back to Harrogate first and hope they would be in time to make the evening service at one of the town's churches.

By mid-morning they had made steady progress and arrived in Wakefield, where they decided to stop at an inn called the Coach and Horses. The armed coachmen kept a sharp eye out for signs of anyone following, which in the driving rain was a thankless task. The Major did remark that the name given to the inn had not extended anyone's imagination too far and offered a number of alternatives. Some of the names amused Angela and the Major felt a sense of achievement as the mood within their party had been lifted. With the horses rested, fed and watered they resumed their journey north. The rain continued to lash down and, at times, it could be heard bouncing off the roof of the carriage. The roads were becoming muddy and puddles disguised deep and dangerous potholes. As they neared Leeds, their carriage then became stalled behind a funeral procession. There was no room to pass and in any event it would have appeared unseemly to do so. This lasted for almost half an hour and when the procession finally turned off and was out of sight, Miss Coutts spoke to the Major.

"I suggest we ask the coachman to drive quicker, Major. We still have far to travel and need to make up for lost time."

"I fear that would be exceedingly dangerous, miss. The roads are becoming more and more treacherous and the last thing we can afford is to hit a pothole hidden by the rain and lose a wheel. Fear not Miss Coutts, even at this slow speed we should arrive in Harrogate with ample time to prepare for tomorrow. Which brings me to my greatest concern; having to hand over these wretched plans. I fervently hope that Captain Townsend has rescued Miss Meredith, thereby sparing us the need to do so."

"I think we all share your hope, Major. I pray they are both safe. On reflection, perhaps you're right, it probably would be safer to travel steadily and avoid any risk of an accident. We lost a wheel on the way up to Harrogate and I would hate that to happen again," said Angela deep in thought, watching the rain wash everything in sight.

A few miles south of Leeds the carriage came to an unscheduled stop, causing the Major to reach for his pistol. He looked out of the carriage and could see a group of men standing in the road, preventing the carriage from going any further. They all wore what looked like oil skin cloaks and hats to protect themselves from the rain which continued to fall heavily.

"Do not move, miss, and hide these plans. It is possible that we are being waylaid," said Major Phillips, quickly handing Angela the plans to the repeating rifle whilst wrapping his cloak around himself in preparing to face the elements. He then checked his pistol and stepped out of the carriage into the sodden landscape.

Angela and Emily trembled at the thought of what awaited the Major and scrambled around the carriage looking for a suitable hiding place for the plans. Eventually they settled for the folds of Emily's dress, believing that no gentleman would entertain searching such a place.

"What is all this?" shouted the Major while walking through the driving rain, brandishing his pistol as he approached the men who blocked their passage.

"The road's flooded, sir," replied one of the men moving toward the Major. "No need for a pistol. We are simply trying to help you."

Major Phillips looked at the coachmen perched high on the carriage who had their weapons handy and so he placed his pistol in his belt and peered through the rain at the road ahead. It was genuinely flooded but how deep was the water and was foul play afoot?

"How deep is the water?" asked the Major, who had moved to within a few feet of the men.

"Can't say for certain, sir, maybe two feet in parts. Perhaps more."

The Major turned his head away from the road as a gust of wind drove the rain into his face. He headed back to the carriage and climbed inside.

"Why, Major, you are soaked through!" said Angela followed quickly by, "Who are those men and what do they want?"

"They are merely warning us about venturing any further on this road due to flooding. It seems that the water is two feet deep or more in parts."

"Do you believe them Major? Can we be certain that this is not just some ruse to get us to remain here or to encourage us to take some obscure route where we would find the Russians waiting?"

"No, Miss Coutts, I cannot give you that assurance, which is why I think we have little choice but to press on and take our chances with the flooded road."

The Major then spoke to the coachmen and explained their intentions, after which the coach lurched back and forth and resumed its journey north.

Owing to the lack of any means of accurately assessing the depth of the water covering the road, one of the coachmen walked ahead, leading the horses through the worst parts. All the while the other coachman kept a constant look out for any signs of an attack. The rain continued to fall steadily. At times the water was two feet deep and once or twice the coachman stumbled as he missed his footing. Only the fact that he was holding the horses' reins prevented him from falling headlong into the brown, murky river which now replaced the road.

The rain gradually abated and the level of water on the road subsided. There were no signs of anyone following or lying in wait. As the condition of the road improved, the coachman resumed his position on top of the carriage and their speed steadily increased. Leeds approached and the opportunity for any ambush receded.

Given the afternoon was now well underway and allowing for the fact that there had been no previous opportunity to stop for lunch, the Major suggested another visit to the Bull and Mouth Inn was in order. A late lunch could be taken there whilst the horses were rested and everyone could have an opportunity to dry out. There was a collective feeling of relief as the carriage pulled up outside Leeds' most famous coaching inn. Angela, the Major and Emily all headed inside, taking the plans for the repeating rifle with them. Two of the armed coachmen followed close behind, as no chances were being taken. Although they were in the relative safety of Leeds with its thirty constables, they could still be out manoeuvred by the Russians at any moment.

Reeves and I were very relieved to leave the Black Bull Inn, Patrick O'Shaughnessy and all. It was about eight o'clock in the morning.

"Didn't think we would get out of there this side of Christmas," said Reeves as the Black Bull faded in the distance.

"Yes, and I was beginning to think that being locked up was becoming a daily ritual!" I replied, reflecting on the last two days, turning my face away from the rain which was beginning to fall quite heavily.

We still had good supplies of food and ammunition in our saddle bags, in addition to the curious timetables for Manchester and Liverpool. Those damn timetables had led me in completely the wrong direction but I remained mystified as to why the man who met with the Russians had carried them. Surely that wasn't part of their plan to wrong foot me? Surely they are not that clever! They couldn't possibly have known that I would deliberately bump into the man at the coaching inn in Boroughbridge.

Our fresh horses carried us easily up over the hills and back into Yorkshire. Patrick O'Shaughnessy's men said very little and Reeves and I were deep in thought, riding most of the way in silence. In spite of having the benefit of an escort, we continued to stick to the coach roads primarily because we had no wish to court any more trouble by deviating from the main highways. The further we rode, the more my hopes turned to Sinderby-Smythe. If he and Private Bates had caught Mr and Mrs Von Benckendorff, we would certainly have something other than the plans for a repeating rifle with which to negotiate. In any event, we couldn't be certain that these plans even existed or that Miss Coutts had managed to obtain them. After a few hours hard riding through the rain, we reached Huddersfield which was mercifully quiet. The hustle and bustle of the previous day had been replaced by a sort of calm. The church bells rang and the few people we saw were dressed in their Sunday best and heading for church. There was no sign of unrest at all.

We stopped at the Waterloo Inn to give the horses a breather and a drink whilst we ducked inside and attempted to dry ourselves by a roaring fire, although we dare not linger and were soon on our way again. Our progress was being seriously impeded by the continued driving rain. I was anxious to reach the Bull and Mouth, where I hoped to find Sinderby-Smythe. On we rode with little being said. I hardly knew what to say to Reeves. He had been a solid ally and I felt I had let him down. In the end, we risked our lives to uncover two corrupt aristocrats lining their own pockets and abusing the powers given to them. The news of Sir William Hamilton's involvement in all this had me hoping that his gunshot wound festered just enough to ensure that he had a long and painful life. Perhaps worst of all was the injury I had inflicted on the Duke of Aldborough, which was something he was unlikely to forget easily. He would be reminded of me constantly and I felt sure he would be another aristocrat plotting revenge.

We passed through Dewsbury and headed on towards Leeds, where the rain began to ease up and by mid-afternoon we arrived at the Bull and Mouth. Despite there being several carriages parked outside, I couldn't help noticing the distinctive crest on the doors of one of them. It showed a stag's head. It was most certainly the crest of the Coutts family and the carriage of Miss Angela Coutts.

At this point we bade farewell to Patrick O'Shaughnessy's men who, as promised, returned our pistols even though I had to remind them to hand over my Joseph Manning knife. While they rode out of sight, we handed our horses to a stable boy and asked him to feed and water them. They had worked very hard this last seven hours or so and were white with sweat and blowing hard. Reeves and I attempted to shake ourselves dry in the best way we could. My arm had bled again and the bandage which had been wrapped around it was now completely soaked in blood. It still hurt and I couldn't move it freely, yet thankfully, I hadn't been hit in my stronger right arm. We walked to the entrance of the inn, passing a young girl carrying a tray of food towards the Coutts carriage. I wasn't sure if this meant that Miss Coutts was still in her carriage, or the food was merely being sent out for the two coachmen who were standing alongside.

Consequently we were uncertain as to whom we'd find inside. Nevertheless, we hoped that whoever else was there, Lieutenant Sinderby-Smythe would be amongst them. Once inside the inn, we could easily see Miss Coutts who was sitting with Major Phillips and Emily at a table by the fire. Two more coachmen were close by, suggesting that the Major had followed my advice. Unhappily there was no sign of our lieutenant.

Both Major Phillips and Miss Coutts looked equally pleased to see us, as we were to see them. Miss Coutts continued to look behind us, no doubt hoping to see her companion, Hannah Meredith.

"Captain Townsend and Lieutenant Reeves! How good it is to see you! Please join us. What news do you have of Miss Meredith? Do you have her with you?

Why, Captain, you have been hurt!" said Miss Coutts, noticing the blood soaked bandage on my left arm.

"It is nothing, miss. I regret to report that I have been out-witted. The coach we chased was indeed carrying the Russians but only Von Benckendorff and his wife, and they disembarked here in Leeds. I sent Sinderby-Smythe and a Private from the 15th Hussars after them and I am hoping that they will bring them back here soon. I had supposed that, as a man and a woman continued west in the carriage, it must be Miss Meredith and the Russian's manservant. We had reason to believe that they may have been meeting up with the man behind this whole evil plot. However, when we caught up with them, we found the carriage contained Mr Beales the banker and Miss Hatherway from the grocery shop and not Miss Meredith and the Russian," I replied.

"I take it that Miss Hatherway is the same girl you purchased the tea from?"

"Indeed, Miss Coutts, the very same! It would appear that the Russians had intended for us to make such a wrong assumption. They have led us a merry dance every step of the way. They laid the bait and, like a fool, I took it. I suspect that they wanted us out of the way in order to leave you more vulnerable and all the while we were heading away from Harrogate, they knew we were reducing our chances of finding Miss Meredith."

"Are we therefore to assume that Miss Hatherway and Mr Beales were part of this conspiracy?" asked Major Phillips.

"No, sir, I think they were being used by the Russians all along. They knew nothing of Miss Meredith's abduction or the ransom demand. It doesn't mean that Mr Beales is entirely blameless, as we established that he was bribing Sir William Hamilton and the Duke of Aldborough whilst also embezzling a large sum of money from the investors in the Harrogate railway venture. We uncovered all this, supposing we were capturing the Russian manservant and rescuing Miss Meredith. Lord Redmayne came to our aid and there was unfortunately some shooting, which is why my arm is bandaged."

"You must let me dress your wound, Captain. Was anyone else hurt?" asked Miss Coutts.

"Yes, I'm afraid so. Like me, Lord Redmayne took a bullet in the arm and both Sir William and the Duke of Aldborough were also injured. I fear that Sir William has a more serious injury than the Duke, although I suspect that the Duke will sport a limp for the rest of his life."

"So he was shot in the leg?" asked the Major.

"Close sir, very close," I said and hoped that was sufficient information for the

Major to work out the precise nature of the injury I had inflicted on the Duke. Given the presence of Miss Coutts, I was reluctant to be any more specific. Had I been pressed for more information, I had thought to draw a comparison with a conductor of an orchestra devoid of his baton.

"Did you manage to get the plans of the repeating rifle?" I added, slightly impatiently, anxious for positive news.

"That we did," replied Major Phillips. "Though I am not entirely sure just how complete they are. Apparently Mr Botterill's claim to have invented the repeating rifle might not be quite true. Regrettably, he may have been provoked by sceptics into saying more than was wise. Unfortunately for Mr Botterill, the Russians heard of his claims, took him at his word and when he wouldn't hand the rifle plans over, killed him."

"So how did you manage to locate them?" I queried.

"Thanks entirely to Mrs Botterill. Following the death of her husband, she moved all his belongings into the attic and despite the Russians ransacking their house whilst he was being buried, they failed to find any trace of the rifle plans and I presume that's why they came up with the idea to abduct Miss Meredith."

"So they are not only cunning but ruthless too. In any event, you have done well to get the plans at all. Have you looked at them closely, Major? Do you think Botterill's invention could possibly work?" I asked.

"Actually, it might work," said Major Phillips with a hint of surprise in his voice. "Basically the rifle butt stores a line of bullets which one by one can be fired using Botterill's mechanism. Brilliant, if it works."

"Then it's still a grave risk handing the plans over to them?" I replied.

"Yes, Captain. But what choice do we have?" questioned Miss Coutts.

"Perhaps we might get them copied overnight?" I replied.

"It's a very precise and delicate mechanism, involving a series of springs which are all very complex. Who can copy such plans at short notice and in such a limited amount of time?" asked the Major.

"I was thinking that Pickersgill Palliser at the post office in Harrogate may be able to help on that score."

"Well, it has to be worth a shot, but the Russians will still have a copy even if we have retained one for our own country's use," retorted the Major.

"Yes, that's true Major, yet we still have a chance to recover them," I said, with a germ of an idea developing in my mind. "The Russians need to get the plans out of the country for them to be of any use and it's a long way from the

Devil's Arrows in Boroughbridge to Russia. Instead of dancing to their tune, I think it's time we had them dancing to ours."

"Please explain, Captain. What do you have in mind?" said Major Phillips.

"What I am saying is that all is not lost until the plans are out of the country. So we need to anticipate their next moves from the Devil's Arrows. If we can intercept them, we should recover both Miss Meredith and the plans," I replied.

"But how will you manage that when they have outwitted us every step of the way? They seem to know what we are thinking before we think it," responded Major Phillips.

"Because Major, I know the area surrounding the Devil's Arrows and I think I can cover all the routes to the coast which they may take."

"Is that possible? Surely there must be many different routes?" questioned Miss Coutts.

"Yes, that is true and we must look like we are covering all the obvious ones, otherwise they will smell a rat. Nonetheless, I think I can get ahead of them for the first time. We are clearly dealing with devious agents who know every trick in every book. Our problem has been that up until now, we have been groping in the dark and chasing shadows. It's time we gave them a dose of their own medicine," I said with growing confidence. Even though there was no guarantee that we would succeed, my spirits rose as I mapped out a plan in my head.

We then gave Miss Coutts and Major Phillips more details of the den of corruption we'd uncovered in Lancashire, and in return, they told us everything they had learned from Mrs Botterill. It was now clear that the Russians had tried hard to get the plans from Mr Botterill and only when all their efforts had failed did they decide to kidnap Miss Meredith. Their scheme must have been concocted hastily as this fortuitous opportunity would have only arisen when they heard of Miss Coutts and Miss Meredith heading to the region. News which must have surely come from spies in London. I presumed that they had chosen to abduct Miss Meredith in order to leave Miss Coutts free to organise their ransom demands.

Miss Coutts had dressed my wound and the rest at the Bull and Mouth benefited us all, but with the afternoon almost over, we knew that it was high time to make our way back to Harrogate. Sinderby-Smythe still hadn't arrived and I really wanted to wait for him as planned. However, there was a growing concern that he may have become another casualty in this villainous plot. If the Russians anticipated we would follow the girl in the carriage, they must have also considered that at least one of us would go after Von Benckendorff and his wife. In which case, they could have ambushed Sinderby-Smythe. All the same, they may not have reckoned on the handy Private Bates accompanying him.

We had waited long enough and were still sixteen miles from Harrogate, so after speaking to Reeves we agreed that he would remain at the Bull and Mouth for Sinderby-Smythe whilst I accompanied Miss Coutts on the rest of the journey. Before parting, I also told him of my plan to thwart the Russians. If Sinderby-Smythe hadn't returned to Leeds by seven o'clock this evening, we must assume that he was lost to us, in which event Reeves was to head north and be ready to carry out my plan.

Miss Coutts and Major Phillips climbed aboard the Coutts family carriage which slowly pulled away from the Bull and Mouth and headed north to Harrogate. Knowing how ruthless these Russians had been, I was reassured that we had four armed coachmen to help us protect both Miss Coutts and Botterill's plans. The Russians may have initially fallen for our trick of posting the plans to Harrogate but, for all we knew, they may have rumbled that by now and be lying in wait to intercept us. That way they could get the plans and still have Miss Meredith with which to negotiate their escape.

Accordingly, the carriage travelled quickly with orders not to stop for anything. Although it had rained here too, it was evident that it had been nothing like the downpour we had encountered on our journey to Leeds. We travelled back along the turnpike road to Harrogate, with me out in front on my horse watching every tree and bush for any sign of trouble lurking. We passed Harewood in good time and all was looking well when the carriage hit a pothole in the road, making the most awful noise. Fortunately the wheels seemed undamaged and the carriage continued on down the steep hill towards the river. At the bottom of the hill we came to a bridge where we slowed down to wait for another coach coming in the opposite direction. The hairs on the back of my neck stood to attention as I suspected this was no coincidence. I took out the pistol from my belt with my right hand and prepared for trouble. The other carriage which was drawn by four black horses came over the bridge and drew alongside us. A man peered out through the window causing the grip on my pistol to tighten only for it to quickly relax as he thanked us for giving way. He wished us a pleasant evening and carried on up the hill to Harewood. Despite its innocent appearance I watched the four black horses pull the coach out of sight, whilst the Coutts' carriage safely crossed the bridge. Confident that all was well, I rode my horse across the bridge and once more took the lead.

After travelling for a further mile along the Harrogate road, disaster struck.

The wheels crashed into another pothole and this time one of them broke off, causing the carriage to lurch to the right, almost throwing off the coachmen. They clung on and managed to bring the horses to a halt. I rode up alongside, jumping down from my horse whereupon I was reminded of the hole in my arm, prompting me to wince briefly.

Everyone was, thankfully, alright.

"Oh no, not again," said Miss Coutts, while I helped her from the leaning coach. We were stranded and it would take hours to get the wheel repaired, by which time it would be dark.

"There is nothing for it but for you to take Miss Coutts to Harrogate on your horse, Captain. We will use one of the carriage horses to ride to Harewood for help. We will meet you at the Queen Hotel whenever we can. And here, you take the plans, just in case something should go wrong and we don't get back in time," said Major Phillips.

Despite Miss Coutts appearing a little shocked at the initial mention of the two of us doubled up on a horse, she soon saw the sense in it. With her safely on board and the plans in the saddle bags, we rode away from the carriage. If we were vulnerable to an ambush before, we were really badly exposed now. We walked slowly and surely, taking no risks. It was imperative that we arrived safely in Harrogate before nightfall. Ordinarily that wouldn't be a problem but with two of us riding one horse, and a tired one at that, this was by no means a certainty.

On we rode and my eyes and ears were everywhere. Miss Coutts was wise to the risks we faced and little was said between us. We reached Buttersyke Bar with its surly gate keeper, as the light was starting to fade. Safety was now only a couple of miles away and on we travelled. Occasionally we would pass a rider or carriage heading away from Harrogate and as each one passed us, my hand kept a tight hold of my pistol. We rode up the hill which welcomes visitors arriving from the south and with just a mile to go, we passed the Travellers' Inn. We were close, so very close and then much to our relief the Queen Hotel came into view.

I rode up to the front door of the hotel where we were met with a flurry of activity the moment the staff recognised their most illustrious guest.

I looked onto the Stray and saw six army tents. I had forgotten about the letter I had sent to the garrison. Miss Coutts noticed them too and we both feared for Miss Meredith at that moment.

"Captain, would you find out who's in charge of the troops and tell them to keep well out of the way. Major Phillips had asked them to stay hidden. Their actions could have serious consequences for Miss Meredith!" said Miss Coutts, looking very concerned. "Thank you so much, Captain. Once again, you have saved me on the open road. I can't tell you how much I appreciate all your efforts to help Miss Meredith. You are a good and noble man and I would be lost without you. Now, it is late and we have the most trying day tomorrow. Might I suggest we meet here at six o'clock tomorrow morning? I will arrange for another carriage and I suggest you ride Tribune. We might be in need of his speed," she said, trying her best to smile.

"I fear that six o'clock will be too late, allowing for the fact that it's a good ten miles to Boroughbridge. Might I suggest we meet at thirty minutes past five instead?"

"Half past five it is, the sun should just be rising then."

"Please accept my apologies for the presence of the troops, as I fear this is of my doing," I said, apologetically.

"Fear not, Captain. Your aunt told us of the letters which Benson had been sent, which is why Major Phillips sent a note advising the garrison at York of the need to remain out of sight."

At which point Miss Coutts looked forlornly over to the rows of white tents and added, "Either the letter never found its way to the right person or else the recipient misread its contents."

A tired looking Miss Coutts then made her way inside the hotel and past the flowers left for Tom Dawson, whilst I went in search of the officer in charge of the troops. It took a while but eventually I found a Captain Thomas who was a pleasant enough chap from Wales. I explained the whole saga to him and divulged most of my plans for tomorrow. I only held back the role I had given to Reeves. Captain Thomas apologised for misunderstanding our requests. It seemed that receiving two messages from two different officers had confused him. In any event, he agreed to stay in the background out of sight and only cover the most likely escape routes from the Devil's Arrows. These would be the main coach roads north, south, east and west. At my request he assigned one of his junior officers to watch over Angela Coutts, assuming the role I had given Sinderby-Smythe. After agreeing that he would pull out of Harrogate before five o'clock in the morning, I rode to the post office to seek out Pickersgill Palliser, all the while continuing to look out for signs of trouble.

I knocked on his door and eventually Pickersgill Palliser opened it.

"Captain Townsend, I am surprised to see you here! We were all under the impression that you were being held prisoner at Constable Hardisty's house."

I had completely forgotten about that episode.

"A misunderstanding, Mr Palliser. The unfortunate constable had been misled in order to cause me great inconvenience."

"I knew it! I told Mrs Palliser it was inconceivable that you would have murdered poor Mr Dawson," he said, ushering me through the door.

"I do sincerely regret this intrusion, but I need you to perform a vital service for Her Majesty's government," whereupon I took Mr Palliser into my confidence and explained the need to copy the plans. Without any fuss he agreed to help and furthermore, as I couldn't let the plans out of my sight, he also agreed to carry out the work at Holderness House. Palliser promised that he would be there within the hour, together with the necessary equipment.

On the way back to Holderness House, I called in at the Granby Hotel. I had to tell the Duchess about the events at her husband's shooting lodge and that I was the one responsible. I must have looked a woeful sight having not washed since Friday, still in the same clothes which had only just dried out and a blood stained bandage on my arm. It was no surprise that I received a less than enthusiastic reception as I entered the 'house of lords'.

Somewhat reluctantly they agreed to raise the Duchess.

Although it was late, she had not yet retired for the evening, which again had been spent in the company of the Earl of Warkworth. In the same way that the hotel staff had looked aghast at my appearance, she too appeared a little shocked. Nonetheless, she was very pleased to see me. I told her the whole story, leaving nothing out and she listened intently and never interrupted. Mary, Duchess of Aldborough had clearly known a good deal about her husband's shady dealings but, knowing his violent temper, had kept his secrets. I detected mixed feelings in her voice. With his philandering days almost certainly over, it was more than likely that she would bear the brunt of his frustrations. I told her that I was intent on rescuing Miss Meredith in the morning and said I would visit her after that if she wished. She threw her arms around me, kissed me on the cheek and made me promise to take care.

Exhausted and drained I rode back to Holderness House continuing to be vigilant all the way. Not only had I the plans for the repeating rifle, more importantly, I also had a plan to outwit the Russians.

Chapter 37

I arrived back at Holderness House to the most emotional reception from my aunt. Benson asked the stable boy to look after Lord Redmayne's horse only when I had taken custody of the saddle bags. Pickersgill Palliser arrived and Benson stayed with him in the library whilst he traced a copy of the plans. My aunt tended to my arm, after which, we had a late supper and I told her the whole sorry tale. She was shocked by the news that the railway venture had been so corruptly managed and vowed to meet with Henry Payden in the morning. The fact that Lord Redmayne had intercepted twenty five thousand pounds which he was intent on returning to investors did little to improve her mood. Such was her resolve that she rejected my attempts to intervene and confront Mr Payden on her behalf. She felt a fool for making the investment in the first place and intended to vent her anger in person. There was no doubting that Mr Payden was in for a torrid time and deservedly so.

Pickersgill Palliser worked diligently for several hours and didn't leave until he had provided us with an identical copy of Botterill's invention. Benson and Cookson were to maintain an all-night vigil, to prevent the Russians making some audacious last minute attempt to steal the plans. Given the extent of their spy network it was eminently possible that they would attempt this in order to avoid handing over Miss Meredith tomorrow. We were now as prepared for the meeting at the Devil's Arrows as we would ever be.

Even though I was exhausted and desperately wanted to sleep, I was terrified that I wouldn't wake and would fail to make the early morning rendezvous with Miss Coutts. Benson assured me that he would rouse me, which turned out to be com–pletely superfluous, as with so much racing around in my mind, I barely slept at all.

Morning eventually came and I was up and dressed in good time to meet with Miss Coutts. I had hoped to feel refreshed, but not surprisingly I still felt very tired and my arm ached continuously. The sun was making its first appearance of the day as the stable boy brought Tribune to me and, after saying goodbye to my anxious looking aunt, I rode away from Holderness House and back towards

317

the Queen Hotel. Cookson and Benson escorted me, well-armed and riding up top on my aunt's carriage. There was little warmth in the sun, leaving an invigorating chill in the air which soon brought me fully awake. I rode steadily across the Stray, checking my pistols on the way. Yet again, a battle loomed and like all battles, the outcome is never certain. It's at times like this when I recalled the great battle cries of victory and glory which were constantly preached in the Dragoons. This was no time for faint hearts, we simply had to succeed with me surviving in the process. That was the only outcome I could accept, and I had to eliminate my fears of anything else completely.

We arrived at the Queen Hotel to find Angela Coutts and Major Phillips waiting with a carriage they had hired for the day. Captain Thomas had departed with his men and all that could be seen was the impression their camp had left in the grass. There was still no sign of Sinderby-Smythe, which did not provide a good omen for what lay ahead. I thanked Benson for his help and he and Cookson returned to Holderness House.

"I am relieved to see that you managed to return here safely, Major," I said, genuinely pleased to see him.

"Yes, Captain, but only just. We spent most of the night in Harewood and headed over to Harrogate at the earliest possible moment," he replied.

"I presume you have the plans, Captain?' enquired Miss Coutts apprehensively.

"Absolutely, both sets," I said, tapping the saddle bags.

"Good, because we are going to need them both," said Miss Coutts, raising the eyebrows of Major Phillips and myself.

"Another letter arrived this morning from the Russians. Somehow they know that Mr Palliser made a copy of Botterill's invention and the price for the safe release of Miss Meredith is that we must safely deliver up two sets of the plans to the repeating rifle."

"How the devil did they find that out?" I exclaimed.

"Presumably like they have known everything else. Spies, Captain, spies," replied Major Phillips.

"Then, gentlemen, there is nothing else we can do. Frustrating as it is, I suggest we make for the Devil's Arrows," said Miss Coutts climbing into the carriage quickly followed by Major Phillips.

In a repeat of yesterday's journey from Leeds, I led the way scouting for trouble.

We made good time covering the ten miles to Boroughbridge, arriving at the Devil's Arrows fifteen minutes before the appointed hour. The carriage stopped about fifty yards from the three stones and after scouting the area, I rode up alongside it.

"What do you make of it, Captain?" said Major Phillips, surveying the open fields through the carriage window.

"There are only the three stones to see, sir. Other than the odd tree there's nothing else in sight. That's why they chose this place," I replied.

"Bloody big stones, Captain," said Major Phillips, marvelling at their height and girth as he stepped down onto the grass.

"Legend has it, Major, that if you walk around the stones in an anti-clockwise direction, you'll raise the devil," I said, remembering my conversation with Virginia when she told me of a similar legend in respect to the four stones of Harlow Moor.

"Maybe the Russians have already raised the devil, Captain," said the Major ominously.

"What time do you make it? By my watch there are only ten minutes to go."

"Mine too, sir," my nerves starting to jangle.

Minutes ticked by slowly as the tension mounted. Miss Coutts looked most anxious and, although our group looked innocent enough, we were all armed to the teeth. I had agreed with Captain Thomas that two of his men would drive the carriage disguised as coachmen. They were his best two marksmen, Sergeant Kitching and Private Kettlewell.

We all repeatedly checked our weapons.

"Perhaps we should have taken Constable Hardisty into our confidence and invited him along?" suggested Miss Coutts nervously through the window of the coach.

"Bringing that man along would be like taking a spoon to a knife throwing contest," I replied, releasing some of the tension that was hanging over us.

Seven thirty came and went, which only increased the mounting concern we all shared and it was a full five pressure-loaded minutes later before a carriage appeared on the opposite side of this vast field. It arrived from the direction of Boroughbridge and seemed to have some sort of storage cover on it, making it impossible to determine its usual livery. When it was within fifty yards of the Arrows it stopped, leaving around one hundred yards between the two carriages with the Devil's Arrows standing majestically in the middle. I took out my telescope from my saddle-bag and saw the one-eyed Russian in the carriage with a woman. She wore a yellow dress, similar to the one worn by Miss Meredith at the races on Friday. Behind the carriage followed a man on horseback.

"They're here," said Major Phillips, nervously stating the obvious and we all waited to see what the Russian would do next.

Nothing happened and both sides waited, watching the other for signs of treachery. After a few minutes the horseman dismounted and exchanged places with the one-eyed Russian who then climbed on the horse and rode to the centre stone of the three. Once there he beckoned me to ride forward.

"Damn, aren't I the lucky one?" I said under my breath as adrenaline suddenly coursed through my veins at the imminent prospect of confrontation.

"It looks like the Russian is ready to trade, Captain. Good luck my boy and keep your wits about you. He's bound to have a trick or two up his sleeve," said Major Phillips, standing by the carriage stroking his whiskers in the same way he did when he first came to my aid outside the Dragon Hotel.

"Be careful, Captain," said Miss Coutts.

I urged Tribune forward and we slowly made our way over to the centre ground. All the while I was on the look-out for trouble with my hand inches away from my loaded pistol. As I neared the Russian I could see that he was totally relaxed, wrapped in a long black cloak. He looked confident and in control, which for the minute, he was. He even had the audacity to light a cheroot while he awaited my arrival.

"Good morning, Captain. We meet at last," he said, as our horses came within a few yards of each other. I prevented Tribune from getting any closer in order to remain well out of arms reach.

"Even though we have not been introduced, I feel like I know you very well. My name is Nikolas Von Benckendorff and I am pleased to make your acquaintance," said the Russian with an air of authority.

"Any relation to Vladimir?" I asked.

"He's my brother," he replied.

"I don't suppose he really is a railway engineer?" I asked.

"No," said the Russian with a wry smile, continuing to draw on his cheroot.

"Now, Captain, I have a long way to go today and so I would be grateful if you would hand over the plans to the repeating rifle, and both sets if you please. Did you really think we would be so naïve as to allow you to copy them?" said the Russian, clearly irritated by my actions.

"The moment I have Miss Meredith, then you shall have your plans," I said, which prompted him to draw his pistol and point it at me.

"You will hand over the plans immediately, Captain," said the Russian, brandishing his weapon ferociously.

"I may have acted foolishly these last few days but do you really suppose I am so stupid as to ride out here with them?" I replied, endeavouring to remain calm.

"Perhaps. I never cease to be amazed at how stupid people can be. Either way, let me warn you, Miss Meredith's life is in your hands. Any tricks and she dies."

He then directed me to look back at the carriage where Miss Meredith was sitting, looking terrified with a pistol pointed at her head.

"You will get your plans when I get Miss Meredith," I said forcefully. "If she's killed, I promise that you will be right behind her."

"Bold words, Captain. Two people have already crossed us and died. Take care you're not the third."

"Then it was you who killed Dawson?" I concluded.

"Mr Dawson became too greedy. He wanted more money so he could run away with that girl you liked. He was a loose gun as you say," replied the Russian.

"Cannon," I corrected. "It's a loose cannon, not a gun.....So he was working for you and I suppose you employed the Irishman too?" I said, unravelling the plot as the smell of his cheroot aroused my suspicions that he was one of the riders who had met with the Irishman in the small farm building just outside Harrogate.

"Yes, they kept an eye on Miss Coutts which was next to useless when your lieutenant arrived, but I am tiring of this. You can work everything out in your own time!"

I smiled inwardly that Sinderby-Smythe's efforts had caused them problems but then felt only anger at the possibility of him lying dead in some ditch, killed by this man's brother.

"Dawson was an obnoxious toad but Botterill was a good man and you had no business killing him. You will answer for that."

"Choose your words carefully, Captain. We should make the exchange before one of us does something reckless," sneered the Russian.

"They are with Major Phillips," I said, pointing to the man standing by our carriage. "He will bring them over to us when Miss Meredith is safe."

"Very well, Captain. Ask your Major to start walking towards us and I will ask Miss Meredith to do the same. Rifles will be aimed at her all the while and my pistol will be trained on you and make no mistake, I will kill you if you try to deceive me in any way."

I accepted his terms apprehensively, not knowing what would happen next and signalled for the Major to walk out towards us.

"For your benefit, Von Benckendorff, there will be guns on you too and if anything happens to Miss Meredith or the Major, then it will be the last thing you see in this world," at which I signalled to the two sharp shooters driving the carriage who immediately picked up rifles and aimed them at the Russian.

There was a real tension in the air as neither party trusted the other and men on both sides of the field held rifles and pistols ready to fire. I feared that the carnage at the Duke of Aldborough's lodge was about to be repeated.

The Russian had waved for Miss Meredith to start walking towards us. She looked frail and terrified and likely to faint.

"What have you done to her?" I growled.

"She is a tough lady and refused to eat. Maybe she thinks that wasn't such a good idea now," answered the Russian.

The Major was making good progress although I could see he was blowing quite a bit, as walking through the long dew soaked grass took its toll. When Miss Meredith was within twenty yards, the Russian shouted for everyone to stop.

"That is far enough, Major. You will now show me that you have the plans."

The Major waved both copies of Botterill's designs in the air.

"Captain, you will kindly bring them to me," said the Russian, attempting to be civil when all the while he bore the look of a predator about to pounce.

I rode the twenty yards to where the Major stood and said to him softly, "Give me just one set, Major." Which he did and I rode back to the Russian, wary of his next move.

I showed him the plans, taking care to remain at arm's length, nonetheless he was sufficiently close enough to see we had the genuine article.

"As you can see, we really do have the invention you want. It is yours when we have Miss Meredith."

I looked over to where she stood and was afraid she might collapse at any moment.

"Very good, Captain," said the Russian looking irritated, his right hand gripping his pistol tightly.

"And now, I think it's time we concluded our business," I said.

The Russian nodded in agreement and then beckoned for Miss Meredith and the Major to come forward.

When she was only five yards away, he told her to stop once more.

"That is close enough. She is yours, Captain, and you will oblige me by handing over the ransom," said the Russian, still holding his pistol menacingly like a venomous snake about to strike.

I turned towards the Major and moved the few yards to take the second set of plans from him. I had to hold them under my injured arm in order to keep my right hand on the handle of my pistol. If shooting was about to start, I intended to roll off Tribune and shoot from the ground.

There was nothing left but to hand over the plans to the repeating rifle. The Russian examined the drawings closely with his lone eye and quickly placed them inside his coat.

"Thank you, Captain, these seem to be in order. My men have rifles aimed at Miss Meredith and if any of you move, she will be shot. After fifteen minutes they will leave, at which time you will be free to take Miss Meredith away with you. Count Zadovich will be very pleased with these and by the way, he asked me to send Lord Palmerston his very best wishes." Smiling in the most irritating way, he turned his horse and rode away at high speed, his black cloak flapping wildly behind him.

The carriage which had brought the Russian did not move and we could clearly see at least three rifles trained on Miss Meredith. Despite being desperate to pursue Von Benckendorff, I dare not risk the life of this poor lady any further. I spoke to her and asked her to continue to be brave as it would soon be over. The minutes passed slowly and I could see Miss Meredith swaying, fighting to remain standing. Miss Coutts was out of her carriage, clearly anxious.

At last the Russians' carriage sped off and the Major shouted, "They're off," at which Miss Meredith promptly collapsed.

"She's yours, Major. I'll get after Von Benckendorff," I said, as I spurred Tribune forward.

I chased the carriage towards Boroughbridge and then it turned north into some woods. I suspected that I was supposed to follow, only I chose not to.

Captain Thomas had men posted on the Great North road, both north and south, which left me free to chase the one-eyed Russian and I was confident that he went east. I headed towards Upper Dunsforth, to the house I saw Von Benckendorff visit a few days ago which seemed like a good place to begin. Tribune was the fastest horse in this part of England, but even he couldn't give anyone a fifteen minute start.

We galloped into the village to see it deserted, save for a couple of farm hands in a stock yard on my right and a fisherman on my left walking back from the river. The cottage which the Russian had visited was on my left and I cautiously rode towards it. I dismounted Tribune and tied him to a fence post. Taking out my pistol, I walked towards the front of the cottage. Knocking on the door seemed like an incredibly stupid idea, nevertheless, it was possible that someone was living there quite innocently. So I knocked on the door. There was no answer, forcing me to walk around to the back. There was no sign of anyone. I then knocked on the back door and still nothing. After trying the handle and establishing it wasn't locked, I pushed it open and went inside. There were the remnants of a fire burning in the grate and a black cloak thrown in the corner. There were signs that Miss Meredith had been held here and there were more half-smoked cheroots lying on the floor.

Searching the house from top to bottom revealed no further clues and so I followed my instincts and rode quickly towards York. If I was right, the Russian had come to Upper Dunsforth not just for the use of the cottage but also for quick access to the river. The river would take him to York and then straight out to sea. I had told Reeves of this and if everything proceeded to plan, he should be lying in wait, ready to intercept Nikolas and rescue the repeating rifle.

I rode Tribune just like he was going down the finishing straight in the Harrogate Handicap Stakes, which quickly had me closing in on our pre-arranged meeting place. Before I caught sight of anyone, I heard shots being fired. Some fifty yards further I could just make out Reeves and Sinderby-Smythe crouched behind trees, firing at a boat. Sinderby-Smythe was alive! Shots were being returned from those on board. Reeves took a bullet and fell backwards as if mortally wounded, prompting Sinderby-Smythe to go to his aid. Shots continued to rain from the boat preventing him from getting too close to his injured comrade.

As I closed in on the scene, I could see the boat slipping away from my two officers. It was being navigated by three men who appeared to be fishermen, one of whom had been hit. Anger rose within me; I was incensed and determined to stop the Russians escaping with the plans. Riding Tribune inland out of sight of the river, I headed downstream to cut them off at the next bridge. The river grew in size and widened as it neared York. Arriving at the crossing ahead of the boat, I dismounted and left Tribune tied to a tree. I ran to the entrance of the wooden bridge with a pistol in each hand and lay flat on the ground. With my arms stretched out in front of me and pistols at the ready I waited. When Von Benckendorff sailed into view, I would shoot him.

The boat appeared with two men standing and one laid flat on the deck, possibly dead. They came closer and closer with their guns searching for trouble, no doubt realising that the bridge would be a good place to ambush them. The current carried them forward and, in next to no time, I had them in my sights.

I took careful aim at Von Benckendorff and then fired. The bullet hit home, yet not where I intended. A man fell overboard and the vessel rocked wildly but Von Benckendorff still lived. The boat passed under the bridge and out of my sight. I scrambled across the width of the crossing, and waited for him to appear and head downstream to York. My forefinger nestled on the trigger of my second pistol, waiting to finish the job. The boat appeared but Von Benckendorff was nowhere to be seen.

Before I could get up to investigate, a voice said, "Captain Townsend, you will throw your pistol away, if you please." It came from the Russian. He had left the river and crept around the back of me.

"You have greatly inconvenienced me, Captain, and deprived me of the sailors who were taking me out to sea. I must now borrow your horse and take a different route. I ought to compliment you, Captain. I underestimated your ability. It is a pity that I must now kill you…" and with that I heard his pistol cock and then a gun fired.

Chapter 38

I don't know what I expected to feel, but I felt nothing; no pain, no darkness. I was still conscious. My hand moved, confirming that I was indeed still alive. I turned over in time to see the Russian tumbling down the embankment and into the river.

Sinderby-Smythe came bounding onto the bridge.

"By gad, sir, are you alright? Looked like the damn fellow was going to shoot you."

"I think you're right, lieutenant. What can I say? You saved my life!" as Sinderby-Smythe took me by the hand and pulled me to my feet. Still coming to terms with my reprieve, I looked down at the Russian, wanting to ensure he had taken his last breath before retrieving the plans, but the river was stealing him away.

"Quick! We must get the plans," I said.

Von Benckendorff's body was steadily floating down the river at an ever increasing pace. We ran along the river bank and then waded waist deep into the cold, grey water. We both stretched out our arms to grab his body as he floated by. I seized one arm whilst Sinderby-Smythe caught hold of a leg and we pulled him towards us. As his face came ever closer, I half expected his good eye to open and for him to tell me how I had fallen for yet another of his tricks. Thankfully his body remained limp and still and his eye closed. By the time we had dragged him out of the river, all the writing on the plans had become so badly smudged that they were rendered totally illegible. The drawings were ruined and Mr Botterill's vision of a repeating rifle was now lost to us all.

We hauled his body off the bank and managed to borrow a farmer's cart which we also needed to help us get Reeves back to Harrogate. We tied all the horses to the back of the cart and Sinderby-Smythe and I sat up front. Reeves had a taken a bullet to his leg which needed to be removed. We had wrapped his belt tight around his leg to stop him bleeding to death but even though he was barely conscious, I don't think he much enjoyed sharing a ride with a dead, one-eyed Russian. It seemed to take an age but we finally arrived back in

Harrogate around mid-day. We left Reeves at Holderness House with my aunt, who was only too pleased to see us all safely back. She sent Benson to fetch Doctor Richardson then Sinderby-Smythe and I, after off-loading the body of the Russian with Constable Hardisty, headed to the Queen to break the good news to Miss Coutts and Major Phillips.

They, too, were delighted that the plans had been retrieved from the Russian and whilst Miss Coutts tended to Miss Meredith, Major Phillips accompanied Sinderby-Smythe and myself into the bar for a drink.

There was a strange atmosphere pervading as we toasted our success. Although we shared a common victory, we were still collecting our own private thoughts. Sinderby-Smythe really was the crack shot he said he was. He had never killed anyone before and in doing so now, had saved my life. I would be forever in his debt. Major Phillips was noticeably fatigued following his interrupted night in Harewood and I suspect he thought his days of active service were long since over.

After toasting the bravery and fortitude of Miss Coutts and Miss Meredith, we all retired to change our clothes and refresh ourselves. I returned to my aunt's, while Sinderby-Smythe and Major Phillips went back to their rooms.

Once at Holderness House, I first looked in on Reeves who I found sleeping peacefully, after Dr Richardson had successfully removed the offending bullet from his leg. I then made my way to the library where I wrote my report to Lord Palmerston. This was the hardest report of all, with the code proving to be an exhausting challenge for my tired mind. When it was at last completed, I passed it to Benson to post. Now I was determined to embark on the most serious night of drinking imaginable.

I had invited Captain Thomas to join myself, Lieutenant Sinderby-Smythe and Major Phillips for dinner at the Dragon Hotel. My aunt had assumed the role of matron and took great pleasure in caring for 2nd Lieutenant Reeves. She also seemed to have enjoyed her meeting with Henry Payden much more than he had done. She was furious, feeling she had been taken for a fool and made Mr Payden aware of that in no uncertain terms.

Henry Payden had confessed to being shocked by the news of his partner's actions and quickly distanced himself from him, although he failed to satisfactorily account for his whereabouts when he left the races half way through the afternoon. He made full restitution of the monies invested by my aunt, which happily included the money she'd invested on my behalf.

"By this time tomorrow everyone in Harrogate will be aware of what has happened and I suspect there will be a long queue of disenchanted investors outside his bank, all seeking their money back."

"And what will become of Virginia Hatherway?" she then asked. "I was sorry to hear that she had become involved with Mr Beales and Sir William Hamilton. That must have hurt, George," she said sympathetically.

"Yes, it did come as a bit of a shock. Although I had received a warning from the Duchess of Aldborough that everything wasn't as it seemed. Having said that, I never for one moment thought she could be referring to Virginia and Beales."

"You should stay clear of women like that, and your Duchess. I know you think me an old fool, but Angela Coutts is the one for you."

I couldn't help smiling at my aunt's persistence. There was no doubting that I had grown close to Miss Coutts, however I believed that neither of us desired anything more than friendship from each other.

Young Harry arrived at the house and offered to take me to the Dragon in his cart but I opted for the comfort of a carriage instead. I, nevertheless, gave Harry five sovereigns and thanked him for all his brave efforts and told him to come and see me tomorrow as we still had the unfinished business of the boys who had attacked him and so brutally whipped their donkeys.

Cookson drove the carriage admirably and I arrived at the Dragon in fine spirits. After everyone else had joined me, we were led to the same private room William Beales had shown me several days earlier. We then ate well and drank freely, spending the night reliving the events of the previous week.

Captain Thomas, having only seen the ending of this saga, was struggling to grasp all the complexities and sought clarification before the wine rendered the exercise futile.

"Please tell me if I understand this correctly, Captain," he started.

"These Russians, old Von Benken what's its… heard about someone inventing a repeating rifle in Sheffield. They attempted to get their hands on it. When that didn't work, they killed the inventor and then ransacked his house while the poor man was laid to rest. In their act of vandalism, they didn't find the plans although they did see that the inventor was heavily indebted to Coutts Bank. Then, hearing that Miss Coutts was coming north to Harrogate, decided to pressurise her into obtaining the plans for them?"

"So far so good, Captain," I said.

"Thank you, Captain," replied Captain Thomas. "Then the Russians head to Harrogate posing as railway engineers and hatch a plan to kidnap either Miss Coutts or her close companion."

"Absolutely right so far."

"Presumably, when they became aware of your arrival, they wanted you out of the way. So they tried to encourage you to leave Harrogate?"

"Yes. Von Benckendorff, after offering the Beales brothers his services to promote the railway, probably met Dawson here at the Dragon. Both William Beales and Tom Dawson were regulars here. And when the Russians heard that Dawson worked at the Queen Hotel, he would have looked like the perfect accomplice for them. A man desperate for money and without scruples who could easily spy on Miss Coutts," I answered, attempting to explain my theory.

"It seems to me that the Russians planned everything so very carefully, but surely Miss Meredith spilling a drink and then returning to the hotel alone to change her dress, was pure luck?" enquired Major Phillips.

"I don't think so, Major. The Irishman, Dunn, who we had seen watching the hotel, was planted at the racecourse to lure me away. They hoped that if I saw him, I would chase after him, which of course I did. Whilst I was wrestling with Dunn, someone, maybe even Dawson, bumped into the back of the tent where Miss Meredith was standing, causing her to spill her drink. They were hoping that she would make enough of a mess of her dress to warrant returning to the hotel to change. I suspect that if the first accidental bump hadn't worked then there would have been further accidents planned. With me out of the way, they would know that Lieutenant Sinderby-Smythe wouldn't leave the side of Miss Coutts, necessitating Miss Meredith to return to the hotel alone, or possibly with the Major. The moment she was clear of the racecourse and alone, they planned to abduct her. At the very latest, this would be when she was changing her dress, as all the maids were at the races too. With everyone so pre-occupied, even if Miss Meredith had chance to cry out, it is very unlikely that anyone would have heard her," I explained.

"Damn Ruski's," said Major Phillips.

"So why was Dawson killed?" asked Captain Thomas.

"I expect it was because the Russians may have seen him as a loose end. He probably knew too much for them to feel safe, and by planting my watch on his corpse they no doubt hoped that I would be arrested, making it far more difficult for us to give chase."

"But what of the girl who was involved with Dawson? Did you not know her, Captain?" asked Captain Thomas delicately.

"Yes, I did know her and I believe that her involvement with Dawson existed largely in his head."

"All the same, I hear that she was prompted by one of the Beales brothers to spy on you. How did they fit into all this?" asked Captain Thomas.

"That was another matter altogether and designed to settle an old personal score for Sir William Hamilton, who was basically selling parliamentary approvals to those companies wishing to build railroads. I gather that making life uncomfortable for me was a condition of his corrupt deal with the Beales brothers. We have history."

"Were they not connected to the Russians in any other way than through the railway?" asked Major Phillips.

"That's correct, sir. The Beales brothers had no idea what the Russians were planning. They were simply being used to disguise the real purpose behind their visit to Harrogate. They each used the other."

"Yet they shared the same carriage as they fled the scene?" queried Captain Thomas.

"Again, they were being used by the Russians. There were three Russians in all and if they had abducted Miss Meredith that would make four people, two men and two women. When Von Benckendorff learned that Beales was leaving in a private carriage, he saw an opportunity to mislead us and so he asked Beales if Vladimir and Svetlana could join him and Miss Hatherway. Once they split up in Leeds, we too had to split up and we then erroneously went miles out of the way to Manchester in the belief that we were following Miss Meredith and the remaining Russian."

"Didn't you think it odd that they were heading west, Captain?" asked Captain Thomas.

"At first, yes, but we observed the Von Benckendorff's at a secret meeting with a man at the Plough Inn in Upper Dunsforth. After the meeting, I followed this man into the Crown at Boroughbridge where I deliberately bumped into him in order to see what he was carrying. Surprisingly, I found that they had been pouring over timetables to Manchester and Liverpool. Why else would he be carrying those if the Von Benckendorff's were not planning to travel there for one purpose or another?" I said.

"I think I can answer that, sir," interrupted Lieutenant Sinderby-Smythe.

The lieutenant then filled us in on his adventure east, which resulted in him catching up with Vladimir and Svetlana Von Benckendorff and successfully capturing them. They had been heading for Kingston upon Hull where they had arranged to meet Nikolas after he had obtained the plans to the repeating rifle. Following which, they would all sail back to Russia. Eventually he got around to answering the mystery of the timetables.

"On the way back to the Bull and Mouth, I queried the point about the timetables with Svetlana, who I have to say was far more helpful than her sly husband. She told me that the man you bumped into in Boroughbridge was indeed working with the Von Benckendorff's and he had taken the timetables to the meeting at the Plough Inn, Upper Dunsforth. However, in addition to bringing the timetables needed to travel west, he also brought those needed to travel east. The Von Benckendorff's kept the timetables needed to travel east, which is why the man they met at the Plough Inn was left holding the ones needed to travel west as they weren't required."

"It just shows that you should never make assumptions as they are invariably wrong. My father always used to say 'believe nothing of what you hear and only half of what you see and never assume anything.'"

"But what I would like to know, sir, is how did you know that Nikolas, the one-eyed Russian, would use the River Ouse to escape and not follow the same route taken by Vladimir and Svetlana?" asked Lieutenant Sinderby-Smythe.

"Once it became clear that Vladimir and Svetlana had headed to Kingston upon Hull and that our one-eyed Russian had remained in the area, I concluded that following the meeting at the Devil's Arrows, he would most likely chose an escape route which took him east to meet up with his brother. Furthermore, the route needed to be one which would not be immediately obvious to any of us. It was then that I recalled them visiting that house in Upper Dunsforth and I remembered from the time I spent in the village as a child, that the River Ouse ran from Lower Dunsforth to York, and then to Selby and onto Kingston upon Hull."

"So why didn't you tell us that, Captain?" asked Captain Thomas.

"Well, I couldn't be certain that I was right, and I was worried that if Nikolas didn't see us blocking the routes which we would naturally expect him to take, he might change his plans altogether. I was fairly sure that if we gave him no reason to think we were aware that the river was a viable means of escape, then there was a good chance to intercept them on the river at some point."

"Bravo, sir," hailed Major Phillips. "I would place a large wager that Lord Palmerston will be promoting you once he hears of this."

"Thank you, sir, but I couldn't have done it without all your help," I replied, a shade embarrassed by his comment.

"Where are the other two Russians now, Vladimir and Svetlana?" asked Major Phillips.

"I left them with Private Bates at the barracks in Leeds, sir," said Lieutenant Sinderby-Smythe.

"It took us a long time to catch up with them, which is why we were late back. Fortunately Reeves had waited for me at the Bull and Mouth and told me of the plan. Otherwise I wouldn't have been at the river to assist you, sir," he added.

"And it's a damn good job you did lieutenant, as I would not be here now if it wasn't for your quick thinking and excellent marksmanship," I said sincerely, raising my glass to him.

"Thank you, sir," he replied, while the rest of us banged our fists on the table in appreciation.

Captain Thomas explained what had happened to the coach and the men driving it. It turned out that the cover we saw on the coach was disguising the fact that it was a stolen mail coach which enabled them to evade the Captain's men. The coach was found abandoned near Selby and it is presumed that they fled east to board a Russian ship. This seemed to just about wrap everything up and before I was too drunk to speak, I visited Mary, Duchess of Aldborough only to find that she had left Harrogate earlier in the day. She left me a letter which confirmed that she still loved me and promised to return to me one day, which was confusing in the extreme.

With my work in Harrogate complete, I was intent on heading back to London with Sinderby-Smythe the instant Reeves was recovered enough to travel. In the meantime, I intended to rest and spend the days with my aunt and the nights in the Dragon. Lord Palmerston had not received my letter advising him of the abduction of Miss Meredith until three days after it had been sent, as he had been spending the weekend at his country estate. By the time he read of the abduction he was also in receipt of my next letter advising him of the outcome, which just left one piece of unfinished business to attend to and that concerned our young friend.

Accordingly, the next day Sinderby-Smythe and I met up with Harry and asked him to point out the two boys who had attacked him. The cuts and bruises they had inflicted had just about healed, but the memories of their actions had not. I was not surprised to see that the two fourteen year old thugs were taller than Harry and dirty and scruffy to boot. Their donkeys were also in poor condition, badly cared for with their ribs clearly visible.

I stayed out of sight with Harry whilst Sinderby-Smythe approached the two boys who were waiting in a small line of carriages and hackney cabs outside the Brunswick Hotel.

"You two!" shouted Sinderby-Smythe towards the boys.

"What? Us?" replied one of them pointing to himself and his friend.

"Yes, you two. I am in need of two donkeys and carts and have two sovereigns to spend," said Sinderby-Smythe, tempting them.

"You've a deal, sir," said the first boy and they both whipped their donkeys, making the poor beasts flinch as they moved the carts out of the line.

"Do you know where Upper Dunsforth is?" asked Sinderby-Smythe.

"Why, yes sir," they replied in unison.

"Then meet me there at the Plough Inn," said Sinderby-Smythe, which brought puzzled looks from the two boys.

"Here is six shillings each and the rest of the money will be given to you when you arrive at the inn. Make sure you are there by mid-day."

"What's the job, sir?" they asked.

"Nothing that your donkeys won't handle easily," he replied, whereupon the two boys took the shillings, smiled at each other and then repeatedly whipped their donkeys as they set off in the direction of Upper Dunsforth.

Sinderby-Smythe re-joined Harry and I as we all went back to Holderness House where Cookson had my aunt's carriage ready to take us to Upper Dunsforth.

We arrived ahead of the two donkey boys and waited in the Plough Inn. I envisaged the Russians sitting at the table by the window, plotting their escape from England a few days previously. Harry sat with his back to the door in case the boys were to come in and catch us unawares.

Eventually I could see the boys arriving and I nodded to Sinderby-Smythe that it was time for him and I to greet them. Harry remained in the pub and watched through the window.

"Splendid, splendid!" I said enthusiastically, as I strode out towards the two donkey carts.

"Two sovereigns you said," I added, turning to Sinderby-Smythe.

"Absolutely," replied Sinderby-Smythe, who then made his way over to the two rather bemused boys and gave them the balance of the money owed to them.

They kept looking at me, Sinderby-Smythe and each other while they tried to establish what was happening.

"Now please unharness those poor animals," I said to Sinderby-Smythe who stepped over to the first cart and started loosening the leather straps of the harness on the nearest cart.

"What's going on?" said the boy holding the reins on the first cart, prompting me to move across to hold the donkey tied to the second cart.

"Why, we want to release our donkeys from their carts," I replied.

"But they're not your donkeys, they're ours!" said the first boy growing angry and tightening his grip on his whip.

"No. They were yours, however you sold both donkeys and carts for two sovereigns which you have just taken in full payment," said Sinderby-Smythe.

The landlord of the Plough Inn, on hearing a commotion, had come out of his pub and was now watching the events unfold.

"Two sovereigns was for hiring the carts, not buying them, you prick," said the first boy readying himself to use his whip.

"No, actually laddie, I said I wanted two donkeys and carts and had two sovereigns to spend. There was no mention of any hire. You both said 'yes' and I asked you to deliver them to Upper Dunsforth," answered Sinderby-Smythe, turning to the landlord who was nodding as if he was a magistrate sitting in judgment.

"That's not right! I thought you wanted to hire them. You'd have to be mad to sell two donkeys with carts for two sovereigns," pleaded the first boy.

"Well, next time I suggest you pay more attention to detail when you strike a bargain. Nevertheless this deal is done, you have been paid, the carts delivered to the agreed address and I will thank you both to get off my carts," said Sinderby-Smythe confidently.

"You can piss off!" said the first boy and directed his whip at Sinderby-Smythe to prevent further loosening the harness on the donkey. The whip cracked yet it failed to strike the lieutenant, who simply caught the whip in his hand then pulled hard on it dragging the boy off the cart sending him hurtling to the ground. The second boy looked to do the same to me but before he could move, I had shifted alongside him and simply snatched the whip from his hand.

"Get down!" I said to him firmly. "Now unharness that donkey."

Resigned to their fates, both boys released their donkeys and I took hold of the poor beasts and tied them to the hitching post outside the Plough Inn. Both animals celebrated their freedom by drinking noisily from the nearby horse trough.

"This isn't fair," bleated the two boys.

"No, it's probably not. But mistreating those poor animals isn't fair either. Anyway let no-one say that we are not fair minded men, and so for two sovereigns I will sell you back your carts," I replied.

"Where's the catch this time?" asked the first boy who was dusting himself down from his fall.

"The only catch is that the donkeys are not part of the deal. Those donkeys have been beaten for the last time. They are now retired from service."

"But how will we get home?" questioned the second boy who seemed to be realising what was actually happening.

"You can ride in your carts," I said sarcastically.

"How can we do that when we haven't any donkeys to pull them?" sneered the first boy.

"True. So do you want your carts back or do I keep them as well?" I said, beginning to tire of this charade.

"No. We'll have our carts back. Here are your lousy two sovereigns."

The two boys then took hold of their carts and, after looking around in vain for some sort of help, walked away pulling the carts behind them.

It was a long way back to Harrogate and for good measure I shouted after them.

"If I hear of you beating a donkey or anyone else, I will be back and next time you won't get off so easily. And while you pull those carts, just think about what you've been putting these poor animals through every day of their lives."

The boys pulled the carts slowly down the lane and after a few minutes were out of sight. We took the two donkeys to a kindly local farmer at the suggestion of Harry who promised that he would look after them and that they would never work again.

We returned to Holderness House, satisfied that at least two poor donkeys had been saved and hoped that news of the treatment we'd given to these two boys might make a few others respect their animals a lot more. When I walked back into the house, Benson handed me a lovely letter from Angela Coutts and Miss Meredith, telling me that they were returning to London and they would very much like me to call in and see them at Stratton Street. That was one appointment I most assuredly intended to keep.

Within a couple of days Reeves was up and about, although he winced with every step. In an attempt to speed up the healing process, Sinderby-Smythe and I insisted on taking him down to the wells to take the waters. Despite his lack of enthusiasm, he managed to hobble manfully down the hill towards the Crown with the aid of one my uncle's old sticks.

As we passed the bank, I was surprised at the continued absence of queues of disenchanted investors which was puzzling, although I presumed that these would form the minute Lord Redmayne arrived, once he had overcome whatever was delaying him.

As we reached the bottom of the hill, the hairs on the back of my neck twitched and I turned around to see Virginia Hatherway walking towards her father's flower shop. She caught my eye and smiled. My heart skipped a beat but before I could return the smile, a young man who had clearly been running, stepped in front of us clutching a letter.

"Captain Townsend?" said the young man, breathlessly.

"Yes, and who might you be?" I replied.

"I have been sent by the Duchess of Aldborough to deliver this to you personally and without delay. I was directed to you here by the butler at Holderness House," whereupon he handed me the letter.

The note was brief and to the point. It was warning me that Sir William Hamilton and the Duke talked only of avenging the actions of Lord Redmayne and myself. Their bodies were still recovering from the injuries we had inflicted on them, yet their minds were obsessed with revenge.

I pushed the letter into my coat pocket, intending to set aside my concerns for the future perils which I must undoubtedly face. Right now, however, I had to brace myself to take another dose of the odious, sulphurous waters with Reeves and Sinderby-Smythe.

The End

Historical Note

Although this novel is fictional, there are elements which are loosely based on a number of alleged historical events, including the visit to Harrogate by Angela Burdett-Coutts in August 1838. Captain Townsend is based on my great, great grandfather who was born in Tullow, Ireland. I was drawn to him after reading through the papers of my late father who sadly died whilst we were researching the background for this novel. Despite the fact that he was not a captain in the Light Dragoons, he was nevertheless an adventurer with a love of horses who apparently made and lost more than one fortune. Consequently he seemed ideal for the role I had in mind. Although his military career is a figment of my imagination, the 11th Light Dragoons most certainly are not and in August 1838 they would have recently arrived back in England from Bengal, India.

The 11th Light Dragoons were soon to be adopted by Prince Albert and became the 11th Hussars around 1840. The regiment had a hand at Waterloo and, more famously, at the Charge of the Light Brigade on 25th October 1854, where British Light Cavalry led by Lord Cardigan charged the Russian guns during the Crimean War. In 1838 the British government really was concerned about the possibility of Russia extending its reach throughout Europe, providing them with a route through which they could invade Afghanistan and then India. The Russians were also making efforts to ally themselves to Dost Mohamed in Kabul (spelled Cabul in 1838) and a Captain Burnes was reported to be in Kabul attempting to steer Dost Mohamed away from the Russians. For the purposes of my story I created three Russians, ostensibly to advise on the building of the railway between York and Harrogate. Count and Countess Zadovich are entirely fictional although loosely based on the Prince and Princess Levien, whose maiden name was Von Benckendorff. I created the Yorkshire Railway Company to build a railway line from Harrogate to York, which must surely have been under discussion in 1838. The first actual railway line into Harrogate was built by the Leeds and Thirsk Railway Company who opened a line from Leeds in 1848.

Miss Angela Coutts (only very close friends called her Angela) was only twenty four years old when she visited Harrogate in August 1838, which was shortly after inheriting one of Europe's leading banks. Despite conflicting reports, the newspaper accounts at the time confirmed that she stayed at the Queen Hotel (now a Cedar Court Hotel). The purpose of the visit was to escape the pressures of London, created in the most part by endless marriage proposals and a constant stream of begging letters. Unfortunately her complexion was said to be poor, however the waters and fresh air found in Harrogate apparently improved her skin considerably. Whilst there she was joined by her faithful companion, Miss Hannah Meredith. Angela Coutts love of the town was passed to her by her late step-grandmother who was an equally a fascinating character. Harriot Mellon was born into a family of travelling players, became an actress and appeared in Drury Lane, as well as countless theatres throughout the country. She met Thomas Coutts when he had sought refuge in Cheltenham, away from the strains of caring for his ailing wife. Thomas Coutts behaved properly throughout this time and remained faithful to his wife, however, such was his fondness for Miss Mellon that he paid for her to live in improved circumstances. Upon the death of his wife, who was also from humble beginnings, he quickly married Harriot. Unsurprisingly, this caused alarm bells to ring throughout the Coutts family and, in particular, from his son-in-law, Sir Francis Burdett (who was MP for Boroughbridge for a time). By all accounts, Thomas Coutts and Harriot were very happy together and he had complete trust in her. So much so, that when he died he left her all his wealth, which included the bank. Unbeknown to the Coutts family at the time, Thomas also entrusted Harriot with the task of choosing an heir from his children or grandchildren. Harriot took this role seriously, spending a lot of time with them all, eventually settling on Angela Burdett, Thomas's grand-daughter. In the meantime, Harriot married the much younger Duke of St. Albans, but despite this, never wavered from her promise to her beloved Thomas Coutts.

As the Duchess of St. Albans, she spent a good deal of time travelling and throwing parties and was a regular visitor to the Granby Hotel in Harrogate. Whilst there, she became a firm favourite with the staff and frequently competed in races with the donkey boys. Many of the donkey boys mistreated their donkeys, much to the abhorrence of some visitors to the town. You can see from paintings and drawings from the 1850's that the donkeys rarely pulled carts and passengers actually rode on their backs. I chose to add carts for the benefit of the story. Jonathan Benn was the owner of the Granby in 1838 and would have met both Angela Coutts and the Duchess of St. Albans a number of times. Such was his admiration for the Duchess that he named his own house which was adjacent to the hotel, St. Albans House. The Granby is now a nursing home and Jonathan Benn's former home has been converted to offices. Coincidentally, I occupied one of these offices whilst writing this story.

One of the terms of the bequest to Angela Burdett was that she should change her name to Coutts and as a consequence became Angela Burdett-Coutts. Predictably she was subjected to many proposals of marriage and the 'coughing' routine she devised with Miss Meredith to repel them, was supposedly true. Her visit to Harrogate in 1838 was made famous by a series of incidents involving an Irish barrister named Richard Dunn. Following his expression of undying love towards her, Angela Coutts did ask for help from London which came in the form of Mr Majoribanks who was a director of Coutts Bank. He came to assist her with his daughter. In the end Dunn became such a nuisance that when she found him her bedroom at the Queen Hotel, she quickly returned to London and Dunn was arrested. However he would not have been arrested by Constable Hardisty as he was created solely for my purposes. The constable at the time was Robert Mills and by all accounts was much more effective than the hapless Constable Hardisty. After his release, Dunn travelled to London where he continued to stalk her. Once again he was arrested and eventually prosecuted under a civil action brought by Miss Coutts. In the end Dunn was placed in a mental institution and was never heard of again. A full account of this trial can be found in the newspapers of the time.

The whole episode understandably distressed Miss Coutts and, given its rather unseemly nature, I opted to have Mr Dunn working for my fictitious Russians instead.

In the 1830s Harrogate was seen to be one of the leading spa towns in Europe and had devoted itself to catering for the spa visitor. The serious business of taking the waters and therapeutic bathing during the day disguised a lively nightlife consisting of balls, music and for some, gambling. As the summer season progressed, the wealthy mill owners of the north gave way to the aristocracy who then dominated the town's hotels and residences for the remainder of the season. There was a rich variety of hotels, such as the Granby Hotel (known affectionately as the 'House of Lords') which catered solely for the aristocracy and the livelier Dragon Hotel ('House of Commons') which was owned and managed by William Powell Frith's family up until 1838. William Powell Frith, having grown up in the area, moved to London at the age of sixteen, where he became one of the leading portrait painters of the 19th Century. An example of his exceptional talent can be seen on the front cover of this book. There was also the Crown Hotel, nicknamed the 'Hospital' due to its close proximity to the sulphur well and the Queen Hotel, which had the alternative name of the 'Manchester Warehouse' reflecting its popularity amongst Lancashire mill owners.

However, rather than the town being full of invalids, Harrogate also attracted a number of young ladies searching for a husband, in addition to young men in search of brides. There was consequently a mixture of invalids of both sexes and all ages, added to those who sought relaxation and stimulation from the fresh air and social exchanges. The details of the hotels, wells and gardens have all been taken from diaries and accounts of visitors to Harrogate in and around 1838. Betty Lupton did indeed serve the water from the sulphur well for 60 years and quite possibly may have served Miss Coutts at some point.

Balls were held on set days of the week, but for the purpose of this story, I altered the order in which they took place. The Dragon hosted balls on Mondays and the Crown on Wednesdays, not the other way around as I suggested. The Dragon was the liveliest of Harrogate's hotels with large sums regularly gambled there including the amounts referred to in the book.

Dining at the Granby was just as I have recounted, with the most recent guests (irrespective of their title) sitting at the bottom of the table for dinner, working their way up the table the longer they remained in residence. Clive of India was recorded as having stayed at the Granby and he was truly famous for avenging the atrocity at Fort William, Calcutta (the Black Hole of Calcutta) when 123 people died overnight, mainly due to suffocation and dehydration.

The shops I mention, with the exception of the Bank of Harrogate, Hatherways Grocer's and Tea Importer's, Harrogate's House of Flowers and Nixon's Optometrist, all existed. Christopher Nixon did establish a practice in Harrogate but not until 1981. I should also confirm that Sue Potter of Yorkshire Farmhouse Eggs was indeed the inspiration for the Mrs Potter I had selling eggs around the town. Mr Palliser did run the post office and publish a visitor's guide to Harrogate, which is a fascinating insight to life in Harrogate in those early Victorian years. He would have been in his early thirties as the Captain speculated, given that he was born around 1804. If anyone decides to look for the four stones of Harlow Moor, I would be interested to learn what they find. There were four large stones on a map of Harrogate dated 1849 and so would have presumably been there in 1838. I have never seen any other mention of them and so the legend of the four stones of Harlow Moor is entirely of my creation, along with the young wife who after walking around the stones, murdered her husband.

All the characters in the book have been invented with a few exceptions: Angela Coutts, Miss Hannah Meredith (Angela's long standing companion) Pickersgill Palliser, Betty Lupton, Lord Palmerston, Jonathan Dearlove, Jonathan Benn and Captain Upton. I have tried to show them favourably in the manner I believed they would have acted should such a dastardly plot been hatched at the time. Angela Coutts, being so young and rich, could easily have been a target for more than just stalkers. But whether she would have used the theatrical experiences imparted on her by the Duchess of St. Albans to disguise her identity, is pure speculation on my part. Although possible, such a step might have been out of character.

The journey taken by Captain Townsend to Leeds and onto Manchester is authentic wherever possible. The 15th Hussars were based at barracks in Chapeltown and there was a spate of soldiers being flogged, which were reported in the *Northern Star* in the early part of 1838. One of the unlucky soldiers was in fact Private Roylance, K Troop of the 15th Hussars, stationed in Leeds and commanded by Captain Upton. They would almost certainly have been involved in controlling Chartist meetings. The largest meeting reported was at Hartshead Moor on the 15th October 1838 which was supposedly attended by 250,000 people. The *Manchester Guardian* later suggested that the number was closer to 10,000. An Irishman did play a significant role in the furtherance of the Chartist movement, however he was called Feargus O'Connor and not Patrick O'Shaughnessy.

One of my favourite scenes in the book relates to the horse races. Races were held on the Stray periodically and the details I have used in this book came from 1852. A horse called Augusta did win a three horse race and the main race would have been the Harrogate Handicap Stakes. All the runners mentioned competed in that race in 1852, with the exception of Tribune which was a horse I jointly owned with a couple of friends in the 1990s. (Tribune was a magnificent horse who won six of his last seven races over hurdles). I came across the information about horse racing in Harrogate from articles written in the Sporting Intelligence of 1852 and 1853. Unfortunately I was unable to locate any images of these colourful meetings, however thanks to the Tate gallery we have been able to include a copy of William Powell Frith's exceptional painting of a much grander race meeting at Epsom.

There is a strong likelihood that there would have been all manner of stalls and entertainers in Harrogate on race days, although despite ice cream having been invented well before 1838, Gianni Bernardi did not start selling his own range there until 2015.

341

The reference to Touchstone is apparently true, he won the St Leger in 1834 and then went missing after a stable lad lost him whilst he was under the influence of alcohol. Rumours then circulated for some time afterwards that various foals in the area had been sired by him.

Gordon's (named after my father and brother) is a club invented for the purposes of this book although there were many noted gaming houses in London at the time. The most intriguing of which was Crockfords situated at No. 50, on the west side of St. James's Street, over against White's, and was built for Mr Crockford in 1827. It quickly became all the rage – every English social celebrity and every distinguished foreign visitor hastened to become a member. Even the Duke of Wellington joined, though it is alleged that this was only to enable him to blackball his son.

Holderness House does exist although it was not built until around 1850. I used it as the home for the Captain's Aunt Violet, as my family presently own the ground floor and basement of the original building which is now divided into a number of apartments.

Theodore Botterill was entirely of my own making, as was the repeating rifle which was a little ahead of its time. Samuel Colt appears to have invented the first repeating weapon, which was a revolver. The first thousand would have been made, ironically, in 1838 in the USA. In August of that year, the British Army would have used single shot rifles which could fire two or three rounds a minute depending on the dexterity of the user. A repeating rifle would have given any army a considerable advantage and with trouble brewing between Russia and England, such a weapon would have been priceless. As I have already mentioned, the unrest between our two countries did eventually turn to war in the Crimea (1854). The Great Game was the name given to battle being played out between Great Britain and Russia for supremacy in Central Asia.

For those readers not familiar with the term 'dissected maps' these were effectively the forerunner to what we know today as a 'jigsaw puzzle'.

Throughout the book I have tried to accurately describe travelling around England at the time. There were some railways already in existence, most notably Darlington to Stockton, Leeds to Selby and Liverpool to Manchester. In all, there were around 500 miles of track laid down in 1838, however there were thousands more yet to come as the golden age of rail was just beginning. The Rotherham to Sheffield railway was nearing completion when Miss Coutts and Major Phillips passed that way. And the Leeds to Manchester line was also well underway. Each new railway required an Act of Parliament and the sponsors needed to show they had the necessary funds in place. Building railways was phenomenally expensive. The Leeds to Thirsk Railway Company are reputed to have spent around one million pounds in building around 26 miles of track from Leeds to Harrogate. It's hard to imagine that all the dealings in railway shares were completely honest as the protections we have in place today for investors were not in evidence in those early Victorian days. Tsarskoye Selo Railway was the first public railway to be built in Russia. It ran for 17 miles from Saint Petersburg to Pavlovsk.

Stage coach travel was still the most widely used form of transportation and with the help of several publications I have tried to piece together the coaching inns that Captain Townsend and Miss Coutts might have used. The only ones I invented were the Waterloo Inn in Huddersfield and the Black Bull in Oldham.

The Royal Mail Coach did arrive daily at 2pm at Gascoigne's Hotel in Harrogate from Leeds on its way to Darlington. The fastest coaches would average around 11mph and the quickest recorded journey from London to York was 20 hours. The stage coach station in London really was St Martin's Le Grand and the 'True Briton' coach did travel daily from Leeds to Manchester at 10am. The boats sailing from Selby to Kingston upon Hull are also genuine as was the SS Great Western which sailed to New York on August 16th 1838.

The village of Upper Dunsforth does exist as did the Plough Inn and the cottage called Homelands. The Crown at Boroughbridge was a most famous coaching inn and would have been very busy in 1838. The Devil's Arrows just outside Boroughbridge are quite amazing and worth a visit. Initially there were possibly more than the three stones which remain today. Each one is around 20ft high with an additional 4ft buried underground and all of them were transported to Boroughbridge thousands of years ago. One has to wonder why anyone would do this and to what purpose.

Wherever I have made reference to an event such as the Barnsley mining disaster (which was horrific, given that only children were lost), the burning of the Tsars winter palace, the Battle of Bossenden Wood and even the cricket match at Lords; these were all taken from newspapers of that period.

All in all, this is a fictional account of something that could have happened in August 1838 but most definitely did not. Having said that, the story is set in a place that really existed and Angela Coutts was in Harrogate at the time recuperating from the trials of being the richest woman in England (save for Queen Victoria). Angela Coutts was my inspiration and she was truly an incredible lady who was described by King Edward VII as being the most remarkable woman in the kingdom after his mother, Queen Victoria. She undoubtedly received many begging letters and appeals for money and nearly all the ones I have referred to are entirely fictional although all very plausible, particularly the reference to Gregor McGregor who existed and his Poyais project happened more or less as Lord Redmayne described. The calculating engine (the forerunner to the modern computer) was indeed brought to her attention by a Charles Babbage and later in 1839 he showed his invention to her. Nevertheless throughout her life, Angela Coutts is said to have given away around £3 milllion for which she became known as the 'The Queen of the Poor'.

The descriptions of the hotels, the balls, the horse racing, gambling and such like, have largely been based on books and diaries of the time and consequently I owe a great deal of thanks to the works of: *Harrogate Great Chronicles, Harrogate History and Guide, Exclusively Harrogate* (All Malcolm Neesam), *William Powell Frith* (William Powell Frith), *Spas of England* (A.B. Granville M.D.), *Harrogate Past* (W.R.Mitchell), *Lady Unknown* (Edna Healey), *Regency Harrogate* (Prudence Bebb), *The Merry Duchess* (Joan Perkin), *The English Spa 1560-1815* (Phyllis Hembry), *Harrogate Story* (W.Haythornthwaite), *The Home Office and the Chartists 1838-48* (Neil Pye) as well as *Palliser's History and Directory of Harrogate* (Pickersgill Palliser) and various newspaper articles published in 1838.

Miss Angela Burdett-Coutts, Harrogate, 1868.

ABOUT THE AUTHOR

Ian Townsend is a businessman turned author who was born in Leeds, England. He now lives near Harrogate with his wife Mandy.